Puccini's Ghosts

Puccini's Ghosts

MORAG
JOSS

SCEPTRE

First published in Great Britain in 2005 by Hodder and Stoughton
A division of Hodder Headline

A Sceptre Book

A CIP catalogue record for this title is available from the British Library.

Hardback ISBN 0 340 82050 0
Trade paperback ISBN 0 340 83094 8

Typeset in Sabon by Hewer Text Ltd, Edinburgh
Printed and bound by
Mackays of Chatham Ltd, Chatham, Kent

Hodder Headline's policy is to use papers that are natural, renewable
and recyclable products and made from wood grown in sustainable forests.
The logging and manufacturing processes are expected to conform to the
environmental regulations of the country of origin.

Hodder and Stoughton Ltd
A division of Hodder Headline
338 Euston Road
London NW1 3BH

Puccini's Ghosts

is for

Sue Chilcott

8 July 1963 – 4 September 2003

whose life, music and friendship inspired me in many
ways although not in the creation of any of the characters
or events in the story, which are entirely imagined.

'Covent Garden was haunted last night. It was haunted by the gentle and immaculate ghost of Puccini . . . who died with the final bars of *Turandot* still imprisoned within his brain, who disappeared to solve an enigma more terrible and profound than any created by the Princess Turandot.

We like to think that Puccini revisited the glimpses of the moon last night to observe the opera's performance in England, where his works are so universally cherished, to watch his tricksy spirits at their revels. We imagined him pleased with the magnificent production and the sensation it created.'

Daily Express, 8 June 1927

BURNHEAD ASSOCIATION FOR SINGING TURANDOT
Presents

TURANDOT

Lyric drama in three acts and five scenes

Music Giacomo Puccini
(completed by Franco Alfano, abridged by George Pettifer)

———

Libretto Guiseppe Adami & Renato Simoni after Carlo Gozzi
abridged by George Pettifer

———

Conductor
George Pettifer

———

Directed by George Pettifer
Designed by George Pettifer and Guiseppe Foscari

The BAST Chorus
Chorus Director George Pettifer
Chorus Master Gordon Black

The Orchestra
Leader Wilhelmina Bergsma

CHARACTERS

Mandarin	Norman Clay
Liù *a slave girl*	Eliza Duncan
Timur *deposed King of Tartary*	Alec Gallagher
The Unknown Prince (Calaf) *Timur's son*	Guiseppe Foscari
Pung *Minister of Princess Turandot*	Sandy Scott
Princess Turandot	Fleur Pettifer
Emperor Altoum *Turandot's father*	Norman Clay

Populace, guards, Turandot's ladies, phantoms, wise men, heralds and soldiers

Now I'm here I begin to sense the trouble I'm in. I'm back at the window but the view has changed. I haven't switched on a light so I'm standing in the dark watching night colours gleam through the glass: silvered wet tarmac, darts of rain caught in the cloudy glow under the streetlights and across the road, garden walls soaked in warm, sodium glare. There are no streetlights on our side – they belong to the new houses – but their orange sheen leaks as far as our privet hedge, staining its green leaves brown. The old road is a street now. At intervals across it there are lumps lying in wait to slow the traffic; even at this hour one or two cars pass. The beam of their white headlamps tilts and dips and steadies as they curtsey over the bumps and then they pick up speed with the fizz of tyres on the wet road, pulling their shadows after them. I follow the line of streetlights stretching through the sky all the way back to the bridge, receding spangles of orange distorted by the rain on the window into a row of tiny bursting suns. Behind me, the room creaks with damp, its emptiness sighs. But I will not turn round yet, nor switch on a light. I know what it would show me. I shall carry on standing here, looking out and feeling ridiculous.

What was the rush? Why did I drop everything and come immediately to arrive so late at night, when tomorrow would have done? When they rang to tell me he was dead I came at once as if, having just died, he might be still within reach, somehow not quite gone. His death reminds me of something obvious that I feel stupid for having overlooked, that he was old and one day would die, and yet how can he leave like this, a man who never did anything sudden in his life? I talked to him in my head all the way here. I told him I was sorry.

I'm sorry, I say again now.

All I hear in reply is his tired voice, Och, Lizzie. His voice comes to me, it seems, from a great distance. He sounds lost and cut-off as if he has got himself stranded somewhere, though he isn't crying for help; he is, if anything, resigned.

Och, Lizzie.

I can't tell if he means it as dismissal or forgiveness.

Maybe it isn't so ridiculous, my jumping to attention now he has died; maybe it's an effect the newly dead have on the rest of us. And am I acting any more suddenly than he did? Off he goes raising a cloud of dust and up I start, needing to move in some direction or another, as if giving chase. It's the kind of thing, scrupulously misinterpreted to feed their hunger for a disgraceful tale, that people round here get their teeth into. I can hear their voices, too.

Doesn't see him for years but she's here fast enough to hear the will read.

I don't know if he made a will. But even while I'm booking a flight, packing, cancelling appointments, I think I make out a shape in the dust as it begins to settle, some dark weight he left behind. It's cumbersome, as heavy as history, and I have no use for it, yet I can't leave it lying unclaimed. It's the past, and now it's mine and I have to do something with it. He's not been dead a day but I intend to be practical about it, as I will be about his other things. Already they are no longer just his things but obstacles of a kind, an affront to order, a challenge to the clarity of what belongs where and to whom. I am unsettled by the sudden knowledge that, for an interval at least, everything the dead leave behind is still theirs and yet no-one's, though I'm not sure if this question of ownership is a trivial or a profound matter. But what a strange hurry I feel to bestow or destroy, as if his belongings might be dangerous if they are not at once attached elsewhere. I don't care where they go as long as I get them off my hands, and it's the same with this story of our past. It's a shapeless load with one straggling thread, its unsatisfactory ending, that trails from it like a fuse. I want it tucked out of sight. I have to find somewhere to dump it, some unvisited place in my mind, a kind of mental cupboard under the stairs for a filled sack of worn-out memories.

They'll expect a show at the funeral. Not necessarily of grief, but they'll expect me to make myself somehow conspicuous; I'm sure there are still those who like to think I'm as bad as my mother. Thinks she's the next Maria Callas your mum, everybody says so, Enid used to say, smirking at the very idea, and I would snigger with embarrassment because my mother did think that. Or believed she might have been if my father hadn't ruined her chances, as she so perfectly rewrote events. In my mother's mind she and my father are Persephone and Pluto; he practically threw her in a sack and bore her down into darkness although he, lacking any authority, makes an improbable god of the underworld. But by the time I'm fifteen I believe completely in her shuttered and powerless misery, which seems irreversible. She lives here as if unable to break out of some truly dreadful contract, under a form of house arrest that leaves her in turn distraught and enervated. All that changes, of course, but I cannot look round from the window now that this recollection is upon me.

Behind me she sits, with Uncle George. They're lingering over breakfast, I'm clearing it away.

I need a day off. The voice is tired, she tells him. I'm tired, vocally.

I remember now, she's in a sulk because he has made her give up cigarettes but is still smoking himself.

He says, But you don't know the part properly yet.

I don't want to get stale.

Come on, Florrie, he says, wise up. If Callas spends every hour God sends preparing a role, why shouldn't you?

He's the one who sounds tired. He has his chin cupped in the hand that holds the cigarette and threads of smoke are weaving up through his hair, silvery blue into chestnut. With the spent match in his other hand he is stirring a little paste he has made out of toast crumbs and leftover butter on the side of his plate, black into pale yellow, over a pattern of ferns.

Don't call me Florrie, she says, waving away the smoke. It's Fleur. And don't talk to me about Callas.

She stands, sets her shoulders wide, looks through this window and arches her eyebrows. Out pours the final phrase of '*Vissi d'arte*' from *Tosca*, minus the words for she doesn't know them beyond the first two lines. I notice how unused her lips are to being stretched, as if they haven't done enough laughing. Uncle George looks away and smiles his private smile with one last drag on the cigarette, which he stubs out in the paste of crumbs and butter. The way it hisses a little seems to seal the point, as far as I am concerned.

Of all those people who said my mother thought she was the next Maria Callas, I wonder how many are still here.

When I arrived, I found the key where it's always been behind the loose brick in the garage wall. I stepped through the kitchen and into the back room that my father's life had shrunk to fit: one armchair, the television, everything else on castors. At once I snapped off the light and came in here to the dining room. In a minute or two I'll find my way upstairs in the dark and grope around for blankets in the landing cupboard. I cannot bear bleak electric light scouring the corners and washing out shadows, showing me how unchanged everything is.

I'll linger here just a while longer. In the silences between cars I listen for the rasp of the incoming water of the Firth up the beach not far behind the house, but maybe I only imagine I can hear it, in the same way that I imagine the moon, invisible tonight behind clouds, pulling the tide across the shore. I like such commonplace movements as these: the coming and going of the sea, the falling of rain, the passing of cars. In this dead room, from behind the glass, I feel I am witnessing a kind of breathing.

———•◦•———

ACT I

THE FIRST RIDDLE

In the dark night flies a many-hued phantom.
It soars and spreads its wings
Above the gloomy human crowd.
The whole world calls to it,
The whole world implores it.
At dawn the phantom vanishes
To be reborn in every heart.
And every night 'tis born anew
And every day it dies!

HOPE.

In ancient Peking, the cold-hearted Princess Turandot has sworn a terrible oath. Her ancestor Princess Lo-u-Ling was ravished and killed by a conqueror and Turandot will never be possessed by any man. But her suitors are offered a chance. She will marry the one who correctly answers her three riddles. Those who fail, die. Calaf, prince of Tartary, incognito and exiled, falls in love with Turandot at his first glimpse of her. His old father Timur tries to dissuade him from attempting to answer the riddles and so does the slave girl Liù, secretly and hopelessly in love with him. But Calaf remains steadfast.

1

The school year fell in a heap as soon as the end of term
exams were over and done with, trapping Lila Duncan
and everybody else under the final shapeless week that
had to be got through. Cupboards were tidied and books
counted in and then Lila's class sprawled on their desks playing
noughts and crosses, bickering in low voices, basking in aim-
lessness. Sunlight burned through the windows and glazed their
hair and dark backs; like giant, stranded flies they fretted and
buzzed as if condemned to perish where they lay, the prospect
of escape – the summer holidays – seeming too distant, too
exhausting and unreal. Over their heads the last days of June
loitered, the hours advancing casually with the drowsy menace
of things trite but unpleasant that were still to come, like milk
turning sour or fruit waiting to rot.

By Wednesday the week had halted. Late morning took all
day. Lila had not acquired the knack of looking forward to
things and now time itself, because there was enough to spare
for her to wonder at it, seemed crowded with tiny, hovering
omens of ill. She thought she could see them, hanging in specks
of dust that sparkled out from emptied cupboards into shafts of
sunlight or washing back and forth in watery shadows on the
ceiling, wafting with the lazy threat of jellyfish in the weight of
the tide.

On Thursday Miss Marten set them an Ink Composition,
even though they weren't meant to do Ink Composition in the
last week. They weren't meant to do anything but wait in a
slump and suffocate in the sitting-out of the term, and in any
case the inkwells had already been cleaned. Miss Marten knew

this as well as the class did, but she hated them after a year of their round shoulders and eyes like greasy stones, their smell of sour wool. You runts, she thought, smiling at the back wall. You'll never see me again.

'Ink monitors Enid Foley and Barry Henderson. Inkwells out, one between two. "The World As I See It Today",' she said. 'To be handed in at the end of this period.'

The class rose from its torpor to stir tired hostilities into the air, and Miss Marten bowed her head over her desk. None of them would write anything worth reading, though one or two of the oddballs and outcasts might try. It filled her with warmth to set work she had no intention of marking. In August she was marrying an air traffic controller called Leonard and she wasn't coming back.

' "The World As I See It Today",' she repeated, placing ticks against an inventory of the books that stood in ruined columns around her. 'And no outer space stuff, no seeing the world from a Sputnik. Crossings-out will lose marks. When you come back and look at what you write today, you might be surprised. A lot can change in a summer.'

Was she really still trying to scratch at their minds? She glanced up again and found herself looking into the faces of people staring as if through smoke and wandering from a battlefield, unconscious behind wide-open eyes.

Lila wrote:

The World As I See It Today

Today as I sit in this classroom on Thursday the 23rd of June, 1960, the world looks a hard blue colour. That is because it is a Thursday. Monday is pale green and unripe. Tuesday is beige, Wednesday is white, Thursday see above, Friday is grey like a man's suit, Saturday is a different blue from Thursday and Sunday is that dark green that old people paint their houses. I would rather not do this but I can't help it. I think if I lived somewhere else that was better and a more definite, proper place,

I might have other things to think about and not get the colour coming straight into my mind the minute I think what day it is. This is the first time I have mentioned this. Other people would laugh and as I get teased quite enough anyway! By certain people who shall remain nameless though everybody in this school knows who they are. I would even get teased for my name, the one my mother uses on me, which is Eliza. That is her sort of name. I don't feel like an Eliza. I stick to Lizzie at school, that's what my dad calls me, an ordinary name. He is ordinary himself so it suits him to use it, but I don't feel like a Lizzie either. I used to get called Lila but that was a long time ago.

Best friends don't tease one another or at least they shouldn't, but I still wouldn't tell even Enid Foley (about the colours), though she is my friend she takes things the wrong way and she's only interested in God at the moment, since Easter she is OBSESSED. She thinks everything is a sin and only Jesus can get you out of it. Most people are obsessed by something, Elvis Presley is one, Cliff Richard ect, who I really like but being obsessed is going a bit far and makes you look stupid. My mother hates them, she only likes classical music and opera, the rest is just noise according to her. My father likes Lonnie Donegan but he doesn't play the records in our house.

Anyway, the world as I see it today, it's a stupid idea because I don't see the world today in any way at all. Nobody can see the world. We only see the bit we're in ie this bit of Scotland called Burnhead. And if you only had Burnhead to go on you would say the world is a dump. Burnhead is neither one thing or the other, and I am the same. Anyway who cares? How I see the world isn't important as I am only me and it doesn't matter what I think, so I will just go on seeing the world my way, you can't change. Why I have to live here I don't know, there must be thousands of places more interesting where people really enjoy living there. But wherever you go you have to take your own head with you. What I mean is wherever you go it's the same you inside. You can't get away from yourself, it all comes down to what goes on inside your own head unfortunatly, changing that is your only hope of changing the way you see the world.

In the staff room on Friday morning, softened by her leaving present of a stainless steel hors d'oeuvres tray with matching coasters and a bottle of sherry, Miss Marten marked Lila's composition. She returned it to her in the dinner hall. On it she had written:

Rather solipsistic! You fail to address the question. Perhaps you will ramble less as you mature. 55%

After dinner, order broke down. Boys roamed the corridors wearing their blazers inside out, they started chalk fights and set fire to rolls of lavatory paper, turned on all the taps and threw dustbin lids on to the roof. Senga McMillan and Linda McCall stripped every twig, leaf and bloom from the line of flowering currant bushes that grew along the path bordering the school field and got the belt from the headmaster for it. Lila waited out the afternoon in the empty library, lulled by the smell of dust. She looked up 'solipsistic' in the dictionary and then the bell sounded and before she reached the gate where Enid was waiting she had forgotten what it meant.

'Can we go to yours?' Lila said. She always wanted to go to Enid's. Enid always waited for her to ask.

'What for? It's only a stupid shop.'

'Just. No reason. Just, might as well, why not?'

'Can't. See Senga? She got three of the belt. You should see her hand.'

'So what?'

'She wasn't even crying. Her and Linda, they're going to the Locarno, they said I could go as well.'

They had come out of school into cloudless sunshine. But the heat in the classrooms had been an illusion of summer; outside, a sharp wind off the sea pulled at their hair and raised swirls of wastepaper and ripped jotters in the playground. Lila squinted in the brightness, thwarted and annoyed.

'The Locarno's tough,' she said. 'Why don't we just go to yours?'

'It's not tough. They're not toughies.'

'They are so.'

'Not when you get to know them.'

'Oh, so you know them? You've changed your tune.'

'So? It says in the Bible you should forgive your enemies.'

'Where in the Bible? Bet you don't know where. And you're the one loves going to church.'

'It's not church, it's the Fellowship of Sinai Gathering in His Name.'

'Senga's been going round behind your back. She says it's not a proper church.'

'So?'

'So. You don't even sing hymns.'

'You don't need to. You speak the Word and that's when the Lord hears.'

'You said you hated Senga. She calls you Holy Foley.'

'So what? That was ages ago. You should come off your high horse.'

'I'm not on a high horse.'

'Well, your mother is. Thinks she's the next Maria Callas, everybody says so.'

They walked along for a while without speaking beside the naked currant bushes. As they went, the wind lurched through the branches, sending gusts of stray leaves and squashed flowers down the path, whipping away the bitter smells of torn blossom and spilt sap. Though she was seething over Enid's defection Lila was pleased; the scent of the flowers had always made her feel queasy and restless.

They followed the wind as it blew a veil of sand across Burnhead Main Street. Shop awnings cracked in sudden gusts and the painted buckets and spades strung up in clusters outside gift shops clacked next to beach balls and rubber rings wheezing against the window fronts. Mrs Dobie brought the bin filled with toy shrimping nets in off the pavement outside Dobie's Hardware & Fancy Goods and replaced it with one of canvas windbreaks.

In the branch office of Kerr, Mather & McNeill, Solicitors & Commissioners for Oaths, Mrs Audrey Mathieson got Hugh Mather out of the office for his Round Table meeting on time, checking his papers, dusting off the hat and clicking her tongue without once letting her smile drop. In the calm after the door closed, she finished some typing – only a letter that took no time at all but, as she said, if she had a thing to do she preferred to be allowed to get on and do it. This was true, but the real reason she rattled out a minute or two of typing every now and then, rather than wait until she had what Mr Mather called a proper batch, was that she disliked the brittle sounds and smells of office work and could not bear the thought of them filling an entire afternoon. She liked to get the snap and ting of the typewriter over with and afterwards she would flap the smells of carbon paper and ink away from her desk with a duster dipped in polish.

When she had finished the letter she sat listening to the silence that sang between her office and the small room across the corridor behind Mr Mather's, where Raymond the legal clerk worked. His door would be ajar. Waves of afternoon stillness lapped from room to room.

Through the ridged glass of the window she saw the bob-bing, blurry shapes of children in school blazers go by on Main Street, beyond the stretch of gravel and low wall that fronted the offices of Kerr, Mather & McNeill. Their voices reached her only in faint, neutral snatches, adding to the pleasure of her distance from them. She looked at her watch. Twenty past three: out early for the last day, most likely. Raymond's Lizzie would be among them, drifting along in the tide of black blazers yet not quite of it; she was like him, dreamy and tall and not an ounce on her, knock-knees in the offing. The mirage of children passed; the dancing pattern through the window faded. Traffic noise was a murmur.

The distance from the street was a feature of the offices that Audrey liked, along with the fact that Kerr, Mather & McNeill occupied detached premises, one of the better double-fronted bungalows on Main Street just before the shops. It had been the home of the senior partner's mother, a powdery lady with a dowager's hump and large buckled shoes who hadn't lasted the war; in 1946 the firm took the house over and Audrey joined them soon after.

It had required explanation, to her neighbours if not to John, an accountant's wife of thirty-seven going out to work. Not that she would ever tell them the truth: she and John, already married ten years and settled back from China and Hong Kong for four of those, had been awaiting the babies that she, silently, never quite believed in. Childlessness had seemed to her apt enough. Punishment in some form, as her missionary parents had taught her, there was bound to be, for John not being 'the first' and for her 'coloured' baby, given away to a couple from the New Territories before she had seen his eyes open; punishment too, for remembering the touch of Wang Hoa's skin and her heart's refusal to feel that loving him was a disgusting and immoral blunder. Her little job distracted her from John's disappointment, his forbearance, his goodness. It helped her to be nearly as kind to him as he deserved. And there seemed less to explain if she worked somewhere that looked like a private house. It's just a small branch office, she would say, and it's only secretarial. Oh, there's a lot of working wives now, people told her, pretending to judge her leniently. They did not need to add mind you, not in St Quivox Drive, but at least no-one alluded directly to the empty cradle.

So Audrey saw to it that the house-turned-office, dignified and aloof despite the new gold lettering and ridged glass in the windows, remained homely. At her desk she hurried through the typing in snatched moments, anxious not to disturb a peace that was essentially domestic. Her suits for work were apricot, mint and powder blue, never charcoal or bottle green; she would not wear clothes the same colour as the filing cabinets. Paper clips were kept in a porcelain sweet dish from Shanghai. It was she who tended the bulbs edging the path between the two squares of gravel up to the front door, and who kept tray cloths laundered for the junior partner's tea tray. She brought in the spherical millefiori paperweights of Vasart glass with brilliantly coloured chips set in their bases in frozen patterns of flowers that John gave her nearly every birthday and Christmas. They accumulated over the years; now there were at least four in every room. She was an excellent secretary.

Her ear picked up a creak from the floorboards in Raymond's office and the burr of the second desk drawer. She covered her typewriter, stepped out to the hall, pulled down the blind over the glass portion of the front door and pushed down the snib on the Yale lock. Then, leaving her door open, she returned to her desk and took the compact and comb from her handbag. She freshened her lipstick, tidied her hair and popped the things back. Holding her breath, she snapped her handbag shut, a loud single shot into the silence, a dart of enquiry to Raymond. With its usual whine, his door opened wider and his footsteps squeaked along the floor to the clients' waiting room at the back. When she joined him there a minute later he was ready for her on the Chesterfield.

'Och, Audrey,' he said, glancing up with his usual slow smile.

'That's your Lizzie out for the holidays, now,' she said, settling beside him and turning to look at his face.

'Aye, eight weeks. Eight weeks getting on her mother's nerves.'

His smile gets wearier every time, she thought. Was it silly to think he was beginning to look old, when he was nine years younger than she was? The gap in their ages seemed to be closing.

'And how are Fleur's nerves just at the moment?' she said.

Instead of answering, he leaned over and kissed her, a dry touch on the mouth. It was the only kissing they did now; at fifty-one she felt too old to kiss him with hunger and he, at forty-two, no longer expected it. What a relief that that peculiar, questing curiosity that possesses lovers about each other's mouths had faded.

He pulled her against him and placed a hand on her knee and cleared his throat with a long murmur, the signal that he would like to make love to her. He didn't often, nowadays. More often they talked or just held hands. The important thing was the space and time they took, the blind drawn over the front door on the days of the junior partner's meetings: Round Table last Friday of the month, partners' lunch at the Ayr branch every second Thursday. Space and time not snatched by stratagems, merely offered by circumstance and taken without greed for nearly fourteen years. They didn't go in for declarations or breathless discussion of what had brought them together to the back waiting room in the first place; they had no zest for an extenuated philosophy of wrong turnings or missed chances. A little space and time in which to rest from their stoicism was all they took.

Audrey shifted to let Raymond reach under her skirt, smiling over his shoulder at the customary murmurs and familiar moves, assisting him in the removal of the relevant clothing. She sighed as he slipped fondly into her, grateful for life's sweet routines: Raymond's respectful use of her body, neither abrupt nor protracted, and then the resumption of propriety – the tucking away of those parts of themselves, the smoothing of cushions – as pleasurable in its way as Raymond's stately, conscientious thrusting, and after she had popped to the Ladies to make herself decent, a cup of tea made and brought by him and a little talk of ordinary things. Adultery was the last thing it felt like. Adultery meant devious and dangerous and uncontrolled, and what they did was kindly, and ceremonious.

'Well,' was all she said, glancing at him as she finished her tea. Like many sensible ceremonies their lovemaking changed very little over time and sealed a bond that was never expressed in words.

'Och, Audrey,' Raymond said, draining his cup.

At a quarter to five they closed the office and walked down the front path. Raymond removed the padlock from his bicycle in the corner behind the wall, put on his cycle clips and rode away with a backwards smile and a ring of his bell. Audrey started on her walk along Burnhead Main Street, nodding to people she knew, scarcely glancing into prams parked in front of shop windows. When she left the busy pavement and made her way up past St Ninian's church to her immaculate house in St Quivox Drive, she began to prepare her greeting for John, who would be busy in the garden despite his lumbago and would look up as she clicked along the pavement and turned in at the gate.

I don't think there is anything reprehensible about putting my mind to an outfit. One has to wear something to a funeral and it takes my mind off being here. They'll expect me in fur and probably sunglasses, so I shall try not to disappoint. Leather is a definite possibility. Black, of course. I packed both, skirt and trousers.

I'm wearing the trousers. It seems a good idea to put them on for a few hours to see if they feel right. My black wool coat will have to do, though maybe it's marginally better with the skirt. I may find an opportunity to mention that of course there is nothing like real fur on a cold day but it's impossible to pack fur in a suitcase and what a pity nobody travels with trunks any more, all of which is true whether one actually has real fur or not. I've brought boots, but if I decide on the skirt with shoes then I'll have to buy tights. There will be tights for sale in Burnhead but they won't be anything special and there's nobody I can send to get them, and somehow going into a shop myself to buy very ordinary ones will reduce me in their eyes. I know that's silly. Whose eyes, exactly? I don't know anyone here any more unless I count Enid and Bill – and I suppose old Mrs Foley, though she's probably dead by now – and I don't.

But there it is, I'm not comfortable. I feel watched. I feel known by the strangers in the low, new houses across the road. I sense an interest in my return, if not from the people who once knew me then from their children, or perhaps by now *their* children, God knows quite who; the labyrinthine, passive interconnectedness of people here revolts me. People in a place like this just have to stand still to proliferate. They reproduce in long invisible strings; they form, they hang and then they drop, like beads of water along the strands of a web.

I'm at the window thinking about this when a young woman comes to the door. I can't judge the age of women under forty any more, especially the blondes – they all look like underfed children – but I guess she's in her twenties. She has a pushchair with a child in it who looks to me too old to be wheeled around. Apparently they live next door. That figures; I noticed this morning that next door's back garden is full of plastic. She's in one of those fleece tops, bright red with the sleeves some other colour, not the sort of thing I think a person should wear to come and offer condolences, quite apart from the fact it's spitting with rain. I don't ask her in.

These people! They fill the little houses in the tidy web of Burnhead streets in long, dripping lines, one soggy generation after another. She can't help glancing past me up the hall.

She says, I'm awful sorry about Mr Duncan, was it your father?

Yes, indeed, I say. Thank you. That's most kind.

Lovely man, your father. A gentleman. And he was still managing fine, right up to the last stroke.

Yes. He was very independent.

I seen him around, you know, when he was still getting out. He was saying you've been moved away a long time. Is it down south you stay?

I live abroad, I say. I have an international career.

Oh aye, abroad, that was it. Sorry, only your dad was saying you was retired, I remember him saying one time. You've lost your accent, any road, she says.

I tell her I have never spoken with the local accent because my mother was English and never would have allowed it.

And singers never really retire, I say. My father may have been confused. I smile to show I don't expect her to understand.

She looks put in her place and a little pathetic, and laughs nervously.

I smile again. I suppose I really don't blame her for being unused to people like me.

I've lived in several European countries, I tell her. In fact these trousers came from a place in Stuttgart where Princess Caroline of Monaco was a frequent customer. I've bought from the finest shops in Europe. Julie Christie, she was a regular, too.

(I never actually saw either of them but I don't say that. They had their photographs up in the shop. While my trousers were being wrapped I told them it was my first season in Stuttgart but they didn't ask for my picture. Perhaps because I was only buying the one pair of trousers. Or maybe because I was in the chorus.)

Stuttgart's in Germany, I add.

She looks rather startled. She's probably never been further than Glasgow. Her kind don't go far, they hang about a place like Burnhead breeding and watching. She's staring at me now. Maybe she sees me as the big, black, jewelled spider that's come back to trample her under my shiny black legs and set the web swinging. No wonder she watches. In a place like Burnhead one never escapes the eyes of people like her.

Well, lovely trousers any road, she says. So, anyway, if you're needing a wee hand with anything I'll be only too pleased.

I'm very busy, I say, to get her to go.

Funeral's one thing but it's the stuff, builds up when you're in one place all your life, she says. I'm Christine, by the way. This is Paris – say hello, Paris! You're never here on your own with the whole house to clear?

When I tell her I am she tilts her head and clicks her tongue. I want to throttle her.

Well, if there's anything at all don't hesitate, she says.

Actually there is something, I say. I need to know where in Burnhead I can buy tights. Proper tights.

Tights? Oh, all over. There's a wee Boots. And the Somerfield keeps them, there's loads of places, plenty wee dress shops. No problem.

I stop her. No, no, no – I'm talking about tights of very good quality, I say. Oh, never mind, I don't suppose there's any-where here that sells very, very good ones. It doesn't matter.

Right. Well, if you're needing a hand I'll maybe can pop in when this one's asleep, she says, nodding at the pushchair. You know, help you out.

Perhaps I'll pop up to Glasgow for the tights, I say. It's only thirty miles and I've got the hire car. But oh, the parking. I don't think I can face having to find parking. How it does spoil one, having a driver!

Sure, well, just you feel free to chap on my door. And Steve's back day after tomorrow so don't go lifting anything heavy, he'll be only too pleased.

Steve? Is that your husband? I'm afraid I don't know the people round here, I say. I have already noticed she isn't wearing a ring.

He's my partner, aye, she says. He's through in Edinburgh on a job next couple of days, he's in IT. Nuisance, 'cause he's got the car. Lucky you've got yours. You'd be stuck if not, the buses are useless.

I have to smile when I say yes, I'm lucky to have the car. Do they never learn? Stuck alone in cheap clothes at Seaview Villas with a child and no way of getting out, and because she's not married she thinks she's keeping her independence. I get rid of her before she can start asking for lifts here, there and every-where. I think she gets the message that I want to be left alone.

I am undecided about the tights. I wonder if I could find my way back to that place in Glasgow – Fenwicks, is it? I think it was on Sauchiehall Street. My mother got a lot of her clothes in Glasgow.

Glasgow. Suddenly it sounds again as it did years ago, when it means the same as dark, alarming, noisy. When I'm small, in the holidays when she has no choice but to take me, I go, too, on the train from Burnhead to Glasgow Central. She always tries to find a compartment that is empty, but even when she does I am not allowed to sprawl beyond the confines of my place. I want desperately to rub the insides of my arms and the backs of my legs all over the velvety seats. I have a memory of Glasgow afternoons filled with coal smoke and car exhaust, the squeal of bus brakes and the rustle of tissue paper and the silent opulence of dress shops and new clothes. From the ladies who bring things to the fitting room I sense a kind of approval towards my mother that extends to me, sitting outside the door on a chair dangling my legs, and although I do not ask, I always wonder why these ladies, who are clearly our friends, never come to our house. And I see a sort of dream of Fenwicks, the revolving door from the street landing us in the shining Perfumery and Cosmetics, hard and dazzling with mirrors and lights reflecting thousands of myself, when I feel quite awkward enough about being just the single me. The enamelled-looking ladies trailing their bright, pepper and powder scents between the glass counters are less friendly than the clothes shop assistants; I feel like a black stone tossed into a pool of crystals. We stop halfway through the afternoon and my mother has tea and I have ice cream in a freezing metal dish with a wafer. The ice cream has chips of real ice in it and for years I will think this is the sign of superior ice cream, chunks of ice big enough to creak when you bite into them, because from my mother's face I can tell the place we are in is superior. I also know that I am tagging along and not the point of the outing but I love the high decorated ceiling and the swift black and white wait-resses carrying tongs and cakestands, notepads hanging from their belts. I don't think these afternoons are planned. I think my mother acts on sudden impulse. There is always a numbness on the journey home, certainly.

I wonder if it's gone now, Fenwicks. If it is still there it'll seem ordinary now. It's Glasgow.

On the other hand they'll think black leather trousers at a funeral – black leather trousers anywhere on a woman my age, no matter how long her legs – are outrageous, and that in itself is enough to tempt me.

I suppose it's not really about the tights.

2

On the first day of the holidays, Lila stood at the dining room window of 5 Seaview Villas and realised that the colours of the days of the week had tiptoed from her mind, leaving it bare. It was raining, the day was Monday, and that was all. *Monday is pale green and unripe. Tuesday is beige, Wednesday is white.* Maybe it was the telling of it that had chased the colours away; writing it down in an Ink Composition had revealed how stupid a habit it was. She was glad to be rid of it, she supposed, though the space left behind seemed to need filling with something else; the colours had simply fallen from the words leaving eight weeks stretching ahead in a cycle of monochrome days, passing and returning. Already she was so heartsick with the repetition she could not move. She hoped Enid would come. She didn't really want to see her, but if she came they might wander into Burnhead and then she could suggest going to see Enid's mum.

She was also rooted by the noise. Her mother, still in her dressing gown and singing along in the title role with Maria Callas, was playing her records of *Turandot* in the music room across the hall. She had turned the volume right up and through the squalling of the orchestra and competing voices came the fuzzy metal spit of the amplifier; blurted explosions of sound hit the air like handfuls of nails hurled at a window. Every few seconds the space over Lila's head cracked with a noise like snapping bones. Yet she stood quite still; it seemed slightly less risky. Her mother's voice, blaring through the walls and eddying round her like hot fumes, made her feel so flimsy and insubstantial she was afraid she might be whipped up and scattered like dust in its slipstream. She could not hear herself breathe. If she were to speak, her words would be drowned. Suppose she were tempted to sing herself, to slide a single note of her own into the roar, the sound would be lost.

Yet the day had started well. The post had dropped through the door with its usual tired flip but there had been a letter bearing the words 'Official Notification' with the news that one of their Premium Bonds had come up. Not before time, her mother said, opening it and then dropping the envelope on the floor with a cry. She made a series of little jumps along the hall in her mint green nylon dressing gown, playful with self-congratulation. *Oh! Oh! Oh! Oh, look! Look!* The sound brought Lila out of the kitchen with the kettle in her hand, and Raymond clattering down the stairs. They had no idea how to behave in an unleashing of glee. Slowly, they began to see it was safe to be happy.

The bond had come up not with the usual £25 but spectacularly, with £500, a sum you never heard of anyone you knew getting, a sum that would get your photo and a caption in the *Burnhead & District Advertiser*. Suddenly they were a proper family, no longer odd and fractious and easily dismayed. They were people to whom a good thing not only had happened but ought to have happened; with Fleur as recipient it felt less random than deserved, somehow. From now on they would wear the lustre of prosperity and luck. Fleur flitted about making toast, insisting they all sit down to breakfast in the dining room as if this was how life would be from now on. No more short-tempered, solitary foraging for breakfast eaten off the draining board. At the table Lila, cautiously elated, poured out her cornflakes and watched her parents.

'At last!' Fleur said. 'Oh, at last we won't look silly any more, having a garage and no car. We'll have a car! A new car!'

Lila could see it already, her mother in calfskin driving gloves and ladies' slip-on driving shoes, happy.

'Once I've learned to drive, I'll be able to take the car anywhere I like!'

Lila's mind sailed on. Enid's mum had no car. Enid's mum ran the remnant shop on Main Street and did dressmaking and alterations and she and Enid lived in a cramped flat above. Lila was ashamed of how much she loved Enid's mum. Sometimes she ached all day to see her. She suspected, especially since last Easter when Enid had taken up with the Lord and the Fellowship of Sinai, that she only stayed friends with Enid because of her, and that Enid suspected it too. When she suggested going along to Sew Right after school and Enid gave her a hard look and said, What *for*? she was afraid that Enid knew exactly what for. Then she would have to pretend she didn't care and drift home to 5 Seaview Villas, aching all the more.

Maybe when the car came she would be safe from that. Oh, I nearly forgot to mention it, she would tell them both in the back shop, in a careful floating voice, we're getting a car. Surely when she and Fleur were out together on lovely mother and daughter excursions she would have no more need of the back shop. She would not crave the smells of cloth and paraffin and biscuits, the sight of Mrs Foley's round, slow body and the click of the sewing machine like an oiled tongue lapping up the fabric as her big hands fed it under the needle. I won't be able to come round after school so much, I'm afraid, she would say. My mum and me, we'll be off out.

Yes, they'd be off places, and she would never again have to worry about how much she wished that Enid's mother were hers instead.

Her father finished chewing. 'Och, Fleur,' he said, shaking his head, 'just you hold your horses a minute. A car's a major expense.'

'Oh, come on!' Fleur cried, her eyes still shining. 'Now we can *afford* it.'

'Aye,' he sighed, 'we could maybe buy it. But we couldn't run it.'

'Oh, for God's sake, Raymond, of course we could!' She picked up the letter and waved it at him. 'Look! Five hundred! What's the point of having a garage and no car? You *said* we'd get a car.'

'Aye, one day. I never said when. We're still paying off the stereogram.'

Fleur's mouth twisted. Lila, recognising dangerous ground, stood up and began stacking the plates. Her father did not believe in hire purchase so her mother had bought the Decca stereogram – glide-away doors, dark walnut finish, three speakers, four-speed auto-changer – by forging his signature on the forms and on the cheque for the down payment. It had cost 95 guineas and the instalments would go on for another three and a half years.

'That's just *typical* of you. What's that got to do with it? I suppose you think I should sit in this dump with nothing decent to play records on?'

Raymond said, 'Och, Fleur, I'm just saying—'

'If it was up to you we'd never buy a thing. Don't be such a bloody wet blanket, we *need* a car. Of course we should get it now, stuck out here! With a garage and no car!'

'I'm just saying . . . There's purchase tax, don't forget. That bumps it up.'

'We've got five hundred!'

'There's the servicing.'

'Oh, typical. You're so mean. You're a mean *bastard*!'

'Fleur! There is no call . . .'

'Oh, for God's sake, Raymond!'

'Well, it's a fact. And there's insurance, and have you any notion what petrol costs? And you've to take into account,' he said mournfully, 'depreciation. You never get your money back on a car. We'd be better seeing to the damp.'

There was a tight moment of silence.

'You mean bastard! You *bastard*!'

Lila stepped swiftly out of the way. Fleur stormed out with a scream about the Last Bloody Straw, trapping a wad of mint green nylon in the door. It muffled the slam and ruined the exit. She screamed again and yanked the material after her, ripping it. Lila sat down again and waited while her cornflakes sank in the milk and collapsed into saturated orange scabs. The music room door slammed, *Turandot* started, and her father went to work.

Lila had watched him cycle past the window and over the bridge towards Burnhead, his pumping feet appearing and disappearing from under his grey plastic cycling cape. Then, bludgeoned by the noise and surrendering herself to a trance of loathing for the wet view, she did not move from the window. Afternoon shadow would crawl into the room and displace the morning's, and she would not move. She did not wonder if from the room across the hall her mother was staring at the same view and escaping into a trance of her own. The rain dripped down. *Monday is pale green and unripe. Tuesday is beige, Wednesday is white.* But they weren't; the days were insubstantial, colourless, nothing more than shadows burning dimly in emptiness, putting out no heat. She felt trapped and erased, and could not move. She would fall away into ash, probably, in the end.

My first thought is just to get people in. Just get a couple of men in and tell them to get rid of the lot; there are firms that do such things. But when I call the solicitor to get the name of somebody who will take it on for me, it turns out I can't. I find that the solicitor requires me to go through 'the deceased's effects', something to do with valuation and tax, and now there's more. They ask me if the death has been registered. I have to call the bank, they need the numbers of his accounts and any cards which somehow I have to find, why haven't *they* got them? And the undertaker suggests I may care to look out a set of clothes for him unless I want him sent off in the pyjamas he was wearing or wrapped in a polyester shroud. They all need copies of the death certificate.

I have to find things. I have to think. I have to organise. I am unnerved, because these are tasks for which I am not equipped and have no aptitude: tasks requiring at the very least completed forms, lists, decisions and in all probability also buckets and bin bags and rubber gloves. Now I realise that with him gone I was imagining this place already empty of anything important. Not that I think that things left behind spill spontaneously out of houses and dispose of themselves, but I am not prepared for discovering significance in the clutter. It's surprising, like raking over a rubbish dump and finding it full of things I want. I'm not talking about discovering treasure. It's the cheap, broken, dirty things – his disposable razor, a comb with oily strands of hair coiled in it, a tin opener sticky with the dark glue of canned foods, objects I don't recognise and never watched him use – that lie in wait and assault me, because I see them in his hands. I see the daily pickings-up and placings-down of objects by those hands, everyday tasks filling year after year and becoming in themselves the main point, the last of his pride residing in such lonely skills as shaving himself unaided or opening a small tin of baked beans. As Christine says, he was still managing fine.

The picture I have of his hands comes from childhood. They are huge, safe paddles, warm and oddly veined and three times bigger than mine. Which brings me to the problem of his body. I have no intention of seeing it; I want to think it's just a container of no further use, of no more interest than an empty eggshell. But I want to see his hands. I must see his hands one last time, so that's another bloody thing I have to arrange.

I brace myself to get on, to concentrate on the surfaces, and I decide to begin with the topmost layer, the room he lived in: taking down the signs of his routines, assessing the objects he touched four days ago, disturbing the last air he breathed. But all I see is how immutable his things are and how eloquent, on the subject of his loneliness and my neglect. His 'effects' exude the silent loyalty of a bereaved dog; there is something stubborn in their failure to reflect that the life they belonged to is over. A *Radio Times* lies on the edge of the hearth by the armchair, folded over to last Wednesday where *Countdown* is ringed in a shaky, ragged circle. The armchair is like an animal's bed, layered and bumpy with extra rugs and cushions, as squashed and favourite as a nest lined with scraps. It still harbours the crumbs he let fall, still waits for his backside and thighs to hover and fold and collapse into the two channels in the seat. Everywhere, on chair arms and light switches and door handles, there's a waxy patina of grey, the pewtery shine of gentle fingers depositing their oil so imperceptibly there is something sinister in it.

I have not yet dared open a cupboard or a drawer. I start with the sideboard, expecting its shelves to harbour sauce bottles stuck on to spilt syrupy rings, and I am amazed to find instead row upon row of smooth glass paperweights with chips of coloured glass trapped inside that look like petrified anemones or bunches of tight stone flowers. There must be over thirty, each one different, each placed on tissue paper. He never deliberately collected anything, nor was his life prone to the incidental accretion of cherishable objects. I want to ask him where they came from, and why, when dirt became invisible to him elsewhere, he has not let it touch these. I see his hands again, turning each glass sphere in warm soapy water and drying it, holding it up to the window to catch the unchanging colours, placing it on fresh paper. Small rays of a simple, ritual happiness in taking care of them still shine from their surfaces. I tell myself that he would like them set aside and kept apart from the grime elsewhere in the house. In death, he is full of preferences and reasons; in guilt, I am full of consideration for them.

And so, I go up to the attic to see if there is an empty box up there for the paperweights, and now I have got myself into something. There are no boxes, at least not empty ones. There are boxes and tea chests, full mostly of papers thrown in anyhow and spilling over the edges, with shadows of dust sloping into their depths like a powdering of charcoal over white hillsides. There are scrunched-up piles of cloth on the floor, heaps of unrecognisable shapes wrapped in newspaper and pushed in one corner next to suitcases; there are dustsheets, a yellow-grey glacier of newspapers in a slow slide against the wall, a row of jars. A thousand doomed mending jobs flung through the barely opened door have landed across the camp bed or have missed it and hit the floor: bits of lamps, a bag of old plugs, coils of flex ending in wire tongues, chair legs, wallpaper, linoleum off-cuts, picture frames with broken glass, an open box full of tools fused together under a coat of rust like handfuls of sifted sand. Standing up here under the attic skylight at the back of the house, I realise I can hear the sea, and then everything in the room seems to have come from there, thrown up in great freak waves and deposited to rot: the washed-up relics, ruined and stranded after the tide.

I turn to go back downstairs but I know I can't. I can't go on clearing out his sideboard, emptying his fridge, sorting his clothes, with all this waiting above. I tell myself it makes sense to change the plan, to start here at the top of the house and in the scene of greatest chaos and decay, but that's not it. It's the sight of the camp bed and a glimpse of the papers stuffed into the tea chests that make me admit that this is what was waiting all along.

And maybe it should, but it does not surprise me that stuff from the *Turandot* summer is still here, though it doesn't look deliberately kept, and certainly can't have been cherished. On the morning after that unforgettable first night it must have been unbearable for him to see it: cuttings and scraps of paper and lists and sheets of music and props and bits of costume and the rest of it all over the empty house, so I guess he bundled it up and just stuffed it up here, maybe for my mother to collect later, which of course she never did. It doesn't look as if anyone has touched any of it since. I wonder if he forgot about it. I can only hope so.

I bring the tea chests down, scratching my shins on the way, and start them in no particular order – my eye caught first, I suppose, by the cutting from the *Burnhead & District Adver-tiser* on the top of one of them.

3

It was Wednesday and *Turandot* still raged from the music room. Fleur's voice had deteriorated to a rasp and now she was singing along with Callas only in short bursts. It seemed to Lila that everything sung by one person to another in an opera was a complaint of some kind – too heartless, too cruel, too jealous, too beautiful, too young to die – and also a waste of breath. It was all supposed to be about love. But wasn't it obvious that nothing would be settled before there was blood on the floor?

And now an old man was singing:

Abbi di me pietà!
Non posso staccarmi da te!

Lila had been put through enough books with titles such as *Opera Tales for Children* to know the *Turandot* story. It was Timur, the deposed and exiled king of Tartary, roaming disguised and unwanted somewhere through Act I, alone but for his loyal slave girl Liù. Have pity, he sings to his son, I can't separate myself from you. Have pity. I cast myself moaning at your feet.

She remembered. Timur has just come across his lost son, Prince Calaf, also exiled and in disguise. But joy is short-lived because no sooner are they reunited than Calaf glimpses the Princess Turandot, falls in love instantly and vows to solve the riddles that will win her in marriage. Timur begs him not to try.

Lila sighed. The story was a fairy tale, full of people who were not very real, yet Timur's frail plea to Calaf brought her own father to mind. Not that *I cast myself moaning at your feet* was the kind of thing Raymond would ordinarily come out with, but Timur sounded more tired than he ought to be and her father, too, cranked his voice into speech with difficulty, as if winding up words in a bucket from a brackish, underused well. By contrast her mother's words were always waiting in her mouth, ready. Lila began to listen as though her father, no less deposed or exiled or royal for being a lawyer's clerk rather than the king of Tartary, were across the hall on his knees in front of the Decca stereogram, beseeching her mint green nylon dressing-gowned mother to have pity on him. Casting aside his disguise of grey cycling cape, her wandering, exhausted father would beg:

Pietà! Pietà! Non voler la mia morte!

Pity! Pity! Do not wish my death!

It wouldn't work. Anything sung from the heart would sound out of place in 5 Seaview Villas; the house was too damp for heroics. It was one of a row of five built in the 1930s, between two wars. There were meant to be more of them; Seaview Villas were to have been the start of a new suburb – high-class, according to Raymond – between Burnhead and Monkton, but for some reason the others never got built. So the five stood detached and shabby along the road in plots too small for them, looking like the abandoned advance party they were and guarding the empty land behind that nobody wanted, a flat stretch between road and sea less attractive or useful than either salt marsh or meadow, where hardly anything grew in the briny wind off the Firth of Clyde. Across this stretch and almost at right angles to the road, on the Burnhead side of Seaview Villas, ran the Pow Burn. Its brown water trickled between banks overgrown with nettles and under the sandstone bridge next to 1 Seaview Villas, and emptied thickly into the sea.

Like the others, number 5 was double-fronted, with ruby and dark green glass in a pattern of diamonds and leaves in the top pane of the downstairs windows, and had been cheap for its size. But it was the only house to have had a brick garage added at some later point on its far side, there being no space between the others for garages. (This small superiority had softened Fleur's dismay a little when Raymond had first brought her here but because, fifteen years later, it sheltered nothing but Raymond's bicycle, the garage now enraged her.) The front gardens were so small that the houses had the look of wide matrons lifting little green aprons clear of splashes from the road that ran by much too close. When Fleur complained from time to time about the permanent garnish of rubbish and grey dust in the hedge, Raymond told her that the houses were built close to the road because of the drains.

'Drains,' she would say, as if drains could ever be a reason for anything. 'For God's sake don't talk to me about drains.'

'Och, Fleur,' he might reply, or he might not bother; his failure to win her over in the matter of drains would be noted whether he spoke or not. If Lila were present Fleur might cast her a glance and raise her eyes and her father would look droopily from Fleur to Lila and back again, getting them no further forward with the drains but implicating Lila in the general exasperation and fixing her firmly in the middle.

Drains, and all matters concerning the disposal of water were often on Raymond's mind, for in and around 5 Seaview Villas there was too much of it. Damp lived there too, and to Lila that also seemed in-betweenish, neither wet nor dry, just *damp*; hinderingly dank like her father, whose fault it seemed. Damp was always nearby, waiting upstairs or in the room next door. They quietly tracked its movements as if it were the owner of the house, a smelly old relation who must be tolerated and whom they secretly couldn't wait to see dead and buried. Raymond made a hobby of it. He called it intramural moisture. It was a minor science, he said. The movement of intramural moisture was predictable because certain materials retained moisture while others drew it – it was a question of drawing the moisture. With pathetic optimism he applied his mind to futile little remedies, stalking the damp and laying traps: rice grains in the salt cellar, a dish of pumice stones in the pantry, a branch of seaweed at the back door. He forbade houseplants, sprinkled talcum powder on the carpets, pasted the downstairs floors with rubberised paint. Intramural moisture was not drawn.

They heard it in the tapping of rain on the hedge, the drip from downpipes, and if they did not hear it they felt it in the claggy weight of clothes left too long in wardrobes. They smelled it in the yeasty gust from a cupboard suddenly opened and they tasted it when a biscuit that should have broken tight and crisp instead clung in a sluggish pulp to the roof of the mouth. Every spreading stain on the wallpaper and fresh patch of mould cast a new pall over their mealtimes, which were anyway quiet but for the excruciating chewing and swallowing noises of people trying to eat silently and Fleur's 'Oh, for God's sake, Raymond!' when he clanged his fork against his teeth. And all the time from behind the walls it seemed that the damp, too, contributed to the hush with the wordless percolation of water through plaster.

'Skirting board's warped,' Lila's father might offer. 'Of course, wood retains intramural moisture. There's a plastic skirting you can get now we'll maybe try.'

Her mother would adjust her immaculate shoulder seams, looking across the table not at Raymond's face but at his hands, which seemed to appall her. Lila didn't know why; he kept them clean and usually remembered to hold a knife to her satisfaction, tucking the handle out of sight inside the palm. But Fleur would watch his hands and shudder as if she were managing, just, not to scream out loud.

'I don't suppose I am ever going to get a holiday,' she might reply. Then she would lift the salt cellar and shake it over her plate and because it was clogged with damp and rice, no salt would come out, precisely as she intended.

Nor did Seaview Villas view the sea. The dining room window faced inland. Lila was looking out at the road and beyond that a kind of bogus farm with tussocky fields bordered by barbed wire and hawthorn, that harboured broken drainpipes and lost hubcaps and in whose corners pieces of metal and piping that could once have been bicycle parts or bathroom fittings were stacked. Today some cows loitered round the pylon in the middle of the field bordering the road, offering their brown and white sides to slanting arrows of rain.

The farmhouse lay at the end of a cinder track that ran past the pylon and down through more fields. Today it was partially obscured by the only tall trees for miles – sycamores, according to Raymond – whose branches were almost black against a sky the colour of cold grease, but for most of the year you could see it, a red-brick house that would have looked ordinary in any street in any unprosperous town, with the farm sheds set randomly around it.

And offering a view in one direction of a farm that didn't look like one, 5 Seaview Villas looked out from the back towards a beach that was not much of a beach. The shore behind the house was not like Burnhead's proper seafront nearly a mile south that drew the Glasgow crowds in summer, with the new coach park, boating pond, putting green and coloured lights along the esplanade, and where a line of semidetached villas not only viewed the sea but offered 'B & B, H & C, Home Baking & TV Lounge' on creaking board signs.

The cross tides met and curled in on the length of coast behind Seaview Villas in a particular way that dumped all the seaweed in that spot; when a west wind blew in hard on a rainy day the smell was like old vegetables rather than brine and seashells. From her bedroom window at the side of the house, Lila could see over the garage roof to the rise of the low dunes where the zigzag wrack of seaweed lay fused to the land, trapped and dead in the sharp dune grasses and dried more by the wind than by the sun into cracked brown shards. And apart from the seaweed and a faint whiff of cow, the air round Seaview Villas smelled of ash from the smouldering heaps of the council tip down by the shore, half a mile further up the coast towards Monkton. The sky, summer and winter, was usually white and empty but for twists of smoke from bonfires on the tip and the hundreds of seagulls that wheeled and dived over it in greedy orbit, their wings flapping to soundless music with the irregular, lazy beat of scavengers on the make.

Now in ancient Peking the courtier Ping was singing

Ho una casa nell'Honan . . .

I have a house in Honan
With its little blue lake
All girdled with bamboo . . .

Lila pictured it. A place, for all that it sounded suspiciously perfect, a real place that knew what it was. A place you wouldn't be ashamed to get stuck in.

I wonder if one ought to wear a hat with trousers? I always think it looks a little odd. I have one with me, in case I wear the skirt.

I am roused to this and other practical thoughts. His death should be announced in the *Burnhead & District Advertiser*. I jot down the names and dates and hope I've got them right. The date of death is easy. But was he born in 1918 or 1919 – his birthday was February 10th, that I do know, but was he eighty-four or eighty-five? Heaven knows where his birth certificate is and I haven't the heart to go looking; I've seen enough for today. My guess is 1918. I may be out by a year but there's nobody to ask which means there's nobody to mind if I'm wrong. Strange to think that if it was 1918 he was a wartime baby like me, and with me being born in May 1945 we were both only just wartime babies, both born right at the end. Never occurred to me before.

I find I don't feel altogether insincere saying 'beloved'. So I will put 'Raymond James Duncan, aged eighty-five, beloved father of Lila du Cann' and leave it at that. I'm sticking to 'du Cann'. I don't need to revert to 'Duncan' just because he's dead and anyway, I changed my name too long ago to switch back now. I won't add 'soprano' or anything, people will probably know. Nor am I going to put after his name 'widower of the late Florence' even though they never divorced, because I can't go as far as 'beloved' in front of 'widower', and its absence would make the whole thing look odd. Is there something else? It feels as if there should be something but I can't think what. My thinking is letting me down, oddly; it's not quite that I can't think, it's that the thinking I'm doing feels a little less reliable.

Anyway, I can't think what else unless it's 'sadly missed'. I don't think 'sadly missed' is called for.

Although, strangely, he is.

I could telephone the paper and give them the wording but I don't trust them not to misspell 'du Cann'. I shall write it all out and take it in person and make sure it's taken down correctly. In any case I could do with an outing. There's nothing here I can eat and there are other errands, too.

The funeral. Before I get as far as the newspaper office I realise what's missing. You have to say in the notices what the funeral arrangements are, don't you? The undertaker did hint something about 'arrangements' on the telephone but I put them off coming to talk to me about them. Why do undertakers always hint? But arrangements must be made and they are up to me, too. He left no instructions.

So I park in Burnhead, in a car park behind a supermarket that never used to be there. It doesn't surprise me that the Main Street's changed in over forty years but I am not prepared for the extra smells and colours and all the glass. Every third place is a Thai or Chinese or Indian takeaway and is a Palace or a Garden or a Jewel according to the signs painted in gold over purple, yellow or red. They all have flat windows reaching to the ground showing interiors full of white light and tiles and benches where you sit and wait as if you're keeping an appointment at a clinic for people with some affliction connected to deep frying. It's funny to remember a time when you could get fish and chips at one end of Burnhead from the Seashell Café, at the other from the Locarno or in the middle from the Central, and you felt spoiled for choice.

Today a low winter sun slants across the street. The pavement on one side is a tunnel of cold shadow, on the other a long row of glass shop fronts burns in the fire of the reflected sun and shimmers as if furnaces blaze inside. Sew Right is no more, of course. In its window hang those vertical blinds like strips of cardboard joined by loops of thin chain, and the place now offers IT Logistics and Database Solutions.

But I'm looking for a church, of which Burnhead used to have at least half a dozen. The South Church has a new porch with a ramp and has become a Centre for Family Counselling and Child Psychology Services. Kingcase looks unchanged, colourless – its walls still craggy and black and its arched windows filled with small panes of plain glass – except that where there used to be a painted sign with Times of Worship there's now an enormous lit-up board telling me about Opportunities for Praise and Thanksgiving. But I do not want to praise and I don't feel grateful. It is no help to me to know that there are crèche facilities on Sundays (bring your children), a service for Young People once a month (bring an instrument!) or that Mums' Flex 'n' Stretch is restarting after Easter (mats provided). I walk on, thinking about the funeral. I don't object to talk of God – what's the alternative? – but I want it unembellished. Suddenly I decide that there will be no singing. He didn't care for music so I think he would approve and I, certainly, would prefer there to be none. I think being here again is renewing my awareness of its power to falsify.

I know it can't still be here after all this time but I turn off Main Street and walk down Bridge Street. It won't be there. Even during Enid's short spell in their clutches there was something rickety about them, her Fellowship of Sinai Gathering in His Name. I don't mean rickety about their convictions. They were so lost in those that they had lost also all sight of themselves, that was the trouble. They were so cheerful and absorbed in their hobby they didn't notice they looked mad to everyone else, like people at dog shows. What was rickety was their grasp of the idea that religious fervour need not preclude caring what you look like. Maybe that was one reason why Enid's fad was so short-lived. Their clothes embarrassed her.

The place where they used to gather was rickety, too, little more than a shack with a corrugated roof and arched windows with railings round it, near the bottom of Bridge Street between the railway line and the back of the post office. It always looked shut up and in need of repainting, and nobody ever did anything about the buddleia and dock and willowherb that grew in the few feet of ground between the walls and railings. If Jesus died so that the Fellowship of Sinai might Gather in His Name, he had every right to be disappointed in how the bargain turned out.

So it is a surprise, not to find that the shack is no more but to see that it has been replaced with a red-brick building, bigger but of exactly the same shape, so new and hard that it looks as if it has not been long out of doors. The bricks have the bright colour and sharp angles of a child's picture. The railings have gone. Instead there is a low double-sided wall that serves as a container for a line of lush phoney plants of the kind that sometimes hang outside pubs, weeping figs and palms, which seem to me appropriate choices for a biblically-inspired enterprise. There is a sign on the wall that says Evangelical Lutheran Fellowship. The windows are set very high and the building has the same shut-up and empty look that the old place had, but I try the door quietly and it opens into a space of blond wood that smells of varnish, and from deeper inside I hear two people, a man and a woman, talking as they set out chairs across the floor. They have American accents, which is another surprise, and as soon as they catch sight of me they come forward beaming white porcelain smiles. Under the strip lights they look newly wakened, as if they had set some alarm clock whose ring coincided with my arrival.

They tell me they are Luke and Lucy and happy to meet me and that Luke is the pastor and Lucy is his wife. When I tell them my name and that I want to arrange a funeral for my father Luke says, Lila, hey. This must be a hard time for you.

He leads me to a chair. Lucy disappears.

This is the Fellowship of Sinai, isn't it? I ask. Because it all seems very different and I want to be sure the funeral will have no singing. I remember the Fellowship of Sinai never had singing.

Luke tells me there has been much prayer and debate on this issue since the Fellowship of Sinai merged with Brothers and Sisters in Evangelical Lutheranism in 1987, when the brothers and sisters came over from Burnhead's twin town, Vandalia,

Ohio, to take up what he calls their 'Scaddish outreach mission'. I move him on from giving me the entire history and back to the point. Is there singing or isn't there?

The current position, he tells me, is that it all depends. The brothers and sisters, while neither down on nor up for singing in principle, feel that music can enhance Scripture and consequently 'our experience of Jesus'. But it is by no means necessary and there remain a diminishing few of the original Sinai Fellows who are strongly opposed. So it's optional. He assures me that the Divine Shepherd will hear every word taken to Him by a person with a humble heart.

So delivery method optional, I say. Kneeling in silent prayer or borne on wings of song, you're not fussy?

He says, Lila, God will know what is in your heart however you speak to Him. In that sense, no ma'am, the Divine Shepherd is not fussy.

Then I want a funeral without singing or music of any kind. That is what I would prefer.

Luke tells me I have come to the right place. He is dying to talk more but I write out my address and number, and the undertaker's.

I tell him, As long as there's no singing it'll be fine. Please just fix the time to fit in with what the undertakers are arranging with the crematorium and let me know.

He asks if I'm sure I'm comfortable with that. Don't I want more input?

I say, No I don't, and you needn't come up with much to say. He was eighty-five and there won't be many there. His name was Raymond Duncan.

He says, Lila, I mean this is kind of a hard call. I didn't have the pleasure of knowing your father.

I know it's hard, I tell him. I didn't either.

I say goodbye and leave, though I have to accede to being prayed for.

———•◦•———

4

Nothing changed. Fleur played *Turandot*, Enid did not come, Raymond cycled through the rain between 5 Seaview Villas and Kerr, Mather & McNeill. He and Lila spoke like prisoners, as if speech were circumscribed and the overuse of words punishable in some way.

Milkman's wanting paying, it's three and eight.

There's five, get the change.

Fleur was still camped out in the music room. She had become nocturnal, timing her forays to the kitchen and bathroom at night whenever she could. Occasionally in the daytime, looking displaced and pale and wafting her green folds after her, she would meet Lila on the stairs and pass without a word. Perhaps to show that she was not utterly mad she would sometimes try to ruffle her hair or pat her backside as she went by, but in brash daylight her gestures were gawky. They carried too much force; she could not help a pulse of aggression entering her hands.

At night Lila would go upstairs leaving her father staring at the television in the back room off the kitchen, or wiping round the sink, stoking the Rayburn, cleaning his shoes. Lying in bed she would hear over the blaring of *Turandot* the slam as he left the house by the back door and sloped off across the garden, through the door in the wall and down to the shore.

On Friday as he left for work he said, with a tired glance at the music room door, 'Aye well, Lizzie. She's gone too far this time. Stereogram'll overheat. It'll blow a valve in the end. Can't be long now.'

It was his longest speech of the week. Lila looked away in

case even meeting his eye might make him think she was on his side. Not that she thought her mother was in the right; she simply never knew whose colours to wear. The choice was too stark, nor did it matter. Her parents argued over real things: the damp, the Premium Bond, but over unreal ones too, such as whether the ants' nest at the back door step was in the same place this year as last or not. They were not interested in the difference, nor in whether Lila agreed with one or the other.

'Then maybe we'll get a wee bit of peace. Eh, Lizzie? Hear it and tremble.'

Lila studied his face and wondered why, when she might be kinder to him, she wasn't. Maybe it was simply that kindness was too embarrassing in a house where endearments were never heard, and too risky, for what if she created in him an expectation of future kindness? She didn't know how much she had.

'The noise isn't the point,' she said.

She meant it. In their house it was the silences that made her head ache with watchfulness; she was alert always to the danger of lips pressed together, an unknowable distance in the eyes, the cardigan adjusted pointlessly over the shoulders. In a perfect copy of her mother's manner, she stood up from the table and with a single, slow blink turned her head to gaze past Raymond through the window. She couldn't deny herself the sting of pleasure it gave her to dismiss him, and what difference would a little more unkindness make?

A few minutes later she watched him cycle off in the rain towards Burnhead. She continued to stand, the remnants of his breakfast behind her. *Turandot* sounded to her now no more than a slanging match. She knew that the opera ended – how else? – in the triumph of true love, but there was a lot of wailing at the moon to be got through before that happened. People had to waste themselves; in the name of love they had to lie down and be trampled on and vow to tear out their hearts, and the idea exhausted her.

By lunchtime she had not moved from the dining room. *Turandot* had been played all the way through and started over again; Act I came to an end with the crashing of gongs. She waited for Act II. Nothing came, then the music room door opened and she heard the clip-slap, clip-slap of Fleur's mules along the hall. The sound faded to a sweet, sudden silence; Lila waited, listening. Only then, as if her other senses had just been allowed to waken, did she take in the crumby table, the used plates and cups and ashtray. She began clearing up, faintly puzzled. Surely breakfast had been days ago.

It was while she was drying the cutlery she began to feel something else lurking under the silence. The atmosphere had changed. The rain had stopped; maybe things were about to get better, maybe some transformation was even now taking place. In a minute her mother would come downstairs and she would be happy. A tingle started in Lila's chest. Such yearning was dangerous, and she tried to catch hold of the fantasy and tie it down. She wouldn't, for instance, ask for her mother to become like Enid's mum. Fleur could carry on being conspicuous and English, she could even go on playing her records and dressing in her youthful and expensive way that was unlike any other mother in Burnhead. But if she could be cheerful, not occasionally hilarious and alarming, but cheerful in a daily sort of way you could rely on. If she could only laugh things off a little bit and keep some good mood over in reserve.

Lila let herself imagine how it would be. Her mother was in her bedroom now. She was washed and dressed, looking in her dressing-table mirror and clicking her tongue at herself, while sun slanted in through the window. The frivolous dressing gown – what had possessed her to buy that? – was cast on the floor ready to be thrown away. A white, solid, motherly kind of dressing gown was folded on the bed. She was about to turn and hurry downstairs; she would appear in the doorway with a dimply smile and take the tea towel from Lila's hands. She would say, Oh here, Lila, give me that, I'll finish up. You pop the kettle on and let's think about what to do this afternoon.

While Lila made tea she would put the dishes away, humming an easy tune, not one of her tragic ones. The day would open out like a story, filled with friendly talk, mellow with hope.

Now it's a rainy old day but that's not going to stop us, she would say. There's time to get into Ayr and back before your Dad's home. You need some summer clothes. Hourston's have some lovely new things in.

Lila gulped. If they were not getting the car then there was, after all, the Premium Bond to spend. Her daydreams varied in the details but they all featured her mother growing kind, her father in the background but vaguely included in the new warmth, and ended with her getting new clothes. And the daydreams failed her every time, returning her to her life unchanged unless a little more tainted and empty. Would she never learn? She tried to concentrate on something unselfish.

We'll make Dad his favourite supper, your poor Dad always comes home tired on a Friday.

Lila would look up and see her mother smiling. She would be as striking as ever with her carved mouth and large eyes, the shapely waist and ankles. But her beauty would be safer to look at. The edges would be softer; she would look warmed up, less easily broken.

She finished drying the spoons and started on the collection of dirty ashtrays next to the sink. Still no music. She peeped into the hall. The door stood ajar as her mother had left it. She stood with the sink cloth in her hand and waited for a sound; it was impossible to move upstairs without making the floor creak. The quiet was absolute. A new thought ticked through her head. How quickly and quietly could a person commit suicide? In an opera you could see it coming and even then it took forever and could be heard five streets away but what if, in real life, it could be accomplished as unobtrusively as popping upstairs for a minute, in no more time than it took to brush your hair? Could pills or razor blades or a noose work that fast? She held her breath and listened again for a cough or footstep, afraid that she might not hear such little sounds over the thudding of her heart. It could not, surely, be happening just over her head. She returned to the kitchen and took up another ashtray. It could not be happening. There would be crying and pain and mess, she reasoned, and there was only silence. At the same time her mind was working guiltily, trying to devise a scale on which to calculate just how desperate her mother was.

She rubbed at the ashtray over and over, raising its sharp, dirty smell. Suppose it could be even more modestly done, without drawing blood or stopping airways or poisoning the heart? It might be possible simply to slip away in the manner of her mother's tragic sopranos – like Mimi, Violetta – who could expire without having to do very much apart from singing about it. Suppose the creeping illness whose symptoms never seemed all that distressing, or the betrayed heart, or the selfless renunciation (or the Last Bloody Straw) were enough to see you off, if that was what you wanted, without the need for anything as crude as a suicide method? Lila threw down the cloth and made for the stairs.

Her mother was not in her own bedroom, nor Raymond's, nor Lila's, nor the bathroom nor the small spare bedroom. Lila paused on the landing and gazed up the attic stairs. Nobody ever went up there. The two attic rooms were full of junk that nobody wanted, and suddenly she knew. Her mother had taken herself off to die in the attic, among the old and useless and broken things. She took the stairs slowly, noticing the smell grow thicker as she went. At the top, she halted. The two doors in front of her were closed. Silence was embedded here like silt, laid down in the dust. Motes swam in the beam of light that shone from the skylight in the roof. She checked both rooms. Empty.

She clumped back down to her own room, her heart tilting uncomfortably. She needed to hide; she needed the secrecy of a confessional that would absorb her disappointment at not having come across her mother dead. To think that she might want her mother to die just so that life would be different made her feel warped and ashamed; she had to re-arrange her mind so that the idea never crossed it again. Life was going to continue in the same way. There was going to be more of it: more being afraid to move from one room all day, more loneliness in her parents' company, more nights lying in bed with her breath trapped in her throat.

She looked out across the waste ground behind the house, now a lurid patchy green after the rain, to where the sea writhed in to the shore. Though her curiosity about her mother's whereabouts was diminishing now that she was not dead in the attic, she wondered again where she was. Had she got dressed and taken herself off for a walk? But Fleur hated the beach, and there was nowhere else to walk unless you roamed along the road and it was impossible to do that without looking stray and half-witted. Lila's eye was drawn from the distance to something almost immediately below. The front double doors of the garage were closed as usual, but the side door into the garage from the back garden was open. Above it, the garage roof seemed to be swaying slightly. When she looked properly she saw that it was the drift of a soft line of smoke rising from the joins between rows of slates that made it appear to move.

She turned and ran downstairs, out through the kitchen and across the grass. Soft rasping noises and whining grunts were coming from the open door; inside, her mother was crouched and weeping, striking matches and tossing them into a high mound of twisted newspapers and sticks set in the middle of the floor. As she moved, the skirt of the dressing gown, gauzy and flammable, floated and sank over the edges of the heap; from her wrists the long sleeves were already waving like smoke. Lila stared at the drifting folds and the crossed sticks of firewood hazy beneath the green shadow and reaching up like open beaks, pulling at the material. She couldn't help waiting to see what would happen.

The paper was refusing to catch properly. With each dropped and extinguished match Fleur cursed, leaned forward and blew hard. Some paper crackled and the pile settled a little.

'*God!* Oh, for God's sake! Oh, this bloody place!' she moaned. She paused and swallowed, crouched deeper and blew and blew again.

'Might have . . . known . . . too . . . oh, bloody *typical* . . . damp . . . bloody *burn*, damn you . . . Oh, *God!*'

She poked at the sticks in the centre of the fire and a cloud of smoke bulged out from the papers and into her face. Weak glimmers of flame flared and subsided. She threw in another match, leaned forward and blew again. A curl of flame gusted at her and she leapt to get away, snatching her dressing gown and pulling out several sticks that clung to the hem.

She wiped her eyes and nose with her sleeve, bringing away a trail of sooty slime, and glared at Lila.

'What do you want? What are you staring at?'

For a moment Lila could not speak. Her mother's face had shrunk to a tiny white mask in which her lips opened and closed over teeth that seemed smaller and sharper than before. Her frayed sleeves hung over her hands; she was like a creature from a fable, a fairy wrecked and grounded after some calamity, her ruined wings in shreds. But the effort of blowing had made her look younger; her eyes were hard and bright.

'Well?'

'What – what are you *doing*?'

'Oh, for God's *sake*! For God's sake, I am so sick and tired, have you no idea? You and your damn father, the bastard, the bloody *bastard*.'

'But why are you . . .'

'Him and his precious bloody garage! I've had enough, I'll bloody show him!'

She barged past her out to the garden. Lila was too frightened to follow and besides, there was the fire; the smoke behind her was already thick and sulphurous. She stepped to the doorway for a lungful of air and turned back but there was so much smoke she could hardly see. Shielding her eyes, she stamped at the edges of the pile on the floor until her breath gave out, then she sucked in another and her throat filled with hot smoke. She stumbled to the door, retching and dizzy. Several more times she ventured back in and tried to stamp out the fire, retreating each time to the door for breath and returning to find that the flames had encroached further. Her eyes were almost blinded by streaming tears and when she coughed she doubled over with stinging, zig-zagging pains in her chest. There was now heat coming off the fire and she could hear ominous crackling noises from deep inside it. Licks of orange brightened the gloom of the smoke. She ran to the outside tap on the back wall of the house and found a watering can already half-full of rainwater, filled it to the top and lurched back with it, water slapping over the sides and drenching her. With the first canful the fire hissed and collapsed a little. She came and went from the tap several times, dousing the flames until all that was left was a wet, burning stink in the air and a sulking heap from which trickles of water snaked out into black pools on the concrete.

Lila went back outside and collapsed breathless on to the grass, rubbing her eyes and shaking. She was shocked and cold and wet; her legs and arms were soaked and scratched, smeared with black, her nose and eyes sticky with smoke. Her hair and clothes reeked of it and she could taste it in her mouth. She lay for a few minutes with her eyes closed until the ground felt so cold against her back that she had to move. She struggled to her feet, paused, and looked round. All was quiet again. There was no sign of her mother. The door of the shed beyond her father's vegetable patch stood open and was moving gently in the wind; she could see that the shed was empty except for the usual gardening tools and the laden, chaotic shelves where he kept his weedkiller, pesticides, turpentine, brushes, half-empty tins of paint and sinister, unlabelled jars. Her mouth dried. How much poison stood on those shelves? Just then came a clatter and a loud cry from the driveway in front of the garage, and she started running.

Her mother was standing in a pool of red. Red ran down her flailing arms and dripped off the ends of her fingers, casting a ragged circle of splashes all around her. So it *was* happening. As Lila gazed, the world seemed to halt and stretch and fall away and everything became very quiet and flimsy, as in a slow-moving dream; her mother receded into silvery white air, the ground between them swelled and disintegrated, leaving her weightless in empty sky. She looked like a statue in a fountain although far-off and less solid, her red drapery shimmering and transparent, her form fluid, scintillating, as if Lila were staring across a bright, distorting distance or catching glimpses of her through water. Then her mother stooped to pick up something – a paintbrush – from the red pool, and when she straightened up and turned, the world dropped back in place. Shapes resumed boundaries and substance, colour flooded in. Time righted itself and began to tick along again, passing with the swift ease of a nightmare. Lila and her mother were back on the driveway under a rainy sky, their clothes stirring in the breeze, faces stained. A pair of seagulls gloated from the ridge of the garage roof.

With a quiet grunt, Fleur pushed one foot at the overturned paint tin and with the hand holding the brush she lifted the hair from her face. Behind her Lila read, in scarlet letters seven feet high across the left garage door,

BAST

Shining beads from the letter B were already glopping off the bottom of the door and staining the ground. From the tin – Lila recognised it as one of the colours her father had used for the kitchen cupboards – a red ooze was still spreading around her mother's feet. If it hadn't been spilled there would have been ample paint left for the

ARD

that she guessed she was planning for the right door to welcome her father home.

It was so nearly funny – the day's havoc ending in such a spectacle as these foolish giant letters, her mother dripping in paint not blood – that for a moment it seemed impossible that anything serious could be happening. But Lila was too frightened to laugh. There had been rows before, of course. It wasn't that. There had been objects thrown and broken, whole days of grand opera at numbing volume. But until now, 5 Seaview Villas had soaked up the arguments and held them in its walls, like the damp. The poisoned air in the house, bloated with spent storms, at least had not escaped, at least nobody *knew*. But this? Such unadorned madness would not be missed by anyone passing by on the road. It was not a busy road, but that was not what mattered: here was her mother out of doors in a rag of a dressing gown soaked in red paint, hair felted to her scalp and her eyes lost in hatred, in front of 'B A S T' seven feet high on the garage door. It was insane and shameful and worse than that, public, and she did not even appear to care.

A memory of *Turandot*'s jagged music was still sounding in Lila's head, reverberating like hollow pain. How shrill and untrustworthy those voices, what lies they told. Love made nothing clear or right. It did not triumph. As she looked at her mother standing on the driveway – ridiculous, filthy, defiant – Lila loved her with such a surge of want and pity and rage that she again wished her dead. This wasn't love the way an opera would have you believe it. The real thing was far too big a mess to fit to music. Lila leaned back against the wall of the house feeling the cold stone scrape against her spine, and buried her face in her hands. Real love could annihilate the beloved; there was in it something smirched and lethal.

When she looked up, she was alone. A pattern of footprints and flicks and scratches like fallen red petals and twigs trailed up the side of the garage towards the back garden. Once again *Turandot* wafted out from the house. Lila didn't much mind. It sounded almost like a return to normality. The rasp of the music and the lies it complained of were preferable, in their way, to silence.

I've been up since six, unable to sleep. I've got an ache in my legs and grit on my feet, as if I'd been walking about all night. The house is warmer than it used to be – all houses are – but all day I've felt the need to keep moving. Done a bit to shift the stuff in the kitchen. Oxfam, mainly.

I get to the undertakers late. It smells, in a chemical kind of way, layered, as if each smell oozes into another, higher one that is trying to mask it. The premises are done out in pale grey and lavender. The carpet has a pattern like scattered pins and there are misty photographs on the walls of mountains and sunsets and rainforests at dawn. I'm put in a waiting room with quilted armchairs and tight arrangements of artificial flowers in ugly colours – turquoise and ultramarine – and boxes of tissues. Wherever you look there are bibles. I wait while they dress him in the clothes I have brought and then they come to tell me he is ready.

He lies in a coffin in a room without windows. There are more chairs and acrylic flowers and bibles, but I don't take in any more detail than that. It's cold. The air-conditioning makes distant, electrical lapping sounds and in the glowing yellow light everything in the room looks buttered. I want to see his hands. One rests over the other across his torso and they look hard and waxy now, but I know them. I saw them lift teacups, wipe his moustache, wash carrots under the garden tap, but the surprising trust I feel about these hands means, I suppose, that they must also have spooned food into me, picked me up after falling, tidied my fringe out of my eyes, though I do not remember. It's an odd thought that his hands won't move again.

I pull up a chair and look at him hard, and am relieved to see that all that was important about his face is gone. He's aged, but considering he is dead he really doesn't look bad. What I am looking down at, dressed in a suit and tie and pillowed in wads of gleaming artificial satin, is not him. But it's a good thing to be reminded of who he once was, especially since I haven't seen him in nearly eight years.

Every couple of years I used to send him his tickets, for the flight and a seat in the stalls. Each time we act it out this way: it's dutiful of me to send for him, generous of him to pretend he is keen to come, essential for us both that the time together is short and that we make no reference to my mother, to Uncle George, or to my never coming any more to Seaview Villas. I make it easy. We do not meet until after the late finish of the performance in the evening and then it's just a drink before his taxi back to a slightly less than convenient hotel, and I always put him on an early flight home. I ring him next day to see that he has got back safely, and then resume the pattern of a short call every three weeks or so. Well, every month. We get quite good at this.

The last time turns out to be my last season in Antwerp, coincidentally, before my semi-retirement. It's a bitchy game, opera. And by then it's a struggle for him, but he still comes. I don't know what he is expecting – he says nothing about the performance except to ask if I am sure I'm in it as he didn't quite manage to spot me. He has never liked opera. I don't try to get him over after that. He isn't up to it anymore, and anyway by this time I am concentrating on building up my pupil numbers. Maybe I could come to see him, and we mumble about this on the telephone from time to time, but I tend to stay close to base and in touch with the opera house in case I'm needed at short notice. Disasters do happen! After all I do have the repertoire and they asked me to step in as Henrietta Maria in *I Puritani* once, in 1992.

I'm on the doorstep, I'm a local resource, use me! I keep telling them. I say, You know you can always call on me in a crisis, I don't mind short notice.

I don't think I manage to make them realise that I don't object to being rung up at any time.

———◦—◦◦—◦———

5

L
ila was stroking one finger through the red paint and wondering if it would come straight off the door with turpentine when Enid arrived. She turned and watched as she freewheeled on her bike through the puddles up the side of the house, feet outstretched and pedals ticking, her small eyes fixed on the doors. She stopped and balanced on one foot, spinning the pedal round with the other. She was wearing pedal pushers made from material patterned with pineapples, and a yellow knitted windcheater. Enid had no hips; the clothes were perfect on her, so light-hearted they made Lila's heart sink.

'Hiya, what's all that?' Enid asked, nodding past her.

'All what?' Lila said, not looking round.

'That. All that mess.' Enid turned glassy eyes on Lila and pulled a bag of Parma Violets from her pocket. She poured a few into Lila's cupped hand then tipped back her head and downed some herself.

'Senga's away to Filey till Wednesday,' she said in a gust of violet-scented breath. 'Senga's dead nice when you get to know her. What's the matter with you? What *is* that?'

'That?' Lila chewed and swallowed. 'Oh, don't you know? That's *Turandot*. It's an opera. My mother's playing records.'

'I don't mean the noise, I mean that. The letters, that all over the door. All that paint.'

'It's by Puccini. It's her favourite.'

'Not the noise – that. I'm talking about *that*.' Already she was preparing to win. Between them, it was always a victory to point out something embarrassing about the other. She leaned forward, peering and sniffing. 'You're filthy. You smell all smoky. Have you been crying?'

'*Crying?*' Lila said, too strenuously. ' 'Course not! No, I was I was just doing a bonfire. Just a minute ago. My mum – she had rubbish to burn, I was just burning a bit of rubbish. Makes your eyes sting.' She rubbed them to make the point.

'Stinks, anyway. So what is that – all that mess?'

Lila turned round. 'That? That was just an accident with the paint tin. It got knocked over. And the paint ran a bit when they did the letters.'

'*Who* though? What for? What's that meant to mean, bast? What's it meant to mean?'

'Oh, it's just this thing. Are they new?' Lila said, nodding at the pedal pushers. She was so envious of Enid's clothes she usually could not bear to draw attention to them, but she had to deflect her; she needed time to think of something.

Enid flicked a hand against her thigh and said, 'Uh-huh. My mum made them.'

Lila's insides curdled. 'Really nice.'

'They're only a Butterick,' Enid said. 'Out of a remnant.' She picked away a loose thread. 'You should get your mum to make you some.'

'Uh-huh.' Lila's mother did not sew. Enid knew this.

'See my mum? She made them all in the one go. Last night. Started when the shop shut.'

'Oh? Right you are, then.'

'If you ask her she'll give your mum a lend of the pattern.'

There was silence.

'Want a lend of the pattern?'

'Maybe.'

'My mum says they're that easy you don't even *need* the pattern. Only four pieces and a zip, five if you want the pocket. Not counting waistband, you can just use bias binding. Could yours not even manage that?'

'Maybe.'

'Can she really not sew at all then? Thinks she's the next Maria Callas. Senga and Linda says so too.'

'She does not.'

'See your mum, where is it she's from again?' Lila's mother was English. Enid also knew this.

'England,' Lila said, in a deliberately tired voice. 'So what?' Enid asked slowly, 'And what is it you said she used to be again?'

'An opera singer. I've told you before.'

Enid was glaring at her. 'Has she ever went to Italy?'

'No. So what? Neither's yours.'

'Ha! So! She can't have been a real opera singer, then. Senga says opera's Italian, you get it in Italy, and your mum's not from Italy. She's never even went!'

'*What?*'

'She's never went to Italy in her life! So how can she be?'

Lila pounced. 'See you? See Senga? You're stupid the both of you. You get opera loads of places, *loads* of places have opera, everybody knows that. You're just stupid. You get opera everywhere.'

Enid was unabashed. 'Not round here, you don't.'

Lila stared at her. She was always underestimating how unashamed Enid was of her own ignorance. Somehow, because Enid seemed simply not to believe in it, it became Lila's problem. She, not Enid, had to work around it.

'You're that childish,' Lila drawled. Enid shrugged. 'And anyway,' Lila went on, 'I'd have thought you're too busy going to church to bother with Senga McMillan. I wouldn't think going to *church* all the time was exactly Senga McMillan's cup of tea.'

'It's not going to church, it's the Fellowship of Sinai Gathering in His Name,' Enid said. 'Senga doesn't go. You don't have to if you don't want to.'

'Doesn't she now? So is she not heeding the Word? Dear, oh dear, oh dear. I thought that was a sin, not to heed the Word,' Lila said. 'That's what you said.'

Enid looked over the garage roof into the sky. 'The Lord is a loving father. He hears his children when they call unto him,' she said.

'And how is it you call, again? You don't have hymns, do you?'

'We do verses. *And* psalms.'

'Don't sing them though, do you? It's stupid. You just say them.'

'Music is a distraction from the Bible Message. Musical performance is a temptation to vanity. The Lord hears us when we speak in humble prayer.'

Lila felt suddenly sick at heart. 'Oh, who cares?' she said. It was tiring, to despise but at the same time envy Enid's certainties.

'The Lord does,' Enid said flatly. 'Anyway, Senga says it's a free country. What *is* that?'

From the front of the house came a blast of brass and strings and Lila's mother's voice, rising with Callas's:

Son la figlia del Cielo!

I am the daughter of Heaven!

'I told you, it's *Turandot*.'

'*No. That*. BAST.'

Lila turned back to the garage. '*B A S T*?' She spoke casually. 'Oh, the *B A S T*? It's this new thing, have you not heard?'

'*What* new thing?'

'This thing my mum's doing. She's doing this thing for opera singing. It's the Burnhead Association for Singing *Turandot*. It's for people that want to sing *Turandot*.'

Enid gazed at the garage door, dropping her bottom lip so that it hung free of the top one and revealed the bulge of her tongue, today stained violet. Lila had often seen her do this and she intended never to tell her how stupid it made her look.

'So why's it on the garage?'

'Because . . . because that's to be the headquarters. They're going to do it up inside.'

Enid's mind was clumsy with anything new. Lila watched her weigh up what she could see and hear against the reliability, or otherwise, of her explanation. For a moment she felt a secret joy in the speed of her own mind, until the difference between them filled her with loneliness.

'In a *garage*?'

'To begin with,' Lila said. 'Just to begin with.'

'Let me see.'

'No! You can't. It's not done yet. There's still clearing up to do.'

'Okay, I don't care,' Enid said. 'So what, anyway.'

'So *what*, what?'

'So what your mum's an opera singer, so what she's started a stupid singing *Turandot* thing. Who wants to sing, anyway?'

Lila said lightly, 'Well, actually, lots of people.'

'Not me. Senga neither. Wait till I tell her. And Linda. They'll die laughing. Want more violets?' She fished for the bag.

'You're just ignorant.'

'Who cares? Want to go down the shore?'

Lila didn't, but they went. She couldn't let Enid near the house.

They loitered for a while around the beach not far from the tip, kicking over piles of seaweed and the usual washed-up tangles of rope, bottle fragments, broken plastic and pulpy rags. Lila always half looked for treasure, hoping for something to glint through the green-black weed that she would spy before Enid did, but the gleam of silver or gold always turned out to be foil from a cigarette packet, a milk top, a tin can. They found the bumper of a car and a broken lobster creel, a table top and the remains of an armchair; they sniggered at the shreds of tampons lying ragged in the debris, bleached by salt water. Further on they found an upturned rear car seat and hauled it over and set it facing the sea next to a bare, washed-up tree trunk. Enid suggested collecting empty herring crates to use as little tables and making a fireplace in front of it with rocks, but after ten minutes neither of them could be bothered any more.

It rained again half-heartedly, in large, isolated drops that pocked the beach like silent gunfire and made a field of tiny craters all the way down to the sea, whose surface swallowed the rain with grey calm. Soon after that Lila fell mute and Enid, resentful at finding herself no less bored than when she arrived, sulked all the way back to the house to pick up her bike, and went home.

Lila saw her off from the driveway and wandered round to the back. The ruined green dressing gown was stuffed in a paper bag next to the dustbin. She fetched turpentine and rags from the shed and did her best with the paint marks on the kitchen floor and then she stood, becalmed in a turpentine haze mixed with the tarry smell from the Rayburn that filled the kitchen whenever rain got in the chimney. *Turandot* was still playing. She wondered if the volume of the stereogram had been turned down a little or if she were at last growing deaf. Exhausted, she climbed the stairs on shaking legs that she hardly trusted to get her to the top, collapsed on to her bed and fell asleep.

Later from her window she saw her father arrive, looking like a soft, battered grey bell under the billowing cycling cape. He set his bicycle against the wall and stared at the garage for a while, then he marched round to the back door, pulling the cape over his head. A few seconds later *Turandot* stopped. From downstairs Lila heard raised voices, and resigned herself. But not long afterwards the shouting stopped, too. A door opened and was closed. A hush settled over the house, but it was too early to tell if the Last Bloody Straw might be capitulating to Gone Too Far This Time. The silence was of the kind that occurs when an engine cuts out but might at any moment be kicked once more into combustible, raging life.

When she had waited for as long as she could, Lila crept across the landing to the top of the stairs. Would she always be like this, afraid to walk through the house? After her parents' rows she was always embarrassed at how long it took her to get used to being in the same room with them again; she didn't understand how they could be so unaffected, why for days afterwards only she remained wrung out by the things they'd said. She waited till she heard conversation before opening the kitchen door, believing that to arrive in the room during an exchange of words would make her entrance less conspicuous.

Her mother was sitting at the kitchen table with a burning cigarette in an ashtray and a cup of tea in front of her. She was wrapped in a thick dressing gown that didn't belong to her and she looked cleaner but bedraggled and nervy, as if she'd been recently plucked from a hideous predicament – pulled out of a pothole maybe, or winched from a shipwreck. She sent in Lila's direction, without catching her eye, the fluttery smile of someone rescued but not yet quite able to believe it. Raymond was leaning against the sink stroking his moustache and smoking, from time to time drinking from a bottle of beer – Fleur's authority in the matter of drinking straight from bottles (boorish, *typical*) having for the moment lapsed. He rose forward on his feet when Lila came in, gave her a nod and went over to the Rayburn. Setting the beer bottle down, he began cracking eggs into a bowl and beating them, holding the cigarette between two fingers as he worked, another of Fleur's strictures flouted.

'I've rung your Uncle George in London,' he said, not turning round. 'He's coming up to stay.'

Lila gasped as a shudder of pleasure and fright ran through her. '*When?* When's he arriving? How long for?' She hadn't seen him for more than two years. He'd be amazed to see that she was no longer just a little girl. He might think her pretty. He had to think her pretty.

'How long's he staying?'

Raymond was melting butter in a saucepan. He tipped in the eggs, set the pan back on the stove and began stirring.

'That depends,' her mother said flatly, drawing on her cigarette and looking at Raymond's back, 'on your precious father,' from which Lila guessed that she expected Uncle George to take her side about the car and to stay until her father caved in.

'Och, Fleur . . .'

'Oh, for God's sake . . .'

'That's enough. We've all had enough now.'

Both their voices were wary. Fleur drank some of her tea, her eyes still fixed on Raymond as he stirred at the stove. Just the prospect of Uncle George's presence seemed to create between them, if not harmony, then a slight benefit of the doubt.

'Eliza, make some toast, will you? Give your father a hand.'

'You leave Lizzie be, I'm managing. Want another cup?'

Lila went to the dining room to lay the table, not wanting to test the strength of the truce. A little later they sat down to eat, her parents grudgingly. Lila, between them, kept watch.

'You'll have to do something about the door. Before he comes. That spare room door won't close. It swings open.'

'It's holding moisture. You just need to push it hard so it clicks. I'll tell him he just needs to push it hard.'

'You'd better open the window. I can't reach it and the room needs airing.'

'There's damn all in the pantry. I'll get extra bread and eggs tomorrow. Lizzie could call at the butcher.'

'There's enough till the order comes. You can get the meat. I need her to help with the bed.'

'George likes an English paper. Is it *The Times* he likes?'

'He likes the *Listener* too. Order that.'

Later Lila asked again, 'How long's he staying?'

'He's on his summer holidays now, he's a free agent,' her father said. 'He's getting off crack of dawn, he should be here this time tomorrow,' he added more robustly, with a slight, head-of-household raising of his voice. Then he sucked his teeth and shook his head. 'Traffic permitting. It's July the first when all's said and done.' He had to tone down anything that might be veering towards optimism.

'But how long? How long's he staying for?' Lila asked.

Fleur raised one eyebrow and looked past Raymond.

'I told him his sister's been having hysterics,' he said. 'Right hysterics.'

'At least he understands,' Fleur said complacently, though her voice wavered. She lit another cigarette and shook out the match. 'George understands what it's like, suffering from nerves.'

Her mother was making every gesture prettier than usual. She nipped the match daintily between finger and thumb while her lips pouted smoke into little feathers over her head. Claiming George's understanding was all she needed to do to excuse herself. As long as George understood, she could call it 'nerves', as if setting the garage on fire and painting giant swear words all over it were just extra, mildly challenging facets of her attractiveness, so quirky and endearing there was no question of their having to be forgiven.

Lila felt sick. It was she, not her mother, whom Uncle George loved and approved of. His visits were so irregular and infrequent that Lila was a different person each time he came and yet each time she was certain, just from the way he looked at her, that his reserves of affection were hers. He was obliged, of course, not to make it too obvious; it was their shared knowledge, private and unspoken. How she adored him, how her love for him squeezed her heart, was her secret alone. She turned from the sight of her mother's cigarette between her long fingers and looked down at her own hands. They looked pink and boneless, unbearably childish. She wanted to be the one Uncle George could really love. Suppose she were just to die? He would never forget her then.

'Aye, right hysterics, and he says he'll stay till she's not having them any more,' Raymond said. 'Sends love to you as well, Lizzie, says *nil desperandum.*'

Lila caught the lifeline. *Nil desperandum* was their phrase. Uncle George had first said it years ago when she was little, bawling over a scraped knee; if he was saying it now he was sending a message to say he understood and remembered how it was between them. *Nil desperandum.* He would be here tomorrow. A shiver of expectation sparkled down her spine and she prayed silently for her mother to have hysterics indefinitely.

It's getting towards four in the afternoon when I leave the undertakers and finish my errands. I register the death, do a little bit of food shopping and go back to the car. It's too late for the newspaper office so I'll have to call them after all.

The sun is going down with one of those attention-seeking sunsets that occur here, great luminous sheets of pink and turquoise billowing up from the horizon. As I drive I find I am rather taken by it, garish though it is. The flat land between Burnhead and Seaview Villas is still empty, but now there is a long lay-by on the shore side of the road. I pull in and park, knowing it is useless to think I can capture the sunset by getting out of the car but wanting at least not to see it through glass, even though the wind buffets the door and I know it is getting cold. At the end of the lay-by I come across one of those clumsy stone tables tilted at an angle, with a map and diagrams of what you are supposed to look out for. Seagulls, apparently. Three kinds. This is news? It tells me also that this stretch of land down to the sea is no longer the pointless, marshy waste ground it was in my day. Now it is designated. They have made paths across it that are marked on the map by lines of meandering green dots. It seems I may not look at this land-scape simply because its empty darkness reflects my present mood or because I am drawn by the sunset. It is now an area of local ecological interest and I can 'access' more information if I visit some bloody website.

So even this small moment, my tiny, unplanned detour into melancholy has been anticipated and catered for and in a manner that seems to me typical of Burnhead: invasive, crass, and beside the point. Whether I'm ogling all the shades of pink or scanning the clouds for a glimpse of the Divine Shepherd or just depressing myself, I can't simply be left for a while to idle in a lay-by and watch the sky; I must count seagulls and be 'oriented' along phoney bark footpaths, grateful to the Burnhead Civic Amenities Trust and a clutch of minor charities. I feel jaded and empty, and I turn to go.

Then I hear it – a little fluting note sounding in the wind, a voice calling a name. A long way away, almost at the point where the flat land becomes the shore, I can see someone walking, rising into the sunlight and dropping down again, following the undulations of the dunes. The glowing light makes the figure almost a silhouette but I think I can see that it is wearing red – is it her, Christine from next door? Is she calling for the child? It comes again: two notes, a sing-song call across the reeds. What did she say the child's name was? Why did I not listen when she told me the child's name?

The roadside is not a bad vantage point. I stand and wait, hoping for a slight, sudden movement or a flash of colour that will show me where the little one is. I cannot go out on to the marsh looking and calling because I do not remember her name. My not knowing what she is called feels part of the reason she may be lost, and I find my mind suddenly crowded with all my names – Eliza, Lizzie, Lila – and I hope for her own sake that Christine's child goes by just one and that it is a name she likes. The person on the dunes – I am sure now it is Christine – calls again. Perhaps there is no note of urgency in it, after all. Perhaps they are playing a game.

But I continue to stand and watch just in case, and as Christine's voice unhurried and faint lilts across the flat ground, I hear also, across a landscape of years, both my parents' voices: hers high and edgy and his a dry, enclosed one that sounds unnatural out of doors. I think I must be remembering a particular day when I was very little, on a picnic or something.

The sun is almost below the horizon now; its rays stretch down the water in a widening, sparkling path of broken stars. Christine has dipped out of sight on to the shore side of the dunes.

I think I have a memory of that day, of the sun shining too brightly. The wind is in my face and my eyes are stinging. They are calling for me. Lila. Li-la! And then there is no sound at all except a roaring in my ears that might be deep water or could be my own gasps. Have I fallen in the sea? Am I crying? From somewhere above I hear my name again – Lila! *Li-la!* – no sooner heard than carried away, voices calling across so huge a distance that I know I have strayed past some important limit. On that day I wander from the place where my name is spoken, and when I hear it being called I cannot believe that a word so lonely-sounding can really mean me. The shock of it is that then I know – know it for certain with an ache that seems for a second to stop my heart – that I am alone. Not that it's a discovery, quite. It confirms something I am born knowing, knowledge that lies in the blood. Did I that day let go of a hand and run, stumble, fall and lose myself, along with my baby name?

I don't remember. I don't know when I stopped being Lila to everyone but myself. It would be some row or another of theirs, not related to any picnic, that would mark me as Eliza or Lizzie, perhaps some theory that I shouldn't start school with my baby name. They probably disagreed about what I should be called instead and then simply ignored each other's opposition. I'm not under any illusion that by calling me by different names either of them was trying to lay claim to me.

Later memories are even less clear. The years from then until the *Turandot* summer bunch themselves into uniform clumps of silence, resentment, boredom. I perform, sincerely but badly, in the roles allotted me by my other names. As Lizzie, I am beetle-browed and sullen with my father and at school I keep in with Enid and fight off the torments of Senga and whoever happens to be in her gang. My mother reminds me that nobody likes a sourpuss and tells me to smile, and then I wear the name Eliza like a showy, embarrassing hat that she – stronger and capable of cruelty – has chosen for me and is insisting I keep on. Her yearning for a daughter to match the name she thinks so sophisticated flits around me constantly, not as a stated desire but like blinking, a fraction's distortion between one frame and the next in the drama playing out between us every day, as hard to catch as a concealed wince. Eliza is the name of the daughter she could be proud of. Lizzie is the straightforward, reliable girl with her feet on the ground. Answering to either one, I feel muddy inside. Nobody knows who I really am or what I am for, except Uncle George.

————•:•:•————

6

Between visits Uncle George became an abstraction. From the moment his car disappeared over the bridge and Lila stopped waving he was again an idea, a private absence. She could almost lose hold of the fact that she knew him personally; he acquired a film star's perfection and distance. And London assumed cinematic grandeur; it was all clean avenues and squares overhung with blossom or drifting with papery fallen leaves, where well-dressed people walked pretty dogs and ladies hailed shining taxis with a gloved finger and were whisked off to the Ritz or the London Palladium. Lila marked his road in a street map he once left behind; it smelled leathery and ashy, like his car. She kept it in her room and took it out and looked at his page often, sprawling on her bed. She memorised the names of the streets and pictured herself setting down her suitcases and Uncle George calling from an upper window, so here you are at last!

When she was little, saying goodbye, she used to cling and beg to go back to London with him and he would promise that one day she would. Wait until you're old enough, he said. She would be different too, in her London life. The sun would not always shine, of course not. But when it rained she would be adorably mackintoshed for it, tight-belted and accessorised like Audrey Hepburn, and the rain would be cleansing and amusing, unlike Burnhead's mucky obscuring drizzle. Buses would swing into view when required. Just the name Crouch End, where Uncle George lived, had a ring of civilised magic.

She never tried to picture the flat precisely but knew it must be high-ceilinged and airy. She would take the smaller bedroom and get a job in a high-class but friendly dress shop, and would come home in the late afternoon to find light pouring through the drawing room windows. She would have flowers in a glass bowl on the low table in front of the fire, always. Uncle George would wonder how he had managed all this time without her cheerful and economical ways. He and his artistic but respectful friends would include her in everything – trips to the country, rolling back the rug for impromptu rock 'n' roll – and they would pay her teasing, affectionate compliments.

One day. Wait until you're old enough, he said. She had waited. There was no reason why one day should not be now.

The real Uncle George could not live up to the perfected version who was forever charmed, forever laughing and in bright sunshine, so his arrival at 5 Seaview Villas required at the very least an adjustment to everyday lighting. When Lila watched his car draw up into the evening shadow that the house cast over the road, he seemed part of the shade. He was crumpled and less tall. He frowned over the bringing in of his luggage and didn't stand straight. Lila came along last, worried in case she did not love him. She had forgotten that the pores round his nose and chin sometimes looked like a sprinkling of black pepper.

As it always was when Uncle George came, tea that day was special. While Fleur had rested, Lila and Raymond sliced cucumber and tomatoes, opened a tin of vegetable salad and spooned it into a dish. Lila's potato salad, tepid, floury chunks coated with salad cream that had turned translucent, sat in a bowl on the sideboard next to a jelly with tinned pears suspended in it. On the table were four plates on which, under wrinkled sheets of lettuce, beetroot was bleeding into slabs of pink ham and halved hardboiled eggs.

George said what a spread it was and how they spoiled him. As he always did, he had brought a bottle of wine and Raymond, as he always did, had put out cups and saucers instead of glasses because Fleur said it was boorish to expect it.

'Oh, Georgie, lovely! Chianti! Oh, are we opening it now? Eliza, glasses,' she said, seating herself. 'We'll need glasses, the proper ones.'

Lila brought four instead of three. Uncle George raised an eyebrow and gave her a nod as he poured. She didn't like the wine. She wanted it to taste of London life, richly perfumed and exciting or at least more like blackcurrants, and this reminded her of damp rubber. But Uncle George was already forgiven for being merely himself. She sipped the wine, relieved that he did not fix her with an exclusive, Rock Hudson gaze full of blistering admiration. He admitted he was tired after his journey and then there was a plain, ordinary silence while they ate. Fleur picked at her food, flipping the lurid ham between her fork and knife and raising a shower of beetroot juice that fell in an arc of magenta dots on to the tablecloth.

She laid down her fork and asked questions: did he still like his flat, were his students doing well, was he still friends with what was the name again? George pushed his plate away and lit a cigarette, making a show of the first drag, moving his hair out of his eyes.

'Oh, Florrie,' he sighed. 'Everything's fine. Life goes on.'

Lila was not interested in his answers, anyway. Nothing her mother wanted to know would figure in her future life with him in London. He taught music in a college; she didn't need more than that to be able to picture him in a grand building with columns and stone steps. The rest – the detail of his life and hers – she could embroider from her own thoughts.

'Stop that, it's *Fleur*,' her mother said. 'And I just like to know. Is that a crime? I worry about you.'

Uncle George cast her a look. 'Don't. You really needn't.'

With a little defeated sigh Fleur got up and started dishing out the jelly at the sideboard. Lila felt safe and pleased. Although six years younger than her mother, and single, Uncle George was without doubt the head of their side of their family, not that Lila, knowing the meagre facts, thought of them as that. They were too depleted, somehow, not robust enough to be thought a proper *family* – more a huddle of people clinging on because they were related and the only ones left. Lila's grandmother had died before the war; the father had been killed in early 1944. There had been a brother stillborn between Fleur and Uncle George, and that was all that Lila knew. Having no memory of them, she had never been able to make these dead people belong to her. No sound, not even the rustle of clothes, came from the sombre pair in the photograph on the piano; she could not imagine words coming from their mouths, nor a cry from the baby on the woman's lap. It was impossible even to connect that baby with her mother, whose life seemed dense with adult misery, so opaque with complication that no simple light from a childhood shone into it.

Fleur said, 'But I do worry, you know I do.'

'Well, I worry about you, too,' George said, a little sternly. 'And, it appears, with some cause.'

'It's my nerves,' she said. Calmly handing round the jelly and pears, she seemed perfectly happy now. Lila wondered why only Uncle George seemed able to affect her mood for the better. For a while nobody spoke.

'So, George, you winching these days?' Raymond said. 'Knocking on thirty, you not leaving it a bit late?'

Fleur let the use of one of his 'coarse' dialect words pass with an indrawn breath; as Raymond had judged, she was in too peaceful a mood to complain.

'Ah well, Ray, you never know,' George said, with a wink.

'Aye, I ken what you're up to,' Raymond went on, pointing with his spoon. 'You've got a lassie down south, eh? Scared to bring her up here in case a Scottish lad sweeps her off her feet.'

Uncle George smiled, pouring a trail of evaporated cream over his top of his jelly. He caught the white drip off the lip of the jug with one finger and sucked it clean.

'I certainly wouldn't risk a girl anywhere near you, Ray,' he said, though he was looking at Fleur. 'Lucky my big sister can keep you in line, you old Romeo. Still the best looker for miles.'

It was so naturally done. Lila knew that her parents' meeting and marrying had been a disastrous mischance, yet Uncle George was casting them as a pair of heartbreakers, and getting away with it.

'Romeo – that'll be the day!'

Fleur and Raymond's laughter was brittle, but for a few moments they were absorbed in this flattering picture of themselves. Just for an instant they were lovers on a cinema poster, propelled by fate towards their final destiny, romantic combustion in each other's arms. George tipped the last of the wine into their glasses.

He said, 'If you ask me it's Missy here we need to keep an eye on.'

'You mean Lizzie? Och, she's young yet,' Raymond said.

'But she's her mother's daughter,' George said. 'I hope the gilded youth of Caledonia are preparing to fight over her,' he added.

Lila was too busy trying not to blush to notice that he had just rendered her as helpless as her parents.

After tea Uncle George sent Fleur upstairs to take a long bath, producing some bath salts that he said were specially for frayed nerves. Raymond washed up, George dried and Lila put away. Then Raymond took George outside to show him how he was progressing with burning the letters off the garage door; afterwards they stood at the edge of the vegetable garden, hands in pockets, talking in low voices. When they came back in Raymond looked exhausted. He accepted George's suggestion that he take himself off to bed.

'Come on, you,' Uncle George said to Lila as soon as he had gone. 'The night is young! Come and show me the sunset. Sun's just going down.'

They walked along the road without talking. A gusting wind had blown the rain out of the sky but more clouds were massing in wads over the sea. When the low sun broke through from time to time, their elongated shadows cut sharply across the black road. Lila could think of nothing to say, tongue-tied because she was only her ordinary, unembellished self. She so longed to be amusing she did not dare open her mouth, and she looked all wrong with her hair blowing into knots, her eyes screwed up against the wind and sun. When they got as far as the Pow Burn they stopped and watched the slow slide of the water under the bridge.

On the Burnhead side, in front of the each of the bridge posts sat two concrete bins. Litter fluttered around them, although they had not been litter bins originally; they had appeared a year or two before as part of 'a drive' to boost Burnhead's chances in the West of Scotland Floral Borough Competition. After a short wet summer when a few flowers struggled and died and their leaves turned yellow in the salt wind, nobody came to plant anything else or take the bins away. It seemed that, by its failure, the effort of communal cheerfulness had left everyone exhausted, and now the bins were used for target practice by any passing motorist who had a bottle, cigarette packet or dog end. Lila's mother complained about it from time to time. They were, according to her, *typical*.

Lila picked up a wooden lolly stick from the ground and leaned against one of the bins, staring down and prodding into it. She turned over a waxed bread wrapper and uncovered a grey lump, mould coating it like fleece. George wandered across the road, brushed the edge of the other bin with his hand and perched on it. He lit a cigarette and dropped the match behind him.

He called over, 'So – Lizzie or Eliza?'

Lila looked up.

'Which is it these days?'

Lila shrugged. Once she would have claimed to prefer Eliza, seeking to like what her mother liked, but now she was less inclined to; the ground under her feelings for her mother was

shifting too much. But if not Eliza then not Lizzie either, in case
that amounted to saying she admired her father. She looked
down and concentrated on stirring the contents of the bin. It
was all going wrong; she wanted to be chatting to Uncle George
with dancing eyes and smooth hair and clothes like Enid's.
They were meant to be laughing, delighting in quick and clever
conversation. There was meant to be light music in the background.

'You know, your face really is very funny when you're cross,'
he called. She looked up and he burst out laughing. 'It's not
designed for it.'

She carried on stirring. 'Enid chucks lolly sticks in here, you
know,' she said.

'Enid?'

'Enid. My friend. She comes on her bike and times it so she's
finishing it just when she gets to the bridge so she can chuck the
stick in without stopping. My friend, so called.'

There was a long pause while Lila tried not to cry. 'I hate
her,' she said vehemently.

'Oh, so she's that sort of friend,' Uncle George said. 'I see. Of
course, certain friends—'

'She makes me feel like screaming,' she said. This wasn't true
but she had to account for the shake in her voice and the noises
coming from her throat.

'Ah well, now, that I can help with. Go ahead. Go on,
scream. Scream your head off. Give me a minute, I'll just go and
warn the neighbours.'

At that Lila burst out laughing, or something between
laughing and crying. She could imagine Mrs McBray at 1
Seaview Villas with her mealy face and pinhead eyes, wiping
her hands and saying, uh-huh, screaming, is it?

'Don't be *stupid*.' Her nose had started to run. She wiped her
sleeve across her face.

George tossed his cigarette in the bin, crossed the road and
pulled her away.

'Come on,' he said, 'we're going down to the beach.'

'What for?'

'What for? So you can have a proper scream, of course. You can frighten the fish if you like. And you can tell me all about the ghastly Enid.'

'There aren't any,' Lila gasped. 'There's no fish. It's not a proper beach. It's horrible. There's nothing down there.'

'Oh, there's never nothing,' George said, lightly. 'Never ever. Come on.'

'I hate it. There's just seaweed and dead birds and rubbish.'

'There you are then. Something after all. Proves my point.'

Lila did not know what to do with Uncle George's refusal to agree that life was awful. She followed him down towards the sea, and the shadows of their walking legs criss-crossed behind them on the scrubland like clashing silent swords. A straight band of steel-coloured light gleamed between sea and sky. Clouds collided and merged above the water and the sun came and went, shifting veils of pink and orange around itself.

'Beautiful,' Uncle George said, and Lila wiped her eyes and said she supposed so. She could not explain that it was just another thing put there to diminish her, another thing to feel separated from.

They made their way over the dunes to the start of the beach, kicking up from the sand its usual smell of briny rot. Now the marram grass broke off in clumps, revealing small bunkers of pebbles edged with reeds. They crossed the broken line of seaweed that marked the high tide and walked along in silence but for the cracking of dried weed and shells under their feet. The tide was miles out and the wheeze of the waves did not reach this far. George sat down on a tussock of grass and shifted over to make room for Lila.

'I don't suppose,' he said, 'that it's really all about Enid, is it? If I were you, I think I'd be screaming for other reasons.'

Lila was silent.

'Suppose we start with Enid, then,' he said. 'What's Enid done?'

'She saw the garage door,' Lila said. 'She saw the garage door and she kept on about it, what the letters were for. I had to tell her something, I made something up. I just made up this thing and she'll find out it isn't true. Then it'll be awful, she'll go on and on. She's always going on.'

'So? Does that matter?'

'Of course it matters! She'll tell Senga! She'll tell Senga and everybody. You don't know what it's like!'

'And what exactly will she tell them? What did you say?'

'I had to say something! She kept asking, she was going on about Senga and her – Senga's always getting people ganged up on me, I hate Senga. So I told her it was about singing *Turandot*. I said it was a sort of club. The Burnhead Association for Singing *Turandot*.'

'A club?'

'For singing *Turandot*. BAST.'

'My God. Did she believe you?'

'I don't know! Oh, I hate it! All the stupid, the whole stupid . . .' Lila burst into tears. 'I hate it! I hate this place!'

Uncle George stared straight ahead and let her sob.

'Oh, dear,' he said after a while, turning to her, 'you're so like your mother.'

'I am *not*!'

He laughed and shook his head. 'But that was clever.'

'What was?' She was still upset but the hint of a compliment at once opened up the possibility that she might be brought round. '*What*?'

'Your whatsit. B A S T – your Burnhead Association for Singing *Turandot*.' Speaking the words himself, Uncle George seemed to find them hilarious. He threw back his head and laughed. 'Bet it shut her up. What did she say?'

'Nothing much.'

George fished in his pockets and lit another cigarette. The

fumes from the match drifted Lila's way, reminding her of railway smoke.

'So what about this Premium Bond? What do you think it should go on? What would you do with it, if it was up to you?'

The novelty of being consulted made Lila's eyes fill with tears again and this time she wept for a long time. 'I wish it'd never come,' she said eventually, gulping. 'They can spend it how they like. As long they stop arguing. As long as she starts being normal.'

George placed an arm across her shoulder.

'I hate it here,' she whispered. 'I want to come to London. Can't I come to London with you? You wouldn't have to pay for me. I'd get a job and pay you rent and everything.'

Uncle George tugged at her shoulder and gave a light laugh. 'Oh come on, *nil desperandum*, eh? Can't be as bad as all that, can it?'

'It's getting worse. She's never been this bad before. I have to get away. Can't I come to London?'

Uncle George snorted. 'I can promise you she's been every bit as bad as this. You were just too young to know.' He made a wry face and raised one eyebrow. 'Quite funny in retrospect, most of it. You think this is bad . . .'

'What could be worse?'

'Oh, there's worse. If I tell you a funny story would it cheer you up?'

'Maybe.'

'Okay, well. This is true, remember. This was one time not long after they got the house. You were just a baby. She ate the housekeeping.'

'What? She what?' Lila clapped her hands over her mouth. 'She *what*?'

Uncle George nodded solemnly, and they both burst out laughing.

'A week's housekeeping. Your dad had just given it to her. They were having a row about money, I gather she was going through it a bit fast. She tore it up, stuffed it in her mouth and swallowed it. To show him how fast she *could* go through it. By the time he rang me she'd been retching for three hours.'

'So what happened? Was she really ill?'

'You mean how fast did it go through her? Oh, nature ran its course. Eventually. She got herself in a real state.' Uncle George grinned. 'Mind you, it was only the notes. Not even your mother went as far as eating the coins.'

When their laughter died away, Lila said, 'I still hate it. I want to go back with you and live in London.'

'Look, these things pass. They always do.'

'This won't. I hate it. It's their fault. I *do* want to scream.'

'Well, scream, then. Go on, there's nobody about. Scream for all you're worth,' Uncle George said jovially, waving an arm towards the beach and the faraway sea. 'Scream at them. Scream at Enid. Shatter their eardrums.'

He was laughing again. To show him she minded, she filled her lungs and tried to scream, but managed only a couple of stifled, breathy yelps. She sounded like a tired kitten. Her mouth was full of gluey, salt liquid; she swallowed a couple of times and tried again.

'Call that screaming? Oh, you are so funny!' He slapped his leg, snorting with laughter. 'Go on! Scream!'

Lila stood up, walked away a few steps and turned from him, took a breath, and screamed. It came out flickering at first, like a guttering light, and then strengthened to a bright blast that cut the air. She stopped, suddenly light-headed, took a deeper breath and screamed again; after a few seconds the sound changed, grew long, high-pitched, sailing. On it went, one steady note with a slight, fluting vibrato, heartless and clear. She knew what she was doing. She was singing, and she intended it as a warning. When she came to the end of her breath she stopped abruptly. She walked back and sat down again, folded her arms and looked calmly out to sea.

'Congratulations,' Uncle George said. 'That was a B flat. I

see I'm right. I thought you might have the voice to go with the temperament. How long have you been able to do that?'

'Since forever,' she said carelessly. 'There's not much to it, you know.'

She didn't quite believe this but saying it made her feel superior. Uncle George stifled another laugh.

'Shut up! You're as bad as her. She goes on,' she said in an angry whisper, 'like it's something special, like you should get sympathy for being able to sing or something!'

Uncle George nodded, not needing to be told that Lila was now talking about Fleur rather than Enid.

'Just because she was a singer once. It's *stupid*.'

'Does she know you can sing?'

Lila had no clear idea of what her mother knew, about her or anything else. Fleur displaced simple knowing – about every-day, ordinary things – with irritation or loathing.

'She doesn't care, anyway. She's not really interested in it, except for singing along to her records.'

'What about at school? Don't they make you sing at school?'

Lila scowled. 'They try. I can't be bothered. I'd only get teased anyway, it's bad enough they all know *she* sings.'

'Senga again?'

Lila nodded. 'And Linda McCall. And Enid, some of the time.'

'But isn't it difficult *not* to sing? Don't you ever just want to, don't you want to take a deep breath like you did just now and just do it?'

Lila was taken aback by how instantly Uncle George had hit upon it. More and more often when she opened her mouth in assembly for some dreary compulsory hymn, she thought that to let the sound burst out of her would be, at the very least, interesting, and probably wonderful. The idea filled her with a sense of danger but also with an intense premonition of safety; she predicted that there might be a kind of sanctuary in the very letting go. She had been glad when the end of term had freed her from the temptation. But now, one long top B flat sung out towards the sea had left her elated. She stared at the beach, poking in the stones with the toe of her plimsoll, and tried to quell a bubbling feeling in her throat.

'Your mum doesn't really mean it, you know,' Uncle George said. 'She's just—'

'—having a nervous breakdown.'

He searched for a way to deny this truthfully and couldn't. 'It's just hard for her . . . The thing is, she wanted to have more of a career, and when people are disappointed, they sometimes . . .'

'Oh, I know! I know! They're allowed to shout and scream and go on and start fires and paint letters on doors! They're allowed to upset everyone around them!'

She got up and marched down the beach. 'He's just as bad, she wouldn't be like that if he was any use! I hate them!'

Her disloyalty felt magnificent and risky, as if something with strong wings was trying to flap its way out of her chest. Uncle George watched her stride around, kicking through seaweed and soaking her shoes.

'Oh, come on,' he called out to her, 'she's not as bad as all that. Your dad does his best. There are reasons.'

'I know! You all think I'm too stupid to notice! I'm not stupid, I've worked it out, I'm not a child!'

'Worked what out?'

Lila returned up the beach and stood in front of him.

She said, 'I know what happened!'

George looked at her while he took the last drag of his cigarette and threw the butt away. 'You do?' he said, shading his eyes. 'Really? Who told you?'

The mildness in his voice perplexed her. She was telling him she hated her parents and knew their dirty secret and he did not seem to mind.

'*You* know what I'm talking about.' Was he going to make her say the words aloud?

'Well I think I do, but maybe you'd better tell me and see if I'm right.'

'*Well*. It's no secret, she met him when she was twenty, she tells everybody that much,' she said, dropping down on to the tussock again. 'Before she had a chance to get famous. He came to hear her sing and *fell madly in love with her and promised to look after her forever*.' She pushed the words out sourly. 'And he told her he was going to be a lawyer, and they got married straight away, a fortnight after they met, and he misled her. He lied to her. He's not a lawyer, he's only a lawyer's clerk.'

She sensed Uncle George was about to interrupt. Quickly she said, 'Look, I worked out ages ago what happened!'

She leaned forward and cupped her face in her hands to hide how red it was. 'I do *know* the facts of life, you know,' she said, trying to sound adult and breezy. She did know them, but having to associate them with her own parents nauseated her.

'Not sure I'm quite with you.'

'You know! August 1944, and my birthday's May 1945. It's obvious! They must've, you know. I must have been a . . . a honeymoon baby.'

George was staring into the sand and appeared not to hear.

'Right? And so that was that,' she said. 'Wasn't it? They didn't even *want* me. She couldn't be a singer, not with a baby, and he never did what you've got to do to be a proper lawyer because they got stuck with me.'

'You were a bit unexpected,' Uncle George said.

Lila said more quietly, 'It's not as if I could help it.'

They said nothing for a while.

'Look,' George said, 'that's not the whole story.' He turned to Lila and scanned her face. 'Listen, if I tell you this, it's because you're old enough now, okay? It's not fair you don't know, I think you're entitled to know.'

'Know what? I'm not adopted, am I?'

'Of course not! No. It's more . . . unusual than that. And if I tell you, you mustn't let on you know, to them or anybody, all right? It's not to spread around. It doesn't change anything, only it might stop you thinking the wrong things about them.'

'Tell me *what*?'

'They . . . Well, your mother . . .' Uncle George began. 'She . . . I mean, look. Have you ever wondered why she only plays her *Turandot* records when she's really angry?'

Lila cast her eyes upwards. 'That's obvious! She was singing in *Turandot* when he met her. Turandot was her big role, or should have been. Anyway, she plays other things, too, now and then. *Madame Butterfly, La Traviata, La Bohème*—'

'Yes, all right,' Uncle George said gently, 'but *Turandot*'s the one, isn't it? But your dad never actually heard her. He didn't go to the opera to listen to her.'

'What then? What do you mean?'

'They were on in Glasgow. It was some touring company from England. Your mother did well to get in. When our father was killed she had to make her own way so she got this chorus job. I was still at school.'

'I know that. She tells people she was the youngest in the company.'

'Probably true. It was no great shakes, the company, just a scratch thing in wartime. And frankly I've never understood how she came to be even covering Turandot at that age. They were irresponsible to let her, it doesn't bear thinking about what she would have made of it. Her voice hadn't the heft for it at twenty, no-one's has. Could have damaged it, permanently. Turandot's a role you shouldn't even consider before you're at least—'

'Stop going on about the *singing*.'

George paused. 'Your father went round the Glasgow theatres. He was working in a lawyer's office and studying for his law degree, hadn't much to live on. Somebody he met via his firm, some kind of merchant . . . anyway this man put some under-the-counter stuff your father's way – this was when there was rationing, you couldn't get nice things on coupons. Your father sold it in a pub. He could have sold anything, he was different then. Plenty to say for himself. Real polish. And he was very good-looking.'

Lila snorted in disbelief.

'So,' George went on, 'he started getting quite a bit of this stuff, it was coming in all the time off boats from Ireland. He sold round the theatres, mainly clothes and stockings. The chorus girls were earning and they liked good stuff and they moved on. Safer for him. Hundreds did it but it was risky, the black market.'

'Black market? You mean he was breaking the law?'

'Look, I'm telling you how hard it was. He was studying and working for peanuts, he needed the extra just to live. He never did that much. He wasn't a real spiv.'

'So what's that got to do with my mother?'

Uncle George paused before he answered. 'Turandot herself doesn't appear on stage till the second act, does she? On the last night the woman singing Turandot was fine, she always was. Vocal chords like steel cable. Your mother was singing in the chorus. After the first half hour of Act I she wasn't needed on stage till well into Act II, so she slipped off with Raymond. He'd got a lot of things, more than he could bring backstage with him. She went along with two empty cases to this pub where he was keeping the stuff. She had orders from everybody. He got her back in time for the chorus's first appearance in Act II but when they arrived the curtain was down, backstage was total chaos.'

'Why, what happened?'

'They'd abandoned the performance, people were demanding their money back. Turandot had fallen backstage during the first interval, tripped on something, a stage weight. She was in agony and had to be carted off with suspected broken toes, and there was no sign of the understudy. Your mother was sacked on the spot. They were travelling on to the next venue that night and they told her she wasn't going with them, they'd manage with the Turandot they'd got if they had to carry her on and off on a sedan chair.'

Lila burned with confusion. The picture of her mother, rejected and afraid, reminded her of herself. 'Well, so what? It was her own fault,' she said. 'Why didn't she just go and join another company? She didn't have to go and get married.'

'Tough luck though,' George said. 'Out of a job, nowhere to go, she hadn't even got digs for the night.'

'All *right*. But if she really wanted to sing she could've. It needn't have been the end of it. You said she was young.'

George sighed and fished for his cigarettes.

She said, 'She just used it as an excuse, if you ask me.'

'Your father's a very kind man, a good man. Yes, he is,' George insisted. 'He couldn't just leave her. He took her for a drink. She drowned her sorrows pretty thoroughly.'

'So? After that she could've gone and got another job.'

George lit his cigarette and paused. 'Okay. I might have known you'd take that line. I'll tell you all of it but you've got to be sensible, all right? No attack of histrionics.'

'What's histrionics?'

'It's what your mother does and one hysteric in the family's enough. So just be quiet and listen, okay? That night she had nowhere to go so your dad put her up. He sneaked her into the room he was renting. Out of *kindness*. They hadn't much choice, either of them.'

'You mean, they . . .?'

Lila had never questioned the version of how her mother's life had been ruined, in which she starred as innocent victim of false hero; such stories as there were in their family never were questioned. There was no telling and retelling of what really happened, no agreeing on the turning points, arguing about consequences, honing the details; only families reconciled to past events can weave tales about themselves. As a consequence Lila had not learned curiosity. With the full-blown egotism of most unhappy children she had not pictured her parents doing much with their shadowy, half-formed lives except waiting for her to arrive and be made unhappy. And yet here they were with things happening all around them, behaving irresponsibly, even dramatically, as if she might never have been.

'That's disgusting. They hardly knew each other!'

'Don't be such a prig. It was wartime. They're human.'

'How could she? Why did nobody tell me?'

'Look, I thought you were mature enough to cope with this. Your parents aren't perfect, they're just human beings.'

'Of course I know they're not perfect! God!'

'The point is your mother had nothing. She had nobody to help her. This happened at the end of August. They didn't get married then, they only say that to account for you arriving in May. They got married in October once you were on the way. Your father didn't hesitate.'

Lila sniffed the air and blew out a long, slow breath.

Uncle George said, 'So none of it was your fault, okay? You're nearly grown up, you've got your own life ahead of you. Don't let them drag you down. But try not to be too impatient with them, that's all.'

Lila wasn't listening. Her face was livid with shame, for all of it, for all of them. She was ashamed even to *know*. How dare they bring her into being in this way, clumsy and drunk? How dare they regret her? But her indignation was stale, for in some way she had always known. She ought to hate them even more. Yet a fragile, reluctant thread, a single filament connecting her to some notional sympathy for the times, the circumstances, their desperation, was tugging at her. It said, forgive them, it could have been you. Forget it was loveless, forget what you know.

'So, yes, the baby,' Uncle George was saying, 'the baby – you – stopped her career. But you see? They got themselves into it. She missed her big chance because she was off buying stockings. A career over before it began for the sake of half a dozen pairs of nylons. Same thing with him, six months in jail and his future ruined over a suitcase of lingerie.'

Lila gaped while George offered her the cigarette packet. 'Want one? You look a bit green. Sorry. You won't know that bit either, I don't suppose.'

'He went to prison?'

'They came down hard after the war on black-market traders. I'm telling you something they've kept quiet all this time, so you've got to keep this to yourself. I want your promise.'

'Of course I promise! Why would I tell anybody *that*?'

'Okay. Well, he was prosecuted. Don't remember exactly when, around the time you were born. And you can't practise law with a criminal record so after that he got a clerk's job. There was some connection, I forget just what, the head of the law firm in Glasgow's wife had been a black-market customer or something, and they knew someone in the firm here. He's terribly overqualified. It changed him. He's never been the same since prison, actually.'

Lila waved a hand. Refusing to care was, she had already decided, the adult thing to do and she wanted Uncle George to credit her with that. 'Well, why should I feel sorry for them?' she said. 'Just because she never got up on a stage again, just because he went to prison. So what? It was ages ago, anyway. Worse things happen to people.' To *me*, she was thinking. What was worse than knowing all this? What was worse than being stuck here with the people her parents were turning out to be?

'Of course, you're too young to sympathise,' Uncle George sighed. 'At your age, you don't make allowances, do you? Mistakes not allowed. You're made of granite at your age.'

'I am not made of granite. I can be sorry for people. When they deserve it.'

Uncle George raised an eyebrow. 'How magnanimous. Can you really not understand it, wanting to sing so much and there's nobody to hear you? Can you imagine what prison's really like? For a proud man like your father?'

'They brought it on themselves.' She sniffed and looked away. If she possibly could, she would forget it all; it was going to be too great a burden, to be so ashamed of her parents she could barely look at them.

'Stand up. Sing me a scale,' Uncle George demanded suddenly. He gave her a note, the same one, B flat but two octaves lower. 'Start there. Go on.'

'Why should I? I don't feel like it.'

'Stop arguing. Stand up and do it. Two octaves. Go *on* – lah, lah—'

Lila shrugged, stood up, and sang it.

'Now this.' He started a semitone higher.

Lila sang that, too, unfolding her arms.

'And this.'

'No.'

'Damn you. *Do* it.'

This time she took a proper breath.

'And hold the top note . . . loud and strong as you can . . .'

Lila did so.

'And now . . . listen. Hold that note but bring it down, not so angry. Make it quieter, gradually, that's it. Don't wobble, release the breath gradually, don't collapse, support the sound, *piano*, down, *pianissimo* . . .'

Lila was finding this more difficult, but she held it through the wobble, righted it, sustained it. The note was thrillingly high. It made her want to sing and laugh at the same time. When she ran out of breath and stopped, Uncle George smiled.

'Now. Sing me something – some music, a song, something you like. Anything you know.'

'No! I won't. I don't see why I . . .'

'For God's sake, shut up and just *do* it.'

Lila turned away, her heart thumping. How could she? How could she sing anything that included words, words that Uncle George might think she meant? The words of all the songs she knew from school were absurd:

O'er the ocean flies a faery fay,
Soft her wings are as a cloud of day

It was unthinkable that she should come out with rubbish like
that to Uncle George, and the hymns were even worse. He
would laugh. But again the elation was almost taking over. Her
insides felt watery. What could she sing that would sound
right? What would be real? Turning to Uncle George, she sang

Signore, ascolta! Ah, Signore, ascolta!
Liù non regge più!

Uncle George sat up straight, recognising Liù's first aria from
Turandot. He opened his mouth and closed it again. Lila had
little idea that, in mimicked Italian barely approximating to the
real words, she was pleading with him to listen to her because
she could bear no more. Glancing at him and then looking
away across the beach, she continued.

Ma se il tuo destino doman sarà deciso,
Noi morrem sulla strada dell'esilio!

She would die on the exile's road, she sang, though her grasp of
what she was saying was vague; she remembered only that Liù
sounded sad and desperate and that in the end nobody came to
her rescue. Long before the end, she abandoned any attempt at
the words, finishing on the long, imploring top B flat. She had
heard it sung so many times on the record that she was
surprised to feel its sadness, still fresh, from her own mouth.

'I don't know exactly what it means,' she said, 'but I know
how it's meant to sound.'

Uncle George nodded, for once stuck for words. 'Well, then,'
he said after a while. 'Well, enough for a first lesson. Come on.'

It was chilly now and they walked back fast across the
wavering grass that was luminous and pale in the last of the
light. They did not say much more that evening.

At six o'clock Luke rings me. He's a fast worker, I'll give him that. He's got everything arranged and may he call in later this evening to discuss it? He speaks tremulously and is slightly hoarse; sympathy flutters in his throat like a trapped and dusty moth. I tell him there is no need, for it is surely a simple question of jotting down the timings which he can perfectly well give me over the telephone. Pause. Am I happy then, he asks, with twenty minutes at the crematorium at two o'clock for the dispatch of the coffin (prayers, committal and blessing only, he apologises, though this sounds plenty to me), then allowing a generous forty minutes to get from there to the Evangelical Lutheran Fellowship for a service at three o'clock, all timings confirmed as accurate by the undertakers? I tell him this sounds fine. He is working on appropriate readings from Scripture for the service, and as he says this his voice grows solid. When he mentions that the service will end with grateful thanks that our departed brother has died in Christ, he is practically heaving with belief in life everlasting and I find myself wondering if it is possible to vomit with rapture. Would I care to pray with him now?

On the *telephone*? I say.

God will hear you, Lila, he insists.

Not convenient, I say. I've got something on the stove.

As soon as I get rid of him I run myself a hot bath that fills the bathroom with steam so I cannot see too clearly the dark grouting of dirt that grows between the tiles and the black blossom of mould on the ceiling. Afterwards I sit by the gas fire with a glass of whisky and eat toast and butter. These are the comforts I have found to be the reliable ones. Moderate sensual pleasures can, with practice, assuage intangible miseries. Temporarily, of course, but then there are always more warm baths to be had, more drinks and scents and tastes. It's a knack.

Later, though, I am in danger of big feelings so I fish out my counted cross-stitch. I never travel without it. On the continent, cross-stitch is not the seedy Laughing Cavalier footstool kind of thing it is here. The Queen of Denmark does it. A lot of people in my business take it up, either that or knitting; it fills gaps in rehearsals and stops you eating. Knitting's not for me. I always feel there's something improbable about a single strand of yarn evolving into a garment. Trusting balls of wool to become cardigans leaves too much to chance. By contrast, there is no leeway in cross-stitch. A piece of cross-stitch is a transparent promise. There are rules. The pattern is counted out and waiting. The threads are coded, a symbol for each colour. No interpretation is required and nothing is hidden. All I have to do is count and stitch and if I do I will suffer no surprises, no colours will stray across the boundaries, no shapes will distort. As regular and contained as a pulse, the needle in my hand bestows its tiny stabbed kisses – criss-cross, criss-cross, criss-cross – not a single one more nor less than is predetermined. Enid's mother would be pleased at my liking for needlework. She might think I got it from her. It is true that I like thread; I pull and it follows, laying its colour down obediently in the track allocated to it. It doesn't spill.

I enjoy the sight of my finished stitches. A visual pleasure, simply enjoyed; why look for more? Balm for the eyes and balm for the soul should not be confused.

When I'm singing to Uncle George on the beach that summer night long ago, is that the mistake I make? Do I begin to fancy in myself a rare and finely tuned sensitivity that sets me apart from the likes of Enid and Senga? Beautiful, says Uncle George, of the sunset. But it is a sunset, nothing more. It was a sunset just as tonight's was, and an aria. Not a symbol or portent but the end of another day and that is all, with a bit of Puccini thrown in. A flash of pink or mauve in the sky is not a glimpse of higher meaning. A top B flat does not reveal a spotless soul. Be dazzled, but do not let bright colours or pretty songs lead you anywhere.

But after Uncle George and I get back that evening I go to my room and stand looking out, wishing I could see the patch of beach where we have been sitting. The sun is going down with that final, burning desperation, and it strikes me how all my old days of the week colours were bland or cold. *Monday is pale green.* At the time they were the right colours for my days, the colours I saw around me, but how could I have overlooked the sky? I somehow missed the reds, pinks and silvers. I was in no mood to be caught up in their exuberance. I suddenly feel less separate from them, less drab in comparison. That evening a brightness seems to be growing, a flame glimmering below the horizon, and it includes me. Anything can catch and burn.

Oh, this is the wisdom of hindsight. It must be an illusion that I had a sense of what was coming for if I had, could I have stood at the window and not been terrified? Would I really have wanted all our lives to change, to be refined the way they were into something perhaps more honest but no purer, something clearer but also worse? I am uncertain. I do know that I took the days of that summer and threw them like sticks into a fire that drew everything to it until the air was tight with heat. Everything flared and was gorgeous for a moment. All of it glittered with significance until it expired in flames and now only I am left, blinking and blinded and giddy.

I'm just starting on this new piece of embroidery. This particular piece has a formal and pleasing pattern like a knot garden, with fleur-de-lys and trefoils and diamonds set within squares, and if I concentrate on it I shall keep hold of a certain perspective, I hope, that this house seems to want to send askew.

7

Lila was glad the next day was Sunday because there would be no Enid. While Enid's mum lay in the flat above the shop reading magazines or doing extra sewing, Enid took herself off and was Gathered for Morning Witness, for Repentance and Prayer and for Eventide Worship. Lila had all but given up a lazy campaign to goad her out of it.

So she was surprised, late in the morning, to hear the bicycle bell and see Enid appearing in the back garden. Raymond, cheerful again, was working in the vegetable patch. Lila came out to stop her saying anything embarrassing in front of him. She pulled her through the gate back into the drive.

'Where's the B A S T?' Enid demanded. 'It's gone.'

Uncle George had been out early that morning and had already painted one coat of green over the burned-off traces of the letters.

'Oh, they might not have the headquarters there after all. It might not be big enough. Why haven't you got church today?'

'We haven't got church, it's the Fellowship of Sinai,' Enid said, sauntering back through the gate into the garden. She spoke with the authority of an archbishop, which they also did not have. Lila was tired of it all.

'Okay, why aren't you Gathered?'

'Bird,' Enid said, turning and walking backwards. 'There's this bird got in and they can't get it out. It's huge, a big seagull, they're all up ladders with the windows open and clapping at it and it just keeps flying from side to side or it sits in the rafters, they can't make it go. So they're hearing the Word in the minister's front room but the young folk got to go home.'

Raymond was washing a handful of carrots at the outside tap, and overheard. 'Right y'are, Enid,' he said, half-turning. 'Act of God, was it?' He stepped into the house leaving a trail of drips.

Enid grinned after him. Lila had noticed before the way she wanted Raymond to like her. 'There's mess all over the Word. It's all over the minister's big Bible, it was on the lectern open,' she called out to him, 'at the bit where Christ feedeth the five thousand and reproveth his fleshly hearers.'

She waited, hoping to be teased further. Then she turned back to Lila and whispered, 'Honest, there's number twos all over it.'

Just then Uncle George appeared and leaned in the kitchen doorway. Lila watched, expecting to be proud of his impact on Enid.

'What's this I'm hearing? No church? Because of a bird? Bird turd? Bird turd on the Word?'

While Enid was still gasping with shock he advanced and held out his hand. 'So *you* must be Enid,' he said, as if he could not believe his luck. 'Hello. I'm George.'

'Hello.'

'So – not at Sunday School?'

'We don't get Sunday School.'

'Oh?'

'We don't believe in Sunday School. The Bible Message is the same for everybody, young and old.'

'They don't get singing, either,' Lila said. 'There's no hymns.'

'Yes, there is, only we've got our own. We recite them.'

'Bet you don't really believe them though.'

Enid's face flushed. Not even Jesus knew that the only one of the recitations she was really interested in was the first one she'd heard, spoken by the minister on the esplanade last Easter holidays in front of a flimsy semi-circle of Fellowship members. Standing under a banner that said JOIN US IN JOY EVER-LASTING they had intoned in unison:

Home come the soldiers of Lord Jesus,
Bloodied from the earthly fight,
Home to dwell in righteousness
Glorious in eternal light.
Weary soldiers of the Saviour
Rest ye in His grace and might.

Enid, at a loose end, had listened from a safe distance. The words reminded her of a picture she'd once seen. She couldn't remember where, maybe in a history book or a photo in the paper, but it was a proper painting, a painting of those very words. It gave them shape. In it an exhausted soldier lay slumped back in a chair, his kilt hanging over his legs, bayonet cast at his feet and his boots half-off. His head was falling back against a woman who was standing behind him and his white neck was exposed; he was so tired, the poor soldier of the Saviour, he hadn't even finished unbuttoning his tunic. But the point of the picture wasn't how tired he was, or how long he'd been away or even how much danger he had been in. In the woman's arms was a baby that Enid knew was herself. *Home come the soldiers*. The point was he was back. He was home, the weary soldier, the dad, the Saviour, Jesus in a kilt. He had come home, and that was all that mattered to Enid.

'That's not proper hymns then, is it? And you don't sing them.'

'We stand up and talk them and we listen to the Word. Music distracts from the Bible Message.'

Lila made a short snorting noise.

'No hymns?' Uncle George said.

'The Lord listens when we to come to Him in quiet prayer,' Enid said, still thinking of the picture.

'But no singing!?' cried Uncle George. 'Oh, isn't that the saddest thing you ever heard? We love singing, don't we?' he said to Lila.

Lila glared at him. 'Don't say that.'

'Well, don't scowl. But can you imagine? No *singing*!?'

Lila caught his eye and she saw that the joke was theirs. It was Enid who was being teased and isolated and who looked suddenly crushed.

'Come on inside, both of you,' he suddenly told them, his eyes glinting with something. 'I've got something I want you to do.'

They followed him through the house to the music room where Fleur was sitting with a cup of tea. 'See, Florrie? See? Here you are, for a start,' he announced.

'*Fleur*,' she said firmly, but with a slight smile. 'Hello, Enid.'

'A willing recruit for you,' he said, pushing Enid forward. 'First of many. There'll be hundreds more.'

'George, you're mad. It's a mad idea,' she said over Enid's head. '*Turandot*'s huge, lots of proper professional companies can't do it. And anyway, where? Where could you do it, round here? There's nowhere nearly big enough.'

Uncle George was walking up and down the room. He waved all this away. 'We'll reduce the forces, of course we will. We can look into all that,' he said.

His looks seemed to have taken on harder lines than Fleur's. He had similar features, the straight nose and sharp jaw, but now his cheekbones glowed and his eyes glittered, as if something were heating up under the surface.

'As to where, there are halls, aren't there?' he said. 'And look, the scale of the thing's the point. It'd really catch the imagination, it'd involve everybody. And just imagine, you'd be singing Turandot. Imagine!'

Fleur looked away.

'Look, I'll say it again.' He paused with his back to the window. 'Wouldn't it help? If you and Ray *did* something? And anyway,' he said, gesturing towards Enid, 'see? They fetch up right on your doorstep. We'll get plenty more – they'll rope their friends in, there's all the choirs, the amateur operatics, orchestras, they'll *flock* to be in it.'

Lila's mother glanced at Enid without much interest and took up some sheets of paper from the spindly coffee table.

'We'll advertise, hold a public meeting,' George said. 'There's a local paper, we'll talk to them. Get the ball rolling.'

'You're mad.'

'I'm just trying to *do* something for you. Fleur?'

'And the cost! That Premium Bond's not boundless riches, you know.' In a low, flat voice she added, 'And what'll he say? Raymond. You're forgetting bloody Raymond. *He* wants to fix the damp.'

'Oh, Ray's fine! I've already told him!' George said. 'As long as you're happy and we're not letting him in for any more expense, he says you can have the whole Premium Bond for the production.'

Fleur looked up in surprise. 'Raymond said *that*?'

'As long as it makes you happy. And he says he'll take his annual leave to fit in with the dates. I've asked him to be stage manager.'

'He said that?'

'Well,' George looked sheepish, 'well, about the annual leave, he hasn't quite said that, not yet. But I'm sure he will when I ask him. He'd be all right as stage manager.'

He started pacing again and Fleur's eyes followed him up and down.

'The Premium Bond. All of it? Did he really say that? Are you sure?'

'I promise you, he absolutely did. You don't give him credit, you know.'

'Well, anyway, that's not the only thing. If – *if* I decide to sing Turandot, I can't do it opposite an amateur. I won't. I will not sing,' she said, 'if an amateur is singing Calaf.'

'Calaf's not a problem, I told you.'

'Unless we've got a proper Calaf it's ridiculous. What makes you so sure this fellow would want to do it even if he's up to it?

Are you sure he isn't just another of your protégés? George? George, are you listening to me?'

'Oh, he's up to it! Of course he'd do it. How many tenors would turn it down?'

Enid was still standing awkwardly in the middle of the floor. She glanced longingly at the door and widened her eyes at Lila, who was staring at Uncle George and biting her lip.

Fleur shook her head. 'He's really up to it, he knows the part? Sounds to me like one of your what's-its. You've got him on one of your pedestals.'

'That's nonsense! Of course I haven't. I know the real thing when I hear it. He'll make a fine Calaf.'

'What makes you think he'd come up here for the whole summer anyway?'

'Look, he'll love just getting out of London, let alone the chance to sing Calaf. He's keeping himself going with a summer job. He could easily come if we laid on bed and board. I'll stand him his fare.'

'Even so. What about everything else?' She began to count off on her fingers. 'All the other parts. Venue. Rehearsal space. Staging. Scenery. Costumes. Props. Lights. Publicity. Huge chorus. Huge orchestra. Scores . . .'

Uncle George shivered and pulled a deep breath in through his nose. 'I know. God, it's thrilling, isn't it?'

'George!'

'The point is,' he said, lowering his voice, 'yes it's huge, it'll take some doing, but I *know* there are enough people out there. We just have to think bold. She really hit on something, you know,' he said, nodding towards Lila, 'she really has. I was awake half the night working it out. We could actually do it. You'd be wonderful and this place is crying out, you're always saying so. I mean God knows there's nothing else happening. You're so bored you're going mad – you think you're the only one? Listen.'

He turned suddenly on Enid, startling her. 'So, Enid,' he said, looking at her hard. 'Dear, lovely Enid. What are you doing this summer? What are your plans?'

Enid's lower lip dropped free of the top one. The question could be either mocking or just meaningless and she couldn't tell which. Lila couldn't, either. Uncle George was moving away somehow, going beyond the reach of sensible remarks, setting the air in a spin. Didn't he know? Plans did not enter their lives. They did what they were told or they did nothing. Plans belonged to girls in the kind of stories that left Lila sour with envy, girls winning scholarships to ballet school, entering gymkhanas or living on barges, not to her and Enid. The room seemed suddenly too small for four people when Uncle George was one of them. How could they keep up when he was whirring with an enthusiasm that nobody else understood?

He said, 'See? Fleur, see? They're bored out of their minds. There are dozens like them, hundreds! It's just what they need. What you need, what *everybody* needs.'

He lunged across the room, pulled Enid forward and positioned her in front of the piano, pressing down on her shoulders.

'Stand there, Enid, hands at your sides, shoulders relaxed. Relax! And breathe!'

Landing hard on the piano stool, he pulled back his shirt cuffs and sent a clatter of notes up the keyboard.

'Now! To LAH! Sing!' Red-faced, Enid sucked in a breath. Uncle George led her in with three chords, singing along himself, and then off she went obediently, piping up the scale in a tinny, pleasant voice.

'Bravo, Enid! Well done!' he cried, when she reached the top. 'Again! Deep breath! Louder!' Enid did as she was told.

He whirled round on the stool towards Fleur while Enid turned to Lila with a look of terror. 'See, Fleur?' he shouted. 'Even Enid's got a voice. Everyone's got a voice. Everyone can sing!'

Fleur raised an eyebrow. 'Chorus material,' she said, 'if that. And unless we've got a Calaf . . .'

Uncle George interrupted with a flurry of notes at the top of the keyboard, his fingers flickering as though he were catching beads tinkling from a broken necklace. 'Sure we need to bring in our Calaf,' he called to her, 'we might need to reduce the number of principals, rewrite the really hard bits. But the chorus and little parts, everyone else we need, we could get from round here. There's bound to be amateur orchestras, we'll ask them – anyway we'll cut down the band. We'd have to find plenty brass and percussion, of course. It'll be great.'

Enid, looking like a stranded cat, blurted out, 'I need to go. My mum doesn't know I'm here. I'm needed at home.'

She turned and ran. Lila followed her out of the door but Enid sped back through the kitchen, past Raymond in the vegetable patch and round to the driveway where she jumped on her bike and tore away. Lila called after her but she did not turn round.

Lila drifted back into the house leaving the back door open, and stopped in the kitchen. Over the sound of her father's spade from outside she heard Uncle George start up at the piano again and then came her mother's faltering and shaky attempt at one of Turandot's arias. When it was over there was laughter from the music room and outside, the chuck of the spade stopped and was followed by solitary, slow applause from the carrot patch.

I want to laugh (and unkindly at that) at the first cutting out of the tea chest. It's a full page from the *Burnhead & District Advertiser* Thursday 7th July 1960.

I remember now. On the Tuesday, Uncle George gets in touch with the paper and they send along Alec Gallagher the same afternoon. He can only be in his early thirties but to me he is already fading, like a watercolour. With that pink Scottish complexion and pale lashes and eyes, he looks diluted.

He brings a photographer with him but he also says that if George has any 'suitable existing photographic material' they might print that too because the paper's short on pictures this week. When George tells him he also wants to place a full page advert for a big public meeting, Alec beams and says he'll almost guarantee him two pictures with the article.

So there we are in the picture, the three of us smiling round the piano in the music room, our eyes almost blacked out in newspaper ink but mine oddly wide and delighted, as if I can see fairies on the ceiling. Quite a good picture, it fills nearly half the page, and far more picture than words, typical of a local rag. Don't know what I'm thinking of with those wads of hair and the clasp on top though to give myself credit I do change my hair very soon after this photo is taken. Over the picture it says:

LOCAL MUSICAL FAMILY'S
OPERA PLEA

Burnhead mother and daughter singing duo Fleur and Eliza
Duncan are aiming for the stars in a bid to bring high culture

to town, with the brand new Burnhead Association for Singing *Turandot* (BAST). Says Fleur (36) pictured left, 'It all
started with my brother George Pettifer (right). Puccini's
never been done here but that's no reason why it shouldn't.
You need trained singers for the principal parts but there's
plenty of scope for amateurs. *Turandot*'s got everything.'
Conductor George (30) up visiting from London where he
teaches music, stresses you don't have to be a Maria Callas or
a Mario Lanza. 'You need vision. There are plenty of voices out
there, enthusiasm's more important than experience. Everyone can get involved. People who already sing in choirs or
amateur opera are very welcome to BAST but we want begin-
ners too.' Like big sis Fleur, a fully trained soprano known in
opera circles as Fleur Pettifer, he's confident that local talent
can rise to the challenge. 'It'll be hard work,' he admits. 'BAST
is a big step up from Gilbert & Sullivan, something people can
get their teeth into. Opera changes lives. I want to help people
see the vision.' Songster Eliza (15) pictured centre, is tipped
for one of the big parts. Has she always dreamed of treading
the boards? 'I sort of knew I had a voice,' she says modestly,
'but I didn't see any point in it till Uncle George came up with
the idea of BAST. There's nothing round here for young
people,' she adds. About singing in public she says, 'With
Uncle George encouraging me I'll do my best. I won't let him
down.'

All is not lost for those whose gifts lie elsewhere. 'BAST
needs instrumentalists, anyone with an instrument is welcome, we'll fit everybody in! We also need help with set and
costumes,' prompts George. He would especially like to hear
from amateur orchestras and bands.

So come on, give BAST your support and enjoy yourself into
the bargain. Don't miss BAST's inaugural meeting on 9 July
(page 18 for full details) ALL WELCOME. No experience
required.

In real life prima donna Fleur is Mrs Raymond Duncan. Mr

Duncan is legal clerk with respected Burnhead firm Kerr, Mather & McNeill.

By Staff Reporter Alec Gallagher

The photographer leaves when he's done the picture but Alec stays. He's smiling very hard at both of them. He's thrilled when George offers him tea. My mother trips away upstairs and brings down the photographs she had taken when she left music college. Uncle George doesn't point out to Alec that they are more than a decade out of date, and Alec either doesn't notice or doesn't care. My mother's pride in these photographs suggests she simply doesn't consider that she has aged at all.

So here she is in the yellow cutting, a smaller picture underneath the first one. She's not unlike Callas in colouring but more nipped in feature as well as smaller in spirit, leaning in towards the camera in an off-the-shoulder frock. She looks feverish, young, tremulous. The twin points of the lipstick bow of her mouth reach up towards her nostrils and her hair is folded over her temples like smooth, painted wings. She is gazing through oily-looking eyes towards, what, Parnassus? Not, certainly, 5 Seaview Villas with Raymond Duncan and a baby. The caption reads:

Soprano Fleur Pettifer in her heyday: Known locally as Mrs Florence Duncan (36) Burnhead's own prima donna will soon be delighting audiences again. Those with highbrow tastes need not go far for she is lending her talents to a local venture as grand opera comes to Burnhead. The Burnhead Association for Singing *Turandot* (BAST) needs your support (see details page 18). Mrs Duncan's career began with the Cercle de la Lune Touring Opera Company in 1944 when aged just 20 she understudied major roles. 'I was exceptionally young but I was thought to have enormous potential,' she admits. When marriage and family came along Mrs Duncan settled in Burnhead with husband Raymond, legal clerk with local firm Kerr, Mather & McNeill.

Don't forget BAST's inaugural meeting on 9th July (see page 18) and join in with this exciting new artistic venture. ALL WELCOME.

By Staff Reporter Alec Gallagher

Poor Alec paid for that 'in her heyday', I remember. For days my mother flared her nostrils at the mention of his name but she forgave him before the next edition was out.

They entrance him from the start. He just falls for them both; they are so elegant and shiny-eyed and attractive and English, and they must make a change from the Burnhead Bathing Belles and the presidents of bowling clubs receiving memorial shields and town councillors' wives opening Coffee Mornings. Alec particularly loves all George's vision talk and says it's in short supply round here and exactly what the place needs. He says the place is full of philistines and he isn't planning on staying that long himself, only with his fiancée Veronica's mum not so well it's a bit up in the air where they'll settle. He personally needs to be around like-minded people.

As the *Turandot* story unfolds in print through July and August the whole undertaking will acquire a glamour that all three of them like. Everything Alec writes will frame Uncle George and my mother in their preferred version of themselves as artists – instinctive, refined, unembarrassed – and they will encourage Alec to take a similar view of himself. If he regards them as demigods, albeit small-town ones, they return the compliment. As well as persuading him that he can sing, they will egg him on as 'a writer'. Before long Alec will be complaining that his editor is a philistine with no vision. He really will think he is in with some sort of élite.

Meanwhile they, after this first meeting with 'the press', are skittish and elated.

Poor Alec Gallagher, how you were captivated. I can still see you, your pale eyes smarting and pink with devotion and your hands studded with sun spots and short ginger hairs like a piglet's back. You are ready to do anything for the vision, as you guide your stubby pencil with surprising elegance over your notebook, spinning out in shorthand a tale that even George and my mother, before you began to write it, scarcely believed in themselves.

It's tempting to claim it was the way the paper has it. Even now, the idea of doing *Turandot* like that doesn't seem so very ridiculous, given how we look in the picture. The reasons George gives Alec Gallagher sound plausible enough. If only matters could just be left like that.

Yes, it's tempting. It's tempting to look at myself in this photograph and think, look at me, I must have been happy after all. One day more than forty years ago – not even a day, only an afternoon fragment – trapped in a photograph, and I want to remember us just as the picture has us. Caught by the camera and look, here's how we are: the lips curled in a smile just so, a scarf lying across a shoulder, a watch on a man's wrist, every detail stands clear. Here's the evidence you want, you can't argue with it. Here is the very moment untouched by the hours and the days that surround it.

If I have to think of the *Turandot* time at all I wish I could remember it as a succession of days like that: single days of one dimension, no leakage from one into the next, each one free to be spent and let go, and on the next I wake up complete and wiped clean. Not a shadow of yesterday will cling, no cloud is forming over tomorrow. There's no binding in of what came before and no hankering in me for the yet to be, and nothing is missing. But time never is like that, like a newspaper report. Days are not like photographs, in which we imagine we felt just as we looked. The real reasons for what we do never are explicable in a carefree paragraph or two, and seldom are there simple words for all that needs to be said.

8

'Who is this person again, George?'

Less than two days into his visit, George was smoking too much. When he answered a question in the tone Fleur expected, an unkind, barely tethered part of him was composing mentally the reply he thought she deserved. He wondered if his sister's voice – so high and spiritless, as if grievance sent it up in pitch – had changed, or if he had just forgotten how irritating it was.

'Because Calaf's not a role for just anybody. I won't do it with just anybody.'

When she spoke he could feel a tightening in himself, like a key turning, locking fury into a cell inside his head.

'Joe Foscari, Italian family. One of the best students.' *I've told you this a hundred times.*

They were sitting at the table while Lila cleared around them.

He lit his third cigarette since breakfast. 'After National Service he decided to do something with his singing. See if he could make a go of it.' *Why can't you just listen?*

'That doesn't sound very serious.'

'He is serious. He had to leave school young and work in a draughtsman's office.'

Fleur murmured a sound of disengagement, and watched George smoking. Lila chinked the dirty crockery and cutlery together, preferring any noise to the silences during which she feared, even with Uncle George here, that the day could slide to a halt.

'A draughtsman?' Fleur said, pushing out her bottom lip.

'I've seen some of his work,' George said. 'He'll be good with sets and costumes, he's done a bit of stage design at college.' *Oh, you snob. Who do you think you are?*

'And what was it you said about the family?' she said lazily. 'They were dukes or something? He'll be far too grand for us.'

'Not dukes, doges. Of Venice. The last doge of Venice was a Foscari.' *Too grand for you? You don't think that for a minute. Florrie, what happened to you?*

He said, 'They're almost certainly descended but they're not grand now, all that's past. I told you.' *You're still not listening.* 'Joe says they actually started off in Glasgow but they're all down south now. They had restaurants.' *I told you this a hundred times, too.*

'What kind of restaurants?'

'Fleur, I've told you. Italian ones. Foscari's.' *If you ask me to tell you again that Foscari's was one of Glasgow's most famous Italian restaurants I shall slap you.*

'Hmm. Wasn't Foscari's one of the smarter ones before the war? Smart for Glasgow, I mean,' Fleur said.

Raymond appeared in the doorway, bicycle clips in one hand and a paper bag in the other. 'Well, that's me away,' he said, folding his trouser bottoms in place under the clips. 'Monday morning. No peace for the wicked.' He scraped outdoor shoes on the threshold. 'Okay for some.'

'What've you got there?' George asked.

Raymond seemed surprised to have the bag in his hand. 'Oh, just runner beans, few carrots. There's a woman I work with's fond of them. She was saying. She doesn't grow vegetables. We've that many. So she's doing me a favour.'

'John Mathieson does grow vegetables. He's got a greenhouse. Last year we had some of their tomatoes,' Fleur said.

'Aye, but . . . well, he's maybe just not brought so much on this year, maybe that was it.'

'Ahhh, Raymond's runners and carrots! She's in for a treat,' George said, foolishly. 'So, off goes the legal eagle, eh?' *Don't you ever smile? No wonder your family's cracking up round you.*

'Aye, right you are,' Raymond said. 'Well, that's me away. Cheerio.' Hesitating with his hand on the door, he said, 'This, er, this wee opera you're to be at – Chinese, is it? I've got that right, set in China, is it?'

Fleur looked at the ceiling. 'Well, *obviously*.'

George said, 'That's right, China.' *Where have you bloody been? Your fifteen-year-old daughter knows the whole thing off by heart.* 'Actually, the libretto says "in Peking in legendary times".'

Raymond cleared his throat. 'Aye, well, I'm thinking, this woman I work with, Mrs Mathieson, Audrey. See, she knows China, she was brought up there from a girl. Her parents were missionaries. She'd maybe help, you know? She's the helpful kind.'

'Ooh, goody! What's she got?' George said. He pounced on the pen on the table and scribbled down the name. 'Anything in silk? Costumes, jewellery, shoes? Or even furniture, or swords or . . . Has she got a gong? Any cutlasses?'

'I'd need to ask. I think maybe. But I was thinking more Audrey herself. I mean, she'll know a lot about it. She's lived in Shanghai. Before the war.'

'For God's sake, Raymond, what has Shanghai before the war got to do with ancient Peking in an opera of a fairy tale?' Fleur snapped. 'Anyway, it's not meant to be realistic. Is it, George? This is opera. Audrey Mathieson probably knows as much about opera as you do. Which is damn all.'

Raymond cleared his throat. 'Och, Fleur. I'll ask, will I?' he said, looking to George. 'I'm sure she'd be only too pleased.'

'Thanks, Ray,' George said, winking. 'You ask her. Mrs Mathieson, we want your Chinese treasures and your fact-filled mind. Don't we, Fleur?'

Raymond backed out of the dining room, nearly colliding with Lila coming back in with a tray.

'So, this Joe whatever his name is,' Fleur said, glaring at the closing door, 'when's he coming? You say he's got family in Glasgow?'

George mashed the end of his cigarette into the ashtray. 'Joe Foscari, and his family's all down south, Bedford area. He's just finished his second year. And he's very good, potentially.'

She shook her head. '*Potentially*? Calaf's not a role for just anybody.' She lifted her elbows from the table to let Lila gather up crumbs.

Conversations since yesterday had been circling and retreating around Fleur's doubts about the grand idea, but Lila could tell that her mother's energy was lessening. Uncle George was wearing her down; the cadences of her replies were growing relaxed. Now she was objecting in a way that made Lila think of someone making up new verses for a song, keeping an endless duet going for the sake of it. She carried on tidying around them. She liked the warm secret inside her that Uncle George was doing all this for her. Already some of his brilliance was rubbing off his hands and on to the idea itself; it was growing too bright ever to have been hers.

He said, 'Well, yes, he's young, but between us we know how to take care of a young voice. Fleur, it's quite straightforward. All I need to do is ring him up.' *Jesus! Will you shut up and let me get on with this?*

'It'll be one more to cater for,' Fleur said listlessly. 'I hope he's not fussy.'

'I'll tell him he'll be appearing opposite the best Turandot he could hope for, so why don't you get some work in on your voice today?' *Get it moving, for God's sake. You've got ground to make up, God knows.*

Fleur sighed with the burden of her talent. 'I'm tired. I don't want to get stale. And Eliza singing Liù? For God's sake, George, I never heard anything so ridiculous. Singing Liù at fifteen?'

'Well, you just wait,' Uncle George said, 'till you hear her sing.' He smiled at Lila. 'Could you squeeze another cup out of that pot for your old uncle?' *Christ, she is only fifteen, poor little witch. I wonder if she'll be up to it.*

Lila skipped off with the teapot.

'And you, conducting? Georgie, this isn't the *Mikado*. Come on, what's the biggest show you've ever done? Something at college – *Orpheus in the Underworld*? *Die Fledermaus*?'

'Of course it's a challenge,' George said tightly. 'I know *Turandot* inside out. Thank you for your faith.'

Fleur gave a bitter little laugh and reached for George's cigarettes. She said, 'It doesn't matter a damn if you can conduct it or not or if Eliza can sing it or not because we haven't got a venue.'

'You,' George said, pulling the packet away from her, 'may no longer smoke. I'm telling you, I'll have a venue and a tenor lead by lunchtime.'

Christ. This is bloody mad. Joe – you've got to come. Say you'll come. It's for you.

Now I'm tired. I have a sore throat, as if my voice has been under strain although I have spoken to nobody. I'm sitting by the gas fire in the empty back room and I'm back at the boxes, looking at papers. Rubbish, all of it, I could just burn it but as it's been here all this time I owe it – or somebody does and there is nobody else left – at least a look-through.

I have George's notes in my hand. Even rough jottings on torn-off scraps of paper are here, silly faces drawn inside the rings left by coffee cups on the edges of notes, doodles on pages from the telephone pad. On one page interspersed with telephone numbers and names in George's writing are his sketches made that first day: a ceremonial sword, a helmet studded with points, a suit of armour with metal wings coming off the shoulders like blades. I am watching him as he works over them in ballpoint. He also writes this:

Town Hall seats how many ?? stage how wide? Lighting rig?
Norrie's Marquee and Banqueting Hire (Glasgow) no!
Mr?? clerk to the whats? – keep trying.

He is waiting for the telephone to be answered, drawing quickly and jerkily. His mind seems set on something far away; I think he is imagining the hoard of Chinese artefacts that he intends to charm Mrs Mathieson into lending him.

He whispers to me as he scribbles, Here look, this is how it'll be – Calaf's tunic. Like this. He carries a sword, something small, a dagger will do as long as it looks Oriental, a curving blade. Something for his head . . .

He etches the drawings over and over until he nearly goes through the paper.

Now the empty house fills with sound, in broken snatches. In the music room my mother puts herself through a succession of ascending and descending scales, singing every vowel on each note. Her sound is not constant. Filling the air for an instant it is then borne away, now it returns. I hear it in random waves as if it is carried on a wind that is always changing direction; no, I hear it as if I am moving from room to room. I suddenly have a idea of myself roaming through the house and half-singing as I go, a soft mewing noise that seems, even though it is coming from my lips, to be following me. I wonder, fleetingly, about my sore throat. My feet were dirty again this morning.

Now my mother's voice again. She is singing more elaborate exercises involving leaps, changes of pitch, consonants, staccato and legato notes. She even sings through her nose, she hums, she sings arpeggios to yo and yah and bow-wow-wow and brrr. Now she is laughing. She plays a few chords at the piano, rests for a minute, and off she goes again.

I hear the roar of the electric coffee grinder that Uncle George has brought as a present along with proper coffee beans from Soho. He sets it going while I clamber up on a stool and pull our coffee percolator down from the top of one of the kitchen cupboards. I smell the greasy metal as I scrub at it, and now the wood and spice of real coffee rises as the pot makes its plocking sound on the Rayburn. George pours, and then our kitchen is exciting in the way I imagine his London kitchen is: it smells foreign, a place of grown-up ease. I taste my coffee and it needs a lot of sugar; it is a little like the wine, better as an idea than as a drink. Bring those, George says, nodding at our cups and striding into the hall, where he pulls the telephone and the directory down from the hall table and on to the linoleum. I join him on the floor with my back against the wall and look up the numbers of all the halls I can think of, which he writes down. I sip my coffee and think that for once I am more like somebody in a book than the real me. Not madly Bohemian perhaps – not living in a castle or enduring hardships cleverly and talkatively – but it is enough for half an hour or so to be living in a way that is verging on the unusual, sitting on the floor with a cup of real coffee and looking up telephone numbers.

Uncle George is on the phone to the Town Hall. I shuffle up closer and he tilts the receiver so that I hear everything. I sit, waiting and tingling.

Oh, good morning. I have an enquiry about the Town Hall.

I listen, picturing his voice floating like fairy dust around the person at the other end and setting him a-sparkle with competence, cooperation, awe.

Name?

He gives it. He adds, And I would need to know the charges involved, of course, but my main query is how big is the stage?

Aye, but who's it for? I mean what organisation's wanting it, because it's only organisations can get it. And then it's at the Town Clerk's discretion, or his designated officers.

Oh, I do beg your pardon. Uncle George lifts his eyes and smiles at the wall, then turns and includes me. I'm calling on behalf of BAST. The Burnhead Association for Singing *Turandot*.

We listen to the whispering of papers being leafed through at the Town Hall.

That one's no on my register.

Uncle George takes a breath to speak.

You're no from round here, are you? Have you enquired before?

BAST is a new organisation, Uncle George says. Brand new. I'm not surprised you haven't heard of it.

His English accent is so reasonable. His words rise and fall like folds of dark brown velvet. All you have to do to believe him is to listen.

Well see, this is the official register, you've to be a properly constituted and affiliated club, association or society otherwise you'll no get on it. An' if you're no on the register you'll not get the hire.

My mother comes and leans on the wall with her arms folded. She sets her mouth in a thin line.

Uncle George bluffs on, giving assurances about honorary office-bearers and Memoranda and Articles of Association.

We'll have all the proper affiliations in place. May we not book now, for August? It's still several weeks away.

Our hearts lift a little, he is so easy to believe.

August? The hall's booked solid for August.

George shakes his head at my mother. He sticks out his tongue at the telephone.

The Burnhead Majorettes Display and the Bathing Belles go in the Town Hall in the eventuality of inclement weather. There's the Land o' Burns Ceilidh and the Accordion Championships Junior Heats. If you'd just said your dates to begin with, the man scolds, you'd have saved all the bother.

He sounds exhausted.

And it's only a twenty-eight foot stage, any road.

George rings off. I shuffle away and lean back against the opposite wall.

My mother's eyes are full of tears. She says, You see now? I told you. That's all you get in this bloody place. Oh *God*!

She spins away up the stairs to her bedroom, sobs juddering out of her as she goes. Over our heads, the door slams and the house goes quiet.

Just the first hurdle, Uncle George says. You're not deserting me, are you?

Now it's just him and me. I look at him sitting on the floor opposite, and I turn away from noticing the little deposits of yellowy stuff in the corners of his eyes. I have my back against the wall and my legs are slightly apart, knees bent; the telephone directory is still open in my lap. I tip my head back and concentrate on the ebbing away of our good spirits. Uncle George is looking at the directory as if it fascinates him. No, he isn't. I realise that the back of my skirt lies open on the floor under my thighs. He can see all of the backs of my thighs, right up to my pants, and not only that. He sees not just a glimpse of the gusset but the crack into which it has ridden up and now clings, the place of which I am ashamed and over which I have so little control that from it, these days, various dark-smelling and unwanted excretions seep and flow for no other purpose, it seems, than to degrade me. His eyes are bleary, wistful with interest and it is my fault, yet in the moment before I swing my knees to the floor and cut off the view, some other feeling swamps my shame. This feeling is impersonal, because I am momentarily in thrall to curiosity itself – to his, my own, anyone's – I am captive to a fascination which is also, for a second or two, mine, helpless in the glow from any greedy eyes and anyone's strange need to truffle between my legs. In that instant I think I would offer no resistance at all to a lascivious inspection of that part of me, and for the first time in my life I am open to the possibility of being unashamed. This thought at once gives rise to more shame, and I blush.

I'll help you, I say. After all, there must be other halls. Of course I'll help you.

I am delighted to have any chance to show him how helpful I can be. I'll make sure he knows that it'll be the same when I'm staying with him in London, and he'll realise he can't do without me.

The gas fire flickers. I push Uncle George's notes off my lap on to the floor. There's a smell in here. It's the smell of dirty old man: gas, matches, crumbs and ammonia, and it makes me angry.

———•◦•———

9

U ncle George tipped back his head to finish his coffee and Lila heard it go down with a wet, secret noise. He pulled a hand across his mouth and half stood to get his cigarettes from his pocket.

'All right then, not the Town Hall. Too small, anyway,' he said, lighting up. 'There are other halls, surely?'

'There's only church halls,' Lila said. 'Even smaller.'

Uncle George tapped his finger on his cigarette.

She added, 'It's no good. I knew it wouldn't be.'

'Don't say that! What about . . . I know, what about doing it in the open air?' he said. 'Like *Aida* at the pyramids. People bringing their champagne and picnics and all that, like Glyndebourne.'

Lila looked hard at him. 'Outside? Here? Champagne? *Here?*'

'Okay, I'm just trying to think. You're right,' George said, screwing up his eyes in the cigarette smoke, 'they'd probably come with limeade and fish suppers.'

'It'd rain. It's always raining.'

'All right. Shut up.'

They thumbed through the directory and tried a few of the church halls. Uncle George rang a marquee firm in Glasgow that had only one marquee big enough, and that was booked out for August to a golf tournament at Turnberry. Lila was slightly, guiltily relieved. In the grip of what was their last chance she had not wanted to point out to him that they had nowhere to put a marquee.

'Don't scowl,' Uncle George said, getting up from the floor. 'Keep thinking. We're not giving up on day one.'

They drifted into the kitchen and washed the coffee cups. There was silence from upstairs.

'Tell you what,' Uncle George said. 'It's nearly lunchtime, let's get in the car and go for a picnic. Let's make sandwiches and go off somewhere, wherever you like, somewhere we can think. I'm going mad cooped up here. Cheer your mother up.'

Lila wanted to believe that life could be like this, that maybe something as simple as a picnic could actually *be* simple. Then she shook her head. 'We can't. There's no bread and the baker's boy doesn't come till three.'

'Doesn't matter, we'll get some on the way. We'll take a knife and butter and things and make sandwiches on the spot.'

'There's nothing to put in them.'

'We can buy meat paste. Cheese.'

'Grocer's closed till two. Anyway, she,' Lila said, raising her eyes to the ceiling, 'she doesn't like picnics. And it's about to rain.'

Uncle George sighed. 'Oh, for God's sake. All right, what have we got here, then?'

'There's nothing,' Lila said.

'Don't scowl. There's never nothing.'

Uncle George seemed to feel he had something to prove. He nosed about in the pantry and came out with an onion held under his chin. In his hands he had a bowl of dripping and the platter with the remains of the Sunday joint and some leftover potato. He opened a jar of Marmite and sniffed at it. Lila watched him, pessimistic about anyone's chances of turning the ragged grey brick and surrounding rubble of yesterday's joint into something they would want to eat; the attempt seemed hardly less doomed than the opera. But Uncle George sliced up the onion and started to sing something silly in Italian and she couldn't help laughing. He threw the onion and some dripping into a pan on the stove, added the chopped-up meat, stirred it furiously, tipped in the potato and gave her the wooden spoon.

'Keep it moving,' he told her, springing away to the pantry

again. He emptied in a tin of baked beans and shook on some Lea & Perrins, took the spoon again and told her to lay the table.

'See? Lunch. There's never nothing. Go and call upstairs for your mother. Tell her we're eating in the kitchen and I want her down here in one minute,' he said, opening the window above the sink, 'and no histrionics.'

Uncle George and Lila kept up a humdrum conversation as they ate but Fleur said nothing. Tears kept rolling down her cheeks and time after time she wiped them away with a movement more covert and modest than any Lila had ever seen before. Watching her, she swelled with guilt. In Uncle George's company she had been beginning to forget to feel accountable.

Afterwards, the afternoon began to press in. Lila was wondering what they'd do once the washing up was done when they heard whistling and then the clack of the gate into the back garden.

'Jimmy from Brocks,' Fleur told George, dully. 'The coke, first Monday in the month.'

Jimmy passed by the window under a loaded sack. Lila heard a pause in the whistling, a rumble as he emptied the sack into the bunker against the back wall, a scrape of boot nails as he returned, folding the sack as he went. He passed backwards and forwards, weighted in one direction and straightening up in the other. A few moments later the face appeared back at the kitchen window. Lila opened the back door.

Apart from a pink patch where he had lately wiped his nose, and the lids of his swimming blue eyes, Jimmy was like coal itself, as if he had been dipped in it and burnished. With a show of gums and sparse teeth he explained that the truck wouldn't start.

'Auld bitch,' he said. There was grey glue in the corners of his mouth. 'Bitch'll no start. No been right all day.' He held out a dirty delivery note with the coal merchant's address at the top.

'Goannie ring this number for us? Need tae get somebody out from the yard tae give us a tow.'

Fleur, as lady of the house, went away to make the call while Jimmy waited in the garden. She came back and arranged herself in the doorway. She seemed to have brightened up with something to do.

'There's nobody at the yard who can come in less than two hours. They say you should try starting her again, maybe all she needs is a minute to cool down.'

They all trooped out to the truck. On the back were a few full sacks and several heaps of empty ones weighted under bricks. Jimmy tried the ignition again. The engine wheezed and died. He tried several more times and climbed down from the cab.

'Bloody nuisance,' he said. 'See they? They're for the farm, last call.' He nodded at the last few sacks and gestured across the road towards the track between the fields. 'They was wanting it urgent. They'll no get it the day.'

He shook his head, releasing a dusty smell that was both human and tarry.

'But they could load the sacks themselves from here if they brought down a trailer or something,' Uncle George said. He and Jimmy were now lighting cigarettes from George's packet.

Jimmy turned his lakes of eyes on Fleur as he took his first drag. 'So they could, right enough,' he said. His black finger and thumb, tipped with ridged grey horns of fingernails, held the cigarette with strange delicacy. 'If they kenned it was here. But they don't ken.'

Uncle George turned and scanned the distance. 'Well, somebody could go and tell them, couldn't they?'

'Canna go mysel',' Jimmy said. 'Got to stay wi' the truck. Mind you, Mrs Duncan . . .' He grinned at Fleur.

'Me? I hardly know them,' Fleur said. 'We never see them.'

He sucked again on his cigarette. 'See me? I hate letting folk doon. And they was wanting it the day.' He looked sadly up the track.

'George, I really don't think we can go barging up there. I don't know them.'

'We wouldn't be barging, it's just neighbourly. We'd be doing them a favour.'

'I'm not wearing the right shoes, I'm afraid.'

Jimmy looked at her light slingbacks, the same toffee colour as the cardigan slung over her shoulders.

'Right enough,' he said.

'But I've got the car, silly,' George said. 'I'd rather walk though, it's no distance. Anyway, Florrie, you don't *possess* the right shoes. There's no need for you to come. You stay and make Jimmy a cup of tea. We'll go, won't we?' he said, turning to Lila.

'All right,' he said as the two of them started up the track. 'What about these people we're about to see?'

'They're called McCarthy, I think.'

'Big family?'

'Don't know. Well, there's a boy. He went to the High School. Older than me, he left soon after I started. Never spoke.'

'Just him? Does he work the farm with his dad or what?'

'Don't know. Think so.' From time to time she saw one or other of them at a distance, in the fields. The question of talking to them, even if she wanted to, never arose.

'Anybody else? Just the two of them?'

'Not sure.'

'Is there a mum?'

'Don't know.'

Uncle George seemed exasperated. 'Listen. Your mother . . . I know she doesn't mix much but does she stop you? I mean, stop you taking an interest? Aren't you curious about people? Or is Enid all you've got?'

Lila shrugged. 'Don't know.'

'I see. Well, wouldn't you like to widen your horizons a little?'

'How can I? *Here?*'

'Well, by doing *Turandot*, for one thing.'

'I want to go and live in London.'

'I'm talking about right now. About *Turandot*. Your mother's desperate to, though she's pretending she isn't. Don't you want to?'

The truth was Lila was ashamed of her excitement about doing anything that involved Uncle George. She shrugged again. 'Doesn't matter now anyway, does it, 'cos we haven't got anywhere to do it.'

Uncle George picked up the pace and soon snatches of *Turandot* started to rumble from his lips. Lila strode along, trying to keep up. He was deliberately putting distance between them; she wondered why he did not care about her sorrow at being left behind.

She had seen the farm from a distance every day of her life but had never been there, so that reaching the end of the track felt like entering a landscape known from a picture, familiar but unfamiliar; there might be different customs here, and a strange language. Together they passed under the trees and entered the yard and stopped, taking in the clutter strewn across what had been the small garden of the farmhouse: choked flowerbeds round a patch of grass criss-crossed with tractor ruts and petering out at its fringe into cracked concrete that led round to the farm buildings. Lila gazed at the front of the house. They were alone, yet something about it suggested they were awaited, as though they were arriving in a story already being played out behind the windows. Around them lay a queasy silence that might at any moment turn out to be no more than a lull between disasters. The day could yet blow open.

Uncle George strode up to the door and hammered with the knocker. After a few minutes he banged on the door, bringing down a few flakes of pale yellow paint. Then he turned away and walked round the side of the house out of Lila's sight. She waited. The trees rustled in a gust of wind and a few crows let out hacks of complaint and flew away. As she looked up, the wind descended smoothly into the yard and sleeked around her, as though the sky were pouring emptiness straight into her. Gooseflesh rose on her neck and arms and she shivered, and suddenly the quiet yawned open, as full of certainties as the stillness in the house three days ago – it felt like weeks – when she thought her mother had killed herself and she had gone looking in empty rooms for her dead body, her mind fighting between horror and desire. Once again time was passing in a way that must belong to the kind of afternoon on which a death might take place, when a quiet person might suddenly kill another with clean, beautiful strength; in the air hung a calm that threatened to end in the taking of a life, a ripping apart of dreams. She ran a few steps in the direction Uncle George had taken, calling out for him. He reappeared and took her by the hand, as if he knew.

'Nothing round the back. Come on.'

They returned to the yard. 'Halloo-oo!' he called, in a womanly falsetto that returned Lila to the world; she snatched her hand away and prayed nobody had heard. Then a dog barked and skeetered into view. It slavered around them as they skirted past it and followed the direction from where it had come, past the side of a low barn and round to the entrance of a newer, higher building behind. The dog overtook them at the wide doors and rustled through a scattering of straw on the floor towards two people leaning into a tractor. A radio sat squealing in the straw like a small dark animal. The building was vast, and seemed too clean to belong to a farm. It smelled of oil and electricity rather than of earth and blood and hoof, and in its echo there was something metallic.

The older man looked up. 'Well, now?' he said, advancing on them with his hands on his hips. Uncle George stepped forward, offering his hand.

'You must be Mr McCarthy?'

'McArthur,' the man said, not smiling. 'I've oil on my hands. What's your business?'

He listened while George explained. The boy Lila had known by sight at school kept his head in the tractor and did not look up. When Uncle George finished, the corners of Mr McArthur's closed mouth tilted slightly upwards. He wiped his hands with a rag from the floor, finger by finger, giving him a long, assessing gaze. Then he accepted a handshake.

'Obliged to you.'

Uncle George looked past him into the shed. 'A pleasure. Sound building,' he said. 'Bone dry. How wide, about forty feet?'

'Five thousand feet square, fifty-five by ninety-five. Doing well, only eight year old,' Mr McArthur said, as if he were talking about offspring or livestock. 'I put it up to expand, there was to be a big expansion. Fully automated.'

From the radio on the floor Mantovani and his orchestra pealed out a tune on high, silvery wires: 'Forgotten Dreams', a spiralling chase after elation and sadness and the chance of love. If she could see it, Lila thought, the sound would lift from the straw and curl up through the shed in plumes of shining dust.

'Good acoustic for music, anyway,' Uncle George said, with a backward grin at her. Then she saw the way his mind was going.

'Aye well. I never got round to finishing. Never expanded the herd, we hit a wee bad patch there. I'll maybe still do it, one of these days.'

'Shame to let it sit empty.'

'Handy for storage,' Mr McArthur said.

She followed Uncle George's eyes up to the pitched roof. The floor and walls were of concrete and breezeblock and the steel struts from which lights were suspended crossed from side to side like rafters at a height of about ten feet. Six square, metal-framed windows, some with broken or missing panes, ran down one side. At both ends of the building, wide sliding doors opened it up like a hangar. Apart from the tractor and boxes of tools, some lengths of timber and a heap of tarpaulin, the place was empty. Uncle George clicked his tongue twice and sang an arpeggio over the sliding racket from the radio. His voice rose and echoed generously.

Mr McArthur cleared his throat and glanced at his son. 'Aye, well. Billy, turn that damn thing off, we've to take the van and get the coal,' he said.

Billy scrambled down without looking at the visitors.

'Are you the music lover, Mr McArthur?' Uncle George asked, as they walked back across the yard.

'I am not. Fair gets my goat.' Less gruffly he said, 'Billy here, he's the one. Got it from his mother, she could sing you back a tune even if she just heard it the once.'

'I'm just wondering, you see – the shed there. I'm looking for a place like that, for a musical venture. Just to use for a while, till August, nothing permanent. No disruption to you. Would you be interested at all – hiring it out, for a musical event? At the going rate, of course?'

Mr McArthur looked baffled. He cleared his throat again. 'Aye well, good of yous to come and let us know about the coal. We'll take the van down now, give yous a lift home.'

He led them over to a van with an open back. 'Your lassie all right on the back there wi' Billy? Billy, help the lassie up,' he said. Then he made his way round to the driver's side and opened the door. 'I'd no be putting up wi' yon Beatniks, mind.' he said, over the roof of the cab.

'Oh, no. No, absolutely not . . .' Uncle George said, scrambling in at the other side. 'Quite the opposite. Let me tell you . . .'

Billy jumped on to the back and hauled Lila up. His hair covered his eyes so he was still managing not to look at her. The dog leapt on too and barked as the van suddenly pulled forward. Lila grabbed a hold of the side and laughed as she lurched around. The wind blew Billy's hair back from his face and she caught his eye; he stared back at her without trust.

'What's its name?' she asked, pointing at the dog.

'Sherpa,' Billy said.

'Nice name.'

'It was Schubert – my dad changed it.'

'Why?'

'Just. None of your business.' Billy looked away startled, as if he had not known that such a question could reasonably follow from what he had said. They bounced on down the track without speaking. Lila pretended to be enjoying the ride more than she was, laughing and holding down her hair as if being blown to bits were pleasurable, and Billy kept his eyes on the fields as if it were scenery. When she knew he wasn't watching, Lila took a look, memorising him so she could tell Enid every detail, already enjoying the edge that meeting a boy would give her. He was about eighteen, solid and dirty but in an outdoors way; about his shabby clothes was a hint of coal smoke and animal and stale bread that she didn't mind in the least. It was easily preferable to the smell of boiled eggs that eddied round most of the boys in her class and his skin was nicer than theirs, too, darker and almost foreign-looking. She liked looking at him, assessing him. It was a relief to let her mind flow away from her thoughts about the farmhouse and back to the familiar preoccupation and still hypothetical anxiety of her and Enid's virginal lives: what you do when you meet a boy. How you tell if he likes you. The ultimate, most worrisome of all: how you find out if he is interested in One Thing Only, except the hard way.

When they reached Seaview Villas Lila jumped off by herself before Billy could think she wanted him to touch her. Jimmy, Billy and Mr McArthur shifted the coal on to the back of the grey van, Uncle George's clothes being too clean for him to help. More tea was made, Fleur by now quite the hostess. She brought it out on a tray and they became a modest street party, chatting and smoking and drinking tea out on the road next to the loaded van.

Lila watched them all, dazed. In the space of a day Uncle George had changed them, doing something as alchemical with them as he had done with the leftovers at dinnertime (just the way he called it lunch made it different). She didn't understand how, but his assurance about everything was part of his power. He wouldn't believe, and wouldn't let you believe either, that a thing wasn't going to turn out fresh and lively and right. Meeting neighbours, chatting with the coalman – whatever he touched, from *Turandot* to beef hash, he turned into a story thrumming with fun and full of connections, people, events.

As Billy turned to go he handed Lila his cup and managed a direct look that was not hostile. Sherpa was whistled back on board the van, Uncle George shook Mr McArthur's hand and told him he would be up in the morning. Mr McArthur said that would be grand and the corners of his mouth tilted upwards again.

I ring the *Burnhead & District Advertiser* and speak to a woman who seems to like her job. She cares about spelling. I carefully dictate the wording of the announcement and by the time she finishes taking it down she is quite jocular.

Aye, we're the old-fashioned kind, she says. Spelling matters to us. We got taught right.

They don't teach anything useful nowadays, I say.

She says, You're right there. Well, that's all in hand for you now, Miss du Cann, I'll just read it back.

I listen.

'On Wednesday January fourteenth 2004 following an illness, Raymond James Duncan aged eighty-five, late of 5 Seaview Villas, Burnhead. Beloved father of Lila du Cann. Funeral Friday twenty-third January Ayr Crematorium 2.00 p.m., followed by service 3.00 p.m. Evangelical Lutheran Mission, Burnhead. Friends, neighbours and former colleagues welcome. No flowers.'

Without realising I am going to, I ask her, Would you mind just adding, before 'Beloved father', the words 'sadly missed'?

I hear the muffled patting, like words scurrying by in light shoes, of fingers on computer keys.

Right you are. That's that done. Now was there anything else I can help you with today?

I can't reply. Sometimes lately when I open my mouth to speak my voice comes out but the actual words lag behind. It's a bit like gasping, as if I'm suddenly frightened of what I might say. At other times my voice seems entirely absent. It's something to do with breath and vocal coordination, probably.

Are you all right? the woman says. She sounds almost worried.

After a little while I say, Yes, thank you, I'm all right.

No hurry, Miss du Cann, she says. I know bereavement's stressful, you take your time. You don't have to tell me, I've known it myself.

But he was bound to die. He was old, I say. *I'm* old.

Ah, doesn't matter though, she tells me with authority. Doesn't matter how old you are, it takes you just the same. Take your time. It's a shock. Was there anything else?

I used to live here, I tell her. I've been away a long time. I had to get away. I'd forgotten how it was.

Aye, a lot of folk do that. You need to get away to get on, there's not the opportunities round here, is there? That's what I tell my kids. I've four.

The *Burnhead & District Advertiser*, I begin, and falter. I don't even know what I intend to say. I try again. The paper, years ago . . . There was a lot in the paper. One summer . . . there was a lot about my family, our family. The Duncans . . . and the Pettifers . . . A long time ago.

Oh, I see. Was your family well known in the area, Miss du Cann? Will I put you through to Features? They'd be the ones you'd need to deal with as regards the possibility of an obituary for your father in the paper.

While I wait to be connected I gather my wits and so am quite ready when a young man announces himself as the Features Assistant. He sounds Australian, which throws me for a moment. There were no Australians in Burnhead when I lived here. I tell him my name. I am not going to falter any more.

I've returned from abroad for the funeral, I say. Just for a few days. I thought it might make an interesting little piece for the paper – I mean there can't be many Burnhead people who go on to have careers in opera! Never mind a career spanning more than three decades. I've been in opera for nearly thirty-five years, there aren't many people I haven't worked with.

Oh? he says. Big names?

And a career abroad, of course, it takes one so far from one's roots. Roots are so important for an artist, people don't always realise. It might interest your readers to hear about that?

Can you give me an idea of who you worked with? The big stars? Pavarotti?

I give him some names, to which he barely reacts.

These are all opera stars, are they? Okay. Thanks.

And Joan Sutherland, I add.

Now I've heard of her, he says. Is she still alive?

She once lent me her limousine and driver, I tell him.

Really? You were mates, were you?

(At last, a bit of interest – the hoops one has to go through!)

I tell him, Actually it was all rather a scream. There was some mix-up. She thought she was free so she'd ordered her car to pick her up outside the theatre but in fact she had a rehearsal, so this car arrived and she couldn't use it. We'd just got off so she gave it to us. Let us have it for the whole afternoon. Complete with chauffeur!

Let *us* have it? Who else, other big stars?

A group of us from the chorus. Though actually I was covering a small part, on *no* rehearsal I might add – in fact Joan was probably appalled at that. Covers did not get anything like proper consideration, she would have noticed that. Anyway, the car took us out of town to a porcelain factory that had a seconds shop. It parked right outside and waited for us, then we drove back. How it does spoil one, having a driver!

He says, Hey, right you are. Well, thanks for your time. I've got your details but it's not actually my decision, so, thanks anyway.

Obviously he's too young to know who he's dealing with.

I'd better have a word with he whose decision it is, then, I say. You can put me through, I suppose?

He's in a meeting, I'm afraid. But I'll pass it on, tell him who you were and everything. Call you back if he's interested, okay?

As I ring off I ask myself what made me mention roots at all, never mind say that they were important, because I never think of them normally, living a truly international life (I don't think he really got that point). I am not sure there really is any such thing as roots, and even if there is, I would rather there weren't.

It's nearly dusk but I haven't been outside today, or I don't think I have, and I need some fresh air. Perhaps if I walk for a while I shall sleep better. That's probably all it is. This wandering about at night that I seem to be doing rather a lot, it's because I'm not getting enough exercise during the day. In Antwerp I walk everywhere. With roots still in my mind I set off under a broken umbrella of my father's. Darkness is already coming on fast and there is nowhere else to go but across the road and up Arranview Drive, into the orange light from the streetlamps. In no time at all I have strayed far from Seaview Villas and deep into the winding and interlocking roads that snake through the rows of new houses. Not so new, now; early eighties and typically unattractive but at least when they went up they brought mains gas out here and he got central heating at last at 5 Seaview Villas. Though it didn't altogether remove it, it made the damp warmer.

These houses are bungalows, mostly, with flat staring windows reaching almost to the ground. As I guessed, there is nobody about on the pavements in this weather and at this time of day. It's cars that come and go along these streets, not people. So I don't bother much that my raincoat doesn't look right over these trousers. Charcoal grey and the milky beige of the coat don't do much for each other but under the streetlights they barely look like colours, anyway. I have a scarf for my head that has both grey and beige in it, and navy and red as well, in a pattern of horseshoes and crossed riding crops and other equine clutter (not Hermès but just as good) so I feel I have pulled the look together at least a bit. Thinking about that cocky little Australian on the telephone made me put on some lipstick so I wouldn't be embarrassed to be recognised and stopped. I'm not finished yet.

I walk by little, low houses skulking in the rain, some empty and dark, others inhabited by fluttering television screens in uncurtained rooms whose light spills out and trembles on wet front lawns. There are houses that show the backs of drawn curtains, pulled in and hugging to themselves all their padded, warm peachiness, flaunting the glow that the room bestows on those within and that excludes me. I leave Arranview Drive and wander along Arranview this and Arranview that: Avenue, Court, Close, Walk, and then I turn back the way I came, past the lit houses with cars sitting tidily alongside and the unlit ones where empty concrete ramps are still waiting. Now I am in High Trees territory; the same looping cul-de-sacs called High Trees this, that and the next thing. There are no high trees, of course; the real sycamores have long since gone. I guess they disappeared some time between the decision to name part of the development for them, and the realisation that nobody had recorded what kind of trees they were before cutting them down. It's impossible to work out where they stood except perhaps by the next name change, as High Trees gives way to roads called Old Farm. I keep walking under the pattering umbrella, my soles making no sound above the rumble of a few cars rolling home at a conscientious crawl.

I am half-looking for their house. If the Old Farm collection of streets bears some relation to where the farm used to lie, I must be near it. It should not be difficult to find.

Part of the deal when they sold the land was that the developers would build a house to their specification close to the site of the old farmhouse. For a few years I used to get, along with their newsletter, a Christmas card with a photograph of the new one, floodlit. Makes a better card than the ubiquitous robin! she would write, and each year I would privately disagree. Then I suppose I moved and didn't send my new address and the cards stopped. In the last year or two I was treated to a view of not just the house but an extravaganza of fairy lights racing around the eaves and a flashing reindeer on the grass, so it was no great loss.

He went into golfing supplies and sports equipment. Her idea. As soon as the land was sold she put him in silly caps and pastel jerseys and shoes with fringed tongues and sent him off, pulling a top-of-the-range, two-tone leatherette caddy, to play golf in the afternoons. He turned middle-aged overnight. Given the company he was keeping it was a natural development that he should spot a 'gap in the market' and start selling the gear to men like himself: foolish great boys as ruddy in the face and as thinning on top, as bored and gadget-hungry as he was. He needn't have turned out that way. The Christmas newsletter would give a tally of the number of outlets: Gleneagles, St Andrews, Harrods. There was talk of Scottish airport concessions and a tie-in with Burberry. He must have gone along with it.

I find it at the end of Pow Drive, a bungalow more than double the size of its neighbours and standing in a plot four times larger than theirs. It alone has a façade of pink faux marble and is surrounded by low walls made from ornamental blocks with fancy shapes in them that make a pattern of daisies, as if someone has been at work with a giant biscuit cutter. The wrought-iron house name on the wall – 'Casa Lisboa' – stands out in the beam of floodlights set into the ground.

The floodlights must be on an automatic timer for the house is shut up and dark. Around the porch sit the hulks of patio plants over-wintering in black plastic shrouds and in the apex of the front gable a burglar alarm winks its alternating red and green eyes. This is just as I expect. I would not have come this way if I thought there was any chance of running into them. I took the small risk of supposing that their habits haven't changed; the habits of people like them don't. I'm confident they still spend January and February in the Canaries. They will still own property – with them, it's always 'property' – in Gran Canaria, and they will have kept the apartment in the Algarve that one newsletter explained they couldn't part with. She wrote, you do get very attached to your very first overseas property! So with two properties abroad there's nothing for it but to take more holidays! But they prefer Portugal in the spring, when his golfing weather is more reliable and she can take her classes on wild flowers in watercolour.

I gaze at the house for a while until I am numb to its immaculate ugliness. I picture the garden of the old farmhouse where lupins and a tangle of roses grew up through rusting machine parts and old tractor tyres and where in Sherpa's water bowl on the front step you would sometimes find flakes of paint from the peeling yellow door when it was slammed. I turn round and head back to Seaview Villas. Going in this direction I am walking straight into the wind and raindrops land in wet explosions on the umbrella that flaps loose where the cover has torn away from three of its spokes. I tip it downward in front of my face and walk fast, looking at my feet. I do know that this is the last time in my life that I shall walk here, but I can't make this feel significant. I can find no mental commentary for the occasion; as I step briskly back down Old Farm Drive, my footsteps refuse to feel historic.

I wonder if the *Burnhead & District Advertiser* will take up my idea for an article. I wonder if I could put into clearer words this feeling – this sad truth, and true sadness – that although you may be exiled from a place long before you leave it you still crave, upon your return, an invitation to belong.

Traces of the old farm exist nowhere now except in my head. The sounds of that day when I saw it for the first time – my mother singing scales above the noise of a coffee grinder, the whistle of Jimmy from Brocks and the rumble of coke hitting the bunker, a barking dog, Mantovani from the Café Royale in the echoing farm shed – mingle in my mind with the day's many other accidents and coincidences. Suppose we had not run out of bread? Uncle George would have trampled over my mother's distaste for picnics and frogmarched us out to some freezing beauty spot with travelling rugs and sandwiches and flasks of tea, and we would not have been at home when Jimmy's lorry refused to start. Then we would never have wandered up the track to Pow Farm and found ourselves a venue – an improbable one, a putative cowshed with a tractor in it, draughty and floored with straw – for *Turandot*.

I might never have met Joe Foscari.

10

Uncle George returned the next day from the farm and told Fleur and Lila that they had 'a space' for the opera.

'Stanley – Mr McArthur – he's converted. All for it,' he said, rubbing his hands, but Lila thought his jollity was forced. 'It is a great *space*, isn't it?' he said to her. 'Tell your mother. Isn't it great?'

They were in the kitchen. Fleur, perched on a kitchen chair, looked papery with exhaustion. She had pulled out the twin tub and started on a washing but then lost heart, and was now watching while Lila got on with it. Lila was used to the petering out of her mother's energy. It came and went like matches struck in the dark – weak, random flares usually ill-directed and almost immediately extinguished. She seldom found any forward momentum for the jobs she undertook because they never acquired enough purpose for her; long before she came close to finishing anything she would succumb to a listlessness in herself that would be even deeper than before the doomed effort was made.

'I'm not performing in a shed,' Fleur said, over the droning and sloshing of the machine. 'I want a cigarette.'

'It won't look like a shed, we're going to whitewash it. Paint the back wall black. We'll do the whole production very modern, almost bare. With drapes and lights and . . . and . . . shapes.'

'Shapes?'

'Shapes, yes . . . to suggest things. Scenery, buildings, you know. It'll be sort of experimental. Though it's been done before,' he added quickly, 'I mean this kind of approach. They use all kinds of spaces for opera now – it's modern.'

'I suppose he's charging a fortune.'

'I don't want you worrying about that,' he said. 'You leave that to me. You need to concentrate one hundred per cent on your part.'

Fleur sighed. 'I'm exhausted just thinking about it. I need to lie down.'

George looked hard at her. 'Why are you always coming out with these *statements* about yourself?'

'I don't come out with statements about myself. I'm just exhausted.'

'You're only just up. It's only eleven o'clock in the morning.'

'I can't help it,' Fleur said, yawning.

George shrugged. 'Well, all right. Go and lie down. I've plenty to do, anyway.'

'You'll manage on your own,' she said, eyeing Lila and sniffing weakly at the wet smells of bleach and washing soap. She pushed herself up from her chair, pressed her fingers into the space between her breasts and produced a deep, solid note that after only a few seconds faded to a sigh.

She said, 'I'm tired,' and let the line of her shoulders sag. 'I don't know where I'd be without you.' She drifted through the door, not caring which of them she was addressing.

Uncle George sagged a little, too, as she passed. 'I should make some calls,' he said to Lila, loitering. 'I should ring the paper and get the ball rolling. If we're going ahead.'

Lila half-turned from the sink where she was holding the draining hose.

'If? What do you mean, if?'

Before he could answer there was a hot grunt from the twin tub and then the pump started to throb softly. The hose reared in Lila's hand as a snake of grey water gushed from its end into the sink, wave after wave of suds raising the smells of wet wool and warm rubber.

He said, 'Oh, of course. It's just . . . I need to make some calls. Have to ring the publisher, we've only got your mother's vocal score. We need to hire all the parts.'

He was tossing a box of matches from hand to hand and

bouncing on the balls of his feet but the little dance of optimism did not fool Lila. She frowned.

'Shouldn't you get your orchestra before you get the music?'

'Don't scowl,' he told her, throwing the matchbox high and catching it. 'We can't delay that long. We have to advertise in the paper for players and singers, for everybody. We'll have to hold a meeting. If we left getting the parts till after that it'd be too late.'

He stood neither in nor out of the kitchen, shaking the matchbox in time to some tune in his head. 'Anyway we still need to get our Calaf,' he said.

'I thought we'd got our Calaf,' Lila said, glaring at the diminishing trickle of water pulsing from the hose. She was disappointed. Uncle George had arrived with at least as many dirty clothes as clean ones and more than half the things in the wash were his, but he didn't seem to notice either the hard work she was doing or how willingly she did it. This was the second load. Standing in all this steam, hauling the sodden weight of washing from tub to tub was exhausting; did he not know that? Was there a washing machine in the flat in Crouch End, or would she be taking his things to a laundry?

'Calaf? Well, we have, really. It's only a matter of getting hold of him.'

He looked at his watch. As if he had just thought of it he said, 'Actually I might be able to get him now. He starts work at twelve. He's working as a waiter, just for the summer, did I say? I suppose I might . . . I might just catch him, before he goes.'

Lila had now attached the filler hose to the kitchen tap and was running fresh water into the machine. She looked up. If he had calls to make then why was he sighing in the doorway? If he might catch this person before he went to work, why wasn't he trying his number right now? He had withdrawn something from her – his conviction, perhaps – and had grown suddenly mean with his certainties. She resented it; he had handed out promises like sweeties and was gathering them all back, still in their wrappers.

She said, 'Well, go on then, for God's sake,' placing in her voice a sharp edge that belonged to her mother's. 'If you're so sure he'll want to do it, why don't you just go and ask him?'

She dragged the dripping clothes from one tub to the other, using the long wooden tongs. Uncle George twisted his hair in the fingers of one hand and stared at the wall.

'Yeah. Maybe I will.'

He looked at his watch again and then at Lila. Her arms were pale and slippery, the ends of her fingers tight wrinkled nubs. A weak sun gleamed through the steamed-up window behind her and illuminated her strangely. Down the thin curtains in cascading vertical lines the pattern of wine flasks, soup ladles and sticks of celery was casting patchy tints of sage and yellow and charcoal across her damp skin.

'Have you . . . I mean, is all that nearly finished? When will you be ready to hang it out?'

'Well there's the rinsing, two more rinses, then it's to go through the mangle.'

'You'll be a while then?'

'I don't mind.' She smiled her forgiveness. 'The mangle's electric, it doesn't take long.'

'You're a good kid. Look, I'm not sure, you see. About doing this. The opera.'

The day lost its balance for a second, threatened to tip into chaos. She said, 'What do you mean?'

'I mean it's a big thing. Your singing, are you going to take it seriously? Are you prepared to take it seriously enough?'

Not just the balance of Lila's day but the rest of her life lurched dangerously. With a tiny indrawn breath she caught the idea that was still as delicate as a gasp. She held it, set it upon its pivot.

'But I don't want to do just the opera. I want to be a real singer. A proper one.' Then, quickly, she said it. 'I want to train properly. At college in London. I want to live with you and go to a London college.'

Uncle George looked at her. 'Well now. Well, that is serious.' He nodded. Lila waited for him to speak and then realised he wasn't going to. But the nod was enough. She knew she must not ask him for any more now, but she would get what she needed. She smiled.

'Hard work,' he said.

She wasn't sure if he meant the singing or the laundry. 'I don't mind,' she said, which was true in either case.

'I'm thinking, you see. You should do some work on your voice today too, like your mother, and it's much better done in the morning when it's freshest.'

'Work on my voice?'

'So why don't you leave all that for now and go and do some scales while I'm on the phone? Might be easier if I'm, you know, not interrupted or anything.'

'But if I leave it now I won't get it hung out by dinnertime,' Lila said. 'If you're on the phone, I won't interrupt. I could help you with the numbers again.'

Uncle George laughed. 'I think I can manage!'

'The rinsing's easy, the machine does it all. I could help you and still keep an eye on it.'

'No. You go and make a start in the music room. I want you to get busy on that voice.'

'But any minute I'll have to empty it again. And then it'll—'

George gave the matchbox a savage shake. 'Jesus! Look. You need to realise something,' he said. 'This opera's not just a little joke that we fit in round everything else. If we do it, it's going to be done properly, you hear me?'

'I don't think it's a joke.'

'It's not too late, you know. You just have to say, "I've changed my mind. I want to do the washing and squabble with Enid and watch my mother going round the bend. I don't want to sing, I don't want to put in the work. It's too hard." Is that what you want?'

'No,' Lila said in a whisper.

'Sure? Because you're going to have to work hard. Starting right *now*.'

'I don't mind. As long as something nice happens in the end.'

That day in the kitchen there are three voices, a trio of strands weaving around one another and each telling a separate story to which the other two are deaf, a story about what each one of us wants and loves and fears.

Snatches of his voice, his modulated deceits: It's only a matter of getting hold of him.

Hers, twisting itself into a disappearing wisp of sound slipping away up the stairs: I don't know where I'd be without you.

My voice barges in comically. I'm the ingénue in the dreadful dress with the wet sleeves, guilelessly wielding the bawdy toys – the hose and tongs – and knowing nothing, not even how burlesque my mimicry of the adults is, for the sniggering has not yet started. As long as something nice happens in the end.

A trio, all of us blind and expectant and for the time being only – this far in the story, in the delicate plaiting of lies – innocent, still unaware of how massive and ungainly our expectations are, how grotesque we look as we go about their concealment and how ugly, in our final disappointment, we will all be.

I have no choice but to leave the washing in a pond of filmy grey water and be led away, placed in the middle of the music room and bullied about my posture. Uncle George shakes my shoulders, makes me breathe in and out so deeply I feel slightly faint. He talks about my spine and my shoulder blades and my diaphragm and the tip of my tongue on the floor of my mouth and keeping it out of the way; he waggles my jaw and pinches my chin and comes out with something about smiling through my ribs (most of which, I will appreciate years later, makes a sort of sense). He makes me think about the space around myself. I wave my arms. I am to claim this air and claim my sound and the right to make it. He gives me a note to start on and a page of exercises: scales and arpeggios and octave leaps to Ay, Ee, Ah, Oh, Ooo. He warns me that he will be within earshot and that if I fail to breathe properly and concentrate on the sound I am making, he will be able to tell. It always shows, he says, if a singer doesn't mean it.

Do I blame him? At fifteen I am a lanky, dull-eyed girl solidified by neglect and on my way to becoming hard; his arrival is pulling me out from the slow drip of my parents' misery and inattention, under which I am gently calcifying. Starting with the singing on the beach and now, with my very first singing lesson, he is softening me up. I may start to leak feelings, but for the moment I must work on my scales.

Even while I am singing my exercises, and in the intervals between them, I listen to him in the hall as he speaks with private urgency into the telephone.

Joe? Look. Of course I'm not changing my tune, you know I have to stay up here.

I do not actively decide to do it, I do not think, but by the time he rings off and comes back to tick me off about my vowels, I have decided that I have not been eavesdropping.

Because she's my sister. Of course I want you here! Of course it'll be better than staying in London, there's a beach on the doorstep, don't forget.

Joe? You've got to come, I need you to.

I have not learned that the gift of making Uncle George happy rests with someone other than me.

Joe, I need you here, I really do.

I have not learned that he put me in here to make a noise of my own in order to get me out of earshot, so that I would not hear him plead. Joe will be here tomorrow, and I am having my first proper singing lesson and the attention – I have never had a lesson in anything all by myself with just one other person before – is intoxicating. That's all I know.

He pops out and makes another call: a man from the *Burnhead & District Advertiser* will be round this afternoon. My mother comes downstairs and is happier than I have seen her in weeks when Uncle George says he hopes she's had her beauty sleep because the man from the paper is bringing a photographer. At last it is safe to re-enter the day and for me to pick up my plans and dreams again.

The sound of Uncle George's naked begging to Joe will be sent to the now quite crowded place in my mind where I keep words that I wish I had never heard spoken. The general clutter of words already in there – the weaponry of all my parents' rows and altercations – is a blessing; Uncle George's entreaties can nestle there unnoticed with the rest of the spent arsenal, his collapsed dignity like a punctured breastplate under a heap of broken spikes and arrows and staved blades.

He shows me my aria written down in my mother's vocal score – the aria I sang on the beach, '*Signore, ascolta!*' – and goes through the words with me and tells me who is singing them and why. He asks me what I like best about singing it, and I tell him it's the highest note, the note on which it ends, the saddest one. The most difficult, he says. Your favourite part is the most difficult part. That means you're a real singer.

When I sing it this time, my eyes fill with tears. I am softening, flooding on the inside; a river has started to flow in me, bearing my thoughts and my feelings and my voice along, swirling and commingled. As I come to the last note my blood bubbles up and my heart is cast free of its moorings and is afloat in clear, fast-flowing water.

ACT II

THE SECOND RIDDLE

It kindles like a flame
But it is not flame.
At times it is a frenzy.
It is fever, force, passion!
Inertia makes it flag.
If you lose heart or die it grows cold,
But dream of conquest and it flares up.
Its voice you hear in trepidation,
It glows like the setting sun!

BLOOD.

The ordeal begins. Turandot poses her three riddles, and inspired by love, Calaf solves them all. He has won her hand. Turandot is overcome with distress; she will belong to no man. Calaf knows he must win her heart. He gives her a chance to defeat him. She does not know his name. If she can discover who he is before dawn she will be victorious and he will die.

11

The next evening Uncle George stopped Lila from coming with him to meet Joe off the train. From the window she watched them arrive, George trudging up the path under the weight of two suitcases and Joe following with a holdall and a smaller case balanced on one shoulder. He swaggered, in search of an audience. Lila kept still. She could tell he was pleased she was watching and she was drawn to him for that alone, for the compliment of enjoying her eyes upon him. She liked the showmanship of the suitcase borne aloft, his display of strength behind Uncle George's struggle with the heavier cases.

Inside the house he took her hand and said, 'I say, how do you do, you must be the sweet little brand-new soprano I'm hearing about, how very delightful.'

His voice was like no other she had ever heard. It was a little high-pitched and had a slight flouriness in it as if he spoke through a dense white cloth, and it was mesmerisingly hard to place. Any accent that might have attached him to a region or a category of person had been washed out by elocution, and to Lila's ears the result, a controlled neutrality in the vowels, consonants quaintly pointed, was enchantment. His words floated from him unhindered by the local grunt that rendered delicate, private things unsayable; Billy with his floppy hair and sideways looks and reticence would never come out with *sweet, little, delightful*. Words like that would not survive in his rough Burnhead mouth to be at her disposal even half-meant when she might need to hear them. In Joe there was a hurry to put words to use. He was anxious to be known.

'Well, all the way from London! You're very welcome. I hear you're Italian,' Fleur said, wiping her hands down the back of her skirt. Her voice clicked oddly.

'Dear lady, indeed! Indeed I am. How do you do?'

'George says you had restaurants. In Glasgow.'

'Ah, did he, did he now? Well, but those are past glories. Oh, how are the mighty fallen!'

Raymond said, 'I never heard of a Foscari's in Glasgow. Rogano's, yes.'

'Oh, *don't*!' Joe said with a strange shudder. 'Oh, the heyday of the Foscaris is lost in the mists of time. It's little more than hearsay now. But I want to hear all about *you*. Tell me, tell me, tell me – all about yourselves.'

Lila felt his urgency had something to do with her, that she was drawing out not just his words but setting loose inside him some thrilling notion of herself. His voice was a road to elsewhere, his words an invitation to her to shed her limitations: her name, her fear, this wrong place where she had somehow got stuck. She resolved to start talking like Joe immediately.

They sat round the table pushing food and drink at him and letting him amuse them, as if he were a strange new pet whose habits they had to learn. He produced a quarter bottle of whisky from his holdall, tipped some into his teacup, swilled it round and tossed it back. As an afterthought he offered the bottle round. Raymond fetched liqueur glasses and took what he called just a wee hoot, but George refused. He looked, suddenly, as if some air had been let out of him; the spinning ideas and the whipped-up energy of the previous few days were in abeyance. Like Lila he watched Joe who, in between nips of whisky, had plenty to say. When Joe was talking his eyes would settle on some object, the cruet, the hedge outside the window, his two thumbs circling each other, and stare at that rather than look in the direction of the person to whom he was speaking. Although short and round and solid – there was a substantial quilt of flesh around his torso – he seemed ready to flap away into the air if startled; his beak of a nose added to the impression of a solitary and alert bird of prey. When he looked at Lila, in the same way that he had stared at the hedge, she felt floodlit, as if there were something in her that he was determined to find in the bright beam of his gaze. His eyes were channels for escaped light, as if a sun blazed somewhere in his body; his skin seemed luminous. He wore short sleeves, and she studied the plump lilac veins in his forearms as they writhed down to his hands under dark, shining hairs. Why had nobody else noticed how startling he was? Her father was half-asleep. Her mother was listening too hard, leaning forward with her chin resting along the back of an arranged hand. Uncle George just sat looking folded up, his hair dull with smoke and his dark eyes, next to Joe's that were the same green-grey as a winter sea, merely blank.

Nothing was to be trusted now. Angles were newly treacherous, objects unreliable, words slippery; what if she were to collide with furniture or drop a teacup or come out with something childish? She was having to learn much too suddenly how to pretend that nothing had changed, when everything had. She got up from the table and began to fill the tray with things to take back to the kitchen, trying to do what she always did on an ordinary day. But Joe's eyes drifted over the outline of her body as he handed her his plate and she needed the shelter of the table again and sat back down. She felt as if he knew something, as if all her seams and fastenings and buttons were showing and now that he had seen them she could be in an instant dismantled.

'Aha! Kind young lady,' he said, tipping his head to one side. He poured himself more whisky and to Raymond he proposed, lifting the cup and draining it, 'A toast, to the daughter of the house!'

Raymond pulled at his earlobe with a finger and thumb and glanced at George. His glass was empty anyway.

Fleur touched Joe on the arm. 'Joe, carry on with what you were saying. You're ambitious, you have a strong sense of direction, do you, about being a singer?'

'I feel something pulling me towards a career in music, certainly,' Joe said, frowning attractively. '*La Forza del Destino*! Whatever the hurdles might be – and oh my goodness, Fleur, you know what *those* are – whatever the hurdles. I simply must sing!'

He flashed a smile around the table, stood up, struck his chest with one fist and launched into 'Ode to Joy'.

Fleur got to her feet and joined in from the other side of the table, lit up with mirth. They sang to Lah, stretching arms towards each other, trading actors' glances; they were both equally proud of the power of their eyes. When they came to the end everyone clapped. Joe pulled Fleur's hand to his lips and kissed it and turned a sparkling look on her. She sat down stroking her hair with both hands as if arranging a veil of his admiration over her head. Across the table she looked at him as if saying calmly, can I help it if I fascinate you?

Lila got up from the table again. Joe's attention was all that mattered now, and she wouldn't have it again this evening. Already she was getting an idea of how hungry life could be when you were in love, how it would call for patience and cunning to live from now on in need, waiting to pounce on whatever thin bones of hope he might drop behind him. With some idea that by drifting up to her room she might leave behind a memory of herself that would be more compelling than her presence, she said goodnight. She knew that her eyes were too hot and bright, her face too pink and young-looking for her to be taken seriously by the adults for a moment longer.

In her room she peeled the clothes off her limbs as if she were undressing a doll, imagining Joe's gaze. She lay very still in bed with her eyes open, straining to hear his voice and waiting to be struck down by a fever whose first symptoms were already creeping through her. The stereogram started up: Act III of *Turandot* and '*Nessun dorma*', to which Joe sang along. There was clapping and more laughter. Somebody, she assumed her father, clanked knives and forks alone in the kitchen and ran water into the sink.

Later, Joe and Uncle George came up to the landing and paused at the door of the spare room across from Lila's. There was some bumping of luggage, doors opening, the rise and fall of their voices. Her father's joined in; she wondered if it were being explained that Joe would be sleeping in the attic room because Fleur (on account of her nerves) had her own room and George was in the tiny spare one. There was a clattering up the attic stairs. Doors opened again, feet shuffled to and from the bathroom, water gurgled, doors closed, the landing light was snapped off.

Lila lay in the dark, glad to think of Joe in the room above, alone like her. She heard his feet on the boards and the creak of the camp bed, and sent silent messages up through the damp-stained ceiling that he was to wake up the next day to find himself in love with her. She had no notion that he was typical of anything or anyone; he seemed freshly invented for her alone, in answer to a long, aching list of things that until now she had barely realised she wished for.

When you go to Venice you see scores of Joe Foscaris. I was a little unsettled on my first visit. I kept accidentally catching the eyes of strangers and opening my mouth to speak – but to say what? Then, the moment I knew there was nothing I could say I would realise it couldn't possibly be him. But he is replicated everywhere, the stocky, squat Italian running to fat, arms swinging, bandy little legs bearing him along with a pugilist's bounce. He sells fish, steers the *vaporetti*, hawks headsquares and keyrings on the Rialto Bridge. Through eyes the colour of the Adriatic he scans yours, without malice, to see the size of the bargain. I remember reading in a guide book about the people of the Veneto, their meeting and mixing with whoever it was – the Phoenicians or some other seafaring tribe, perhaps more than one – and the attractive genetic accident as east and west conjoined: the aquiline nose, the dark hair and black lashes fringing eyes the colour of the lagoon. You never truly see through the milky greeny-grey to what lies below.

Paris. The child's name is Paris. She is quite an engaging little thing, twisting in Christine's arms as she stands at the door this morning, and staring at me from under a hat that looks like the toe of a sock. She holds a rag of striped brushed cotton up to the space between her top lip and her nose, and rubs it gently against her skin. Her eyes are glazed and distant; she sees only the secret landscape of the comfort it gives her. She doesn't even hear when Christine tells her to say hello. Christine can't get her Stripey away from her, she says. She supposes she'll grow out of it but she's looking forward even more to the day when she grows out of needing so much picking up, she's a dead weight. Paris comes to, grins and turns to hide in her mother's neck. Christine is holding a carrier bag as well as Paris and looks rather burdened. I tell her she may come in as long as she takes me as she finds me.

Paris made you some chocolate krispies, Christine says, putting Paris down among the papers and boxes and chests in the back room. Didn't you, Paris?

I warn her to watch the child because there is no guard round the gas fire but actually Paris can't get near it for all the stuff. Christine takes a deep breath and I notice a smell of hot cardboard that I don't think was here before.

Christine looks at me. Are you not well? I didn't get you out of your bed, did I?

I don't understand the question.

I mean, you in your dressing gown. Are you all right? Still turning stuff out?

I'm fine.

You look tireder than you did before. Is it getting to you?

She raises her voice as she says this because she is on her way into the kitchen with the chocolate krispies. I hear her putting on the kettle.

I'm making you a wee cup of tea, she says. See when you're on your own – you sometimes forget. I'm the same, I don't look after myself. Oh, is there no milk?

She pops home to get some while I wonder how to be friendly to Paris and she stares back at me from behind Stripey, her eyes full of suspicion. Just before she starts to cry, Christine comes back with the milk and a plastic container with a lid.

I brought you a drop soup, she says. You don't look very well. If you've no much appetite I thought still you maybe can manage a wee drop soup.

She pronounces it 'seup' and I want to smile.

Instead I say, Oh, you Scotswomen! You and your soup! If in doubt, make a pot of soup, eh? Soup, soup, soup!

Christine stares at me. It's out of a carton, she says. I'll put it in the fridge.

She pours our tea and brings it in and we sip at it. She has put sugar in mine. The dark clumps of Paris's chocolate krispies sit on sideplates in neon-coloured paper cases. I nibble a piece and find it hard to swallow. Then I see on Christine's face another impending outbreak of compassion so I draw attention to the half-empty, upended tea chests, some of whose contents are littering the floor. I pick up a cutting, the full page advert Uncle George took in the *Burnhead and District Advertiser* on 7th July, the same day they published our photograph and the old one of my mother.

What do you think of that, then? I ask, holding the page up to her. The paper is filthy, the edges frilly with rot and damp. I sneeze, twice.

She cranes forward and reads it.

I wouldn't know, she says. What's it meant to be?

I don't answer because suddenly she exclaims, Paris! Paris, come out of there!

Paris has got hold of my cross-stitch, pulled it out of its bag and is making a kind of cat's cradle out of my silks. I jump to my feet. I don't want it spoiled, she's a sticky-looking child. She may have chocolate on her fingers. Plus there's a needle in it.

Christine gets there first and pulls the work gently away from her. Paris wails, plonks herself on the floor and returns to Stripey.

Hey, brilliant, Christine says, smoothing it over, did you do this? It's brilliant.

She turns it this way and that. Honest, it's really good. What's it meant to be? What way up does it go?

It's not meant to be anything, it's stylised, I say. It's not meant to be anything, it's just a symmetrical pattern. Just shapes.

BAST

BURNHEAD ASSOCIATION FOR
SINGING TURANDOT

Needs

YOU!!

COME AND JOIN IN this thrilling amateur production
of Puccini's *Turandot* taking place in Burnhead 26th, 27th
and 28th August under the baton of top London professional.
NO EXPERIENCE NECESSARY. We need the following
VOLUNTEERS AGED THIRTEEN OR OVER:

. . .

PERFORMERS

Chorus: (all voices, no auditions, just bring your enthusiasm!)
Principals: (some amateur experience desirable)
Strings, brass & percussion players
(own instrument and stand preferred)
Dancers, jugglers, acrobats – any style,
all other special skills also very welcome

. . .

PRODUCTION

Carpenters, painters, technicians, general helpers, front of
house, costumes, makeup, props, production assistants.
Electrical knowledge helpful. ALL HELP WELCOME

. . .

WHATEVER YOUR AGE OR EXPERIENCE

you can join in and have lots of fun. Come to an INFORMAL
MEETING to LEARN MORE at 5 Seaview Villas, Pow Road,
Burnhead, Saturday 9th July at 6.00 p.m.

ALL WELCOME   **FREE REFRESHMENTS**

Christine doesn't know what to say to this, so as she sits down again she picks up the cutting and looks at it.

My God, she says, this is over forty years old. People hang on to stuff that long, don't they? She waves an arm over the boxes and papers on the floor. It's daft. I mean what would you want to hang on to stuff like this for?

I wouldn't know, I say.

When she goes I sit among the cuttings and papers and they feel like old wrappings, the crumpled and torn tissue round precious things so long ago put by that the reasons that made them worth keeping have disintegrated silently inside their coverings. Treasures shrink with time, as do the objects of all youthful ecstasies; unwrapped and recalled later, they are mystifyingly undeserving of preservation. Although those paperweights in the sideboard may be the exception here. I bring the paperweights out again and set them in a row along the sideboard. Clean and pretty things make a contrast in this house.

My father was a mild man – a gentleman, as Christine says – mild to the point of powerlessness, unable to put up much resistance, but still I ask him now, aloud, over the purring of the fire: Why did you allow it? When Joe Foscari came that night, did you not see? I saw you watching. Surely you saw me fall for him. Why was there nothing in me that inspired your protection?

No answer comes. I see his face in old age when his mildness had deepened and he had grown whimsical and ambiguous. No answer will come now.

All right then, I say. All right, just tell me this. Were you not in the least concerned about the way they came and took us over – all of us? Were you not at the very least concerned about the money? You always worried about money. Did it not bother you, the whole Premium Bond being wasted on an amateur opera?

Ah, wasted? It was wasted, you think?

I see him, his hands draped over the arms of his chair like empty, hanging gloves. I could never actually have seen him this way in life so I must be imagining what it was like for him afterwards, late that night, that botched night when everything disintegrated and everyone left.

Yes, I think it was wasted. I lick my fingers clean of chocolate, pick up the cross-stitch, rearrange the skeins of silks, take up my needle and work by the glow from the fire. I don't want bright light.

Christine grows bolder. This afternoon she is back. Paris has just been deposited at the Pow Little People's Paradise – a wee playgroup kind of thing, Christine says – and she is dropping in to ask if I enjoyed my soup. My eyes are hot and dry from my sewing. Her lips tighten a little when I find myself unable to answer and she walks past me to the kitchen and starts to bang around looking for a pan to heat it up in. She rests in the doorway while it's on the stove and asks if I'm all right for bin bags, because if I like she can pop home for a couple and give me a hand to get some of this mess tidied up.

No thank you, I say.

She sighs. It's just, I seen it in the paper at lunchtime, she says. The paper, the *Burnhead Advertiser*, it's out today. Mr Duncan's funeral's in the paper, the announcement? So I was kinda wondering.

Wondering what?

You know. Wondering where you'll be going after, Christine says, as if such a concern is natural or obvious. After the funeral, for the refreshments. The announcement never said. I'm thinking if you're having them back here you'll need a wee hand to get tidied up first.

Refreshments? I haven't thought about refreshments, I tell her. There won't be many there. There may be no-one.

Christine disappears into the kitchen and comes back with soup in a mug. It is far too hot and smells of compost but something tells me she's not leaving till I've eaten it.

Listen, she says. When her voice drops like this, it's pleasant enough. I watch her over the rim of my mug. Listen, it'll mainly be old folk, it'll be a cold day. You need to give them a cup of tea. It's expected. It's what you do.

The soup tastes green and salty and makes my eyes water. I fish about for a tissue. Christine finds one on the floor. There are, in fact, many paper handkerchiefs on the floor, among all the other papers.

I've got this friend that does wee functions, teas and parties and that, Christine says. She works from home, does all her own baking. Want me to ask her? She'll do it all nice for you, brings the urn and cups and everything. She's not dear either, not like the hotels.

She pulls a business card from the pouch in the front of her fleece. On it there's a picture of a pie with 'Sheena's Party Fayre' and a telephone number written underneath. In a cloud of steam coming out of the pie it says in fluffy letters: Function catering in your home. Complete service. Large or small. All fresh made.'

I wonder what this has to do with me.

Here? I say, looking round.

Christine is looking at me carefully. Uh-huh, she's got a wee van and everything. I'll help you get straight. I'm thinking, maybe, she says gently, maybe Mr Duncan would have liked folk back here. He was the gentleman.

Maybe, I say.

She is catching me off guard, this girl, easing herself sideways into my business with bloody soup and chocolate krispies and that blonde, blank child and now, pictures of steaming pies.

See, I'll help you get tidy. Want me to phone Sheena for you? Will I tell her tea and sandwiches and cake and maybe a dram? For about a dozen, or maybe twenty?

I don't stop her. It'll be something to work towards.

12

Audrey entered the clients' waiting room and saw that Raymond was frowning. That meant it would be one of their talking days. She liked those, especially after one of the other kind; it allayed the sound of her mother's voice that could sometimes still, even now, start up in her head, telling her she was plain oversexed and a shame to her parents (there being no shame like that of missionaries with a daughter in trouble), just the type to get caught in a trap of her own making, a web woven from her dirty wants, her cheap compliance and her graceless soul. No man'll ever respect you, she said. After all these years Audrey found this information wearying, but not much more. She was safe from the worst consequences of it, even supposing it were true, but still she liked to see that Raymond was as anxious to talk to her as he sometimes was to have her splayed, as decorously as she could manage, on the leather Chesterfield. He was frowning at the *Burnhead & District Advertiser*.

'Paper's just out. Would you take a look at that,' he said, folding the page back for her to see. They studied it together.

She said, 'So they're really going ahead with it?'

'Daft,' Raymond said. 'They're dead set. We've the young fella up from London now, moved in for the duration. Tenor. Fancy talker.'

'Well, what Fleur wants Fleur gets, isn't that usually the way?' Audrey said easily.

On and off she tried to get Raymond to stand up to his wife a little, for his own sake, but the pattern of her encouragement followed by his failure to act on it was by now reassuring and neither expected any more of it than that. It was a marker, that was all, of how things were and how things were done, like the cool paper smells of the office, tea cups washed as soon as finished with, pencils sharpened: daily, expected, approved. Raymond lived by such measures and so did she.

'Aye, well. Well . . .'

His voice tailed off. Audrey waited, without expectation. He often tried to feel his way forward like this, with little murmured observances that carried no meaning. He would let the potential of words expire in a sigh of exhaled breath, compromising the moment when he might speak by letting it pass with a shrug because it always turned out to be not the right time, after all, when he might come out with a speech about what he really felt. She didn't regret his lack of rhetoric any more.

He said, 'It's not just Fleur, mind you . . . it's the lot of them. They're egging each other on. I'm to stage manage the thing, so I'm told.'

'Stage manage it? Can you do that?'

'I'm to get a team to build the stage. In the evenings. I'm to talk to a firm about lighting, I'm to look at drawings for the set. I'm to ask, no, I'm to *tell* Mr Mather I need to take my holidays to fit in with it.'

'You'll be busy, then.'

'I've tried to tell them! I've tried to say I can't do this kind of thing but George won't hear a no. Fleur's not listening at all, the Italian fella just smiles and swings his arms about. I mean, what'm I supposed to do?'

'You're not to worry. They can't expect you to do it all by yourself, can they? They couldn't, surely.'

'Och, Audrey.' Raymond hesitated. 'I don't know. Maybe if, how about if you come in on it, too? Maybe help with the costumes or something, just so's maybe . . . maybe I'd not be so much on my own?'

Audrey took Raymond's hand and gave it a squeeze. 'Well, maybe I could. Though there's John.'

Another moment passed with a faint clearing of the throat from one or both of them, and a small sigh of respect for John. The anemones on the low table that he had grown and that Audrey had brought into the office on Monday were open and curling now, the petals gaping inside out to their polished hearts, stamens purple and smoky like the remains of a private, burned-out pyre. A dusting of sooty pollen lay on the cloth under the vase. She didn't know whether her deceiving of John were important or not, in the wide sense. Conducted so modestly that Raymond, beyond the door of the clients' waiting room, was shy of asking anything of her at all, her infidelity felt like a discreet grace note in her life in which she was permitted to take a small and private pride, such as the filing kept up to date, the placing of cloths under vases.

'John'd help too. He wouldn't want to be left out. And he's practical enough,' she said.

Raymond murmured, then withdrew his hand from hers and hit at the folded page of the newspaper. 'Ach I mean, look at it,' he said. 'How am I supposed to know what to do?'

Audrey pulled the paper away and folded it up and tucked it out of Raymond's sight. 'Don't worry so much. We'll come to the meeting, John and me.'

'That's good of you.'

'And what's Lizzie making of it all?'

'Oh, Lizzie.' His incomprehension became even more burdensome. 'We're to understand from George that Lizzie's got this voice, a real big voice. He's got her full of it. She wants to get properly trained.'

Audrey raised her eyebrows. 'Like her mother?'

'Or so I'm told. I've never heard her on the subject. Lizzie never speaks to me.' He sighed. 'She's living in a world of her own. I think she's away with the fairies.'

Audrey thought for a moment. 'Well, it's probably her nature. I was like that once.'

'Her head's in the clouds.'

'She'll be all right. As long as they're *her* clouds,' she said, 'and nobody else's.'

I go to bed in my old bedroom, and I dream. Though I am there in the dream, I am not doing anything except watch, nor am I utterly myself. It is some more valid person than I am who is doing the watching; through my eyes and from inside my own head she is looking out and seeing my parents and somehow me as well. This nearly-me, beside-myself person wonders if she is asleep or awake.

What she – or I – sees is a fragile picture. It comes and goes in light that is full of tricks and keeps changing and is the colour of neither night nor day; in an unsteady glow that could be from sun or moon the picture flickers and could evaporate altogether if stared at too long. In the dream I know that it is 1960, so it is another trick, then, that the dream is playing this picture back to me as if it were a memory, for it is impossible that I ever did see my parents like this in 1960, or ever. But there they are, staring as from a photograph, my mother at the end of her rope and my father dull with bewilderment. Their eyes, impenetrable circles of darkness, are larger than in life. They are standing in the garden and all around them on the ground lie the splintered remains of something they have broken, and they are sick at the loss and waste of it. They look ready to end their lives, and it seems arbitrary – a question of timing only – whether they will kill themselves or each other. But in their eyes sits the knowledge that one way or another the whole sorry business will soon be over and the hush surrounding them has something to do with respect for this fact. The waiting must be borne out with decorum.

Now I am lying down and staring through darkness towards the ceiling. I rise and take myself to the attic where at night the air smells even older than in daytime. The light of the bare bulb glares on the camp bed, which is still strewn with things piled up in a bank against the wall. I start to remove them, methodically at first, ferrying armloads to unfilled patches of floor, imagining that I am sorting things out. But all I want is the bed cleared, so I start to push stuff off and fling it around anyhow. Under all the junk, the surface of the dusty bedcover is still its original indigo blue. I ignore a fleeting, dark movement across its surface; something swift and scurrying has already vanished with the lightness of blinking. When I give the cloth a shake I find woven into the underside of its folds little silky white swellings that are powdery to the touch, the remains of ghostly, fled cocoons. Where more than forty years of light from the square skylight has fallen on the edge of the cover as it spills over the side of the bed to the floor, the colour has faded to a dim lilac.

I pull back the cover and get in and surrender to the embrace of the cloth and also to my own disgust, for it smells, and is heavy with damp and sticky with the layers of years; it feels like a coating of death. No trace of Joe remains. Not a breath or a hair nestles in the brown-stained ticking of the pillow, no memory of his skin is held in a whiff of talcum powder or aftershave between the cover and the rank mattress. Yet here is where he lies night after night while in my room below I stare upwards. I have to know how he sleeps. Is he on his back staring up too, not at the ceiling but through the skylight at the moon? On his side? Are his legs straight or scissored and are they covered or bare, does he grasp the bedcover between his thighs? Does he think of me and touch himself, imagining my hands, as I am trying to make my fingers feel like his body, opening mine? Does he listen for the sea or turn at once towards the wall and dream? It seems that I am still lying awake and burning in the dark, tormented by the heat in myself.

Now I see him. As I watched my parents so I watch Joe, simultaneously witnessing my invisibility to him. He is here in the attic but lying in a high, carved, baronial bed, the kind of bed I imagine his family owning. Uncle George is in the doorway with his back to the room, explaining something to my parents, who are out of sight. What he says is making them unhappy. Joe sleeps. I fancy George is talking about him. Nobody sees me.

A dream and not a memory, but this is how it was that summer. My watching with nothing to do while others talk, talk, talk, stretches of time when I hesitate between rooms, unsure whether to go towards or away from the sound of voices. Spells of loitering, waiting for Joe to turn up and give shape to long, senseless hours. Days filled with the single purpose of awakening a part of him that doesn't really see me, to bring him alive to the necessity of me. Day after day when I fail to rouse him beyond a vague, drowsy friendliness and into a revelation of what I mean to him, when I squander hours devising excuses for his being unaware that his life and mine are unbearable unless we are together.

I am wrong to try to remember that time as if I saw one thing leading to another. Memory tries to insist that there is a kind of inevitability between events but even if there is, it is hidden at the time. But that summer, we really are marooned and voiceless until Uncle George comes along. He makes everything possible, even easy; swinging to our rescue the way he does, he seems to explain to us who we are. Above all, he disguises the preposterousness of it: an amateur production of *Turandot* mounted in nine weeks with a cast of kids, oddities and thwarted also-rans. How blind I am not to see that Uncle George is just as blinded, and chasing just as hard after what he himself wants. But I don't care to go over and over it.

Now I sneeze and the blue cover fills my nose with a smell like pepper and dead leaves and is rough against my face, like a prison blanket. I struggle to my feet and try to wave away the frowsty air around the bed, protesting. I feel things crawling in my scalp. My eyes water under the bright light that casts a blade of shadow along the sloping ceiling of the attic and now I really am awake, scratching at my arms and shivering on the bare floor.

13

L ila woke up with two hot patches high on her cheeks. In the bathroom she washed furtively and afterwards hid her flannel and toothbrush because there was nothing pretty about them. She kept the taps running while she used the lavatory and then she tipped bleach down it and waited ten minutes in case the next person in the bathroom should be Joe.

Back in her room, she looked at herself in the mirror. Reflected behind her she saw clothes draped over a chair and behind that the stale and wrong things that she had accrued, outgrown and stopped noticing: her old dolls' house with painted ivy wandering up its walls, the shelf of school stories and ballet annuals, a flaking black metal tin of broken geometry tools. She owned nothing that she still wanted. Overnight she had become herself, arriving in her real life at last only to find that she had got there burdened with possessions with no point, and dressed as someone else. She had no clothes she could bear to appear to Joe in. Somehow she had been surviving under a shadow that obscured how unacceptable she looked.

But the tragedy of her clothes could not be played out now, on a Thursday morning in Burnhead. She could smell burning toast from downstairs, she heard the back door bang as her father left for work and the sound of the taps running again in the bathroom and the rippling of her mother's voice, trilling and turning Italian phrases. A gusty wind blew outside, squeezing an ordinary, everyday draught through the window frame. She had to join the day and get dressed in something, however thwarted her changed self would be in it. She pulled on her dirndl skirt. It had a pattern that reminded her of half-beaten eggs but it was reasonably new; Enid's mum had run it up for her at Easter at the same time as doing one for Enid in red and white stripes. (Two's as simple as one, she said, handing it over to Lila and waving away thanks.) If she pulled her white belt in tight it looked better, but the yellow aertex shirt would not do. It would never do again. She put on her reasonable white blouse with the Peter Pan collar and bows on the cuffs, and spent a long time practising how to move: she turned sideways to the mirror, straightened her back and thrust out her chest, imagining through Joe's eyes the combined impact of her bust and her glancing smile. He had to catch sight of her like this, bashful and skittish, just at the moment when a tiny, breathy laugh escaped her lips.

She was still barefoot. The flat sandals would also have to go, permanently, but she had little else apart from school shoes and plimsolls, only a pair of tan pumps meant for special occasions. They would have to do, with American Tan stockings. She undressed again in order to put on her suspender belt which was ointment pink and needed a wash, but at least she would not have to worry about Joe's eyes judging it.

The stockings and smart shoes did not look right with the high colour in her face and her hair flattened childishly under Kirby grips. She damped down the pink in her cheeks with some Max Factor but it looked strange, sitting on her face by itself, so she put on mascara as well, scrubbing a paste off the surface of the flat black cake with spit and stroking it into clumps on her lashes with the little doll's brush. She scraped her hair back hard to make her eyes look Chinesey and startled, and then she backcombed it into a thick, felted swell and tied it high at the back of her head in a yellow chiffon scarf. She was amazed at how long all this took. But she had to count herself now among those who knew the true purpose of dressing to the nines. Realising she could never again be a person who wasn't prepared to go to such lengths, she felt initiated and dismayed.

Uncle George and Joe were in the dining room. Going in, she broke an atmosphere, as if opening the door snapped threads lately spun between them. She poured herself tea in silence, not sure if their eyes were on her or on the trickle into her cup that meant she was emptying the pot.

'So, *buon giorno, la bella*!' Joe said, loudly and suddenly.

Lila lifted a hand to the scarf in her hair.

'So, today, *la bella* Liù, may I enjoin you to give me a tour of my new surroundings?' He stretched out a hand that remained too far away for her to touch, had she dared reach for it.

'La *what*?' she asked, unconsciously dipping her head to receive the garland of her own special name. '*La bella* what?'

'We have a great deal to do,' Uncle George said. He sounded as if he were repeating himself. 'We have a public meeting here the day after tomorrow. The three of you need vocal coaching every day, and on top of that you have to be able to sing your parts in your sleep. And all in a matter of weeks.'

'Yes, Maestro, but I don't see why that means we have to hang around all morning,' Joe said. Lila giggled.

'There is no need to be hanging around. You should be working on your parts, on your own. Without over-taxing your voice, naturally. Then we need to start thinking about the set, do some drawings, start thinking about materials. You said you were keen to design it. I'd have thought at the very least you'd want to go up to the farm to see the space where you're performing.'

Joe widened his eyes. 'Ah, may I remind you, the set's all up here,' he said, tapping the side of his head with his index finger. 'I told you, that's the way I work. I could get it down on paper in ten minutes. How you fuss! Doesn't he, *la bella* Liù?'

Uncle George lit a cigarette and looked at his watch. Joe screwed up his nose and waved the smoke away. 'Really, Maestro, I don't know why you get so het up,' he said.

'At 9.15 I shall give Fleur her session. At 10.15 you will have yours, and at 11.30, after a fifteen minute break, it'll be her turn,' George said, nodding at Lila. He got up from the table. 'You will each work for at least four more hours every day learning your parts. At 2.30 every day we shall meet and discuss what else needs to be done. Understood?'

'We're not students now, you know,' Joe said, looking at Lila for support.

'Exactly. You're taking on something that even professionals would baulk at. You should also,' he said, now fixing his attention on Joe and dropping his voice, 'rest for at least an hour and a half every afternoon. You need to build up stamina. I expect you all singing your parts, word-perfect without scores, in two weeks' time.'

He set his cigarette in the corner of his mouth and left.

Joe said, 'He's not being fair. I just need time. I know the part already, most of it. I need to mull ideas over in my head. My . . .' He spun a hand in the air. 'My ideas for the set . . . they are buds. They need time to flower. You understand, don't you?'

'Oh, of course,' Lila said. 'I understand.'

'*He* doesn't,' Joe said. He seemed to be waiting for her to say something.

'I know. Typical.'

'Come on,' he said, standing up. 'We'll go out. We'll just forget all about him, shall we?'

'Out? Where?'

'Anywhere – you choose. Take me anywhere you like,' he said, putting on a smile and spreading his arms.

Lila's heart thumped; he didn't care where he went as long as it was she who took him. 'But Uncle George, the dishes . . .'

George was now at the piano across the hall, stabbing out the chords of the chorus at the end of Act I:

> *La fossa già scaviam per te*
> *Che vuoi sfidar l'amor!*

> We are already digging the grave for you
> Who want to challenge love!

The sound rose and punctured through Fleur's whooping and swooping voice from upstairs.

'Forget him! Come with me. You're not scared of him, are you, little Liù? He's not Bernstein, you know. We've got to stand up to him.' He made for the door and opened it noiselessly. 'Come *on*,' he whispered, reaching out a hand.

Without having to discuss the need to avoid the front door, they left the house by the back, crossed the garden and slipped through the gate in the wall into the scrubland that stretched down to the shore. The wind almost toppled Lila's hair and she raised a hand to steady it while with the other she grabbed her skirt that was suddenly full of treacherous, billowing life. The weather infuriated her. She had to get used to the new way she looked; she did not want to have to concentrate on keeping herself in one piece and stopping her stocking tops from showing. Now the wind was making her eyes water and soon her mascara would run and she would be weeping indelible, soot tears in front of Joe.

'There's nothing to see,' she said, watching his eyes scan the shoreline and the windy sky. 'It's a rotten place.'

He was taking deep breaths in the manner of inland people about to say something about sea air. 'No, it's not the Riviera, is it?' he called over the wind. 'George exaggerates so.'

'I hate it. I'm not staying, I'm moving to London.'

'Still, I wasn't expecting much,' he said, taking a few purposeless steps. He turned back to her. 'So! Now Joey is in your gentle hands. Show me round! I'm interested in everything. I want to see it all.'

Lila pushed her skirt down, trapping its folds between her thighs. What did he mean? He had, strictly speaking, asked her out, so why was it up to her what they did? Could this be a date, on a blustery Thursday morning? Was this the material on which she was to build memories for saying, for the rest of their lives: *Do you remember the first time we went out together?*

'Suppose you take me down to the beach?' he said.

She couldn't possibly take him to the beach. To get to the beach you had to cross the dunes with sand stinging your legs, and the dunes, as everybody knew, were where couples went at night to make little shelters in the marram grass and writhe privately in the dark to the sucking of the tide. Joe was in short sleeves again. She could see the hairs on his arms, ruffled by the wind. When she looked at his open top shirt button and saw the hair sprouting there at his throat, a ragged flutter of warmth ran through her. She blushed, thinking of One Thing Only, the thing that all boys wanted and that certain girls were apparently prepared to go the dunes for. Joe might think that was what she wanted. She turned away. It had never occurred to her before, but what if some couples went to the dunes in daylight and they were to stumble across one? Until now she would have thought it impossible because what took place was so embarrassing surely it could only be done in the dark, but she was getting an inkling of powerful reasons why people could throw off that kind of shyness. And hardly less awful than stumbling upon *that* was the thought of Joe and her together catching sight of the things she and Enid occasionally came across on the beach and that Lila was ashamed of knowing the purpose of: the limp, discarded evidence of One Thing Only lying like pink emptied maggots, sometimes delicately knotted at the end.

'Well, what about showing me the glorious sights of fair Burnhead?'

His gaze was now drifting over Lila's head. Was he regretting coming out with her?

'All right,' she said, 'come on, we'll go this way!' The carefree laugh she tagged on to the end of the words was lost on the wind.

When they emerged on to the road next to the bridge over the Pow Burn, Lila stopped. It was nearly a mile's walk in one direction to Burnhead, a mile in the other to Monkton, where there was even less to see, and she was in her pointed court shoes. Joe wasn't equipped for a walk either; he didn't seem the type who ever would be. He was wearing pointed shoes too, come to that, black leather ones that curled up slightly at the toes, and the belt round his jeans pulled him in so stiffly it was hard to imagine him striding carelessly along the sea road. They loitered moodily for a minute or two.

She was about to suggest that maybe they should go up to Pow Farm after all, when Joe called out, 'Hey, look, a bus!'

Lila looked up and saw it in the distance, rocking along the road from Burnhead towards Monkton, going the wrong way.

'Quick! There's the stop, come on!' Joe yelled.

He grabbed her hand and suddenly Lila didn't care where the bus was going. Even running with splayed feet, terrified she would lose a shoe, she was storing the moment away: *Do you remember the first time you took my hand?*

The bus pulled to a halt. Joe clattered upstairs and Lila lurched behind, thrilled at how willingly she could abandon decency and follow him, for upstairs on a bus was a place where only a girl who wanted to mix with chain-smoking men playing with themselves would go. Joe marched up to the very front seat and slumped in it. A minute later they rumbled past Seaview Villas, almost level with the drawn curtains of Fleur's bedroom window. Lila, laughing, sent the house a little wave.

'Byesie-bye, Fleur, byesie-bye, George,' Joe said, turning and wiggling his fingers. 'Byesie-bye, *Turandot*.'

The conductress clumped upstairs and took their fares. Joe paid, as was only right on a date and besides, Lila had no money. Then he leaned across and gave the ends of her yellow chiffon bow a little tug.

'You're coming undone,' he said. 'You've come undone running for the bus. You're falling to bits. Turn round.'

He took the ends of the scarf. '"A sweet disorder in the dress . . ."' he said over her shoulder, laughing. 'D'you know the rest?'

'The rest of what?'

Joe took his time adjusting the scarf, lifting it and fluffing the bow, primping the ends.

'That's better now, *la bella*, oops, just a minute . . .' With one finger he lifted a loose tendril from her neck and pushed it upwards into the mass of dark hair under the scarf.

' "kindles in clothes a wantonness." Or so they say. Done – there you are!'

He patted the top of her head and turned back. Lila, breathless with the sensation of his finger on her neck, hardly heard what he had said. She sat letting memories form – already memories, already she was starving for more – of his hands touching her hair, grazing her skin. She had to fix them in her mind. She had to edit and interpret them too; that pat on the head, for instance, he must have meant to be tender rather than casual. There couldn't have been anything brotherly in it. She turned to look at him. He was staring straight ahead now and lifting and lowering his eyebrows as if practising facial expressions or conducting a silent conversation. She must be patient. For the time being the rules confined them to gestures and looks. Words would come later. She saw a series of arches through which she and Joe would pass, gradually shedding the layers of rule-keeping – the pretence of indifference, the perfected indirectness – until their true feelings could be admitted. Soon after that they would be engaged and she would be able to say: *Do you remember the first time you touched my hair?*

Of course I do, but what I really wanted to do was kiss it. Lila looked at him again, surprised. Now she was inside his head and seeing herself: she felt the chiffon under his hands and her warm hair tangled in his fingers, knew precisely his impulse to lean forward and breathe the scent of her shampoo and taste strands of her hair drawn through his lips. She knew the sparkle that went through him when he touched her, all the magazine talk of destiny, romance and encountering True Love melting in a single, tyrannical leaping of the blood.

The bus rolled along, slowed and stopped. A man came

upstairs with a cigarette in his mouth, pulling a greyhound on a lead. Its claws tapped like falling stones along the deck between the seats. If he had not come, Joe might have kissed her. 'So, where is it you're taking me, then?' Joe said, after a few more minutes. 'Where exactly are we?'

She tried to explain. 'The bus only goes one way. It goes the wrong way, it comes along our road away from Burnhead and goes up to Monkton and back round all the little roads to Burnhead by the long way. The road's not wide enough for buses to pass, that's why.'

'Oh.'

'So you have to go nine miles in the wrong direction to get where you want that's only one mile away.'

She failed to make this sound amusing. They sat in silence for the rest of the journey and by the time they got off the bus Joe seemed to have forgotten that the outing had been his idea. He dawdled a little behind Lila as if he were indulging her by consenting to follow. They joined Burnhead Main Street and walked along past the mix of gift shops and tearooms – *Ice Cream made on the Premises, Sugar Novelties* – that sat side by side with the butchers, chemists, ironmongers and churches. Lila longed for him to assert how things were meant to go; the responsibility for making the day special was beginning to crush her. With a pang of sorrow she led him past Sew Right. She wished he were more curious about her because then she might be able to explain, at the very least, about Enid's mum. But a single glance at him told her they couldn't possibly pop in and see her together. She wasn't sure why.

They followed the path through the public gardens between the beds of wallflowers and the children's putting green and still they said little. Lila wondered what she was supposed to do with him now. If they could just stop marching along, if they could only come to a halt and look at each other and talk with nobody else around, all would become clear between them. But there were no places designed for them. There was nowhere they could linger and be out of the wind and away from other people, except perhaps certain notorious park benches where Senga McMillan's initials were etched with several others and at which no right-thinking girl could suggest pausing.

Families defeated by the weather and giving up on the beach for the day limped past them, laden parents with faces cured pink by brine and wind, hauling behind them urchin offspring in sopping plimsolls, shivering and clutching their crotches and whining for a place to stop. A number of them lodged on the benches next to the swings and rubbish bins to eat their jam pieces and swig from Thermos flasks – dinnertime brought forward to half past ten for want of anything else to do – not far from the sinister, red-brick conveniences that were set back at the end of a path lined with thorn bushes studded with discarded papers.

At the point where the path joined Station Road and led down to the sea, Lila and Joe turned and wandered back up to Main Street.

'Well,' Lila said, slowing by the bus stop. 'Well, that's Burnhead. See, there's nothing to do. We might as well go back.'

'We've only just come!' Joe stood with his hands on his hips, looking round, his eyes suddenly, newly bright. 'I suppose it's too early for a drink. How's about a coffee? Where's your usual haunt? Where do all the lovely young things go?'

There was nothing for it but the Locarno. These days the Chit Chat was soaking up the clientele the Locarno no longer wanted: the more prosperous sand-covered families from the beach who had the money for choice of sausage roll or fish and chips, orangeade or tea, and solitary old people dropping jammy scones in their laps. Nobody of Lila's generation went there any more. The Locarno was the place, the set high tea off the menu and newly done up, the dark panelling and bentwood furniture stripped out. Lozenge-shaped Formica tables with lethal metal trims were now screwed to the floor and brash lighting buzzed from the ceiling where the plaster cornicing and ceiling roses had been chiselled away like icing off an old cake. There, Burnhead's teenage sophisticates sat numbed by the jukebox while condensation from the new, hissing coffee machine poured down the plate-glass window. Joe's kind of place. They went in. He ordered coffee for them at the counter and sauntered towards a table. He knew without being told that the waitress would bring it.

Enid was sitting in a bay with Senga McMillan, Linda McCall and Deirdre Munro, one of several bovine quartets of girls slumped and chewing on their empty mouths or on straws poking out of Coke bottles, while their eyes travelled round for the subject of their next sneer. The boys, commandeering the jukebox in knots of four and five, shoved and showed off, breaking into laughter and catcalls that carried sometimes a sudden unfettered high note that was giddy and female. Lila raised a smile to Enid as she went by and sank into a seat opposite Joe.

The four girls leaned in and whispered and broke into laughter. Senga called over, 'Look whit the cat's brung in! Who's yer friend, got yoursel' a fancy man?'

'And who do we have here?' Joe asked Lila, turning round and sending them a lazy smile.

'Don't look round! They're my friends. *Supposed* to be. I hate them.'

'Look at the state of her. Haw, Lizzie! I seen your mum's picture in the paper. Goin' to gie us a wee song?' Linda said.

'Tra la! What's your favourite opera? How'd you cry it again? Touring-whit?'

'Aw, 'scuse me, my Italian's a wee bit rusty, what's Italian for fancy man?'

'What's Italian for fancy hair-do?'

'What's Italian for whaur's yer knickers?'

Three of the quartet collapsed into more laughter; only Enid looked uncomfortable. Lila stared at the table, her face hot and red under the Max Factor, and folded her hands over her head to try to hide the scarf. Then, before she could stop him, Joe got up and walked over slowly, thumbs hooked into the front pockets of his jeans. The girls shifted, composed their faces and shook out their hair.

'How do you do, ladies? Allow me to introduce myself. Joe Foscari,' he said, planting himself in front of them. 'And how are yourselves, ladies?'

He proffered a hand but none of them dared take it.

'I hope I shall have the pleasure of seeing you all on Saturday,' he said, looking round at the other tables, assessing the attention. 'Full details, as you say, in the paper. I trust you *are* all coming on Saturday to join BAST?'

'Well, hawdy hawdy haw. Opera, you kidding?' Senga said. 'BAST? Is that that shite you was telling us, Enid?'

'What?' Enid said. 'Oh. Uh-huh. It's some thing of Lizzie's.'

Joe said, 'It's a great chance. We'll be needing young ladies like yourselves.'

Senga turned lazy eyes back to Joe. 'You – have – got – to – be – kidding. Opera's shite. You wouldn't catch me dead.'

A squabble broke out over by the jukebox. There was some pushing and complaining, and then 'A Big Hunk O' Love' began blaring out of it.

> *Hey Baby, I ain't askin' much of you*
> *No no no no no no no no baby*

The boys fell silent and grouped round, some of them pumping from the hips with their eyes closed, lips pushed out; alerted, in with a chance, jerking with adult stealth to the universal beat of lust, the thump, thump, hump of an easy pick-up. Senga dropped her mouth open, pulling taut a sheet of gum between her top and bottom teeth, snapped it, flipped her tongue round it and joined in with the song, smirking at Joe:

> *Well you can spare a kiss or two and*
> *Still have plenty left, no no no*

The boys looked over. The girls giggled.

> *Well I ain't greedy baby*
> *All I want is all you got, no no no*
> *Baby I ain't asking much of you*
> *Just a big-a big-a hunk o' love will do*

The song finished and another one started up. Senga sucked up a mouthful of Coke and stared at Joe without blinking.

He said, 'Dear me. That's a most grave error you're making. Opera's not what you think. You'll be missing the time of your lives.'

Senga tried to engage the other three in an exchange of sniggers but now they were all watching him, trying to work out how, while being so polite and friendly, he was managing to make fools of them.

'You surprise me, up-to-date ladies like yourselves,' he said. 'Opera's the in thing. Everybody'll be there. You'd better come or you'll miss your big chance.'

Enid said, 'Big chance of what? Singing in a stupid opera?'

Joe glanced down the aisle at Lila. 'No, I mean your chance – your glorious chance – of appearing on stage with the tenor, Guiseppe Foscari. That's me.'

'Haw! Fancy yoursel', don't you? Whit's so great about you?' Senga said. 'That's a stupid name, anyway.' The others gasped. She would always go further than any of them.

Joe smiled and turned to Lila again. 'Hear that, Liù?' he called over. 'What's great about *me*?'

Just then the waitress came along with their coffee. To give her room to get past, Joe turned back to the girls' bay and pressed himself hard against the end of their table. The edge pushed into his thighs. Even Senga had to look away.

'Ah! What's so great about me?' he said softly, easing himself back on his heels. 'That, ladies, I shall demonstrate.'

The last verse of 'Please Don't Tease' was bouncing from the jukebox. Joe took a few steps down the aisle and waited while

the song died away. Then he turned and fixed his eyes somewhere above the girls' heads. He was on stage; he placed his
fingertips on his ribs, took a deep breath and from his mouth
came a caramelly slick of sound that coated the steamy air of
the Locarno:

> *Ma il mio mistero è chiuso in me,*
> *Il nome mio nessun saprà!*
> *No, no!*

It was '*Nessun dorma*', though to Lila's ears, pitched a couple
of tones lower. The hairs rose on the back of her neck at Joe's
effortful, insistent sound. It was over in a matter of seconds.
People turned to see if they'd heard right. There were murmurs,
snorts of laughter, raised eyebrows. A few people peered
round, whistled and stamped, then they turned back. Talking
resumed.

Lila's face burned. She could have told him Burnhead people
were the most heart-sinking on earth. Joe deserved cheering
and clapping and most of them hadn't even taken their straws
from their mouths. Then the Locarno's proprietor, Mr Loca-
telli, appeared from the back. He wiped his hands, raised an
arm and laughed. 'Bravo, bravo! Bravo, *signor*!' he called.
Conversation stopped again.

Joe bowed towards him. '*Prego*. Ladies and gentlemen,' he
said, 'come and sing in an opera! Details in your excellent local
paper! And now if you'll excuse me, my coffee's getting cold.'

He slipped on to the bench opposite Lila, beamed at her and
reached for the sugar. He seemed refreshed. The jukebox began
again. While Lila waited for him to finish with the sugar, she
glanced round. She was beginning to enjoy herself, nervously;
being with Joe filled her with an uneasy, though pleasurable
sense of importance.

After a while Enid and the others got up to leave. They
loitered at the door, calculating interest in them. Joe called out,
'See you on Saturday, ladies!'

All of them sailed out except Enid, who hung back, came over to their table and sat down. She looked embarrassed.

'They're away to get cigs. I'm not going. My mum'd kill me.'

'Well, quite right,' Joe said evenly. 'Sensible young lady.'

'See my mum?' Enid turned to Lila. 'She saw the advert in the paper. The BAST what d'you call it. She says I'm to join, it'll keep me out of the wrong company.'

'I thought singing was supposed to be against your religion,' Lila said.

Enid clicked her tongue. 'That's only when we're Gathered, stupid,' she said. 'Otherwise music is one of God's gifts, except Elvis Presley. Anyway, my mum says I'm to join.'

'Well, how splendid!' Joe boomed. 'You must come and sing!'

Enid considered. 'I can't. I can't sing . . . you know, yon way. Like you. You're dead good. Are you the star of it?'

Joe laughed. 'I am singing the tenor lead, yes! But leave the tough stuff to us. You don't need a big voice for the chorus, just come and sing.'

Lila said, 'I'm singing one of the main parts too, did you know that?'

'*You*? How come?'

'One of the best natural lyric soprano voices you'll ever hear,' Joe said gravely. 'Totally astonishing for her age. She could have a great future.'

Lila murmured, adoring Joe's adoration enough to forget that he had not heard her sing so this assessment must be Uncle George's. Her insides were rocking joyfully at the sight of Enid having to hear him speak admiringly of her. Enid had never managed a fraction of that kind of compliment from anyone, not even a slow-eyed Burnhead lout, let alone a handsome and devoted man like Joe Foscari.

'My mum,' Enid went on at last, 'she says if you want any help with the costumes you just need to ask. She can get you material wholesale if you want.'

'Her mum's the manageress of Sew Right. She can make anything,' Lila said. 'She's dead good.'

'Splendid, splendid, splendid!' Joe said, raising both arms. 'Your kind mama's contribution is most gratefully received! Please do convey to her our thanks. And, so, young lady, we look forward to seeing you on Saturday!'

It was a dismissal, and Enid left.

It was then that Joe's perfection almost faltered. While Lila waited for him to say something, he sucked the dregs of his coffee from his spoon, belched, and turned to look vacantly through the window. Then she realised he was being natural with her. Soul mates do not put on performances for each other. He belched again.

'Pardon,' he said. 'Shall we be getting along?'

When the bus came he led the way inside without explaining why he was abandoning the lark of going upstairs. He sat saying nothing as the bus lurched along, and Lila's doubts gathered again.

In quiet terror she asked, 'Penny for them. What are you thinking about?' giving him the chance to say I'm thinking about you, and dispel the clouds.

'Nothing.'

'You must be thinking about something.'

'Well, yes, I am in a way,' he said frowning. 'Nothing important.'

They rode on in a silence that was deeper and now as much Lila's as his, while her mind raced to find excuses for him. It did not occur to her to put his withdrawal down to simple boorishness; she was disproportionately respectful of other people's silences. At 5 Seaview Villas she had waited out enough of them to know that silences were not merely one of the things that adults imposed on children. They were a mark of separation between the two states; it was one of the privileges of adulthood to clam up and control the atmosphere, a ploy by which children were kept halted, guessing, on the edge of grown-ups' lives. So she reminded herself that Joe was five years older than she was and probably just further on than she in the mastery of unfathomable behaviour.

They had got off the bus and were walking over the bridge when she could bear it no more. The glitter of the morning was falling away, spoiled. She had had him to herself all this time and she had wasted her chance, and now she was about to lose him in the crowd made by Uncle George and her mother. They were claiming him back before she could find out why he wouldn't speak to her.

'What's the matter? Joe, what's the matter? Is it *me*?'

Joe stopped. 'What? Nothing's the matter!' He spoke as if she had been pestering him for hours. Then he saw that she was about to cry. 'Look, of course it's not you! Sometimes . . . things . . . they get on my mind. That's all. Things you don't know anything about. Things I have to think about, okay?'

He started to walk away and Lila grabbed his arm. He shook her off gently and kept going. 'Hey! Come on, look, I told you . . . I've just got things on my mind, okay?'

'Tell me! I want to know. What things?' she bleated after him. 'I want to help! How can I *help* you if I don't know?'

At heart she knew that she was not making an offer of help at all, but a plea to be included.

Joe stopped, exasperated. 'Look. Just . . . this thing, this whole thing George started. I mean, other things as well. There's a lot to it. You won't understand.'

'Yes I will! I do understand! I know it's a lot to organise, I know we need to get lots more people! I know it'll be hard work! That's the point!'

'I didn't . . . Look, that's not what I . . .'

'Okay! Okay! I know! There's casting, tickets, publicity, the band, the lights, the set. The costumes. Headdresses. I know!'

Joe shook his head. 'Aw, Jesus! For God's sake. That's not what I'm talking about.'

'Well, *what* then?' Lila shouted. '*Tell* me!'

Joe took her hand. She let him, though it was a humiliation to be so ready to be appeased while not yet knowing if appeasement would be offered. She waited in terror for him to drop her hand, to reject her for the sake of whatever secrets were whispering in his head. But he raised it and touched it with his lips.

'You're quite a little fireball. Forgive me, *la bella* Liù,' he said. She pulled her hand away. '*La bella* Liù. The Princess Turandot is no contest for Liù. Allow me to pledge to you,' Joe reached for her hand again, 'my undying respect.'

Respect did not sound quite right. Lila could hear the same tone with which he had mocked Senga and her gang, and he had put a certain look in his eyes. She withdrew her hand once more.

'I don't believe in pledges,' she said, mimicking his grandeur. 'Why should I?'

'Ah, *la bella* Liù requires proof, a token?' Joe said, thumping his chest, still acting. They started walking again and now he was darting to and fro in front of her. It was impossible not to laugh. Any of their neighbours might be looking out of their windows. *Oh, aren't they a lovely couple, I remember when they first met.* They would all be on the pavement in front of the church to see the bride come out.

'*La bella* Liù shall have . . . what? What does Madame Liù desire?' Joe cried. This time he took both her hands.

Lila said, 'Desire? Nothing. I don't want anything.'

She blushed. She wanted everything, could he not see it? She knew that wants on the preposterous scale of her own must be kept hidden, for now. Still, she was imagining his first, shy gift: a little vase, a book of poetry, a shining, unreal jewel. Something in silver perhaps, a tiny object about which a modest and tender poem could be written. There it would be in times to come; the two of them would hold hands as she explained to their lively and artistic friends: *This was the very first thing Joe gave me.*

He said, 'Well, I shall think of something. And you must promise to keep it as a little memento of me! Promise!' Then he dropped her hands and dashed on ahead.

Lila followed him slowly, watching him disappear up the side of the house. Why would she need a memento of him when she would see him every day? He must mean a memento of him as Calaf, or a memento of the time they met. She would get used to it. Her life would soon be full of little events deserving of tokens of commemoration. *Keep it as a little memento of me. Promise.* He did not hear her whisper after him, once the dizziness in her head cleared, that she would promise him anything he cared to ask.

She could not expect to understand yet what it all meant: his changes of mood, the banter that faded away when she was the only audience, the holding out and snatching away of little signs. Already she accepted that being confused was another thing that was now her due, a trial to be passed on the way to forming herself into the perfect template that would fit over Joe's nature precisely. At that point she would merge with him completely, but meanwhile there were bound to be occasional rough corners and misunderstandings to be honed away.

It's Christine's doing, I have no doubt, that brings pastor Luke to the door. She knows from the announcement in the paper where the service is being held and she's rung and tipped him off to come and see if I'm going off my head. Luke's not in holy clothes this time. He's in jeans and a checked shirt with a white T-shirt showing at the neck, a padded jacket and a hat with earflaps. Hands in pockets, stamping on the threshold.

He says, Hey, it's a frosty one, isn't it? His breath forms a cloud around his head. At this rate I guess it could even snow, it sure feels cold enough.

I know he thinks to catch me off guard, dressed like that, and means to sneak in a prayer before I can stop him.

I'm not expecting you, am I? I say. I could have been out.

Well, I tried calling you, he says, but no-one's been answering. Are you okay, Lila? Hey, you okay? You look a little upset.

Well, maybe, I say, wiping my eyes with the bundle of papers I happen to be holding. Maybe you telephoned but maybe I don't always answer. I'm busy. I'm busy now, in fact.

Good! That's one reason I'm here, I thought maybe you could use a hand. His teeth really are very impressive. He stamps his feet again and blows on his hands.

Oh, all right then, I say.

He follows me inside quickly and I take him into the music room. You can tell it's a music room because the piano is still there, though of course the Decca stereogram has gone. She had it sent down.

Fine piano, Luke says. Do you play?

Needs tuning, I say.

We look around for a while. Luke is searching for a way, I can tell, to bring God into it, into these stale remnants, the quiet wreckage left by people – and among them I count myself – who had their chances once and squandered them so long ago that it should not still matter. Luke will want to insist it does matter and I predict that his attempts to proffer higher meaning will offend me, because the way I see it God is either inattentive or plain uncooperative and either way it adds up to the same thing. I wonder if it daunts him. God I mean, not Luke. Maybe even God realises that where his presence hasn't been noted within living memory is a place he isn't wanted, though that realisation would entail an unexpected degree of humility on his part. More likely, to me, is the thought that he just *isn't*. But to spare Luke that view into the void, I start to tell him a bit about the piano.

Our eyes are now fixed on it, perhaps because it is the only object in the room that retains any possibility of life. The chairs and the spindly coffee table look somehow extinct.

You call it fine, I say, but that night, that night when everybody comes to the first opera meeting, my mother's Decca stereogram outclasses that piano by a mile. That's what people notice.

Decca stereogram? Luke laughs. That's going back some!

I turn away. It's in the same place as always, right here along the wall. It's her favourite possession: a walnut-veneered rectangle of pure status. It stands on black legs with brass rings at their bases, it's got slide-away doors and a panel of dials like a dashboard that lights up all greenish, the latest thing.

The stereogram eclipses the piano completely, I tell Luke. Do you understand what I'm saying?

I hear what you say, he assures me. You're talking about a long time ago, right? About stuff that's gone. It's not here, right?

But I see it, here in the crowded room. I stay where I am and

Luke goes away somewhere, I have an idea he's putting on the kettle. I know the room: the carpet that does not go all the way to the skirting board and shows linoleum in a herringbone pattern of olive green and yellow at its edges, the lampshade overhead of thick, pale green glass, the empty grate in July. A smell of linseed and dust.

People – more people than have ever gathered here before – occupy all the dining chairs and every stool we can find. They are squeezed up, two in every armchair and more on the arms, others are leaning, perching where they can and the younger ones sit cross-legged on the floor. Our chairs are mortifying: wartime brown with wooden arms, now re-covered in red and charcoal, but the room is so crowded tonight they can hardly be seen. (He hung on to two of those chairs and here they are still, re-covered again in stretch nylon in a pattern of dark green leaves.)

How many people are here? I hear their voices murmuring small, balanced remarks over cups of tea. These people are nearly all dead now, their quirks and mistakes and stupidities evened out and neatly put by as if their lives were a pile of ironing. But I am here, too, yellow chiffon scarf in the hair and the dirndl skirt all over again, anxious in my wrong clothes, watching the door. Joe walks in, moving slowly. When Uncle George asks him to go and find more chairs, he looks sullen.

Do you think, Uncle George says through his teeth, I can do everything myself?

Joe glares and exits. He and I are still somewhat in disgrace for skipping off to Burnhead on Thursday but Joe is brazening it out, claiming that he was drumming up support for the meeting. The thrill I am getting from sharing a bond of criminality with him outweighs any fall from grace in Uncle George's eyes. Uncle George sometimes looks a little seedy and unwell, now. He says *nil desperandum* too often. I do not meet his eyes because I am afraid that there may be a look in mine that will reveal to him how I have changed. But whenever I remember about going to London with him, I feel nicer about him, and try to be helpful. Maybe I should feel confused about this, but all I feel is powerful.

The trickle of arrivals for the meeting thickens, and slows again, and by twenty to seven there are well over three dozen people crammed into the music room.

Enid is sitting with her mother. I am glad to see that Enid's mum is as placid and solid here as she is at Sew Right, behind the sewing machine. I have an idea she is the same everywhere. Enid sticks her tongue out at me. Behind her, to my dismay, sit Senga, Linda and Deirdre. They kick and poke and giggle behind their hands.

My mother glides into the room like a knowing guest, like a visiting priestess. The other women are in cotton skirts and twinsets; she is in oyster chiffon that drifts around her body like smoke. She does this. Her clothes are not just superior, they are antithetical. When Burnhead womanhood is wearing tiny floral prints she's in pared-down black and white. They turn out in tweeds and she's in bias-cut crêpe-de-chine, get them in navy check and she'll be in caramel zig-zags. I'm not sure if it's deliberate. She presents herself like an exhibit, some untouchable artefact from an exotic and distant civilisation. Her value is not explicit and to guess at it would be vulgar and irrelevant.

She finds a stool at the back of the room. I think she feels awkward about our house filling up with people she knows slightly or not at all. She doesn't have friends as such; her dealings with people are skewed and unnatural because she wants too much and expects too little. She is not quite at ease with those by whom she would like to be regarded a social equal, the wives of the town's professional men – Moira Mather, Delia Hunter the doctor's wife, who are both here – but nor is she quite friends with ordinary folk like Mrs Mathieson and Enid's mum to whom all she conveys is her sense that deference is due to her, along with faint surprise that they turn out to have perfectly nice manners after all. She is only really comfortable giving orders to the shopkeepers, I think.

I recognise Mr McArthur and Billy from the farm, Billy looking young and pointless. I discover a ruthlessness in myself, thinking what a narrow escape I am having and what a mistake a farm boy would be; what a mistake any fat-fisted, flat-eyed Burnhead oaf knowing nothing of Life and Opera and Art would be. I glance at the door through which Joe has just disappeared to remind myself where my true destiny lies. Thanks to Joe, 'true destiny' is the kind of phrase I am quite comfortable with now. Alec Gallagher is here with his notepad open on his lap and next to him is his fiancée Veronica. Her hair is dyed and lacquered into a yellow helmet. She has fat knees and she chews the inside of her cheeks. Next to them are Mrs and Mr Mathieson. She has quick eyes and no neck and a spreading body with a comfortable undercarriage. Mr Mathieson sits with his brittle ankles crossed and his arms folded. Although he is old he looks more like a fledgling; he has the thin skin and damp, sorrowing eyes of a creature lately cast from its shell.

Oh, now Luke is back, asking me about milk and sugar, which I don't believe I have. He hasn't taken his jacket or hat off. Oddly, he brings a crocheted blanket that belongs on my father's chair in the back room, and he places it round me. Still not a word about God.

My father is nominally in charge of refreshments and goes between the kitchen and music room with a tea towel tucked into his trousers between the buttons of his dreary braces. He brings in plates of sandwiches that he made himself but the butter was hard and the bread tore, for which he apologises as he hands them over to the Bergsma sisters and Mrs Mathieson who are on their feet now and helping with cups and saucers and plates, possibly because they are ill at ease watching a man do it.

Everyone in Burnhead knows the Bergsma sisters and knows

their story, though probably they never tell it themselves. They don't need to. In Burnhead, people's histories are attached to them like invisible signs round their necks. What happened to the Bergsmas is like all other common knowledge, and in a place like this there's a lot of common knowledge: for example, the path running up between the Bergsmas' barber and hair-dressing premises and the building next door is called Kyle's Wynd, but there's nothing there to tell you that. There's no actual sign round the Bergsmas' necks. It's common knowledge.

Kyle's Wynd? Luke says, puzzled. What are you talking about, Lila?

It's still there but the Bergsmas' place isn't, I tell him. It's all knocked down now.

In my mind the Bergsmas are typically Dutch. I picture the whole of Holland full of old-fashioned spinster sisters like Joanna and Willy (short for Wilhelmina), though of course nobody my age calls them anything except Miss Bergsma. Joanna's hair is wound in plaits around her head and Willy has a bun that is glossier and darker than the surrounding cloud of her hair; it sits like a Bakelite light switch in a nest of jute. But this is not the most remarkable thing about Willy. One side of her face is a slip-sliding disaster of flesh that pulls her eye down so that it is constantly red-rimmed and teary. The skin on that side looks melted and is both pinker and bluer than the rest of her face, like a patch in a related but not identical material that has been stretched and crudely tacked over the torn original. It's from when their house in Rotterdam was bombed in the war. Enid's mum says Willy got burned rescuing her mother's silver and tortoiseshell dressing-table set. This is part of their history and Burnhead's common knowledge. How and why they got to Burnhead from Rotterdam isn't.

Yes, war is a terrible thing, Lila, Luke says. He sighs and mutters something I don't catch.

I don't know if Willy Bergsma had a choice and went for the

dressing-table set instead of the mother but like everybody else I know the mother died in the fire and I also know I'm frightened of that watering eye. It may have weighed up the silver and tortoiseshell against an evil-tempered old lady and if it did, well, we know what happened next; it's common knowledge. Any minute the terrible things that eye has seen might start to ooze out of it and down Willy's cheek.

Joanna does most of the shaving and trimming at their barber and hairdressing place while Willy keeps the appointments book and sells brushes and combs, compacts, travelling cases and shaving requisites. She seldom leaves the front shop, she calls through from the counter if she has something to say. Maybe she doesn't like the mirrors in the back reflecting to her from every angle her ruined face.

Lila, you okay?

Luke brings in the tea and joins me on the floor. I don't remember deciding to sit on the floor, but here I am. As Luke speaks, his breath forms a cloud and I notice that the room is cold.

There are others here, too: Jimmy Brock the coalman, scrubbed into ordinariness, Sandy and Lydia Scott, stalwarts of the Ayrshire Amateur Operatic Association, wearing badges that say 'AAOA Committee Member'. In addition, because he is President, Sandy wears a medal on a chain. There's a woman with two children dressed for Scottish Country Dancing in kilts of acid yellow tartan with velvet waistcoats, lace jabots and pumps, who are clutching their certificates for *1st Runner-up: Formation Sword*, and *Highly Commended: Flora MacDonald's Fancy*. To my embarrassment Mr Black, the principal music teacher at Burnhead Academy, is here with his wife and his stuck-up daughter who goes to a fee-paying school in Troon where Mrs Black teaches Domestic Science. Mrs Black has tight hair that's bumpy on the surface and is neither fair nor grey. The colour looks boiled out of it and reminds me of porridge.

Uncle George stands behind the piano making over-hearty

gestures of greeting. He is unnerved that the glorious idea has come to this: a crowd of ill-assorted people who in the very act of turning up may be marking themselves out as the oddest in Burnhead. The idea – my idea – ran away with him and now he is aghast. I think he has it in mind to make a speech.

Welcome, ladies and gentlemen!

Who are you talking to, Lila?

Now Joe comes in last, making George wait. He picks his way over to where I am leaning against the wall. My heart jumps because he is singling me out to stand next to. From here we can see nearly everybody but more important perhaps, to Joe, is that nearly everybody can see him. George watches me watching him watch the room.

Thank you for coming. We are all here, as you know, for a purpose.

You're welcome. And indeed we are, Lila. We Evangelical Lutherans believe that firmly. We believe that we are here because Jesus Christ . . .

Uncle George stands there, unsure what to say next. We wait. My heart is thudding. It is terrifying to watch the slippage of a dream. Is anyone safe, ever, once they have laid eyes on what they want? How long before it becomes what they need, and if they have to go without, what then? All George's London confidence is blurring. He is shrinking, losing buoyancy. Beside me, Joe shifts against the wall, pinches the end of his nose between finger and thumb and looks at the ceiling.

So do we, I mean, is anyone – anyone at all, familiar with *Turandot*? At all? Uncle George asks, but he has no idea what to do about the thick cluster of hands that goes up, among them my mother's, the Scotts', the Bergsmas', the Blacks'. Even Billy's is half-raised.

Right, he says. Very good. Well.

He clears his throat and looks at his notes. He picks up some papers and waves them vaguely. We wait again.

Mr Mathieson stands up.

I'm John Mathieson for anyone here doesn't know me. See – George, is it? – I'm thinking, George, maybe we could do with a wee committee. Get ourselves going. Get organised kind of thing, eh?

Lila? Lila, are these papers important? Is there something you want to show me? Luke says. What is all this? It's all just scrap paper, isn't it?

Uncle George's notes of the meeting are still bunched in my fists and lying in my lap and on the floor around me.

Of course it's not scrap paper. Here, I say to Luke, and I shake the papers at him. This is what happened. Here are the notes, this is a *true record* of events.

He pulls my fingers open and takes them from me. He places a mug of tea in my now empty hands and the warmth of it makes me sigh.

I watch Luke gather the papers up. The writing is worn away in places and it's hard to read, I admit that, but I think he makes particularly heavy weather of it. He looks only at the first couple of pages. The first five lines are in pen, George's attempt at an agenda some time before the meeting. Everything that follows is in pencil and written fast.

Mtg 9 July
Introduce – self. Intro others. Intro opera. Does anybody know Turandot???
THE TASK AHEAD.
What we need to achieve: make list.
Ask people. Split into groups?

COMMITTEE?
Orchestra sub-cttee: JIMMY Brock (coal) t b in charge of band. JB plays coronet & trombone. NB now rtd from mine but still in colliery *brass band* – can get other band members, min. 12 players, all exp'd, most vg. JB can transpose parts!!!

Will work with GORDON BLACK – will get school orchestra members to join, maybe another 12. Can borrow stands and lights. AYRSHIRE AMATEUR PHILHARMONIC Orchestra – he will contact, bring on board.

– Strings – cd. be prob. – J Bergsma played viola as girl. **Willy Bergsma USED TO TEACH VIOLIN!** NEED MORE PLAYERS PERCUSSION WOODWIND

Chorus sub-cttee:

REHEARSAL PIANIST V IMPORTANT – GORDON BLACK available hooray!!! **WILL COACH CHORUS**

CHORUS – Sandy SCOTT – President of Ayrshire Amat. Opera. Assoc. says WHOLE CHORUS OF AAOA MAY BE WILLING. On summer break, no commitments – individ members always keen to sing. Mrs Scott says ditto her ladies choir – 65 members – she will persuade (consider definite)

ALSO – S Scott offers loan props/costumes of AAOA!!!!!

Costumes & props sub-cttee:

Stella Foley (M of Enid) – gets material wholesale, + trimmings, beads etc. Can make anything, needs designs, sketches will do. YES will tackle headdresses. Needs team helpers . . . tb arranged. ?Chorus make own??

Joe – prod: concept modern & simple, muslin drapes etc. lighting min. NEEDS CLOTH – QUANTITIES??

Chorus = peasants: pyjama style, black pumps. Principals = Silks, colours, more elaborate. S Scott – AAOA has FULL MIKADO costumes.

So this is how it happens. Mr Mathieson's frail and mournful surface dissipates. He's a fiend of an organiser. He comes to the front of the meeting and takes charge and soon has the whole room confessing to skills and contacts and signing up to do special favours. There is nobody he does not commandeer. It's all written down; he gets promises that he intends to see kept. In no time he is Production Manager and Mrs Mathieson is

Production Secretary. Uncle George is happy just to scribble notes.

People grow trusting and optimistic and talk as if they have been waiting all their lives to be useful. They form committees and sub-committees for this, that and the other. Mr Mathieson scolds us to be brief and keep to the point. Just as I think there can't be anything left to talk about, Uncle George whispers a few words in Mr Mathieson's ear. He nods.

He says, And now George here reminds me of another crucial matter and that is fund raising. We need to raise money . . .

More hands go up. We hear more ideas and make more lists. The *Burnhead & District Advertiser* might publicise any fund-raising events for free. Some of the ladies will organise a raffle. The shops will have collecting tins on their counters. Mrs Mather will suggest to Mr Mather a donation from the Round Table.

Aye, fine, Mr Mathieson says, but we need something bigger, a big event that'll raise a good sum. It's dear, opera.

And soon there's talk of a ceilidh. It's to be in the shed at the farm, once it's painted. A date is set, ticket prices decided. Folk will flock to support such a good cause, tickets will go on sale throughout Burnhead. Trestle tables can be arranged, plus a few chairs. Mr McArthur can find straw bales for extra seating but insists it'll have to be soft soles only; boot nails could spark on the concrete. Jimmy Brock's brother-in-law in Annbank lives next door to a man who gets up an accordion band every Hogmanay and Burns Night; he'll do it no bother for beer and expenses and maybe a wee fee. The ladies will do a tea. Tea will be extra so we'll make a bit more that way.

Sounds like a real old-fashioned barn dance, Luke says. I've been to plenty of those! Lila, is the gas connected here? Does this work?

No mention in the notes, of course, of my heart boiling with jealousy as Joe's attention wanders. I can see him out of the corner of my eye but I sense it anyway, his focus lengthening across the room and alighting on Senga and Linda and Deirdre. He doesn't need to wink though I can see he may want to. They're drawing themselves up straighter and turning about to show themselves at better angles, as if he jerks wires tied to their ankles and wrists. They whisper together, mouths behind hands, eyes on him. He tips his head back against the wall and inspects them down his hawkish nose. He shifts without taking his eyes away, pulls his arms apart and clasps his hands behind his head, glances once at George and then looks back to them. The room has grown stale. I cannot move away from the tang that now comes raw from his armpits – in fact I draw closer. The smell is rank and urgent and, this late in the day and in a hot room, not quite clean. I want to roll in it. I will stand inside the circle of his odour if it chokes me, in the space around him that nobody enters without invitation, the territory of the air he fills with sweating and breathing and base male habits I suddenly want to know all about. Blood is rushing in my ears so I barely hear what is being said but I will occupy this space because it belongs to me. Across the room Senga and Linda and Deirdre squirm and preen, the sniggering tarts. He's only doing this with them because they don't matter. It's a compliment to me.

Hey! It works after all, Luke says, and there is a burst of orange in the room as the gas fire whups and sighs. I blink and my eyes smart in the sudden brightness. I have not noticed how, without the lights on, the air in here has descended and enshrouds us in charcoal gauze.

Luke says, So hey, no need to sit here in the cold. Let me get you some more tea. Lila, wanna let me get rid of some of these papers?

The meeting goes on, words swill around me. It's been a clear day and the music room curtains have not been drawn. The sky is darkening from turquoise towards the amethyst dusk and the Pow Farm fields at the horizon are the colour of a deepening bruise. This window faces east so I can't see the sun going down behind the sea, but in the sky over Mr McArthur's land the moon and the first few stars appear. It's getting late when people finally leave. Joe does not join in the goodbyes, but disappears upstairs. People spill down the path and on to the road and linger. They stand and talk, voices rising softly in the air; any excuse to breathe in the smell of the cooling land in the gloaming and the freshwater scent of the night to come. Senga and Linda and Deirdre and Enid circle round Billy and one or two other straggling boys who can't be older than thirteen. Their muttered and breathy words mingle with the grown-up talk. I watch from the doorway. My mind is elsewhere; part of me is with Joe upstairs, of course. But I am thinking too of the sharp marram grass at the shore's edge and imagining a campfire burning in a hollow dip in the dunes and I picture Joe there, free from the tugging eyes of those girls. He is with me and there is nothing to fear. Wrapped together in the firelight, we are alone and separate from the others, swaying in obedience to some tide, some warm, gathering wave of optimism, a pride that pulses through us – it is nothing less than youth and love and the promise of more tides of love to come, swamping us and washing us away – and of all these he is talking to me softly under the moon, with a sweet curling of his mouth.

14

G eorge tried to instil some discipline. He began sentences with 'Speaking as the producer and musical director'. At odd moments he pulled out the folding baton he now carried at all times and practised his conducting technique in front of an invisible orchestra. He addressed Lila, Joe and Fleur by the parts they were singing instead of their names and gave them written schedules: the mornings on private practice and coaching with him, and part of the afternoon on other tasks, rest or quiet study. He gave each of them a tuning fork and taught them how to practise alone without the piano. Evenings were taken up with proper rehearsals with combinations of principals, chorus and band. In between times he was overseer of the set, lighting, costumes and publicity. He never stopped.

Lila felt sullenly that if she obeyed his rules it would be because they coincided with her wishes. She was still obliquely grateful towards him but Uncle George was no longer in command of his glamour; it seemed not so much his own as a reflected gilt that belonged, really, to the London world he seemed less and less a part of. But she had to remember that she needed him as a springboard from which to launch herself on her London life with Joe. Late one night when the house was quiet she pulled out the largest of the suitcases from the cupboard under the stairs, took it up to her room and hid it under her bed. No need for declarations. By stealth and in tiny stages she would pack and be ready to leave with him. She would share Uncle George's flat until she and Joe could get married. Lots of students got married. They wouldn't wait until everybody thought they could afford it, they would just do it and be happy even if poor (she knew she would be marvellous at managing on very little). She tried not to let her spent love for Uncle George – more often now just plain George – show in her eyes. Even as a toppled idol he was, for the time being, essential.

If she had had to, she would have invented ways of throwing herself into Joe's path. But it wasn't necessary; they were tumbled in together to 'the production' and its demands – no life outside it was much thought of. Sometimes Lila minded the lack of a decent courting distance between them. If only she could have retired to a cool room sometimes, miles from where he undressed, washed, shaved and slept and where she could not see him, or hear him sing or talk or laugh – if she could have kept a small space for recovery from so much of him so soon – she thought she might, though she had already lost her heart, be able to lose it a little less abjectly. For there was no escaping the risk, run a thousand times every day, that he could by some jokey or ambiguous remark or unconscious omission – a cue for a small compliment not taken, an elusive reference to the rest of his life that seemed not to include her in it – plunge her into hours of private misery, hours spent shaving an inter-pretation out of his words strip by strip until she exposed the buried place where she decided that he had said more or less what she needed him to have said.

There were days when she woke up feeling over-exposed and fearful, thrown out of sleep with unbearable abruptness; the light reaching through her window cast much too bright a beam over her love for him and threatened to reveal it as hopeless. Then she would hide under the pillow and wish for a few more hours' relief from the effort of getting him to love her. But soon she would hear from the room above his cough, a grunt, the squeak of the mattress, and then her heart would start pounding and the day would quicken with meaning. By now she knew how to time her own comings and goings so that at the foot of the attic stairs she would happen upon him tousled, stripped to the waist and smelling of bed and skin. She fancied that in his extravagant Ah, and a very good morning to you, *la bella* Liù! and his accompanying, rippling scale to *lo, lo, lo, lo*! he puffed out his chest just for her. And then she felt that some unnamed, benevolent force at work between them made it inevitable that one day she would wake up with his adoration glittering like a star over her. She would be glad, watching his thick bare back as he strolled away down the landing, that nothing could stop her imagining both of them naked in the same bathroom, even if she stopped just short of imagining them there at the same time; while she was learning to accommodate the notion of Bliss of Union as opposed to One Thing Only, location was important. Neither the sand dunes nor the bathroom, which seemed a kind of opposite, was fitting.

George collected the orchestral parts from the station one afternoon and the house filled up even more. The number of boxes sent by the publishers took everyone by surprise; it was sobering, what quantities of music there had to be, how many volumes and pages and hundreds of thousands of notes it took to capture on paper the floating sounds of the opera that to them had been, until now, essentially airborne. *Turandot*, from the stereogram or sung by Fleur, Joe or Lila or played on the piano by George, sounded through the house all day long, and the music had grown easy on their ears, almost simple. Judging by the written music, Puccini had not found it simple at all.

Lila helped George unload the boxes and stack them along the wall in the front hall. Space was already running out. Gordon Black, now appointed chorus master, chief rehearsal pianist and part arranger, had borrowed twenty music stands from Burnhead Academy and they lay in a heap of folded metal just inside the door. Raymond had come home with a Chinese ornamental cutlass, on loan from the Mathiesons, carrying it in a string shopping bag slung over the handlebars; that and a brass gong lent by somebody else lay in a large box labelled

'PROPS'. Enid's mum had ordered thousands of yards of white muslin for the set from the wholesaler in Glasgow, who delivered it direct to 5 Seaview Villas. Bales of it were stacked in the hall waiting for somebody to come up with a way of dyeing it red. (Though he had no idea how it was be done, there had to be red drapery, Joe said, to express Liù's sacrifice of blood. There was also to be white drapery and a huge white paper circle to depict Turandot's coldness and purity and the moon. The only other colour would be black. Black was for death, he said. George said he didn't know about that but a coating of black would flatter the workmanship of the set, which was likely to be shaky.) Meanwhile 5 Seaview Villas was beginning to resemble a badly organised warehouse. Nobody swept around the accruing piles of stuff or opened a window or wiped a surface. The air was sharp with damp, tobacco and musty cloth.

Several of the chairs that had been brought into the music room for the first meeting stayed there. George said he needed them because people were coming and going all the time and he had to be able to sit them down and deal with them in one place. So the back room off the kitchen remained bare, a place where nobody could sit any more unless they perched on a kitchen stool, not that anybody did want to settle for long. It had become no more than a space that people crossed on their way to somewhere else, adding to the sense of transit.

Visitors seemed to arrive in no obvious pattern and often without apparent purpose, and George, who tended to make arrangements without writing anything down or telling any-body else, was at times bamboozled by the traffic. They came for auditions and stayed and talked about costumes instead, or they turned up to discuss transposing the trumpet parts for coronet, or to hand in props or donations of paint, and found themselves singing one of the principal roles. Sometimes they arrived just to be friendly and to see what was going on, they brought cake and then stayed to have some. They brought their curious friends, most of whom found themselves persuaded by George into swelling the ranks, as he put it. The numbers signing up for shed painting, set building, front of house, backstage, chorus and band grew and grew. Within days, at least twenty people knew their way round the kitchen well enough to take over and make pots of tea.

The frequent arrivals and departures dislodged the already precarious domestic rhythms of the house. Fleur's small tyrannies in the details (no drinking straight from bottles, use the butter knife and ketchup ruins decent food) masked an indifference to actual housekeeping, and now that she had the distraction of visitors coming and going, kettles on, expeditions to the farm with George, long sessions of singing, chats on the telephone, she ceased even to pretend to care. There was no discussion about it. She simply took it as read that Princess Turandot was exonerated from household responsibilities.

'I hope nobody's expecting me to know what's for lunch,' she would say around noon, to whoever might be present, 'because I haven't the foggiest. Just help yourselves.'

She was too busy to bother, too happy holding court amid the passing waves of new people which now included Moira Mather and Delia Hunter, who declared her a scream and whom she now called 'the girls'. She had had no idea, she said, what a scream those girls were and how much they all had in common. Nicknames and catchphrases developed. Whenever any two of the girls were together at Seaview Villas they would telephone the absent one to make her feel included, holding the receiver out to the whole room and getting them all to shout hello.

Arrangements in the house collapsed for any or no reason: the hot water gave out because nobody had stoked the Rayburn, in the morning Raymond would iron a stale shirt and wear it again because the laundry was behind. On the day there was nothing but baked beans for tea because there was no bread left for toast, Fleur waved her arms and said, 'Well, just have beans on beans, then!' Her speaking voice was now a little breathy, not unlike Delia Hunter's.

Every day they ran out of something. George made inefficient emergency excursions in the car to pick up milk or cigarettes or lavatory paper. Once or twice Raymond, acting on sudden initiative, would call in at the butchers and arrive home with an oozing parcel of mince that he would disown as soon as he got in, thumping it on the draining board as if it had come into his hands by means he preferred to forget. Sometimes when Joe was working in the music room and she knew she was not squandering any opportunity to be with him, Lila took some of the housekeeping money from the kitchen drawer and went to Burnhead, striding there and back if there was no bus, slipping quickly in and out of the shops and never succumbing to the temptation to pop into Sew Right. Away from him, she would imagine that all that needed to happen for Joe to realise he loved her was for her to walk back into his line of vision; this little break in their proximity was going to be all it took. So she would arrive back laden and breathless, only to find the disorder of the house sliding further towards chaos. A hope that she would deal with it would, in her absence, have hardened into expectation. Still there was no let-up in the flow of visitors. In the lulls between the door closing behind one lot and the sounding of the doorbell, the atmosphere could be a little accusatory.

Enid says, See Joe? You fancy him, don't you?

No.

Away, you do so.

I do not.

You do so. I seen you.

Seen what?

Seen you fancying him. See Joe?

What?

Would you let him go all the way?

I would *not*! Anyway, you fancy Billy.

I field these questions nearly every afternoon. I suppose she notices the change in me from pessimistic little sloth to busy household bee, from aertex and bare legs to back-combing and chiffon accessories, and jumps to the right conclusion, proving that stupid people do well, on the whole, to run with their instincts. It's all they have. Those with more powerful brains too often distrust first impressions; they addle them with the wrong mix of qualification and interpretation until the impressions split into something useless, ideas that refuse to bind and are fit only to be thrown away, like ruined mayonnaise. That is how my mind works, now. It cannot make thoughts and feelings smooth themselves into memories that are clean and whole and assembled unselfconsciously into something that makes sense.

But at least I see what's happening here. I see the need to get a grip on myself, oh yes. I can't go on like this, as if a simple funeral and a houseful of junk are the stuff of opera. They're Life and that's all. And thank God it *is* only in opera that people exist in such idiotic, heightened states and not in Life, unless of course, we put quite tremendous efforts into being inconsolable. I will calm down, because with what feels like my last scrap of common sense I know I have to. My cross-stitch is coming on nicely. People die, of course they do.

Though in between bouts of embroidery I can't just ignore what's in these boxes. There's this:

Burnhead & District Advertiser Thursday 14th July 1960:

BAST director says, 'Look, we've borrowed a tenor!'

Guiseppe Foscari (20) as his picture reveals is the real thing, an Italian tenor with the looks as well as the voice tailor-made for Puccini's famous heroes. Grins George Pettifer, musical director and founder of the Burnhead Association for Singing *Turandot*, 'If you need a tenor and you don't have one, you've got to borrow!' Brought up from London to sing the lead role of Prince Calaf in BAST's upcoming production of *Turandot*, Mr Foscari is challenged but not daunted. 'It is every tenor's dream to sing Calaf. I'm absolutely thrilled to have this opportunity.' And not only is he the real thing, he's home grown! Or almost. Born to Italian parents, his family first settled in Scotland only to abandon these shores for the South. Mr Foscari says the move down south was necessary for family reasons but it is a decision he regrets even though it was long ago. 'I'm absolutely thrilled to be here. Scottish folk are the best in the world and Burnhead is a wonderful place.'

By Staff Reporter Alec Gallagher

Alec Gallagher makes quite a fuss of Joe. He and the photographer spend nearly a whole afternoon together. There isn't a lot to show for it in the paper but Alec says that's not his fault, he wrote a big piece and it got spiked. It's his editor, who says he's not running a fan club.

You can't deny it's a good face even in a blurry photograph, but what it doesn't reveal is that Joe's only five foot five, a good two inches shorter than my mother. When she's in her heels and headdress she dwarfs him and he's sensitive about that.

He's sensitive about his voice as well. Quite often through the music room door I hear Uncle George trying to talk to him about it and then the day comes when he loses patience and shouts sarcastic things about a modicum of accuracy in pitch being a fair expectation. Afterwards he walks around conducting jerkily with his baton as if swatting flies, glowering like an animal you'd know better than provoke.

But I love Joe's voice. I love it all through those wet days in July when rain tips down outside and we all work hard, when among all the comings and goings – the doorbell, the visitors, the telephone – there is always the sound of at least one person singing somewhere in the house. In my room I listen for Joe and I arrange my own practice to coincide with his. Even though we are singing from quite different parts of the opera most of the time, I feel close to him. I love the cloistered, dedicated feeling; even the damp makes me mellow and serious. Outside, summer pleasures that in Burnhead are at the best of times enjoyed under a sun that bestows little heat are rained off altogether; it feels like a kind of approval of our undertaking that the weather tempts nobody out of doors. Gutterings drip and ooze. I listen to the rain and the voices. On the quiet I am selecting and preparing my London clothes, though getting them dry after washing them is impossible in the wet. I filtch from my mother's cupboards, picking things I'm sure she won't miss: nylons, a green silk blouse she's gone off and a white sweater with a spot on it, black Capri pants, her old red patent leather belt, a nearly empty compact, old squashed lipsticks. My case is filling up. I perfect my plans.

Sometimes George summons us to sing for the visitors, to get us used to an audience.

He calls out from the piano, Liù, over here, you first. Let's have '*Signore, ascolta!*'

Everyone is staring at me. My heart hits so hard on the inside of my throat I think I shall choke.

He whispers, Breathe. Forget them. Do it like on the beach. Remember to breathe, sing out past the room.

I fix my eyes on the field beyond the window and sing to Mr McArthur's cows. It's only about two and half minutes long, '*Signore, ascolta!*', and even if you don't know the story of *Turandot* you know from this pleading little lament that nothing nice is heading Liù's way and you want to cry out and warn her. Not that it will help. It's rather in the nature of opera that people don't see these things in time. I do not sing it as well as I can, but there's a burst of applause when I finish and Uncle George is on his feet too, clapping and nodding and showing me off as if I am all his own work, as if he carved me himself out of a piece of driftwood picked up off the beach. My feet are crying out in the pointy shoes but my knees are shaking with joy, because Joe is looking at me.

Now Joe sings '*Nessun dorma*', standing with his feet splayed. Let no-one sleep, he sings. He presses one hand against his chest and offers the empty palm of the other in a turning motion, describing in the air the waves of a gentle sea.

> – *O Principessa,*
> *Nella tua fredda stanza*
> *Guardi le stelle*
> *Che tremano d'amore*

Oh, Princess, he sings, in your cold room you are looking at the stars that tremble with love.

I am only Liù the slave girl, but I know that by *Principessa* he really means me, not Turandot. I know the cold room is mine. He thinks of me lying there below him. Let no-one sleep. I can tell we are both thinking of the same thing, of last night, when again I heard him on the attic stairs in the middle of the night. I lay frozen and unable to breathe, wondering if my door would open. It didn't. We both know that. I lay there while he paused on the landing, his hand just touching the handle. I see his face as he fears to come any closer and decides to retreat once more, and it is not another failure of courage but another triumph of respect for me over his true wishes. But it will not always be so. I picture him turning with manly anguish and regret from my door. Soon I am half-dreaming again for I do not follow the direction of the footsteps after that, only later I hear the soft squeal, like gagged mice, of the attic bed as his weight presses into it again.

He's singing out of one side of his mouth and raising the eyebrow on the other as if for balance, and he girds himself for high notes and prefixes many of the words with a kind of extra half-syllable 'huh-ynn' that helps him locate the note. '*Huh-ynessun dorma*', he sings. At times there is a pushing quality behind the sound as if he is trying to force a small potato down one nostril. His voice cracks on the top note and although his face is already red he blushes even deeper. I think him magnificent.

My mother jumps up and joins him in their final Act III duet '*Che è mai di me?*' and I listen with tingles running up and down my back. Calaf has kissed her and Turandot's struggle is over; she submits, transformed by love. I marvel how opera transcends such trite considerations as the relative ages and heights of the singers: my mother at thirty-six, statuesque and striking with her powerful though unpractised voice and Joe, short, round and an eagle-faced twenty. He can't live without her and she can't hold out against his heroic charm. They sing combatively, locked in a duel to out-express each other. Then Joe advances on her, rises on tiptoe and holds her against his chest. He gazes over her shoulder with a look of faraway longing and then sinks his face into her neck. He's awkward because he does not really want to be doing these things with my mother. It's me he wants. As I watch, our music room evaporates and dawn breaks over the Imperial Palace of ancient Peking. Love conquers all.

And I'm very calm again. Christine has been organising me and now I have a list. She's given me the name of a hairdresser who she says is the best one in Burnhead. I will want my hair tidying she says, since I'm not shampooing or doing much to it myself at the moment.

And you need a skip, she tells me. The council takes paper on a Wednesday as long as it's in green bags. And if you ask them they'll do a special pick up, anything at all you want rid of but they will charge, oh and keep organic matter separate, she says, tapping the list. I've got green bags I can loan you. I'll leave them in the porch, will I? You just need to ring them. Or will I ring them for you?

I'll get round to it, I say. When I'm dressed.

She leaves it at that and after she goes I think, now she's been, there's no hurry after all. I settle to a bit of cross-stitch. I don't know where the time goes.

So when I do ring the number for the bin men I get an answering machine telling me to call back in office hours. And Sheena the caterer who is on the case (as Christine says) for after the funeral but who has a query about the ham sand-wiches has an answering machine that starts, Hiyaaaa!!! I feel foolish leaving a message about mustard and no mustard and white and wholemeal so I ring off before I finish.

When I call the hairdresser it rings and rings and rings. Is everyone on holiday?

Now I'm in the mood to get on, though, and I won't be discouraged. Christine's got me fired up. Some bin bags seem to have appeared from somewhere. Not that I'm about to start just shoving papers in them. There is far too much sorting out still to be done. I don't want to throw anything away that I might later find I need.

15

With Fleur no longer much present, let alone in charge of the kitchen, Lila seized the chance to satisfy Joe's stomach. It would be demure and wifely and an endeavour he would surely love her for, though thanks to Raymond she found herself having to do it far too often with mince. Twice she produced it stewed in the ordinary way, serving it up in a bumpy grey slick.

The third time Raymond dumped mince on the draining board she knew she had to do something. Once they were in London they would never touch it again, but how could she convey to Joe now that mince was the last thing she would cook if she had any choice in the matter? She had to surprise him. She wanted to deliver to him on the end of a fork mince that revealed her originality and cleverness. Her cooking would make him curious about her, and having got him intrigued she would preserve the aura of mystery and feminine authority around herself by revealing none of her culinary secrets.

Fleur's two or three basic cookery books only confirmed the limitations of mince, but one line at the end of a recipe for making rissoles caught her attention: 'Cooked, finely diced chicken may be substituted for the minced beef.' She remembered seeing, in 'Broadcast Suggestions for the Housewife' (the only page she could understand) in George's current copy of the *Listener*, a recipe for Summer Chicken. Chicken was too expensive, but if mince and chicken were interchangeable then she could make it with mince instead. She fetched the *Listener* and made a shopping list. The recipe contained a great many other things as well as the chicken, some of which she had never tasted, and it sounded different and exciting enough for Joe.

Nobody ate quite everything that they found in their Summer Mince. Joe left the prawns and the green pepper (that Lila had had to go to four greengrocers to find), George left the pineapple and Fleur the spring onion, but only because of her breath, she said. Raymond did best, leaving only a small, generalised heap on his plate, but his lips swelled up from the paprika and chilli powder. Lila looked at Joe. She knew that her eyes were shining too hard, as if enamelled or like dolls' eyes, because she needed his praise too much.

'Did you like it, Joe?' she said.

He said, 'Aah! Such splendours! The splendours of the continental kitchen! Dear Liù, what wonders you have performed, and would I could do you justice. But alas, I am not *pisciverous*.'

He pushed with his finger at one of the curling grey prawns on his plate, pretending to be surprised when everybody laughed. 'I mean only what I say. I am not pisciverous, a fish-eater. Indeed I am, you might say, not a savoury person. I am a *sweet* person. I have a very, very sweet tooth.'

So Lila turned her attention to puddings. With everything else that was happening she had no time for all the weighing and mixing and baking and steaming that the proper recipes called for, so she stocked up on packets promising, at a fraction of the trouble, a blancmange or a whip, a table cream or chiffon – *desserts to please the whole family*. Dessert rather than pudding would be more in line with Joe's tastes anyway, she felt, and she liked the pictures on the packets of a hostess in a perfect apron bearing to the table her trophy, an airy froth piped into minarets and studded with exotic fruits. And they were so easy! They made her feel modern and carefree.

The packets spilled their contents in a trickle of pastel-coloured dust, dry and silky as talcum powder and smelling the same, sometimes with tiny sharp crystals of something that looked like glass. When mixed with the animating liquid – milk or water, sometimes hot, sometimes cold – and beaten, the powder burst into life, coagulating into lurid gobs that clogged the whisk and ballooned up to the top of the bowl, releasing fumes more redolent of a colour, often pink, than anything edible. Lila would feel as she placed it in the pantry to set that she was leaving it in peace to calm down.

But her desserts, no matter what she did to them with glacé cherries and tiny silver balls and hundreds and thousands, tasted of sugar and chalk with a whiff of perfume, and were not the focus of anyone's interest. She soon gave up telling them, as she brought one to the table in the manner of the lady on the packet, how thoughtfully she had chosen today's flavour or how carefully she had placed the decoration that she was about to destroy with one plunge of the spoon. When Uncle George bothered to look up he was usually weary and watchful of Joe, more inclined to smoke than to eat and too busy making lists to notice what was on his plate. Her mother, humming from her latest conversation on the telephone, seldom had more than a few moments to spare. She would always be just off out; the girls would be arriving any minute in Moira's car to pick her up for some excursion: talking to the printers, buying trimmings for the headdresses, choosing outfits for the ceilidh. Having just touched up her lipstick, she would take only a mouthful or two off the end of her spoon, gingerly and with a show of teeth. But because she was happier she was not unkind, and showed Lila some spasmodic appreciation: *I don't know where I'd be without you.*

Since her offerings were not really for them, Lila did not mind. But Joe turned out to be a shoveller. She put his apparent lack of table manners down to superior appetite and found it slightly thrilling to watch such relish. In the congealing lull afterwards she would scrape plates and let the inevitability of the coming afternoon settle on her. She tried to be at the sink with her back to him so that she did not have to see him rise to go. But she would hear the scrape of the chair and have to turn in hope of a smile or a look, and once he was gone she would stuff into the most meagre half-glance all the meaning she could make it hold and try to let it be enough. But she hated the afternoons. When, still standing at the sink, she got a glimpse of how deep her desolation might go in the space of the hours that stretched ahead, she would seek out company even if, as it usually was, it had to be Enid's.

Enid comes round on Sundays, now, and on it goes. See Joe? What about him? You fancy him, don't you? I do not. You do so. She seems not to be Gathered very much any more, but I don't want her to think I'm interested enough to ask why.

One day we wander up to the farm, on George's instructions. I am to get a feel for the space. I go reluctantly because Joe might be around later and I might miss him, and because I resent doing what Uncle George tells me.

Enid gets bored early on and we walk in silence. Sherpa the dog meets us and bounces along and we talk to him instead. The yard is deserted but the yellow door of the farmhouse stands open. Sherpa lopes over the overgrown grass and stands barking into the narrow hall, his whole body twisting. I peer in. One dim, hanging bulb fails to light the place but manages to stain the air. Mr McArthur appears, holding a length of rope. He is too big and looming for the doorway and in his farm clothes and boots he seems unsuitable, generally, for indoors, even an indoors as shabby as this.

Aye well, girls, you're here just at the right time. Come on, he says, and turns and disappears back into the house.

We are too sullen with each other to express any suspicion about what dire thing involving rope we might be here at just the right time for, so we follow across the mud-scented hall and through a flat door with a ochre patina of grime and smoke. Billy stands in the front room. Both his arms are stretched around one end of a tilting upright piano that is resting half-on and half-off a low platform on castors. He looks hot and fierce.

Hiya there, Billy.

I am showing Enid that I know him better than she does, staking my claim. Even if he is just a farm boy he is mine to say hello to first.

He nods at me and says, I'm needing a hand. I cannae lift the back end on, the wheels keep slipping. Dad, get the rope round it again and pull from the front.

He grunts and nods at Enid and says, You, hold the wheels steady. Don't let it run away.

To me he says, Here, you help me lift this end.

I go to help him with a slight simper. With a couple of pushes and pulls we manage to get the thing up and balanced on the set of wheels.

From what feels like a long way off I hear a noise, a small scream that even so may be coming from me, and I feel a tightening and a tugging as if a long, invisible piece of my clothing has got caught under the bottom edge of the piano. Nobody says anything.

The space the piano leaves against the wall is brighter and cleaner than the rest of the room and shows that the flowers on the paper were once two colours, lilac and green, before they faded together and aged into shadows of themselves. On the newly exposed area of floor weightless rolls of dust eddy over the linoleum in the air disturbed by our hauling and panting. The smells of a trapped past lift into the room: camphor and book covers mix with candlewax and the old bready scent of wallpaper stuck on decades ago with flour and water. Age and neglect smell the same everywhere, I think; this place reminds me of Seaview Villas. Enid straightens up from crouching by the wheels, and claps her hands. I feel the smack of palm against palm as if they are my own.

We're no finished yet, Billy says. It's going out. It's to go in the shed yet.

Mr McArthur says, You're daft, Billy, I'm telling you.

Billy glowers. It's my piano and it's going where I please.

Mr McArthur turns on me. See your man, your George? After one thing and another, now it's to be a piano. A piano for rehearsals, a bloody *piano*. I've a farm to run, I've no time to go shifting pianos.

But how can he do the opera without one? I say, protective of Uncle George for the first time in a while.

This is no a bloody concert hall.

We just need to get it to the shed, Billy says. Pay no attention.

It's not my fault, I say. Or Uncle George's.

Mr McArthur glares back at Billy across the top of the piano. Well, you'll no be wanting me now you've got the lassies here. Eh, Billy?

He looks angry and strong enough to lift the piano single-handed and hurl it across the room. He slaps the top of it with the flat of his thick hand and strides out. We listen to the tramp of his boots, the clatter of clawed feet and a bark as he curses the dog. The front door slams.

I can feel my hand stinging as though it were mine that slammed down on the cold lid of the piano. I raise it to my lips and stroke it across my mouth. My poor hand is sore and trembling.

Enid tosses her head prettily. She has seen Doris Day do it exactly like this. Billy makes his eyes deliberately sleepy and looks away.

Your dad, he's maybe just in a bad mood, I say.

This is how I used to explain my mother's behaviour to myself, before *Turandot*. I want to tell Billy that I understand what it is to live with an unpredictable adult.

It's because of the piano, he says. You just need to leave him. It doesn't last.

I think it's very rude, in front of us, Enid says.

I see the effect she's after. She thinks it's attractive to flounce and insist on feminine privileges and nice manners. The Doris Day tricks are embarrassing the way she does them, like an overgrown child still playing in her mother's shoes, too old to play dressing-up but fooling nobody because she clearly isn't doing it like a proper grown-up either. I seem already to have marked myself out as separate from all that where Billy is concerned, I just want to talk to him as if he were real, but I feel a sudden flush of embarrassment because what if this is what I'm like with Joe?

Just you shut up, Billy says to Enid. You pull from the front and keep the door open.

I half expect her to storm off but her eyes are gleaming back at him and she gives one elaborate finger brush of her hair and does as she is told. The piano rolls forward with a squeak and a boom from its insides that sounds like a guitar strummed in a cave. Enid helps the trolley over the doorjamb, while Billy and I push.

It is extraordinary how cold I suddenly feel, although when we walked up the track it was a warm day. And how heavy the load, as if nobody else is helping. It is so heavy. I feel as if I am moving this thing all alone.

Laboriously, slowly, we make our way down the hall, the castors sticking on the linoleum. When we ease the piano over the front step there is a wild, stray planking of jammed notes that raises a flurry of small birds out of their secret places in the garden and up they go, little frayed parcels of bone wrapped in feathers swooping over the wire fence and across the field. Away from the sick light of the hall and in the bright air of the afternoon, we pause. Billy lifts the piano top, peers in and pokes around with one hand to check that none of the hammers is stuck or broken. A fustiness belonging to the house clings to the piano; a smell of rusty strings and dead coal fires rises from the carcase like a dying exhalation. In the bleached outdoor light the shadows that hide in the corners and under the slope of the keyboard lid are revealed as simple dirt and the once polished surface is a yellowy grey as if the sulphurous air of the front room has soaked into the wood.

I notice that Enid has not exerted herself enough to get her face shiny never mind sweaty, but she draws a hand across her forehead and widens her eyes at Billy, stretches her arms up behind her head, lifts and drops her hair, and sighs with exhaustion.

Billy says, Keep her steady. I'm just away to get some sacks.

I stand there keeping her steady. It is delicious following orders, and I feel a pang that it is Billy and not Joe telling me what to do. Enid tests the length of her arms and examines her nails from a distance. I lift the keyboard lid and pick out my aria with one finger until Billy comes back with an armful of sacks, head down as he walks along, assessing the ground we have to cross. The shed seems a long way away.

We'll put these down where it's rough, he says, setting the pile on top of the piano.

We trundle our load across the yard, manoeuvring the tiny castors over cracks where camomile and vibrant willowherb sprout – weeds so jaunty and bitter-smelling they seem ferti-lised on neglect – around dips and hollows in the concrete where slicks of rich emerald slime grow across the oily surfaces of puddles that never dry up. Billy places the sacks carefully to avoid filth and uneven patches. We go slowly, the squeak of the castors mingling with the suck of the wind in the sycamores. We are too wary of one another to pretend we are having fun, or perhaps we are all too desperate to be taken seriously to draw attention to how silly we must look.

Still I have a lonely feeling, as if I am doing all this by myself.

Sherpa appears and sniffs around the piano, escorting us in this way until we reach the shed. We push the piano up a ramp of ribbed concrete at the doorway. It shudders all the way, notes rattling from inside in hysterical disorder. Enid laughs. I catch a look of pain on Billy's face.

It'll be all right, I whisper. You can get it tuned again.

Billy makes a face. My mum'd kill me.

I thought you said it was yours.

It is now. It was hers.

Enid is still doing Doris Day, as if everything in the world has

been put there just to enliven her. She laughs and plays with
Sherpa as if she's never seen a dog before or as if Sherpa is, of
the species, uniquely and irresistibly captivating. She jumps up
and runs forward with him and yanks at the high sliding door
of the shed. It grinds open, she disappears inside, switches the
lights on and out comes a high yelp of surprise. I strain to see in
but can't. Enid comes back and I glance at Billy and dart away
to the entrance myself, leaving them steadying the piano on the
ramp.

What makes me gasp is the transformation from farm shed
to the cool hangar where I now stand. I take a few steps in,
gazing. The breezeblock walls have been splashed with bucket-
loads of whitewash and are so vibrant they almost buzz. The
metal spars above my head are now free of cobwebs and wisps
of plastic sheeting, the floor is clear of straw, stacked timber
and tarpaulins, and every trace of spilled engine oil and dirt has
gone. Here and there are freshly laid concrete patches and the
whole place prickles with the tang of new paint and disin-
fectant. And it is huge.

I see for the first time in my life that it is possible to be excited
by whiteness, by nothingness, by mere space. I want to clasp
Uncle George's hands and tell him that now I understand, and I
believe. I believe in space and emptiness and the white desert in
which anything can happen because here, nothing is confined
and there can be no concealment. I want to run and shout and
sing in all this air, in this joyful *availability* of air, this space that
is waiting to have my sound spilled into it. I try a few scales and
each note swirls and melts into the one that follows, in a
rushing, ecstatic whirl of echoes. Something else, something
strange is happening. If even the white space has limits, those
limits surround me like mirrors. I am seeing myself from the
outside, as if free of the constraint of also being me, and I think
I see a person who is very nearly relevant, whose presence in
this white space may even be called for. I skip into the middle of
the floor and whoop. It does not escape me that reaching into

this space alone and leaving Billy and Enid somewhere in the dark behind me is an important part of my excitement. I laugh back at them, too loud, to try to include them, but only as my audience. But still I cannot rid myself of the feeling that they are not really there. Surely I am alone.

Billy calls from the entrance. Come on. We're nearly there, a wee bit further and we're in.

Together we shove and the piano slides over the top of the ramp, rattles down and rights itself on the floor of the shed, but I hardly notice that we have got it in safely because my foot is caught underneath. The full weight of the piano rolls over it. Enid and Billy and the cool white shed disappear.

I hear a crash like boulders falling and a noise like a bomb going off inside the piano. But it is my head that feels like the crater, exploding with ringing notes from deepest bass to the highest, shrill and desperate. A real scream rises from my throat and I am suddenly awake with pain, standing in nightclothes outside Seaview Villas and under a dark sky. My mother's piano is upturned and split on the patch of front lawn, its innards disgorged and vibrating with twanging sounds that mix with the pulsing glare of the streetlights across the road. In the orange light my foot is spilling bad brown blood and a cold wind flattens my dressing gown against my body.

Hands tug at me. Christine's. Something quilted that makes a glassy noise and smells of cigarettes is pulled around me, someone's anorak. I hear mention of reasonable limits, of fucking four o'clock in the fucking morning. Back into the house we go.

———•◦•———

16

Billy and Enid stood by the piano in the doorway and watched as Lila whooped and twirled and danced and sang.

Enid pursed her mouth and said secretly, 'If you ask me she's not right in the head. She's just showing off.'

Billy glared. 'No she's not. *She's* not the showing off type. Not her.'

Then he called through the doorway, 'Come on. We're nearly there, a wee bit further and we're in.'

Lila returned to the entrance and all together they shoved. The piano slid over the top of the ramp, rattled down and righted itself on the floor of the shed.

Enid marched into the middle and looked round. 'There's no stage,' she announced. 'Where's the stage?'

It was a sensible question, to Lila's surprise. She hadn't thought of it.

'They're building it straight after the ceilidh,' Billy said. 'Out of beer crates.'

'Beer crates?'

'Aye. They're after getting thousands of beer crates. Your Uncle George says wee travelling companies used to do it with beer crates and we're to do the same.'

Lila didn't understand but left it to Enid to say so. 'What do you mean, *beer crates*? What have beer crates to do with it?'

Billy was strolling around the walls, scratching at the paint and rubbing his fingers together. 'They need to be the old wooden ones, of course,' he said nonchalantly, turning to answer Lila. 'They're all getting the fancy plastic ones now, the breweries, they'll give you the old ones for nothing. You turn them upside down and nail them together on the inside, like you're making a big raft. Loads of them, hundreds, thousands, you can make it any size.'

'Oh, that'll look just dandy,' Enid said.

'Mr Brock's lending the coal truck to get them brought. You cover them with cloth or canvas or something and then you paint it,' Billy said. 'You can make hills. Steps. Even buildings. 'Course, you use other timber as well, to fix it all together. But mainly it's crates.'

He made his way back to the piano and stood with his hands hovering over the keys. He nodded up to the far end of the shed. 'And then they're to hang cloth down the back there to cover the wall and the back doors, and they're putting loads more cloth at the sides. And lights, they're to be hanging lights up in front, proper stage lights.'

Enid seemed more pleased with this. Billy looked up from the keyboard, smiled at her and played a chord.

'Right,' he said, closing the lid. 'C'mon out of here.'

They wandered back to the house. None of them was able to say anything that would either prolong or end their time together; the only sound was the breeze in the sycamores. In late July their leaves were already a dark, bitter green and against the white sky they flapped to and fro like black rags. It was the kind of day with no real weather except for the wind that blew all other features away, a day when the sun would push neither light nor heat through the clouds. Everything betrayed its truer listlessness; the sparrows that flittered around the tree trunks and pecked in the yard seemed elderly and disappointed. They gathered on the fence and waited for the day to end like creatures sagging in a queue, too ballasted with weariness to hold themselves straight. The smell of manure dust from the yard mixed with a sour green scent off the fields.

Enid pranced ahead across the old garden in front of the house. Picking her way over a heap of tractor tyres and balancing on a tipped-over zinc tub almost lost in the long grass, she turned to check that Billy was watching her, and then she stretched into the dingy wreckage of the flowerbeds and squealed as a rosehip caught her sleeve. She pulled at lupins and catmint that were either dead or gone to seed. Billy, from a distance, did watch.

Lila looked away down the track towards Seaview Villas. She was picturing Joe in the attic, his eyes closed but not asleep and lying not on the camp bed but on a bed more appropriate to Joe and to Prince Calaf: something carved and grand, a soft, noble, romantic bed that would bless them both when they lay in it together. She tried to make him open his eyes and think of her and remember her face, but she could not make it work. She felt isolated and jealous. Uncle George would be standing guard, idling in the hall with his plans and lists, talking on the telephone and frowning against the smoke snaking up his cheek and into his eyes from the cigarette that was now always in his mouth. His lips had altered, thinning at the corners into tight shadows deep enough to hold the smouldering stump permanently in place.

She was wearing again the dirndl skirt with the white blouse but had reverted to her flat sandals because the court shoes had blistered her feet. Staring away down the track, she wanted to be dressed in anything else in the world, to be standing any-where in the world other than here on pocked concrete with her hair whipped in her face, her confusion exposed by white, shifting darts of light slanting down through the trees. She craved any sky, even one ready to split with lightning and storms, rather than this *nothing* sky; she wanted thunder and trouble to pit herself against. She closed her eyes. If she could just be out of clothes altogether, out of these garments designed for some mistaken idea of her, out of the big wrong shoes. She felt a touch on her arm.

'You'll be needing something to drink.'

Billy turned back towards the house without waiting for an

answer. Enid looked up from her flower picking and scuttled after him through the front door. Lila heard her laughing down the hall. On the grass she set the zinc tub straight for a table, sat down on one of the tyres and pulled at the sorry bunch of flowers Enid had picked and thrown down. Sherpa padded over and lay at her feet, sniffing once or twice as she chucked leaves and petals at him. Billy came out with orange squash in three different glasses on a tray, Enid followed with biscuits. It was a self-conscious picnic to begin with. Enid rolled around making a daisy chain and when it was finished Billy refused to wear it so she threw handfuls of grass at him and attached the daisy chain round Sherpa's neck. They all laughed. They fed biscuits to the dog and Billy raised his glass and said cheers and then clammed up.

After a while Enid said, 'So your dad gets mad just about moving a piano.'

'He's not mad, he's upset because it was my mum's,' Billy said. 'She passed away.'

'I thought that was ages ago,' she said.

'Eight years. What's that got to do with it? People get upset when somebody dies, haven't you heard?'

'Yes, but they get over it after a while,' she said, informatively.

Billy scowled at her.

'Maybe if it's true love,' Lila said, using the chance to be the sensitive and operatic one, 'you never get over it.'

'I don't ken about that, I was only ten,' Billy said. 'Anyhow, that's no the point. My dad gets upset when he sees stuff that reminds him.'

'But he must see the piano every day,' Enid insisted, 'in the house.'

'We're never in the front room. It just sits.'

'Well, maybe it's better putting it in the shed and people getting the use,' she said. 'Maybe he'll be pleased once he gets used to it.'

'That's what I told him!' Billy said. 'I told him it'd be good to get it played. I told him a bit of music wouldn't hurt. That's why he's letting the opera in the shed. Plus he likes your Uncle George, says he's a character.' He bit off half of a biscuit and chewed it with his mouth open, then fed the rest to Sherpa. 'He doesn't like thinking about my mum, that's all.'

Lila recalled the stale face of Mr McArthur and thought that he might not be old at all, just tired.

'Believers don't get as upset as ordinary people,' Enid said. 'Believers know that people don't really die. They get gathered unto the Lord's eternal embrace.'

Billy and Lila looked at each other.

'You're to be happy for people when they die, the minister says.' Enid always tried to make things sound simple and tidy when she was cornered, and cornered was what she was – the only one in her class to be deprived of a father by the war. Others further up the school whose fathers hadn't come back had taken the brunt of the teasing, though Enid was still sometimes singled out for not even having been born when he died. Though she clung to the simple and tidy idea that she was lucky for never knowing him (for how could you miss what you'd never had?) she knew her ignorance of him and his absence for what they were, a double loss.

'What do you know about it?' Billy said. He dipped his head so that his hair covered his eyes. Sherpa edged further along the grass towards him and pushed his snout under his hand. 'Nobody believes that rubbish, anyway. My dad doesn't and I don't either. See church? It's rubbish.'

'That's blasphemy. If you don't repent that you'll be cast from the loving presence,' Enid said smoothly. 'And we're not a church, we're—'

'Aw, Enid, just shut it,' Lila said. 'We don't need to hear all that again. You know you don't go any more.'

'Well, *that's* nice. Oh, pardon *me*, just because I'm missing Gathering and doing you a favour instead,' Enid said, rolling her eyes, offering Lila a chance to stay on her side. Lila looked away and pulled at the grass. For a while nobody spoke.

Enid got up. 'Well, I'm away then,' she said, planting her feet and folding her arms. 'I'll just be off.' She waited. 'Somewhere I don't get insulted. For my beliefs.'

It was Lila's last chance. 'Cheerio, then,' she said without looking up. 'See you.'

Billy had hold of Sherpa's front paws and was shaking his head into the dog's grinning face; their silky hair mixed and tangled together.

Enid, with a final glazed look at Billy, stalked off. Lila watched her swing down the track, heading, no doubt, straight to the Locarno and Senga McMillan.

In the lull that followed, Billy kept his face buried in the dog's neck. Enid turned around twice, walking backwards for a couple of steps before spinning back and striding on. The third time she turned Lila lifted a hand and waved, then she took up the broken daisy chain and began shredding it in her fingers.

Billy looked up. 'So, that your friend away home in a huff?'

'I don't care. She's a pain,' Lila said. She wanted to go, too, but she would have to wait until Enid was too far away to see her get up and leave. She might loiter at the end of the track until Lila caught up.

'She's just a bit daft,' Billy said.

Over Billy's shoulder, Lila watched the tractor roll across the back of the yard and stop. Sherpa pulled away from Billy and fixed his attention on Mr McArthur as he swung down from the seat. Billy turned round.

'That's him getting in the straw for the ceilidh,' he said.

'What d'you need straw for?'

'Never been to a ceilidh? Straw bales, for sitting on, round the side. For falling over, if you've had a few too many. Eh?'

'There's not to be a proper bar, there's only to be soft drinks and tea. Mr Mathieson says we've not got a licence and things get out of hand if there's drink.'

Billy laughed. 'Aye well, we'll see. Mr Mathieson won't
know what's going on round the back, will he? Maybe some
folk'll bring in a wee bottle or two. For private consumption,
eh?'

'You're not going to get drunk, are you?'

'All depends. You'll be going yourself, will you?' he said. It
was a statement with no possible answer, somehow less than
either a question or an invitation.

'Uh-huh, I might,' Lila said, trying to sound faraway. 'I
might, I suppose.'

She wanted Billy to think she had the ceilidh under consideration, that she might have a choice, but Joe would be there
so of course she was going. She had already cast and directed
the event in her head in the same way Uncle George moved her
about during rehearsals, pushing her around, making her look
one way when she sang this, lifting her eyes here, hands there,
to sing that. The ceilidh night was to be not just the first time
she and Joe danced together – *Do you remember our first
dance? Oh, of course I do* – but the night of their first kiss and
proper declaration. They would whisper the words, their faces
still warm from the dancing. As was natural Joe would say it
first, having led her outside away from the music and lights,
holding her hand tight as they breathed in the grassy, cool air.
Oh, Liù, I love you. And she would whisper back, *Oh, Calaf, I
love you, too,* and then they would kiss, a powdery and
fragrant, dreamy, private kiss; no wetness, no cat-calls in
the background, only music. Lila had already chosen the spot,
avoiding the slimy trough up next to the fence with the
permanent cloud of midges above it. She would steer them
clear of the nettles on the verge so that they could pause
naturally by the field gate where there was a clump of mea-
dowsweet and a spriggy briar rose that would, since this was to
be perfection, offer up its scent to lovers and the night air. It
would not rain.

It was deflating to look at Billy and be reminded that other people would be there too, milling in the background with their eyes fixed on the same surroundings, degrading the scene.

'Are you coming or no?' Billy said.

'Oh. Well, I'll be going I suppose, right enough.'

'Right, well. So. I'll get a dance with you, will I?'

Sitting cross-legged, Billy leaned towards her a little, stretching his forearms on to the grass in front of him, close enough for Lila to smell his skin. She was horrified by how acutely she felt that he was already touching her, through air. He wore a jersey that looked scratchy but his arms as they came around her would be soft over the hard muscle, the hairs fuzzy and sweet.

'So you'll give me a dance?'

She must be making a mistake. She could not want Billy this close. She wanted the smells of all Joe's soaps and bottles in the bathroom cabinet at Seaview Villas, the sweet mix of them with the sharp sweat of Joe's skin, clove and Elastoplast and something rich and spiced and antiseptic, like very clean marmalade.

'I'm not staying here!' she announced.

At once Billy leaned back and got up. 'Aye, right. Right, off home then, are you?' he said, scraping his feet on the grass. He nodded over towards the tractor and trailer. 'I need to go and give him a hand, anyway.'

'No, I mean I'm not staying here,' Lila said, as she stood up. '*Here*. I'm away to London. I'm going as soon as the opera's finished. I need to go.'

'I'm not stopping you. See you.'

It was not until she had almost reached Seaview Villas and could hear Joe's voice swimming out from the music room that Lila managed to clear her head of the atmosphere of Billy, his salt and animal skin, the scents of both sea and earth. She crept into the house and up to her room, seeking peace.

I hear you've been a bit restless at night. Have you ever consulted a doctor about this? Has this been a long-term difficulty for you, the noctambulism?

Dr Chowdry has her hair in a bun and wears a crossed pink ribbon pinned to her front. She has large spectacles with red frames.

The what?

The restlessness at night.

Nessun dorma, you mean?

Dr Chowdry blinks.

No-one shall sleep, I translate for her. *Ma il mio mistero è chiuso in me.*

I'm sorry, I'm not with you.

But my mystery is locked in me, I explain. Till the riddle's answered, anyway.

I'd like to talk to you about your sleep-walking. Noctambulism. Has it troubled you before?

I've hurt my foot.

She listens to my heart and lungs, takes my blood pressure, looks at the whites of my eyes and all the time my foot is throbbing and she isn't interested. Then she pulls up a chair and places her hand on my arm. She has been trained in the skill of appearing to care.

It's my *foot*, I repeat, when she asks me if I have been eating.

She looks up at Christine hovering in the doorway of the kitchen, who says, See when she first arrived, she wasn't like this. Were you? she asks me, raising her voice. And you've lost weight. You're skin and bone.

233

It's my foot, I remind them. I've hurt my foot.

But I already know Dr Chowdry isn't interested in the real problem. When she arrived she just took the bandage off and pressed here and there and told me to wiggle my toes and bandaged it up again.

Christine says, Sure you want me to stay? Will I not go so you can talk to the doctor in peace?

Stay, I tell her again.

Dr Chowdry smiles at Christine. Your husband did a good job strapping it up last night.

Lucky he's a trained First Aider, Christine says. We tried to get her to A & E but she wasn't having it. We didn't press, we didn't want her any more upset. She was quite confused.

Oh, there's no harm done. And he's a better bandager than I am!

What I don't understand, Christine leans forward to ask, is you wouldn't think she had the strength. It's like she was superhuman.

Dr Chowdry nods, looking at me.

I mean it's on castors but a piano's that heavy, I don't see how she could do it all by herself.

Dr Chowdry says, I think it's a bit like a form of hypnosis. The body does what the sleepwalker's mind believes, you know? Same as people under hypnosis.

She hypnotises herself, you mean?

Maybe. In a way. Under deep hypnosis, for instance, if you tell someone you're slapping their face their cheek can actually turn red, they'll even get the finger marks. It's because the unconscious mind is in charge. Mind over matter, I suppose.

Christine says, Really? I thought it was all fake, those hypnotists on the telly.

I don't know. But maybe if a part of your mind is telling you you can move a piano, then you can, even if only a little. Eh, Lila? What are you up to, Lila, eh, when you should be asleep in your bed?

Two of my toes are round and purple and split like ripe grapes and I've also hurt a muscle in my shoulder. My back aches.

What about my toes? My toes hurt, I say.

Dr Chowdry says, Your foot is bruised and cut. It looks worse than it is. Nothing to worry about if you stay off it for a day or two, now the bleeding's stopped. A & E might've put a couple of stitches in if they'd seen you last night, but you're borderline. Just painkillers and antibiotics to be on the safe side, okay?

She says the last bit in an extra-smiley voice, patting my arm. And a tetanus jab just to make sure, okay? I'll call in and do it for you here, easier than getting you down to surgery. It doesn't take a second.

We tried to get her to go in but she wasn't having it, Christine says again, more quietly.

They both look as if they are waiting for me to explain myself.

So you're not sleeping, Dr Chowdry says. Why do you think that might be?

I'm restless, that's all.

Christine has made tea and hands me a cup as if it is some kind of truth drug, a tool of persuasion.

Here. You're up all hours, you know you are, she says.

I have a lot to do, I say.

Bereavement is very stressful, says Dr Chowdry, shaking her head. Bereavement's certainly a difficult time, it rates right up there. I wouldn't automatically resort to medication but there are things that can help short term, if you feel it would be helpful. I would need to know if you're taking any other medicines.

There is a silence, filled with polite bafflement and tea-sipping.

You know, maybe it's even a wee blessing in disguise, Christine offers, nodding at my bandaged foot. You'll maybe not be so restless if you can't get around so much. You'll need to keep the weight off it. Accept a wee bit of help. I'm only too willing.

Is there anyone else nearby, any family? Dr Chowdry says in

a perfect whisper of empathy. Is there anyone else? Somebody who can come and help with things for a while? Any friends?

Friends? No, there was only Enid, I say. And Enid's mum – Enid's mum looked after me. When I got ill, that summer.

Dr Chowdry and Christine exchange another look. Christine shakes her head.

Enid's mum? Is this you going back over things again, is it? she says.

Enid's mum was very good at sewing, I say. She could make anything. She sat and sewed and listened. She let you get on with it.

And Enid, what about her? Enid herself, is she still in the area at all? What's her other name?

Enid? Foley . . . oh, but no . . . it was Foley, now it's McArthur. Mrs Bill McArthur, now.

Oh! Dr Chowdry says, her eyes lighting up in Christine's direction. I know who she means, I know the family. She turns back to me. You mean Enid McArthur, the McArthurs in the big bungalow, do you? House with a Spanish name. They're on the practice list, she whispers to Christine. The mother's a patient as well.

It's Portuguese, I think you'll find, I say. They used to go to Portugal.

I think they still do. They're away a lot, Dr Chowdry tells Christine. She bends closer and talks to me in a slow, loud voice. So you remember old Mrs Foley, do you? From a long time ago?

Enid's mum. Isn't she dead?

Mrs Foley's fine. She's still in Burnhead. She's in sheltered accommodation.

Enid's mum, she didn't mind anything. She sewed and listened and let you get on with it, I tell them. I suppose you could say she was a banal sort of woman. I suppose by this time she'll be soft in the head.

17

L ila woke early with the idea that during the night a pair
of tiny crusty sea urchins had climbed into her mouth
and lodged themselves high up in her neck under the
jawbone. When she tried to swallow they clung on, tearing up
the lining of her throat and bringing it with them. She ran a
hand up her neck and prodded at the two swellings under her
fingers and her eyes watered with pain.

She lay and reminded herself what she was in for: today, a
high temperature and possibly tomorrow, for a while, even
higher. She would stay in bed and hope that by lying still she
would not need to drink. She would spend hours trying to talk
herself out of thirst until she was parched, and then she would
rise on one elbow and sip some water and fall back after the
effort, her throat stripped raw by swallowing. She would lie
worrying that her ears and eyes were getting in on it, too. She
would wonder why a disease of the throat should make her legs
and arms feel as if they were rolls of cloth badly stitched to the
rest of her body. By the third or fourth day the symptoms might
be taking their leave, subsiding over the next few days and
leaving her tired out and with a scoured, fragile throat. But she
was too exhausted to imagine it with anything but calm. As
long as it did not make her ugly (because suppose her illness
brought out the Florence Nightingale in Joe?) she could almost
welcome a dose of tonsillitis; she liked the idea of staying put
for a while. Already feeling an invalid's detachment, she
watched the light through her window change from a blue
dawn to the yellow of a rare, hot, cloudless day.

Her father was first up. He clicked his door, cleared his

throat softly on his way to the bathroom on bare feet, slipping from night to day as imperceptibly as he moved through all his plain routines of living. She heard him go back to his room, clicking the door again, and then she forgot about him. Uncle George was next, starting up like a motor and pounding around on the landing, thumping downstairs, calling out to Raymond as he went, not so much waking up as announcing to an anxious world his resurrection from sleep. Lila fell into a doze and woke with her throat drier than before. Birdsong reached her from the garden and filled her room with a strange, clean sweetness. Later she heard the creak of Joe walking above, his descent of the attic stairs, and then she heard noises from the bathroom that made her quickly cover her ears with the blankets. She would not think about such splutterings from unthinkable parts of him, or from herself for that matter; after they were married all that kind of thing would happen off-stage. Their bathroom would be safe from all that, a fragrant place sparkling with hygiene. She turned her mind to the little flat they would have and how she would scold him good-naturedly for leaving the bathroom so steamy, and fold the towels up neatly after him.

Some time after that, her mother stirred. Lila imagined her floating progress from nightgown to clothes, seeing to the needs of her body as if it were not quite hers but an article entrusted to her aloof, appraising care. After that, the upper floors fell silent again. Lila lay and let her throat and face burn. They would notice, surely, that she had not come down?

After what seemed a long time her mother tapped on the door and opened it. Around her head she had wrapped a scarf like a turban and she wore a strand of thick beads the size and colour of walnuts; the look was arty and high-minded.

'Eliza?'

Lila rose on her elbows. 'I've got tonsillitis again. My throat's sore. I'm all hot.' Her voice sounded as if it came from behind a closed door.

'What? Oh, for God's sake, not now! Your voice!' Fleur backed on to the landing and made her way downstairs, wailing. 'George! George, she's gone and got tonsillitis!'

A few moments later Uncle George came tramping up. Fleur followed, fingering her beads with a thin, cold-looking hand.

'What's this? Poor old you,' George huffed, landing heavily on the end of the bed. He was carrying a torch and a teaspoon. 'Oof, I took those stairs too fast. So – what's up? A dose of Soprano's Delight?'

Lila slumped back on her pillow and stared at the ceiling. She'd had tonsillitis before but it hadn't really mattered. Enid's mum said everybody had their weak spot: with Enid it's cold sores, with you it's tonsils, she said, nothing you can do about it. But Lila felt she was being awkward. It was now her responsibility, she realised, to play down how ill she felt.

'Just tonsils,' she said, with a grunt that she intended to come out like a sigh of boredom rather than pain.

'Let's take a look. Open wide.' Uncle George leaned forward, pushed her tongue to the floor of her mouth with the handle of the spoon and peered in, moving the torch from side to side. He snapped off the beam.

'Red and raw,' he said, cheerfully, 'but *nil desperandum*! You just need to stay put and get dosed up in time for the run-through on Sunday.'

'She'll be all right, won't she?' Fleur asked, rubbing the toe of her shoe up and down the back of one leg. 'We won't have to cancel the run-through or anything?'

'Oh, no, shouldn't think so. You'll pick up, won't you, Liù? Liù will muddle through?' He laughed his disparaging, own-weak-joke laugh.

Lila didn't care much about the run-through on Sunday. The ceilidh was on Saturday. She had to be better by Saturday. Five days.

Counting off on his fingers, Uncle George turned to Fleur. 'First thing, you and Calaf stay away, she might be infectious.

239

Two, she needs aspirin. And put the kettle on, she should have hot orange squash. Cold flannel for the neck, bring down the inflammation.'

Fleur was turning to go, still playing with her beads. For the first time since she arrived she took her other hand from the doorknob, and gave a delicate finger wave. 'Well, you take care of yourself,' she said.

Uncle George got up and patted Lila's shin under the bedclothes and told her, 'You'll be better soon. After all, you're young and strong!' Then he broke off in a fit of coughing that made them all laugh.

The day passed. Uncle George came and went with orange squash and aspirin. Lila slept and woke and dozed. She thought she heard Joe singing, somewhere far away. The telephone rang. Two flies circled her room in a maddening metallic-sounding duet, as if they were flying around in an empty tin. When she absolutely had to, she drank, turning her face into her pillow to wipe the tears that came every time she swallowed. Outside, the sun burned fiercely, the first hot day in weeks. The next time Lila woke there was a thick, briny taste in her mouth and she felt bloated and crabby. The room was hot and bright and the house beyond her door was full of a flat, dreamy silence that belonged to afternoon. She got up and ran a tepid bath. While she waited for the tub to fill she brought down Joe's bottle of Gentilhomme Debonair from the bathroom cabinet, removed the stopper and stood sniffing it, shocked at her pleasure. Surely when she was this ill it should be impossible to feel so alive? She tipped a little, not enough to be missed, into the water, and Joe's scent rose into the air as if he had quietly entered the bathroom and closed the door. She sank into her bath feeling that he was with her, watching.

She returned to her room to find it cool and dark. In her absence the window had been opened wide and the curtains drawn, and her bed re-made. Although she was touched – so far Uncle George's nursing had been unrefined, only aspirins and orange squash – Lila was too exhausted by the bath to feel more than mild surprise. She climbed into bed with Gentilhomme Debonair still on her skin; smeared with essence of Joe, she felt owned and happy. Then, sliding one foot down the sheet that was now smooth and without ridges, she remembered that Uncle George had gone up to the farm for the afternoon. Her mother was down on Burnhead beach with the girls. It was Joe who had made her room nice.

The sun was burning lower. It glared straight through the thin brown material of the curtain and cast a tremulous filter of shadow on the wall opposite, setting it a-shimmer with runnels of watery, amber light. A gash of escaped gold hit the floor directly under the window and leaked across the linoleum to the corner of the rug, one elongated, fluttering edge of light moving like a frilled skirt as the hanging curtain stirred in barely moving air. Beneath the clean sting of Gentilhomme Debonair murmured a sweeter, older scent, the drowsy melancholy of summer flowers. On her bedside table next to a glass of lemonade – that had not been there before, either – stood the little blue and white Spode jug filled with plum and gold pansies, almost blown over, their petals velvety in the softened light, some already shed and lying like dusty curls of silk on the table top. Happiness swelled in her like a bubble. Joe must have picked them from the front of 1 Seaview Villas where Mr and Mrs McBray, who were away for a week in a caravan at Loch Lomond, grew them behind the low wall along with their petunias and lobelias and primulas. *The first time you gave me flowers.*

For a long while she just lay. With the window open she could hear gulls, so far away over the sea that their calls sounded offhand and less cruel, and from the back garden came the chuck of the hoe. The yellow slice of sunlight on the floor under the curtain had paled and lengthened. It was after six o'clock and her father must be home from work, now in his shirtsleeves and his braces hanging at his sides, weeding again in the vegetable plot where so very little grew.

As the light burned down deeper the sounds from the garden stopped. Inside the house people were now about, there were doors opening, greetings, voices in the hall. Lila was content to be out of the life downstairs, even though it sounded as if she were not being missed. It would be like this if I were dead, she thought, as long as I have a soul and don't just die. Even if she were quickly forgotten she would still be present yet hidden, eavesdropping in this ghostly private way. She wondered how long it would be before anybody came.

Later, Uncle George appeared with a tray with a cup of tea and a plate of bread and butter.

'Thank you,' she croaked, when the tray was settled on her knees, 'for everything.' Her eyes were stinging.

'I haven't really had a minute, I'm not long back. Here, can you eat something? You should drink the tea.'

Lila drank in sips, watching him. His eyes were electrically bright.

'I've been up all afternoon at the farm with Gordon Black,' he said. 'He's already rehearsing the chorus up there. And I popped in to Sew Right, Enid's mum was asking for you. Enid says to tell you she'll maybe come and see you tomorrow.' He looked at the flowers. 'They're nice.'

Lila's eyes sparkled in the shadowy room. 'Somebody put them here while I was in the bath.' She was keeping her lovely secret for the time being. Joe must be the first to know that she knew they were his gift.

'Your mother's caught the sun. She's covered in calamine and lying on a wet sheet. Mmm, pansies,' George said quietly. ' "Pansies, that's for thoughts." They don't last in water, though.'

'Pansies for what? They're for what?'

'Thoughts. Don't you know, in the language of flowers? Ophelia, in *Hamlet*. Pansies mean "I am thinking of you", I think that's right.'

'Really? Where's Joe?'

'Joe? Huh, *Joe*. I only got two minutes' notice myself. Joe,' Uncle George's voice grew tight, 'Joe appears to have gone.'

'*Gone?* Gone where? When's he coming back?' Lila cried, pulling herself up straight.

'He left a note. He's gone up to Glasgow, about the head-dress trimmings and the material for Timur and Calaf and the Emperor Altoum. Apparently.' Uncle George pulled a hand over his face and sighed hard, longing for a cigarette. He glanced at the door. 'He's after proper brocade. He says there's trimmings and brocade he can get in Glasgow that Stella can't get here. He says he has to choose it personally.'

'Oh.' Lila looked over at her flowers. 'Did he not want to say goodbye? Did he say how long he's to be away?'

'He said goodbye in the note,' Uncle George added, working to keep his voice level. 'He said he'd be back in a few days.'

'Why *days*? Why's he away so long?'

George shrugged. 'He said in the note he needed a break. Says he's feeling the strain.'

Lila's head started to pound and she lay back, desolate. She wanted Uncle George to go so that she could get under the covers and sob.

He said, 'Look, *I'm* not going to worry, I can assure you. So you certainly shouldn't. He'll be back in a little while.'

'In a little while? In time for the ceilidh?'

'Oh, I'm pretty certain he'll be back for the ceilidh. I don't suppose you'd catch him missing that.' George's lips puckered and squirmed for a cigarette. 'Not a word about missing rehearsals, as if that doesn't matter. I mean, I should really kick up a fuss. Talk about *selfish*.'

Lila was not really listening now. Joe had said everything, anyway, and so shyly and delicately that only he could have said it. Nobody else in the whole of Burnhead would know that pansies meant 'thoughts'. He had stolen into her room with the flowers while she was bathing, and then he had taken himself off so that she could get better in peace. What else could be meant by the leaving behind of thoughts, and his scent, and his promise to be back for the ceilidh?

The weather continued hot. Over the next few days Lila let herself be borne along like a rag, bobbing on the surface of hours that passed and receded, washing her in and out of sleep. The sky flared with heat. Sunlight burned in every day through the curtains and melted in a trickle of yellow-white over the sill of her window, and was consumed, as night came, by shadows that solidified into a cold grey-blue at dawn, when she would wake shivering in a fit of fractious coughing, pulling up blankets that felt wiry and foreign in her sleepy fingers.

After three days she was not that ill anymore – it felt as though her throat were being scratched by stiff feathers, nothing more – but she had slipped into a mood of detached, almost religious waiting, blessed by a kind of patience that seemed to have been dormant all this while in the shadows in her room and that she could now invoke and bestow upon herself. All around her, get-well cards appeared: from Mr and Mrs Mathieson, Enid, Mr and Mrs Gordon Black and stuck-up Gillian, Jimmy the coalman, and even 'Alec and the gang' from the *Burnhead & District Advertiser*. Willy and Joanna Bergsma came by on early closing day, with a gargle that they swore by and said you couldn't get now. The bottle was nearly empty and Willy herself solemnly measured out three brown drops, her wet eye watching them fall into a glass of warm water. It had a taste of tar and scorched rubber that made Lila think of the burning house in Rotterdam. Enid's mum sent Enid with a rice pudding that she said would slip easy down a sore throat, and Enid managed to slop most of it in her bicycle basket. Delia Hunter and Moira Mather brought grapes. Fleur, finding the role of visitor bearing a gift more natural than that of nurse, gave her an excitingly large bottle of eau de cologne. Senga, Linda and Deirdre clubbed together for a big bag of barley sugar.

Lila had never been so fussed over before but she took it all calmly. She thanked everyone nicely, but did not really need the attention. She was content to abjure the world until Joe should return, counting her get-well cards and listening to the sounds, lapping through each day, of her visitors coming and going, sounds that belonged to other lives and so were essentially meaningless to her and Joe, the lives of other people being to both of them now peripheral. Voluntarily alone and only temporarily exiled, she basked in the certainty of her life to come. She was in no hurry. She luxuriated in her clarity and faith and was a model patient; she sipped and gargled as expected and sent the visitors away feeling glad that they had come.

By the end of the week she was not very much worse than she had been before the tonsillitis. She came downstairs bathed and dressed late on Saturday morning, aware of a glide in her movements, not consciously copying her mother's way of holding herself but sensing that something of that elegance was now in her possession. It was a surface smoothness only, a subterfuge to hide the workings of a mind that had pre-empted all obstacles and was now simply anticipating events, because how things were going to be was decided. A timetable for the rest of her life had been drawn up. She was finally in control of the cast of her own mind; there was no need for her to draw attention to herself, to make any noise, to bound downstairs or flap her hands. A drowsy, final look had settled in her eyes.

Now at last I'm getting somewhere. That busted piano still out on the front grass, an eyesore! Can't leave it that way.

Further down one of the tea chests I find wads and wads of muslin: Joe's experiments with dyeing. I remember him in the back garden with tubs and buckets borrowed from all and sundry, dipping lengths in red ink, poster paint, pigments of one kind or another, in search of his true Chinese red. Cherry won't do, apparently, nor will vermilion nor cerise nor scarlet nor crimson. Chinese red. The truth is he quickly loses interest and leaves these yards and yards of dreary experiments hanging around all over the place. He gets other people to deal with it. Enid's mum sorts it out in the end, I don't recall how.

I pull out yard after yard of it. The cloth holds the colour reluctantly; fragments of red are flaking off everywhere, smelling of chalk and salt and dead minerals. He never did get a proper red and now the muslin is the colour of old insect blood and it's filthy after years bunched in heaps in the attic. It's full of pink dust and black broken bits you can't name, as if smashed wings and shells and legs as thin as threads are all wrapped up in it, as if these great lengths of muslin have been used to wipe a giant windscreen clean of mortalities after a long journey. There has been massive loss of life and spillage, but long ago; the stains are too dry to associate with anything recently alive.

My foot is a trouble to me, I won't deny, but I can hobble about when my mind is set on getting to a place. I gather up the muslin in my arms and shift myself out to the front garden, where I unwrap folds of it in and around the broken frame of

246

the piano. I arrange the cloth so that it pours in motionless floods of red around the ruin and makes it look like what it is, a corpse. Dried entrails. Christine will be pleased with me, for I add also some of the papers, the early newspaper cuttings and George's jottings, his handwritten sheet music, jamming them tight into the gaping holes in the piano so they won't blow away. White, fluttering paper birds come home to roost like memories – they stop its twanging, broken mouths with some of the very notes this piano came out with and the very words we sang: promises, lies, threats and desires all set to music.

I also find near the bottom of the chest a large bag of buttons and beads. Surplus to requirements. Everybody in the production is asked to provide at least thirty buttons or beads, for decorating the principals' costumes – red for Turandot, gold for Calaf, black for Calaf's old father Timur. Liù doesn't get beads. The Mandarin and the old emperor Altoum and the courtier Pung are going to wear *Mikado* costumes with Chinese adjustments, though most people won't make the distinction. I put my hand into the beads, lift them in dry handfuls and let them run. The rattling coloured river of them makes an old sound, like rain on the privet.

There are close to two hundred people connected in some way to the production now: we've got four boy scout and girl guide troupes roped in as the chorus of boys, though we are letting the girls sing too as seems only fair, and the boys are helping with the shed painting and the set. Most of my school orchestra and Ayr Academy's too are enlisted, as well as more than half of the Ayrshire Amateur Philharmonic Orchestra, and dozens and dozens of people from choirs and the two amateur operatic societies, several music teachers and their star pupils. It really does seem as if all these people were just waiting at a loose end, desperate for something to do. George is permanently nervous and his mood alternates between thrilled and ratty. It is Mr Mathieson who keeps us organised and who follows through George's and Joe's whims and flights of fancy over the set and costumes. Getting everyone to donate a few beads and buttons is another of Enid's mum's ideas, practical and simple. Lots of people donate lavishly, and we are awash in them.

There are more papers at the bottom of the chest, impacted into a clump that sticks to the base. They are smeared with red and stuck together as if once they were the first thing to come to hand after an accident. I suppose the muslin was shoved in on top before it was quite dry, and seeped colour on to them. I have to lean right in with a torch and I can read only the page on the very top, through a film of pink like dried, blood-streaked saliva.

Burnhead & District Advertiser Thursday 28th July 1960:

Opera Hopeful 'Not Serious' Says BAST Maestro

Common Complaint

The high hopes of BAST (Burnhead Association for Singing *Turandot*) were struck a blow earlier this week when leading hopeful Eliza Duncan (15) succumbed to the singer's classic complaint: tonsillitis! A condition which on occasion renders even the greatest sopranos speechless. Maria Callas herself is notorious for announcing, minutes before the curtain, 'I can't go on!'

Show Must Go On

George Pettifer, BAST's Conductor and Musical Director, assured *Burnhead & District Advertiser* reporter Alec Gallagher that Miss Duncan, singing the part of Liù in Puccini's *Turandot*, is made of sterner stuff. 'It's not serious. It's quite common among singers. With proper rest the voice will be fine long before the first night.' Miss Duncan, Mr Pettifer's niece and daughter of Fleur Pettifer who is singing the lead role of Princess Turandot, can certainly boast an operatic pedigree! She commented, 'I'll be right as rain in a day or two.'

Well Wishers

There has been a steady flow of visitors and well wishers to Eliza's home at 5 Seaview Villas. 'News travels fast!' she smiled. 'I want to thank everybody who asked after me and sent cards and presents, it honestly feels as if the whole of Burnhead has been wishing me better.'

Performance to Remember

Miss Duncan added, 'The rehearsals are going superbly well and my being indisposed hasn't disrupted the schedule at all. And it certainly won't affect my performance. When I finally get up on that stage I shall be singing the very best I can. I want to repay everyone's kindness by giving a performance to remember!'

By Staff Reporter Alec Gallagher

Well, does that sound like me? Not a word of it is mine. Either I'm asleep when Alec Gallagher pops in to get the story or I'm overlooked, being upstairs and out of the way. Uncle George supplies him with news of what I think and feel.

The tea chest has a raw metal edge that scratches me as I lean over to read. Not badly, just the skin snagged and broken at intervals in a line of red dots and dashes running from side to side under my breasts. Later I lie back in a hot bath and the line of the scratch looks like a pulled thread in fine knitwear and from here and there along it tiny, stinging little plumes of blood escape. But I'm all right. I'm even managing to keep my bandaged foot dangling over the side out of the water. A bath calms me. Then I'm going to do some cross-stitch and then, taking care not to cut my hands on it, I'll haul that filthy tea chest out of the house. It can join the pile on the front grass.

18

George pulled a stray sour thread of tobacco out of his mouth, threw the cigarette end away and spat into the grass. Something about fresh air raddled the taste of a cigarette and reminded him too much of burning leaves which, although that was all it was when you got down to it, he found an unpalatable thought that put smoking in almost the same category as eating grubs, a savage habit. He did not like the picture of himself hunkered down, lapsed and apelike, sucking in fumes just for the corrupting trickle of nicotine in the blood, but that was the kind of smoker an outdoor fag made him feel like and that he feared he must look like, crouching to take the weight off his legs and keep out of the wind in a corner of the field bordering the yard of Pow Farm.

To be more truthful, he was also keeping out of the way of the Mathiesons. The Mathiesons and all the rest of them: the ladies, the helpers, the 'useful pairs of hands' who were setting up for the ceilidh. He could hear Mrs Mathieson calling out to people as they arrived – *Mrs Burnside, would you butter gingerbread with the Misses Bergsma? Trestles to the shed, please! Are those macaroons, Miss Anderton?* And over the hedge Mr Mathieson was going to and fro from the boots of cars with a pencil behind one ear, unloading crockery on loan from the Townswomen's Guild, counting out plates, cups, saucers and spoons and marking numbers down on a clipboard. If Mr and Mrs Mathieson ran the world it would be, George felt, better organised, though with more inventories and home baking than people were used to. He wondered why, when these people contributed so much, they made him feel so weary, as if their energy sucked away all of his.

He hadn't been able to put Joe out of his mind. It wasn't that he was worried because he didn't know what he might be getting up to, he was in a slough of quiet despair because he knew exactly what. All week he had found himself hanging around Seaview Villas in the hope he would walk in; he'd made himself late for rehearsals and meetings because he was reluctant to leave, feeling superstitiously that his not waiting in the house would somehow prevent Joe's coming back. He hadn't come. Now it was Saturday and George was bracing himself to discover, whenever Joe might deign to re-appear, that his fears about how he'd spent the past five days were well founded. He was too tired to conceal from himself any more how much it wounded him.

This morning he had eaten some bread and marmite and waited again, listening for the sound of his arrival. He'd done some more work on the score (there was still so much cutting and changing to do to arrive at a version that this cast and orchestra could perform, never mind what he was capable of conducting) but still Joe had not come, and by then George's spirits had sunk so low he had been unable to stay in the house another minute.

He'd come up to the farm and found Billy hosing and brushing down the yard, sweeping off dust and cow muck and tall weeds, and he'd hovered for a while and offered to help. But Billy wouldn't ask him to do more than put a few buckets and brooms away, and when Mrs Mathieson appeared there had been in her voice, George thought, a hint that he might not be pulling his weight. *Oh George*, she had said, *do I spy you empty-handed? I've an urn needs lifting and going in the shed, there's a table up waiting for it, it'll need filling.*

Yawning, he felt acid rise in his gorge and a slow pain spread under his ribs. His eyes watered and he swallowed a mouthful of bile and spat again. Rubbing his chest, he straightened up and strolled up the field, turning out of the wind to light another cigarette as he went. He leaned over the gate and inhaled and held the smoke for as long as he could, but he still felt hollow inside and sick with yearning. He sighed the whole chestful of smoke back into the air.

It didn't help being hungry, and he didn't suppose there would be lunch to speak of. He needed some proper food, not the plateloads of stuff these people ate. From the field he watched the ladies, most of them in small workaday hats, bustling with towered cake tins and covered plates. One or two arrived on foot and some had come on bikes with filled baskets and bags slung from handlebars. He caught snatches of talk and sometimes a gust of surprisingly excited laughter.

It wasn't quite fair to call it a sugar orgy, he knew that, but he had been surprised at the scale and seriousness of the under-taking that had become the ceilidh tea. There was a kind of sumptuous finesse in it, he discovered. There had to be three kinds of scone: plain, fruit and cheese, and gingerbread both dark and light, and if Dundee cake then also, for balance, cherry Madeira. He found them strange and touching, these people who with their thick legs and broken veins seemed constituted to go overnight from childhood to middle age, the desires of young, crazy hearts shelved before they were out of their teens in favour of decency and responsibility, yet who would be hilarious within ten feet of a cake stand, giddy on Viennese fancies, raspberry kisses and butter icing.

George felt a sudden longing for Chez Hortense in Soho, a bistro rather than a restaurant (a distinction that appealed to him) that aspired to being French, though it was enough for him that it was foreign. It was a place he liked when he was in the mood to find roughness amusing; it smelled of scorched meat and mus-tard, the salads were full of raw onion in thick chunks, the steaks were bloody, the wine cheap and the waiters ham-fisted, friendly Greek thugs. He had taken Joe there. In fact, dinner at Chez Hortense was probably all they needed now to set things straight.

He shivered, feeling desperately homesick. It was a mistake, standing here long enough to let his fears crowd in, and he tried to remind himself why he couldn't just leave. Poor Florrie. Chez Hortense would appeal to her too, or would have once. She was probably too brittle and precious for it now. There were glimpses still of the Florrie he was losing, but they were rare; there was a fragmented, obscured quality to her as if she lived in a cloud of disappointment, sidestepping joy when it crossed her path, distrusting it, preferring her familiar shadows. How hysterical and disillusioned she was, and how bewildered and emptied of resistance Raymond had grown. Singing *Turandot* might be bringing her round somewhat and even Raymond seemed to be enjoying himself but even supposing they pulled it off, what would happen to them when it was over?

At the whistle and the yip of a dog's bark he turned and saw Stan McArthur, hands in pockets, in his slow, rolling walk across the yard. Sherpa bounded ahead of him to the gate and George stooped down and rubbed his ears through the bars.

'Band's on their way,' Stan said. 'That's them just off the phone.'

He turned and leaned his elbows against the gate so that he and George looked across the yard, not at each other. The ladies came and went.

'Billy's in the bath. Splashing away and singing, stinks like a tart's boudoir. You never heard the like.'

Their eyes followed Sherpa as, nose to ground, he tracked in a wavering line the path of Mrs Mathieson who was marching past on neat unsuitable shoes, bearing a tray. She was carrying it almost at chin level to allow clearance for her bosom that sat like a high, padded bar across her chest, pointing the way forward. With her head tipped back to see over, she seemed to be following it, while her bottom swung eagerly behind.

'Aye, good effort,' Stan said. 'Good spread, by the looks of it.'

George pulled out another cigarette for himself and offered the pack to Stan.

'Naw thanks,' Stan said, shaking his head. 'I'm a pipe man.'

Sherpa gave up the trail, trotted over and lay down. After a pause Stan said, still with his back to George, 'See that dog? Name used to be Schubert.'

'Sherbet?'

'*Schubert*. Yon composer.'

'Really?'

'Aye,' Stan said, his voice clipped. 'He wrote songs. I thought you'd have kenned that.'

'Nice dog.'

'He was the wife's. She got him young, just a puppy. Called him Schubert. I says that's a daft name, she says, I like it. I wisnae bothered, tell you the truth.'

'But you changed it?'

Stan stared into the sky and tried to make his voice casual, as if he hadn't thought about the question before. 'Aye well, the wife, see, the wife died. Eight year ago. It wisnae expected. She was a young woman, she was a *well* woman. Twelve year younger than myself. But she took a bad stomach, couldnae eat, and at the finish-up they said she'd a growth. Nothing they could dae.'

'I'm awfully sorry,' George said. He didn't know how to sound as if he really meant it, though he did. 'How terrible.'

'Aye well, she didnae linger. They tell you that's best. Thing was, right after, I couldnae stand it, the dog. Only a puppy still, crying for her. The noise, day and night like it felt worse than me, a bloody *dog* and she'd only had it seven weeks. I'd been married to her eleven year. I was ready to shoot it, tell you the truth.'

'Dogs do feel things, though, don't they?' George said, feeling inadequate. He took his cigarette from his lips and studied the smouldering end. 'They can get awfully attached.'

He meant this as a drawback. He didn't much like animals;

their devotion could be only an inconvenience. He didn't want
to hear any more about death, either. He had never lost a wife
and wasn't qualified to comment, and however sorry he might
feel for Billy it was in the way of things for children to lose
parents, and sometimes young. George was thirty now and
couldn't remember how it had felt when his mother died,
beyond an empty feeling that he supposed he had learned to
live with since he didn't think about it any more. George the
child was as distant to George the man as his mother now was:
a dim figure from a past that he thought of as belonging to
other people, a scratched reminder on a stone over an untended
grave in some place he would no longer be able to find.

'Well, see, the bloody dog . . . I dragged it out in the yard
here one night, I had the shotgun, I was out my mind wi' the
bloody thing, and here Billy comes crying after it, *Schubert,
Schubert*! He was only ten. And I'm shouting back, I was that
mad I couldnae stand to hear its name, and Billy's crying and
bawling away – No don't, don't, he says, I'll take it, I'll change
its name, don't kill it. See, what I'm saying is—'

'Hmm?'

'Billy. He says, don't make the dog die *as well*.'

George could not find a reply.

'What I'm saying is, I'm no proud of that night. Billy was a
wee boy.'

'Yes, but you were very upset. When people are upset they—'

'Aye, even so. Anyway, he trained that dog to a new name.
That's no easy.'

'I'm sure you were just upset.'

'What I'm saying – see, the dog, how I see it, the dog was
getting it oot its system. An' see me and Billy? We never talk
about it. Still.'

'Well, he probably knows how you feel, don't you think?'

'But it's that quiet. See him and his mum, they were the ones
for the music. And see if she was here, she'd be that pleased,
with yon opera and that. She'd be tickled pink.'

'Yes, Billy's a great strength in the chorus. And so willing, with the set and getting the shed ready.'

'No, what I'm saying is, him up there in the bath singing away, it's *good*. See what I'm saying? Me getting to do something for Billy just like his mum would have done. See what I'm saying?'

'Yes, I think I follow,' George lied.

Stan cleared his throat, started up from the gate and set off back to the yard, clicking his fingers at Sherpa. Still walking, he turned and said, 'Ach, the hell you do. I'm trying to thank you, you wee bugger.'

My first day up after the tonsillitis and I have much to do before I will be ready for the ceilidh tonight. I'm meeting Enid because she is lending me her turquoise dress. (I know, secretly, that it looks better on me with my dark colouring than it does on gingery Enid.)

When I leave the house I see that the boy scouts have been busy. In the field adjoining the farm track there is now a painted sign that says:

Saturday 30 July 7.00–10.30

COME TO A CEILIDH
All Welcome

Dance to Jackie Shenley's Accordion and Band
Tea   Refreshments   Raffle
Tickets 5/- and 3/- on the night or in advance from
leading Burnhead retailers

The ragged edges of the entrance to the farm have been scalped. Skeins of lopped grass tumble over the mown verges and branches of hawthorn and torn bramble are strewn across the track, which seems wider now. The hedges look startled, stripped by the cutter down to short twigs like fingers ripped to their white bone tips. At intervals along the verges small boulders – from the beach, probably – have been set in the grass and whitewashed to form a pale and lumpen guard of honour all the way up to the farm. Is this all it takes, I wonder, a bit of mowing and a few white stones? For the place is transformed. It looks prosperous and poised, less homely but oddly, more welcoming. It looks unlike Burnhead and is somehow operatic, my mother's kind of place.

I'm too tired to walk, so I catch the bus that takes the stupid route round Monkton and in to the wrong side of Burnhead. The noise and motion of the bus lulls me back and forth between memory of the time I made this journey with Joe and anticipation of seeing him at the ceilidh tonight. When I meet up with Enid outside Woolworths she asks what that look on my face is for. We go in and edge our way around Beauty Accessories. From the tannoy next to the record counter Kenneth McKellar's voice sounds scratchily over our heads:

> *The birthplace of valour, the country of worth,*
> *Wherever I wander, wherever I rove . . .*

A dozen of his new record sleeves are pinned in a fanlike display on the pegboard wall above the counter; a dozen pensive and kilted Kenneth McKellars, chin cupped between finger and thumb and one foot resting on a log, gaze over a purple hill.

I finger scarves and hairbands. I shake minute puffs from tins of powder and open bottles of scent, sniffing with closed eyes as I try to guess which one will drive Joe wild. I'm not inspired by any of the labels: neither a moonlit Eiffel Tower (*Nocturne de Paris*), a desert island (*Girl Friday*) nor an almond-eyed beauty in furs and diamonds (*Casino*) strikes quite the right note. The one that smells the best (*Rodeo Princess*) has the worst picture of all, a blonde girl in a pink Stetson. I put the bottle down. Kenneth McKellar's voice sails on, chased by massed, echoing accordions:

> *My heart's in the Highlands, wherever I go!*

Enid is shoving Parma Violets in her mouth every few seconds and flipping and turning through racks of nylons on a revolving stand.

She says, See my turquoise dress? That I'm wearing tonight? I'm getting the exact right eyeshadow for it, Rimmel's got the *exact same* colour.

Your turquoise? You said I could borrow that.

Oh, did I? When?

Wednesday. You said I could borrow it for the ceilidh.

Oh, but that was when you were not well and I thought you wouldn't be coming. I need it now. Anyway I never promised. You can borrow the pedal pushers.

You can't wear pedal pushers to a ceilidh, I tell her.

I turn away and look at hairnets, which I never buy, so she won't see I am about to burst into tears. I have nothing else to wear, nothing I can stand.

See the eyeshadow? I seen it in the Ayr Woollies but I'd no money on me. They'll have the exact same one here, not think so? Okay listen, you can borrow something else, okay?

How can a turquoise dress, or the lack of it, produce such despair? Kenneth McKellar is singing something to a dance tune now. He has no idea. It's so cheerful I want to lie down and curl into a ball until it stops. My ribs are folding in on themselves, like a roof collapsing.

Look, Enid says, I need the turquoise, I just do, okay? You can get it another time, that's a promise. C'mon. You can still borrow the eyeshadow. Hey, the green skirt, want my green skirt? You can have that if you want.

I don't want the green skirt because there's nothing to wear with it except a white blouse that isn't any more ceilidh-worthy than pedal pushers. It is a matter of so much more than what I will look like. It is a matter of having in my hands the turquoise dress, the means of bringing Joe to his senses, and being required to give it back. I'm getting an old feeling in my chest that I used to get a lot before this summer, like something shrinking, and I pause for a second, wondering what will happen if this time I don't rise above it. I finger the bottle of *Rodeo Princess* and wonder what the point of rising above it is, what the point ever is.

Not think so, the eyeshadow? They'll have the same ones in all the Woollies, won't they?

Uh-huh. Maybe.

It's the exact same colour, the *exact same*. It's Rimmel. I'm not getting Evette. I hate Evette.

Right.

See after, want to go and see my mum? She was saying she's not seen you in a while.

I want to refuse. Not just because of the dress, but because nearly everything Enid says, what anyone says these days, comes to me in another language, and I don't want to risk Enid's mum sounding foreign to me, too. Other people – Uncle George, my father, my mother, never mind Alec Gallagher and Mr Black and all the others – never quite stop annoying me. Even when they are being nice, there is something about their ignorance of what I am really feeling that makes me despise them and I worry that it may be the same with Enid's mum. But the back shop of Sew Right is the safest place I know and I need safety now.

Okay, I say, feeling weak and angry. Can I borrow your white sandals, then? Enid pops another handful of Parma Violets into her mouth and crunches fragrantly.

She says, Okay, you can have the sandals.

My attention is drawn by the rattling noise of the peanut dispenser that sits next to the weighing machine just inside the entrance. It's a rectangular metal box with a glass case on top like a fish tank, in which a greasy dune of peanuts glistens under a light bulb. It's been here all my life and now I think it looks smaller than it used to. Two boys, brothers probably, are squabbling over who's putting the money in, who's pressing the button, who holds the paper cone.

Listen, Enid says, her breath coming hot and scented, we still

need to get one, nail varnish. Two, hairspray. I'll get the nail
varnish, you get the hairspray, okay?

As long as I get your white sandals.

I said you could. Just for the night.

I feel too old, suddenly. I don't want to buy hairspray. I feel
weary for the lost Saturday afternoons spent bloated and parched
from scoffing a coneful of peanuts, immoveable grease on my
fingers, my scalp itchy, my mouth salt-puckered. I can't remember deciding not to get peanuts any more. I just drifted away and
spent my pocket money on other things, I suppose. I watch the
two boys and remember feeding the pennies in and pressing the
button marked 3d. I remember the hum from inside the machine
and then the thrilling part, the first sigh from deep in the nut
mountain and the first movement, a mere shifting as two or three
runaways trickle and settle. Then comes the tumble of nuts
through the chute and into the waiting cone. Will the avalanche
stop before the cone is full or will the entire hillside rattle out and
bounce all over the floor, a catastrophe that will be my fault? I
had no idea then that I will recall this time with the feeling that
something precious came and went before I took proper notice of
what it was. Not freedom from anxiety: what, then?

They're all over the kitchen floor now, multi-coloured hail-
stones all over the floor, red and black and gold. The beads and
buttons – Calaf's, Timur's, Turandot's – they're everywhere. I
must have spilled them somehow, though it seems to me the
bag practically emptied itself. I'll be picking them up for days.

But I can't be bothered with them now.

I feel better. I'm dressed after my bath. My hired car is an
automatic and the hurt foot is my left, so I can drive. Christine
will think it a bad idea but she needn't know, she hasn't been in
today, or for a while, as far as I recall. Maybe her interest in me
is waning. I have to keep my hair appointment. After that I
shall go and see Luke.

19

The bell of Sew Right tinged and they wandered past the empty counter, through the curtain to the back shop and found Enid's mum on the floor, sitting in the foothills of a calico mountain that billowed in peaks around her.

'It's yourselves,' she said, pulling out a line of pins from between her lips and sticking them into the lapel of her cardigan. 'Long time no see, Lizzie. If it's a cup of tea you're needing, away and get it,' she said, amiably. 'I've that many numbers in my head, don't talk to me yet.'

Enid pushed past to the kettle and sink in the passage that led out to the back door.

'What's all this for?' Lila whispered. Enid's mum gave her a warning glance. Her mouth was working fast and silently as she pulled swathes of calico across her lap. Lila slid on to the floor and began gathering it up in folds and feeding it across to her hands.

Enid's mum said, 'Hold on, shoosh just a minute.'

Drawing out the edge of the calico between her fingers and extending one arm as a measure, she counted, 'One yard, two, three, four, wee bit for luck, *pin*.'

Keeping the place pinched between thumb and forefinger, she pulled a pin from her cardigan and stuck it in as a marker on the selvedged edge of the material. She started again, 'One yard, two, three, four, extra for luck, *pin*.'

'What are you doing?'

'– two, three, four, *pin*. I'm measuring out for the chorus costumes,' she said. 'See over there? There's one made up.'

She nodded towards a hanger suspended from the door of

one of the tall cupboards that lined the wall. On it was a pair of calico trousers and a jacket with no fastenings, streaked reddish brown and looking worn and crumpled, like the suit of a convict who'd been breaking rocks all day.

'I've made up a pattern and instructions and done a wee drawing and the chorus get four yards of stuff and they make their own. Oh, they'll moan, some of them, but there's nothing to it. See? Trousers – straight up the outside leg seams, drawstring casing, up the inside leg, round the gusset, down again – done. No need for hems, even. Get me that pin off the floor there, will you? Jacket – bat sleeves, no shoulder seams, wrist up to under the arms and down the sides, no buttons, no finishing. Then they've to put it all in a boil wash with a pair of black socks and a pair of brown socks and then hang it to dry but not iron it. You get it good and grimy-looking that way. My idea, that. Fair enjoyed myself, thinking it all up.' She smiled.

'But there's no buttons,' Lila said. 'How will they keep the jacket on?'

'Everybody's to get something of their own. They can use a brooch as long as it's plain, or an old belt or a cord or thin rope even, or a sash if it's not too fancy. Or they can use a sharp stick or a bit of bone and pin it through. That way, no two's the same. Similar but not the same, like what folk are.'

'Eh?' Enid picked her way across the mound of calico and began fingering the suit on the hanger, lifting and peering inside it. 'That? I'm not wearing that. It's not *clean*.'

Lila and Enid's mum exchanged the glance that two people share when a third person isn't keeping up.

Enid's mum said, 'Och, don't you get on your high horse. Everyone's in the same boat. You've all to be in keeping.'

'Don't see why we've got to look horrible.'

'You're one of *La folla*. The crowd. You're peasants,' Lila said helpfully.

'Don't see why that means we have to be *scruffy*.'

'Because you're peasants. You're poor.'

'So? Poor doesn't mean dirty. It doesn't mean we have to be filthy – you won't be filthy.'

Enid's mum sighed. 'It's in keeping, dear, it's China in ancient times. Ordinary folk didn't have bathrooms then. Everyone'll be the same.'

'It's true,' Lila said. 'Standards were different in those days.'

'Everyone?'

'Everyone in the chorus,' Lila said.

Enid ignored her. 'But not Lizzie, though. So what's Lizzie wearing?' she demanded. 'What's *Lizzie* getting?'

'You know quite well what Lizzie's getting, you've seen me making it. She's a principal, she's got to have something different. That tea made?'

Steam was pouring from the kettle. Enid disappeared into the cloud in the passageway and clattered about with cups. Mrs Foley glanced behind her, then leaned across to Lila and said, 'Yours is done. Half of it, any road. Go and see, the cupboard there, just behind. Shift that awful thing out the road.'

Lila got up from the floor, lifted the hanger with the calico suit and hung it on the next cupboard handle along, and opened the door.

She could not speak. By opening the door she was inter-rupting something, some piece of blinding, uncompleted magic that involved the impossible: moonbeams or stars plucked from their proper places and trapped in the stock room of a remnant shop in Ayrshire. Hanging from a hook in the roof of the cupboard in front of bales of tweed and blanketing was a long, straight dress in the palest, most glossy material Lila had ever seen. It was of so luminous a shade of silvery yellow that it had the gleam of lemon pith. She reached out and touched it and just the stroke of her fingertip cast into its folds a shadow with the translucence of melted butter. She withdrew her hand and watched the surface slide back again to slippery cream. She could not take her eyes from it. The silk neither reflected nor absorbed light, it engaged it; it pulled light in and played games, it chased it across its surface and let it loose, ghostly and flippant and fugitive. A soft darkened edge ran down the length of the dress, the shadow of the time the cloth had been left folded. Here and there it was marked with tiny, rusty spots. All around Lila rose the smell of pear drops and funeral flowers.

Behind her on the floor Enid's mum was at work again – *one yard, two, three, four, bit for luck, pin* – but Lila could tell she was watching her. Her voice was different, fluttering slightly.

She stopped counting and said, with a sigh, 'That's satin for you. Proper heavy pre-war satin, ordered for a wedding. Wedding never happened, aye well, so the wholesaler says. Couldn't shift it during the war, not even after. Folk hadn't got the coupons then, now they haven't the money. You don't see that quality often. Most folk round here wouldn't know it when they saw it.'

'Oh, so it's *old*, then.'

Enid's mum looked sharply at the dress. 'Aye, I suppose to you it's old, it's not that long ago for others. It's quality. Still, you couldn't get a wedding dress out of that material now, all foxed and light damaged.'

She went back to the heap of calico. 'It'll be all right for a stage costume, marks won't show from a distance. It's a wonder the moth hasn't had it. But the man said he couldn't bring himself to throw it away, not satin like that, not that quality.'

'It's the most beautiful, beautiful material I've ever, ever seen.'

Enid's mum stabbed another pin into the calico and pulled more from the bale with a series of soft thuds on the floor. 'Like it?' she said. 'It's nice stuff, right enough. That you've got there's only the top. There's to be trousers as well to go underneath, don't ask me why, your Uncle George and your Joe what's-his-name say it's to be tunic with trousers underneath. I said what, frock and breeks and on a girl, and they said that's what they'd have had in those days. I'm not arguing. You like it?'

'Like it? *Like* it – it's, it's the most—'

'It's quite nice,' Enid said wanly. 'Will she get into it, though? It looks awful small.' She turned away down the passageway and poured out their tea, singing a snippet from the opera in deliberately Scottish Italian so that

Diecimila anni al nostro Imperatore!

sounded like

Deechy Miller Annie I'll no strimp a rat tory!

Lila glowered after her. '*Is* it my size?' she whispered to Enid's mum. 'Are you sure it's my size?'

Enid's mum laughed, clambered to her feet and dropped heavily into the chair at the sewing machine. 'Have I not run you up enough bits and pieces to know your size? I just made it a wee bit bigger in the chest. You've more bosom than Enid and then I was thinking you'll be needing a bit of leeway. You've to take big deep breaths, haven't you, singing? So I gave you a bit of room. Want to try it on?'

Enid, smirking, came in with their tea. 'Go on, then,' she said. 'Let's see if it's big enough.'

Mrs Foley nodded. 'Go on, I'm dying to see it on. Slip it on and let's have a look at you.'

Lila said, 'Please. Oh please, Mrs Foley, please can I just take it home? Can I take it away to try on at home? I'll be careful, I promise, I won't let anything happen to it. I just want to try it on at home, is that all right? I'll bring it straight back tomorrow.'

Enid's mum laughed. 'You're a funny one. What, Lizzie, are you shy? Aye, if you want, I suppose, take it away home. It's tougher than it looks, silk. There's brown paper under the counter, wrap it up in that. If it doesn't fit you, bring it back. There's plenty more stuff.'

Lila found some brown paper and some tissue, slipped the dress off the hanger and folded it up into a parcel. Enid watched her, her bottom lip hanging loose. Lila went about wrapping it feeling big and indelicate, afraid of leaving fingerprints where she touched the dress, afraid to breathe too close in case she dulled it.

'Er, right, that's me away. I need to go now,' she said. 'Thank you very much.'

Enid's mum inclined her head gently and told her she was welcome. Lila hesitated. She wanted to fall into Enid's mum's arms and declare love and gratitude but the right words were not available.

She said, 'Thank you. It's really, really lovely.'

The right words belonged to opera and to Joe. Not even Enid's mum would understand if she tried to say them. Lila squeezed the parcel to her chest and her eyes filled with tears.

'Away now, you're welcome,' Enid's mum said. 'Off you go, you try it on and let me know how it fits.'

Enid said, flatly, 'Not want your tea? It's poured.'

'Er, no, I won't bother, thanks. See you tonight.' She paused. They had agreed that Enid would come to Seaview Villas at six o'clock so they could do their makeup together. 'I'll just see you there, okay? Half past seven.'

'We're meant to be doing our makeup. What about the nail varnish? Half's yours, remember.'

'Oh, no, sorry, I can't. I forgot. I'm to be ready early. My mum says. She's in charge. I'm to be on hand to help with refreshments, they'll want a hand putting plates out.'

It was not a good lie and both Enid's and her mother's silence made that plain. Fleur was never in charge of anything, nor did she take sufficient notice of Lila to organise her movements or commandeer her help. Ashamed, Lila left them in the back shop and made her way swiftly past the counter to the door. She had almost reached it when Enid called out from behind the curtain, 'Hey, what about the sandals?'

'*Oh.*' Lila had forgotten. 'Oh, just bring them with you, okay? I'll see you there and get them then.' She pulled the door open and launched herself through it so that whatever Enid yelled in reply was lost in the clanging of the bell.

I find my way to the hairdressers all right, on Main Street not far from Woolworths, although Woolworths is now a Pet Supplies & Aquatic Centre, which seems odd. It's a very big place for selling Winalot and goldfish.

They're a bit surprised to see me at the hairdressers, I can tell, maybe even impressed; I bet it's not every freezing day in January that a woman with a walking stick and one foot bare but for some bandages (which I admit are a little grubby now) keeps an appointment. They are not very well organised and seem to have lost any note of my appointment but they have a stylist free, they tell me, as if I should be grateful. The girl who does me doesn't see *me*, of course. She gawps in the mirror and addresses my reflection. She lifts my hair in strands and asks what I want. I can't find the words, and she's bored already.

She sighs at the mirror, So will I just give it a shampoo and trim and a tidy and a blow dry and finish, then?

She asks me how my hair has 'been' lately and is disappointed by what I say. She washes at least three kinds of shampoo into it and rinses them all back out one after the other. She tells me there's a Senior Citizens' discount before she asks if I'm retired. But her movements are gentle. When she takes the weight of my head in her hands and her fingertips travel into my hair and over and over my wet skull I feel soothed as if by a lover. She snips in silence, smoothes my hair into an acceptable coating for my head and by then it is almost dry. She wets it again with a spray and dries it herself. At the very end she sprays something on it. Across my forehead, when

I leave, there's a tight hot band of bright pink from the blow drying and my head is buzzing with perfumes and my neck prickles.

Next to the hairdressers is a tiny shop, no more than a stall really, selling hot doughnuts and cookies and I think that perhaps Luke, being American, might like a doughnut, and I am slightly peckish myself. I buy six.

When I arrive quite a bit later at the Evangelical Lutherans, Luke is busy. He is counselling, I am told by a young woman who looks rather like his wife Lucy but isn't. She wants to know if I'm all right which is a silly question. Who seeks out a priest when they are all right? She tells me I can wait and I admit I'm glad to rest my throbbing foot. When Luke is ready there are four doughnuts left. I hobble into a hot little room full of books with a desk, and armchairs grouped round an electric fire.

Luke's face is full of hope that he's got me now.

Hey, *Lila*!

Then he takes a proper look. Oh Lila, oh, my. Here, sit down, you get that foot up here, now. There. You want a cushion under there? Looks real painful. You want me to fix that bandage? You sure you should be walking around? Shouldn't you be home, resting it?

I told you I didn't really know him, but there are things about him that could be said, I tell Luke. When you asked me about him before, I wasn't very helpful, I realise. But there are things that one might say.

About your dad, right? That's just fine, you can include anything you want, we've still got three days. But Lila, I would've come to you any time you asked – there wasn't any call for . . . okay. Okay, now you're here, Lila, do you mind if I just take a minute?

Before I can consider whether I mind or not he's straight in with it: Lord, uh, this is Luke, your servant. I pray, Lord, bless all communication today that helps me give wise counsel and to listen prayerfully and to offer your hope and comfort and balm to our sister Lila whose spirit may be in trouble at this time, send her peace in your holy name O Lord Jesus Amen.

You shouldn't give counsel and *then* listen, I say. Listening comes first, or it should, I would have thought.

Luke laughs. Lila, you're right. I'm listening.

All right. There are things about him that could be said. For instance, he served time in prison. I didn't know that myself till I was fifteen. It was kept quiet.

You sure you want *me* to know that?

Not that he was a criminal. It was only a bit of selling during the war. Black market. He got six months. When he came out he was a changed man. Never the same. Lost his spark.

Lila, really, it'd be kind of nice to know things I could say at the funeral. Memories of your dad, the kind of man he was. I'm not sure this is the kind of stuff you'd want me to say.

I'm talking. *You* should be listening. That's why he was a clerk all his life. He wasn't allowed to practise, not with a criminal record. I don't think that was fair. He brought his wife and baby down to Burnhead and bought his house with money he inherited from his father. By that time the daughter was three months old.

The daughter? You, Lila? You mean you?

Have a doughnut. Go on. His wife, by the way, loathed him. She only married him because she was pregnant and even then only because she thought she was marrying a lawyer. It came out in the end, him being in prison, along with a lot of other things. A lot of things came out all at once, really.

Luke is looking desperate now, poor man. He thought he was going to hear about my father's love of gardening, his kindness to small animals, his quiet faith, and he's getting this. He doesn't know why. Not sure I do.

I allow him a minute to think.

I guess things have a habit of coming out in the end, he says, and I nod. He goes on, I guess the truth will always out.

I believe that the ultimate truth is God's truth. The truth, Lila—

I interrupt: – will set you free? Ah, but will it? Will it, though? That's where you're wrong. It's the illusions that keep us going. Illusions and delusions. Stories. Fairy tales. You haven't eaten your doughnut.

Illusions and stories? Is it illusions that keep you going, Lila? Don't you want to shed illusions and let God's truth into your heart? Don't you want to hear the greatest story in the whole world, the best *true* story of how Jesus Christ died for you?

He's getting down to business now, not that I blame him. This is the kind of thing he does.

But that's what I'm telling *you*, I say. A true story. Or a story about the truth, anyway. Because in this story, it comes out in the end. And my illusions, and a lot of other people's too, they don't survive the story. Some of the people don't survive, either. My father only survives it in a way.

What are you talking about, Lila?

Everything comes out. The brother-in-law goes to prison.

Your father's brother-in-law? You mean they were in it together, the black-market deal?

No, no. The brother-in-law goes for something quite different. And it kills him, prison kills him. My father takes it hard. And it doesn't help, though this comes a little later, the wife killing herself just before her fortieth birthday.

He still hasn't touched his doughnut.

The wife, he says. He says it so gently, as if he knew her, that I think about crying. The wife. Your mother. Your mother, Lila.

There is another long pause and I sense he wants to give me this silence for some purpose, but I don't want it.

The wife, I repeat.

Okay. Right, Luke says quietly. So, the daughter. What happens to the daughter, Lila?

The daughter? Oh, let's not concern ourselves with the daughter.

You say you want to tell me a story about the truth. You came here to say things about your father. Are you sure it's not the daughter you need to talk about?

Of course I detect the therapeutic timbre of the voice. It's counselling tone, loud and clear.

Oh, the daughter survives it, I say. And there's nothing else I want to say, after all. Eat your doughnut. Do you like my hair? Do you have any painkillers, by the way? I seem to have left mine at home.

Sadly for me Luke does not believe in painkillers, not in tablet form. I let him run on for a while about Jesus being the best cure for just about everything he knows, and then he asks how I'm getting home. He insists on driving me back in my car himself. He takes me all the way up to the front door of 5 Seaview Villas and even comes in with me. He switches on lights and turns on the gas fire and then he has to go and take a prayer meeting at which, I am assured, I will be remembered. From the dining room window I watch him set off into the twilight, turning his collar up. He waves. It is nice of him not to mention that it is a long, cold walk back to Burnhead.

20

L ila waited at the window of her bedroom until the house grew quiet. Outside, the sun was sinking. Long threads of cloud slanted across the sky in careless strokes of silver and the dune grass bobbed and shivered in a mist of sand thrown by the wind up the beach. Inside the house the sounds of doors, telephones and voices had stopped. Her mother had called upstairs for her to get a move on and Lila had shouted back that she wasn't ready and would make her own way, they need not wait.

Now she had to hurry. The snap of her door latch made her jump – what if the house *wasn't* empty? It was already nearly eight o'clock. She crept along to the bathroom. Her mother had taken one of her endless, greedy baths so Lila bathed quickly in a few inches of tepid water and when she ran more into the basin to rinse out her shampoo it was stone cold and made her head ache. She was so late and foolish and afraid. She had not even tried the dress on yet – she had to be clean first – and what if it didn't fit? What if she tore it before she'd even got it on? Still Joe was not back. What if he walked into the house right now? She listened, her heartbeat hammering in her throat. No, she decided, she was safe; this late in the evening he would go straight to the farm from the station. He was probably already there. She took a deep breath and tried to decide whether to use the *Rodeo Princess* or pinch some of her mother's *Shalimar*. But why had Joe left it so late? Was he coming at all? He *must* be already there, and now she was the one who was late. Could she get her hair looking all right in time?

But the dress, slipping easily over her head with an exciting noise, restored her nerve. It fitted well except for a tendency to billow up round her bust (Enid's mum had overdone the bit of leeway) but she smoothed it down and it seemed to settle, for a moment. In any case it didn't matter because raising her hand and lightly pressing the space between her breasts was the kind of feminine gesture that Joe might like.

She had not really noticed when the dress was on the hanger that the side seams were slit to a point well above her knees. She tipped her dressing-table mirror downwards and inspected her legs. There was quite a flash of skin when she whirled round, which of course you couldn't avoid doing at a ceilidh, so she might sit out the wilder dances – the Eightsome Reel and Strip the Willow – during which the girls always got flung about. Anyway, the only dancing she wanted to do was a slow, gliding journey across the floor in Joe's arms. She twirled some more. They were only legs after all, and the dress was narrow; if the slits weren't there she would hardly be able to walk. It was meant to have slits and swing out. There was nothing wrong with it, it was just a bit unusual for round here. She leaned in towards the mirror and studied her face. The satin of the dress made her skin glow. Her dark hair, loose down her back – there was no time to do anything with it – shone like wet coal against it. Lila smiled. She would arrive like Cinderella. Joe would be waiting for her. Other people in more mundane finery would almost fail to recognise her but Joe's eyes would light up and everybody would applaud when he took her by the hand and led her to the floor to dance. At that moment the white farm shed with stark overhead lights would somehow be draped in warm velvet and chandeliered, the accordions and fiddles transformed into a tidy little Viennese octet. By the end of the evening she and Joe would be engaged.

Meanwhile she couldn't wait to see drop-lipped, slow-eyed Enid in her matching turquoise dress and eyeshadow, with midges stuck in the hairspray that would be gluing up her wiry red hair.

But she had almost forgotten again that Enid was bringing the sandals. She would have to go up the track in her black school plimsolls, so it was a mercy she was late, after all. Nobody would see her arrive and Enid would probably be looking out for her, so she would be able to change into the sandals outside in the field without appearing in the plimsolls at all. And if Enid had 'forgotten' the sandals, or actually had forgotten them (either was possible) she would dance in bare feet. She liked the idea of herself dancing barefoot, careless and free-spirited. How Joe would adore her for flouting convention.

Before Lila got close to the farm she could make out Mr and Mrs Mathieson up ahead on the track, stationed on picnic chairs behind a pair of trestle tables. Mr Mathieson was counting and thumbing through papers and did not look up; Mrs Mathieson, adjusting a cape round her shoulders and lifting a cup from its saucer, watched her approach. Lila felt her face turning red. It was bad enough the plimsolls being seen by the Mathiesons but worse, there were people milling around in the field. Terrified of being seen by Joe, she snatched glances through gaps in the hedge as she picked her way over the track. They were quite far away, lingering in groups of two and three high up near the farm buildings, mostly men and boys and some in shirtsleeves, but there were girls, too, turning and preening in their coloured dresses. In the low sunlight Lila could make out objects in people's hands and a blue film of smoke over their heads. Of course, why had she not thought of it? The ceilidh shed was full of straw bales. People were coming outside for cigarettes, and for drink, too, she could see, watching heads tip back and dark shapes lifted to mouths. Probably beer was being sold out of crates round the back, a blind eye turned to 'intoxicating liquor' being swigged out here as long as it did not taint the gentility of the shed, where the urn would be simmering and the shortbread doing the rounds.

There was a sudden burst of shouting from the field. Some horseplay started up; drink was being sprayed and thrown around, people scattered roaring and yelping. A group of squealing girls moved away and then turned back and edged in close again as the boys regrouped in a rough, wide circle a distance away from the buildings. A raggedly organised mock-joust began, the boys squaring up to one another, challenging, advancing, swerving, the girls watching at a distance from which they could be sure they were still being noticed. Lila saw Billy swing across the grass in a low, loping run and take a leap on to the back of another boy and together they spun around, turning and turning until they fell and the group roiled around them, laughing. They tumbled over and over, pulling at one another's hair and clothes, until they lost interest. They got to their feet, slapped each other on the back. Bottles were passed round. The girls moved closer around the group of which Billy was now the centre, brushing himself off and tucking in his shirt. Lila was furious.

She had reached the table now. Mrs Mathieson nudged Mr Mathieson.

'I forgot my money,' Lila said. 'Please can I pay after?'

Mr Mathieson looked up from his cash box and papers. 'I'm all cashed up now,' he said, with a purse of his bluish lips. 'We were just away in, we only stayed out in case we'd gatecrashers. You're a bit late.'

'It wasn't my fault,' Lila said. 'I couldn't help it.'

'Mr Mathieson just means you're missing yourself, dear,' Mrs Mathieson said. 'They've been going over an hour. So you'll not be needing a ticket, will she, John?' She gave him another nudge and nodded towards the book of tickets fluttering on the table. Lila shivered and rubbed at the gooseflesh on her arms. 'John, she doesn't need to pay now, does she?'

Mr Mathieson scratched the space between his eyebrows with one finger. 'Well, everybody else paid,' he said. 'We're trying to raise money here.'

'Yes, and we've already made what we thought we would,' Mrs Mathieson told him. 'And everybody else has had over an hour already.' She turned to Lila. 'You warm enough? I've a cardigan you can borrow. It's grey, it'd go fine over your dress.'

'No, no, I'm fine!' Lila said, not managing to conceal the horror of the idea, a grey cardigan borrowed from an old person. 'Thank you very much, anyway.'

'Well, away you go in then. We'll be right in after you.'

Mr Mathieson nodded. 'On you go, then,' he said. 'I'm going soft.'

Lila was staring ahead. A single string of lightbulbs had been suspended between two of the sycamore trees, making an archway in the yard. The lights glared a strangely dull electric white, caught in the sun's last falling rays. The shed was still out of sight behind the barn. She could feel it waiting.

'Is everybody else here? I'd better hurry. Thank you,' she said, skirting past the trestle table.

'Wait!' Mr Mathieson called her back. 'Here. You'll be needing a tea voucher as well.'

Lila took it and thanked him even though she had no intention of having anything as ordinary as tea.

'You have yourself a nice time now,' Mrs Mathieson sang after her. As soon as she was out of earshot, she sighed and stood up. 'She looks ready for a party, any road,' she said.

Lila walked slowly under the arch of lights in the direction of the music. She was nearly level with the long side of the ceilidh shed now. Soon she would round the corner and find the wide doors standing open and a wedge of bright light hitting the ground in front of it. The music grew louder, a flippant tune she didn't recognise; it drove on brusquely. She shivered again. The sky was changing rapidly now. The slow blazing-down of the sun would soon be over, leaving the sky empty and waiting for the inky wash of the dark.

A figure loomed towards her from the dark alley between the barn and the back of the shed.

'Joe?'

'Hey, you. That you?' It was Billy.

'Hey, where've you been?' he said. His voice was not friendly but Lila felt a moment's gratitude; even hostile recognition might help her feel less lonely and conspicuous. She felt out of place, too bright and too big and exotically plumaged, a flamingo in a flock of starlings.

'You promised me a wee dance, didn't you? You trying to avoid me?'

He came up close, swaying a little and staring through watery, exhausted eyes. His shirt, coming loose from his trousers, was badly grass-stained. Almost as a gesture of sympathy, he brought up one hand and took hold of her shoulder, though he seemed also to need the support.

'You all right?' he said. 'Where've you been?'

'Have you seen Joe?'

'Joe?' The other hand came up on her other shoulder and he pulled her against him. 'What's it with you? I thought you weren't coming.' Over his beery breath came the smell of grass and sweat. Bringing his mouth close to her face he said, 'I was waiting on you coming.'

His arms were tight around her. Her damp hair had been spun by the wind into clumps and he worked his fingers into it, stroking, until both his hands were entangled. She tried to withdraw, though only a little.

'Ouch! Billy!'

They staggered together and almost fell and then Billy found his footing, dragged her up straight and pushed her over to the wall. He pinned her against it, one hand cupping the back of her head. Lila knew this was something she was not supposed to allow, never mind want, but Billy sank his head into her neck with a little moan and began nudging gently at her face with his mouth, making soft cries. She gave a gasp. It was a kind of mewing, bewildered and weak. He was beseeching her, as if she were the one with the power. His lips on her neck and cheek were warm and dry and nibbling. How could she push him away when he wanted to cling to her, when he sounded how she felt so much of the time?

But this was Billy. She squirmed as his hand in the small of her back slipped lower and turned her head sharply away from his mouth. Then he pushed himself hard against her and murmured something and she felt giddy and warm again.

'Well, excuse *me*! Am I interrupting something or can *just anyone* join in?' Enid, emerging from the alley between the barn and the shed, stood in front of them, arms crossed. Billy sprang away. Lila pressed the palms of her hands into the wall to stop them shaking; she was trembling in case anyone, Billy included, might guess what she had been feeling. Had come close to feeling.

'*Well?*'

Enid's engorged mouth was a bright, labial mauve. Someone else's mouth had been giving hers such a mauling that it was pulpy and tender and seemed no longer suited to speech; her lips moved as if her tongue had thickened and was pushing against the back of her teeth and trying to loll its way out. The only vestige of her lipstick that had not been sucked away was smudged across her chin and in the turquoise wreckage of her makeup her eyes were black dots. Her hair was dragged downwards in sticky tufts.

'Did you bring me the sandals?'

'Oh, I forgot,' Enid said, glaring. Actually they were in a gingham slipper bag on the floor under one of the tea tables at the back of the shed, next to a box of spare tablecloths. She and Lila stared at each other. Across the yard Mr and Mrs Mathieson strolled past on their way to the shed, Mr Mathieson humming along to the dance tune as he went.

'I forgot, sorry,' Enid said.

From the shed they heard the accordions start up with 'The Dashing White Sergeant'. The notes flickered and raced along, fast and fluttering. Lila knew she couldn't possibly dance without shoes. Her feet would be trodden and crushed, the concrete floor would lacerate them.

'Billy, you coming?' Enid stepped forward and stood next to him.

There was hardly any light now. Lila could see only the angle of his head and a gleam from the whites of his eyes. She turned away from the sight of the pair of them, pushed herself off the wall and walked away. She did not want to watch Enid pulling Billy back into the shadows.

Inside the shed about fifty people were dancing and dozens more stood or sat round the walls, chewing through piled platefuls of food. Everyone gleamed with sweat. The kilted men danced with sombre faces as if to counterbalance their comic, elderly legs, but the women bobbed and bounced with flat smiles, mouths fixed open and showing double rows of dry dentures that shone yellowish against the white surroundings. Hairdos flopped, armpits wore dark damp grins, stockings were shredded. Lila stared past the revolving bodies. She was in the wrong place. Everyone of her age was out in the fields, probably doing the same as Enid and Billy.

'The Dashing White Sergeant' came to a finish with a long, emphatic *harrumph* from the accordions; the dancers sighed, drew breath and clapped and made their way to the water jugs, the straw bales, the tea tables. A few people looked in her direction and turned away. She needed Joe here. Maybe she did look a little odd, hovering alone on the edge of things without him to make it clear, by his admiration, that she was meant to look like this. But Joe was somewhere else. From the back of the shed she became aware of movement, and looked up.

'Oy! Oy, Lizzie!'

Threading his way towards her from the back of the shed came Uncle George. She beamed at him. He was coming to rescue her. He would know where Joe was. She wasn't in the wrong place after all.

'Uncle George! Where's Joe? Is he here?'

'Lizzie!' he bellowed. 'What the bloody hell are you doing? Just what the bloody hell are you up to?'

She could hear his words but she had no idea why they were being addressed to her. He was accusing her of something, so there must be some kind of mistake. How could she have made him so angry? People in Uncle George's path melted to the sides and her mother strode along just behind him, dressed perfectly in a red flared skirt.

'Jesus Christ, Lizzie! Have you no sense? You'll *ruin* that!' he thundered. 'You stupid child! Suppose you tear it? Do you think this whole thing's a game? Do you think this is about dressing up?'

Lila's mouth opened and closed. The lights of the shed were striking too brightly off the walls; the shapes of people were losing their edges, moving in a silent, confusing dream. Heat poured through her and burst in a wave of sweat over her skin.

'Jesus Christ! I'm trying to do something to a *professional standard* here. Don't you know we're up against a deadline, most of the costumes aren't even half-done, and you jeopardise all that work for the sake of *dressing up?*'

Still she could not speak. Though surely she was being misunderstood, she felt like a criminal. Fleur laid a hand on George's arm. Lila looked at her. *Stop him*, she begged her mother silently. *Explain. Speak for me.*

Fleur gently pushed George away and came forward. 'Just what do you think you look like?' she said. Her voice was soft and deadly. 'You've got proper clothes, haven't you? What do you think you're doing, appearing like that, you silly girl? Honestly! You look like . . . like a . . . demented bridesmaid!'

She looked round, bringing the other women into it. Her voice cracked in a short, hard laugh. 'Honestly, kids! Who'd have them!'

'Please . . .'

Uncle George said, 'No, but honestly, Lizzie, you've gone too far, it really won't do . . .'

Lila looked round desperately. Mrs Mathieson had handed her plate to Mr Mathieson and was ambling over to the band. She leaned over and spoke to the leader, a man with sleek black hair, and he nodded to the others and off they sailed into a new swirling tune, releasing everyone. Mrs Mathieson caught Lila's eye with a look of calm goodwill and walked slowly back towards Mr Mathieson. Before he had handed back her plate, Lila had disappeared.

It was now quite dark. Lila ran as hard as she could under the swinging lights in the yard and down the track, not slowing until her short sobbing breaths and the high rasping of the silk as she went were louder in her ears than the grinding of the band. Inside the bright shed it was Ladies' Choice. As Raymond and George looked on, Fleur swished her skirt around her ankles and took to the floor in a Canadian Barn Dance with Mr McArthur. At the same moment, Enid ran out into the dark from the space between the shed and the barn and fell on her knees, belching up cidery gas and crying with shock at what Billy had got her to do. She tried to gasp out a prayer, her first in weeks, but she knew it was too late for that. The Lord wouldn't want her now, a tainted Eve cast out from even this improbable Eden, kneeling in a thriving clump of Ayrshire nettles that were stinging her legs all the way up to her thighs.

Behind her, Billy picked up the cider bottle and retreated back to the alley and further into the dark. He sank down against the wall and drained the bottle. He thought he might be sick, later, but now he rammed his hand into his open trousers and with his eyes glassy and teeth clenched, he turned his face towards the moon and concentrated on pumping himself to a hot, raw finish, racing ahead of the throb of the band. Overhead, the sky poured darkness over the sighing sea, the dunes and the scrub grass, the Pow Burn and the banked shapes of Seaview Villas. Across the thistles and abandoned tyres and the patient hulks of Mr McArthur's cows grouped for the night round the pylon in the field, the beat of the music followed at Lila's back until she was enveloped in the dark and her sobs lessened. The track, abandoned again under the night, fell silent.

ACT III

THE THIRD RIDDLE

Ice which gives you fire
And which your fire freezes still more!
Lily-white and dark,
If it allows you your freedom
It makes you a slave.
If it accepts you as a slave
It makes you a King!

TURANDOT.

That night in Peking, no-one sleeps. Turandot's guards go through the city issuing the royal decree. Under pain of death, whoever knows the strangers' name must reveal it. When Turandot learns that Liù the slave girl knows it, she is put under torture. Liù, rather than be forced to betray her love, seizes a sword and kills herself.

Her sacrifice moves even the icy Turandot. Calaf places himself in her power, telling her who he is.

As the sun rises, everyone in the city assembles to learn the prince's fate. Turandot proudly announces that she has discovered his name: it is Love.

The betrothed lovers embrace and the crowd rejoices.

I 'm well down the second tea chest now. Another cutting, another big photograph. Christine would like this:

Burnhead & District Advertiser Thursday 4th August 1960:

CEILIDH IN SUPPORT OF
BAST 'OUTSTANDING SUCCESS'

Leading lights of the Burnhead Association for Singing *Turandot* pictured (L to R): George Pettifer, conductor and musical director, Fleur Pettifer ('Turandot'), Raymond Duncan (Stage Manager), Audrey Mathieson (Production Secretary), John Mathieson (Production Manager), Moira Mather (chorus), Sandy Scott ('Pung'), Veronica Clarke (chorus), Alec Gallagher ('Timur' & BAST Press Liaison Manager). Also pictured are Stanley McArthur of Pow Farm and Jackie Shenley whose band played for the dancing. A substantial sum was raised.

By Staff Reporter Alec Gallagher

The picture shows them in a line, arms linking arms or hooked over shoulders. Looks as if the photographer told the women to show a bit of leg.

Come on now, ladies, big smiles please! Let's have a bit more of those lovely pins?

Moira Mather and Veronica are making a big effort but my mother does it best. She's a natural. She's lifted one knee and made a little quarter turn of the leg inwards to show a fine gleaming shin and the line of a strong thigh under the flared skirt. She has pointed her raised foot like a ballet dancer's. She's not a tiny woman by any means, she's curvaceous, heavy breasted, but she has delicate ankles and she looks like a glossy, high-stepping thoroughbred. In contrast Mrs Mathieson, her arm locked on one side in Mr Mathieson's and on the other in my father's, looks homely. She is content to stand with just the back of one foot lifted a little from the floor and she is smiling without showing her teeth. George, on my mother's other side, is making such a silly pouting mouth to the camera that I wonder, now, who is taking the picture. Mr McArthur and Jackie Shenley the bandleader watch from the side.

It occurs to me that Christine's gone missing. I haven't seen her since she brought that doctor here and I'm not sure exactly when that was. I wonder if she likes doughnuts, Christine. I've got three left.

When she answers the door she's in very big pyjamas and she looks a little rumpled and she doesn't smile. Behind her, her house is very hot and bright. I hear a television. It's got very pink inside, that house, since old Mr Henderson's dark green and cream days.

Do you like doughnuts?

The bag is all greasy now and as I proffer it I can see she thinks there's a catch, or maybe something wrong with me.

Come on in, she says. You'd better come in for a minute. You shouldn't be up and about on that foot.

I follow her down the hall. Washing drapes the radiators like bunting; lines of coloured garments are hardening over the heat and the air is sticky with scorching polyester and the tang of washing powder. Steve is lying in an armchair in front of the television, his chin resting on his chest. He seems about to slide to the floor.

It's nearly eleven o'clock at night, you know, he says without turning from the screen. Time folk were away to their beds.

Steve, don't you start. Then Christine says to me, Never mind him. You're all right for a minute, we're still up.

Is it really that time? I don't have a watch. I was thinking maybe Paris likes them, I say. Doughnuts, I mean.

Paris isn't very well, Christine sighs, otherwise I'd have been in to see how you were doing. She shifts a mug and some magazines off a chair. Sit down a wee minute. You're welcome to stay a minute. Though I'll not be up that much longer, I'll be away to my bed.

Steve looks over at her and says, I told you over an hour ago you should be in your bed.

What's wrong with Paris? I ask. Is she all right? I was thinking she might like a doughnut.

Just a wee cold, says Steve. She's all right.

It nearly went on her chest, Christine says, frowning at him. It *is* on her chest a wee bit. She's sleeping now.

Sleeping? Oh, can I see her? I'd love to see her asleep. The words are out of my mouth without warning, before I even know it's what I want. I say, I won't disturb her. I promise I won't make a sound.

Steve says, Jesus, what now? and looks hard at us both. Eh? What next?

Christine says, Well, I was just going up to check on her. You can come up and see her, and then I'll be going to my bed, okay? You should get to bed yourself, she says, peering at me in her usual worried way, which I no longer object to. I may even have missed it.

We climb the stairs, me with my stick, taking them one at a time, resting now and then on my good foot. As we go the smell of carpets gets stronger. Paris's room is full of shadows. There are hundreds of tiny luminous moons and stars and planets studded all over the ceiling.

Oh! I whisper. Oh, how pretty! How magical, all those stars! The moons!

Christine frowns. You get them in packets, she says.

Paris is snuffling, curled up on her side like a little human comma. She's lying under two mobiles suspended over the bed: one is of sheep, the other's composed of shapes I can't make out. They hang utterly still. Her puffy feet are turned in like resting flippers and the palm of one hand lies open, her little flakes of fingernails scraping the pillow. In the other hand she is clutching Stripey, or was; her hold has relaxed and Stripey has fallen away from her lips. Her eyelashes are soft, tiny fans placed carefully upon her cheeks, and her mouth is open and damp. At the side of the bed is a glowing green lamp in the shape of a tree. Bathed in its votive light she lies, small and calm on her green shrine. Christine looks at her and her daily fight to be brisk and practical and all together melts out of her. Sedated by love, she smiles and yawns and sags, and the room swells with adoration. As she arranges the covers around the child I can tell she is resisting an urge to lift her up and hold her in her arms until dawn. She touches Paris's cheek with one finger, smiles and yawns again and pushes me gently from the room.

When we get downstairs Steve is in the kitchen. That you away home, now? he asks. Here, let's fix up your bandage before you go.

He has kind hands. When he's done with the bandage he walks me back to number five. I have my stick in one hand and he makes me take his arm and we go slowly.

Well now, he says at the gate. Let's get you safe in.

Up the path we go in the orange light from across the street, past the broken heap in the garden, the piano and tea chest and papers and all the sodden drapery.

To stop him saying anything about it I tell him, You have a sweet little daughter.

Aye, wee Paris. Just three, time goes that quick, he says. Christine was saying you never had kids yourself, that right?

No, I never took the plunge, I said.

Never married, then?

Too late for that conversation, I can't open the subject now. We have only a few more feet to go.

Well. I came close once or twice, I say.

Shame, he says.

But not that close, I say. So not a shame.

Aye, doesn't suit everybody, I suppose.

I think I'm living in the wrong era. I should have been born in another time.

Steve seems nervous at this.

I mean, in a time when a woman being a spinster wasn't the oddest thing about her. There used to be lots of spinsters. I think it's odder than it used to be, not getting married. Not having a partner, rather.

Is that right?

On the other hand, these days it's not getting divorced that's the real oddity.

Steve laughs gently. So with your dad gone, is that you the end of the line, then? There's nobody else left but you.

We reach the front step. I have a sudden clear picture of next door's pink walls and homely smells and the precious child of the house asleep upstairs, and my heart flutters and sinks like a little falling leaf. I catch my breath, thinking of the many and various messes that await me behind this door. They are all of my own making, which doesn't help.

That's right. He was the last to go, I tell Steve. I've seen them all off now. Goodnight.

To my great surprise and I have to confess, pleasure, Steve kisses me tenderly on the cheek.

Never you mind, he says. Goodnight.

———

21

'Toilets?' Fleur said. 'For God's sake, Raymond, don't talk to me about toilets.'

Raymond closed his mouth and pulled off his boots, stooping in the back doorway. Thick drizzling rain hung in the air like mist. It had started early, as he was setting out for the farm to help clean up after the ceilidh, and after nearly two hours of picking bottles and rubbish from the track and the field he was soaked through. A silvery film of water glistened on his hair and moustache and face; shining drops like tiny glass beads stood out on the shoulders and sleeves of his dark jersey. He straightened up and brushed himself down, sending a shower sprinkling across the floor.

'Stop that!' Fleur hissed. 'And for God's sake get that door shut. You've brought in enough damp as it is.'

Raymond skulked to his place at the kitchen table. Despite himself, he filled the room with his soggy bulk and the out-doors, wide-awake smell of rain. His skin shone pink and cold and clean.

His freshness put Fleur in a rage. She rubbed a hand over her forehead and pinched at the flesh under her chin. She felt slack and tired. Her face was bed-wrinkled, her mouth furry. Often now in the mornings she was afraid she was getting a glimpse of herself as she would soon look and feel all day. Nobody had warned her how short and cruel this interval was, the decade between the ages of thirty and forty, and how she would be more than halfway through it before she realised how much of her life had passed while all she had been aware of was how the years dragged.

She was wearing her new dressing gown, bought from a divine and exorbitant shop the girls had put her on to, but it was failing her, as clothes could these days. When she was younger, beautiful clothes delighted her; she used to succumb and overspend and feel guilty, but she would cherish her lovely things until they wore out. Soon after she was married she turned defiant about the cost; the sums that Raymond sighed over were simply what it took to look half-decent and her expensive clothes were no more than her due. Now their expense was the main point. But the surge of happiness she got in the shop from spending more than she ought to was short and cheap, no more than a gambler's thrill. It never lasted the journey home; by the time a new garment was unwrapped at 5 Seaview Villas, Fleur would know from a sourness in her heart that neither it nor she was worth it.

The dressing gown was all wrong for getting breakfast. The sleeves were gathered at the wrist in floppy cuffs and even when she pushed them up past her elbows the ribbons kept falling in the lard. Not wanting to get the frying pan too hot (the stink would cling to her hair all day if the pan smoked) and trying to keep a safe distance, Fleur cracked the eggs from shoulder height into a pond of barely melted fat. The yolks burst on impact and lard splashed down her pale blue ruffled frontage. She clenched her teeth and watched the egg whites, gashed with orange, spread coolly to the edges of the pan and solidify silently with none of the lively spit they gave when Eliza cooked them.

She turned and glared at the table. George was unshaven and smoking before breakfast again, sitting with his back to the wall and looking even worse than she did. Raymond was still going on about toilets.

She said, 'Will you get some plates and shut *up*.'

'I'm afraid he has a point, though,' George said. 'I don't know why I never thought of it.'

Raymond fetched the plates and returned to the table.

'Aye, toilets have to be considered.' In an odd way, he liked a plumbing problem. Getting down to brass tacks made him secretly cheerful. 'Let's face it,' he said. 'Last night we got off lightly. Stanley McArthur's saying with the best will in the world his cistern can't take it. As it is he needs a new ball cock after last night's traffic.'

'And we had how many at the ceilidh?' George asked.

'Och, less than a hundred and fifty,' Raymond said. 'Maybe a hundred and twenty.'

'So if we're putting in seats for over two hundred,' George said, 'and if we get a full house—'

'And then there's the cast and orchestra and crew, that's an awful lot more.'

'Oh, God,' George sighed, sucking the last out of his cigarette and stubbing it out.

'Aye, and don't forget last night it was only the girls went in the house,' Raymond said morosely. 'The lads mainly used the hedge.'

'Well, that won't do,' George sniffed. 'Not exactly savoury, is it, a big night out at the opera and you have to pee in a hedge.'

'For God's sake, George, must you?' Fleur said, pushing at the eggs.

'Aye, there are limits,' Raymond said. 'A hedge can only take so much.'

'Oh, for God's sake!' Fleur snapped. 'Must we discuss this at the table? Why hasn't somebody thought about all this before?'

'We're not *at* table,' George said, swallowing a painful belch. 'Or nothing's on it, anyway. I'm starving. Florrie, aren't those done yet? Isn't there any toast?'

'Oh, eat some bread, it's in the bin. I've only got one pair of hands, if you want toast you can make it.'

George got up and brought the loaf, and butter still in its paper, to the table. Raymond, his eyes on Fleur's back, fetched a bottle of HP sauce and set it down gingerly, as if it might be a small bomb.

'I *am* thinking of it,' added Raymond, taking his seat again and watching her slide the eggs on to cold plates. 'I'm thinking of it now. Where's wee Lizzie?'

'Never mind her,' Fleur said. She brought the plates and passed them over. 'Let her cool her heels. She's probably too ashamed to show her face. Or she's sulking.' She lifted a strand of her hair and stretched it as far as her nose. '*Damn*, I'll have to shampoo my hair. I can't believe I'm expected to sing a whole run-through this afternoon *and* cook and slave for all and sundry.'

Moving quickly, Raymond upended the sauce bottle over his plate and gave it a couple of sharp slaps. Before anything had come out, Fleur's hand flew out and snatched it away.

'Oh no, you don't. That's an insult to the cook,' she said. 'And least of all at breakfast, *if* you don't mind.'

'Och, Fleur. George likes a bit of HP, too,' Raymond said, looking for solidarity. 'Don't you, George?'

'Sorry, you're on your own this morning,' George said. The very thought of vinegar made his guts shrivel. 'So look, Ray, what do you think we should do? About the, er . . .' Fleur glanced up from buttering her bread and gave them a warning look. 'About the facilities,' he said.

Raymond cleared his throat. 'Elsan,' he told him, carefully. 'Like you can get in caravans, or camping. The chemical solution.' More eagerly he said, 'We'll need to get on with it though, arrange for the hire and so on. And we'll need the proper tents, with dividers. Duckboards. No time to waste.'

'Do they really work?' George said. 'Can they cope?'

'Oh, aye. The Blacks now, Gordon Black was up there this morning helping – he says they're nothing short of miraculous. The Blacks have been camping to the Lakes more than once. He says they're –' Raymond stole a glance at Fleur, who was flipping a slab of egg white into her mouth – 'completely inoffensive.' He lowered his voice. 'Both liquids and sol—'

'Oh, for God's sake!' Fleur cried, banging her fork down. 'Enough! Shut up! I mean it! I don't want to hear another *word*.'

So it was that a few minutes later Lila slipped into the kitchen and was met with nothing but dogged chewing from the three at the table. Assuming that she was the cause of the awkwardness and that she was not forgiven, she was turning to leave when Uncle George said with false brightness, 'Now you're here, Liù, would you fry another egg for your old uncle?'

She did so happily, and also did another one for her father who decided he could manage one as soon as Fleur had left the room to go up for her bath. He covered it with HP sauce and left a large leftover dollop on the side of his plate. Afterwards, scraping everything into the bin and washing up the dishes and the congealed frying pan, Lila reflected on the kindness she had been shown. It was clear to her that Uncle George had not really wanted the second egg because he left at least half of his first one on the plate. In asking her to cook him one he was showing her there were no hard feelings. It did not occur to her that the awful silence in the kitchen might have been caused not by her but by something more important.

A few hours later, Lila heard the whump of the front door and was out of her room and at the top of the stairs in an instant, peering over the banisters. George came out of the music room and confronted Joe in the hall.

'What time do you call this?'

Joe looked ragged and sullen. In reply, he dropped his holdall on the floor. Lila could not bear his letting it fall there as if he were undecided about staying; it looked so temporary. She wanted to tear downstairs and run up to his room with it.

'You know what, Maestro? You sound like an old woman. What time do I call this?' Joe's voice was thick and deliberate. 'I call it on time. I call it punctual. You said the run-through was at two. Well, here I am.'

'You've been drinking.'

Joe looked past George up the stairs and grinned, but his eyes were tearful. 'Well, well! Hello, hello, Liù! And how are you?'

He set his hands on his thighs and shifted his weight on to one hip.

'You're cutting it a bit fine, aren't you? Ray's already down there, so's half the band,' George said, his voice rising. 'You're not even warmed up. I bet you haven't done any practice. You've been on a bender, haven't you? Joe, I'm talking to you.'

Joe ignored him. 'Well, Liù, you're looking happy, anyhow – I'm glad someone round here's happy to see me. So how are you-ou, little Lee-yoo?'

'Oh, Joe, I'm fine! I'm better! My tonsils are fine now.'

'Tonsils? Tonsils! Good news, wonderful, I'm delighted! Ready for a sing this afternoon then, eh?' He shuffled his feet for a moment and with one hand reaching upwards he sang an ascending scale, 'La-la-la-la-la-la-la-la!' He cracked the top note with a lift of his eyebrow at her, an invitation to exclude George. Lila took a deep breath and sang back down the scale, her voice floating easily above Joe's. George crossed his arms and waited while Joe leered up the stairwell and sang:

Ah! Tu sei morta,
O mia piccola Liù . . . !

Lila, leaning over the banister, faltered. A smell of whisky rose from his mouth and he seemed unaware of what he had just said: *Ah! You are dead, o my little Liù . . . !* Could he have forgotten that this was the point in the opera when she dies? Liù has just seized a dagger and plunged it into her bosom, and all for him. Lila shook her head and gazed at him.

'All right, all right, all *right*,' George said, glancing between them. They were looking at each other like two spoiled, unguarded children waiting to receive a surprise, each mistaking the other for the indulgent grown-up holding a treat behind the back. 'That's enough.'

'Oh, I love the way you sing that. I think your voice is lovely . . . it's perfect,' Lila said. 'It's *wonderful*.'

Joe bowed. 'Oh, *oh*. Well, my goodness, Liù, *thank* you!' he said. 'How nice to have one's talent appreciated!' His face, suddenly pinker and brighter, told George that he at least had got what he wanted.

'That's enough fooling around,' he said. 'Save it for the run-through.'

'Hey! Hey,' Joe said, turning to him, 'it's only a bit of fun. No need to get into a paddy, Mr Maestro!' He gave George's shoulder a gentle shake. George could tell he did it to point up the contrast between them: tense, irritable George, big-hearted, lenient Joe.

Lila brought her hair round one shoulder and tipped forward so that it hung into the stairwell. Could Uncle George not see he was in the way? How could either of them speak with Uncle George standing like a wall between them?

'Please, Uncle George, Joe's done nothing wrong. Don't be mean. It's not fair. Let him be.'

'Nothing wrong? He's been away for days, he's missed rehearsals and now he turns up in this condition for a crucial run-through with only minutes to spare,' George said with a rising squeak in his voice. 'It's grossly unprofessional. It's disgraceful.'

He frowned up at her. She was squinting down, flopping over the banisters like a cross-eyed rag doll, pulling her hair around in a way that reminded him of a slipping-off wig. Was she going mad, too?

'I'm here now though, aren't I?' Joe said. 'And did you even really notice I was gone? You haven't noticed me properly for weeks. *Did* things fall apart because I wasn't here?'

George's voice tightened. '*Haven't noticed you properly?* What do you think all this is *about*? How many hours a day do I spend—'

'All you think I am is a *voice*, you don't really care about *me*. And you haven't answered my question – did things fall apart? Of course not.'

'That's not the point. Things are okay, no thanks to you, but that's not the point.'

'I told you I had to get away.'

Lila said, 'You did get all the things you went for, didn't you, Joe, all the brocades and the silk trimmings and everything? You did get those?'

Joe leaned over and opened his holdall. 'Nope,' he said, 'I didn't.'

'*What?*' said George. 'Then what the hell have you been doing?'

'One of the warehouse places I never found, the others didn't . . . well, I wasn't inspired. We'll have to make do with what Stella can get hold of. It won't matter.'

'I asked you what the hell you've been doing. You've been away nearly a week. You've done nothing! And you were meant to be back here last night.'

Joe straightened up and spoke slowly. 'Well, there you are. I've been doing other things. Nothing you'd be interested in.'

'I take it I'm not supposed to ask where you've been staying? Or who with? And just how much have you been drinking?'

'No, as a matter of fact, you're not.'

'How dare you!'

Fleur came out of the back room into the hall. Her head, wrapped in a scarf, was bulging with hair rollers and had doubled in volume. She let out a shriek and brought up her hands to cover her face.

'You mustn't see me like this!' she said. 'I can't bear it!'

Joe winked and clicked his tongue at her, then bent over and rummaged in his holdall.

'Naughty boy,' she said, gliding past. She flipped out a hand and gave his backside a little slap. 'Running away like that.'

'Ah, well, *Principessa*,' Joe said, 'but I haven't come back empty-handed.'

'You shouldn't have done that to poor Georgie. He's been beside himself. Weren't you, Georgie?'

George said, 'Fleur, that's enough.'

Fleur patted her rollers. 'So much rehearsal you've missed, we've covered so much ground. You've got a mile of catching up to do.'

Joe fished for another moment in his bag and brought out a small, heart-shaped box. He waved it vaguely. 'Chocolates,' he announced to none of them in particular. 'Here you are, chocolates.'

'Oh well, *chocolates*. Well of course that changes every-thing,' George said, tightening his folded arms around him-self. Joe had made no show of offering him the box so he would not dream of reaching for it. He was not yet nearly sorry enough. George's anger ignited inside him; Joe was not sorry at *all*. 'As a matter of fact,' he said, 'I think it's rather inadequate of you.'

Fleur drawled breathily, pulling her hands down her hips, 'Oh, George, stop being so mean. Lovely chocolates. Char-bonnel et Walker, mmmm. I adore chocolates.' She sighed and smiled encouragingly, waiting to have the gift thrust upon her. 'Oh, my downfall, I shouldn't, really . . .'

Joe was confused. He probably did feel a little guilty or he wouldn't have thought of getting a present, but he hadn't gone further in his mind than just bringing the damn box into the house. He had no particular concern about *giving* it, and he certainly had not meant it to arouse feelings one way or the other. It had been going cheap in a shop near the station, old stock left over from Valentine's Day. He'd imagined himself handing the box over and joking that the chocolates might already be stale, and then being scolded a little. He didn't see why they couldn't make light of it. He was back, wasn't he? But it was impossible to joke about it now. He looked round for somewhere in the cluttered hall to put the box down. He wanted to forget the whole idea, disown it, lose it.

Lila watched him, and ached. It was obvious he wanted Uncle George and her mother gone so that he could give her the present privately. She took a step down the stairs. Joe saw her and pushed the box at her over the banisters.

'There you go, then,' he said, glancing up and stepping back, wiping his mouth.

She clasped the box to her chest and smiled radiantly through the v-shaped gap made by the dent in the heart. His awkwardness in giving the gift showed how sincerely he meant it.

'Oh, *Joe*! Thank you!' she said. There was nothing else she need say. It would be meaningless to add something about the actual chocolates, because who cared what was in the box? Joe could feed her worms if they came from a heart-shaped box.

'We'll be late,' George said. 'Come on, we've got stuff to shift down to the shed. People will be there already. I should be down there now.'

Fleur was feeling under her scarf with both hands. 'Not me,' she said, coolly. 'I'm still damp. I'll see you about half past three.'

'Half past three? The run-through's at two! You *know* the run-through's at two! Full cast. I said full cast!'

Fleur stepped back across the hall and patted George on the cheek. 'Yes, yes, sweetie, I know, but I'm not on till Act II.'

'But you're *seen*. The whole cast and the audience have to see you. Your presence at the end of Act I casts a shadow over the next two acts. It's important.'

'Well, this time they'll just have to imagine me there. You can't expect me to sit around all afternoon just to *appear*. George, you shouldn't get so worked up,' she told him, drifting towards the stairs. 'It can't be good for you. Anyway, I was going to vocalise but now I must lie down, my head's just aching with these big heavy things. Byeee.'

She disappeared upstairs, leaving the others to load up George's car in the rain, with music stands, folding chairs, band parts and Thermos flasks.

Dr Chowdry calls again though I didn't ask her to.

I submit to my tetanus booster and then she says I may as well take the bandage off my foot now. It's healing all right. Since I won't stop walking around and the bandage keeps coming off there's not much point, she says. I don't think I'm walking about much but the bandages do get wet and dirty and my toes do throb even when I haven't been anywhere I remember going.

She looks around the room, and then a little crossly at me, and says as if it's a joke, Well, well. So now it's all the old clothes you're going through. Have you been dressing up? What's this?

She picks up Liù's pale dress between one finger and thumb and in her hands it looks like nothing but a crumpled, filthy rag that's been stuffed in a box for over forty years. She has no idea that it's proper pre-war satin and you just don't get that quality any more. She has no idea it is the most beautiful garment I ever owned.

That was specially made for me! Give me that back!

The more startled she is the harder she smiles, Dr Chowdry. Oh now, no fuss, no fuss, she says. Here you are, I haven't done it any harm, it's all right.

And you're still drowning in papers, she adds after a minute. Still raking over all these old things. Are you looking for anything in particular?

I have to think about this. She calls at inconvenient times, Dr Chowdry. I'm never dressed. This time I may have nodded off in my chair and she walks in the door anyhow which, no matter how you look at it, is a liberty.

No, I'm not. But I may be trying to find something out.

And what might that be, do you think? She is putting on the very careful voice again. She sits down. Do you have any thoughts about what that might be, what you're looking for?

Not the foggiest. Do you like doughnuts? I've got three. They seem a bit smaller than when I bought them but you're welcome. How is Paris now?

Paris is as right as rain, very nearly. I'm popping in on her in a minute. And—

She leans forward with a widening smile. And I have something for you, or rather, I have someone. If you feel like it. I hope you don't mind, but there's someone waiting in my car to see you, if you'd like to see them. It's Mrs Foley, do you remember Stella, Mrs Foley?

Enid's mum? Oh, Enid's mum, I whisper. I stroke the satin dress between my fingers.

I am not and never was the Paris kind of child. I never did inspire in my mother what I see in Christine. This is something I know. But all at once I'm back in the warm and sleepy land of Enid's mum – Sew Right, the back shop and the flat above – and the smell of cloth bales and paraffin and sweet tea which are to me the smells of acceptance, which is a precious thing when you haven't encountered much of it.

It's the September following *Turandot*. I am being looked after. At my most feverish I blink my eyes and warm brine runs from them and splashes down my face. I remember Enid's mum saying rubbing will make them worse and I must let the tears fall. She strokes Vaseline on my cheeks and says it's a layer of protection. I remember the bliss of not needing to move unless I really feel I can.

After those first two acute and delirious weeks of glandular fever which I can barely remember, I spend a drowsy month on the divan in the sitting room of the flat, lulling myself into an understanding that I really am quite ill. We drift into October. The situation is not ideal. It's the fifth or sixth week before I am properly aware that I have ousted Enid from the divan and that she and her mum are sharing the one small bedroom where Enid's mum usually sleeps alone. I think there may be only a single bed, and cushions on the floor for Enid.

Dr Chowdry whispers that if I'm ready she'll just go and bring her in from the car, she needs a hand, she's not so good on her legs.

But in the way she seems never to worry about anything, Enid's mum seems not to mind the overcrowding and anyway, given what I've done, it's impossible for me to stay at Seaview Villas. Unless you count my father, which nobody much does, there is nobody left there to look after me. I have seen to that. My mother is in London with Uncle George, and where Joe has gone is anyone's guess. I can't bear to hear Joe's name mentioned. I also become distressed when the thought of my father crosses my mind. His disgrace clings to me and I am suffocating in my own as it is. It was Enid's mum's idea to bring me to the flat after I came out of hospital.

Well, it's yourself. Look at you, Enid's mum says from the doorway, as Dr Chowdry goes ahead moving furniture and lifting papers from the floor, clearing a path for the walking frame. Why are you not in your clothes, dear? Are you ill? Look at the state of you.

I'm fine, I say, but I don't get up. Bits of my face start trembling and I put up my hands to control it. It's creasing and collapsing and folding into its former childish, tearful shape.

But I want to add, Look who's talking. I wouldn't have known her. She's almost doubled over and the hair she has left is crimped white and dry. Her legs are massively swollen and one of them doesn't seem to bend at all. With Dr Chowdry's help she gets across the room and eases herself into a chair. Her walking frame is placed to one side with her handbag slung over the top bar. Dr Chowdry disappears to the kitchen and returns with a tray of coffee and I realise she must have sneaked in and switched the kettle on before she went back out to her car. She

tells us she's making a call next door and another across the road
and will be back soon to take Mrs Foley home. Enid's mum
removes her blue-tinted glasses and lets them dangle over her
bosom from their chain. She tips her face up to Dr Chowdry and
smiles the beatific, dentured smile of an ancient child. Her blue
eyes have faded, as if someone has added milk.

She says after the door closes, Well, long time no see.

She looks around the room. I hear he passed away. I'm very
sorry. It's a loss. I had my hair done to see you. They're very
good, they come on a Tuesday and a Friday and they'll do you
in your room if you can't get to the place downstairs.

I hadn't seen him in a long while, I didn't get back, I tell her. I
haven't been back much at all.

And do I hear you're not so well yourself? Upsetting yourself
over all that old business. Where's the use in that?

There are things to sort out. I have a lot on my mind.

I had my hair done to see you, she says, tucking a hand under
her curls. I was sorry to hear about your father. I hear he passed
away.

He was a good age.

She nods around the room. So you're having a clear out.
Only thing to do. I'll soon be eighty. I'm seventy-eight now.

Oh. You always seemed older. I always thought you were
older than my mother. She would've turned eighty this year if
she'd been alive.

Your mother? Aye, well, she did look younger, she took care
of herself. I mean, she did take care of herself. She sips some
coffee and looks at me. I probably felt older than your mother.
It wasn't so easy then.

I drink a little coffee. I say, It was because you were always in
the same place. Like an old person. You were always in the
shop, or in the flat. You didn't move, you hardly ever went
anywhere.

Aye, well. I had my work.

You were a person people went *to*.

You mean you did. I didn't see many folk, mainly just customers. It was quite lonely. It's all different now. I think it's gone too far the other way, now.

What's gone too far?

She doesn't reply at first. She's staring at the carpet, or what she can see of it under the strewn papers. Her attention is held by the ceilidh picture.

Well, maybe there's my point, she says. She sighs and leans forward but can't get near it. Can you pick that up, I want to see that. I maybe remember that picture.

I hand it to her and she fishes in her bag for a different pair of spectacles. You were always so calm, I tell her.

Enid's mum looks up from clucking mildly at the picture. Calm? Aye, well, who wasn't calm, next to your mother? You and her were a pair. See anything in that picture?

I take it from her and look at it again.

Well, the people. All of them, we knew them all. The ceilidh wasn't really like that but it doesn't matter. There's nothing else.

Nothing else, no, maybe not.

We smile and lay the cutting aside and sip coffee. I wonder why people pretend to like instant coffee when it is so full of bitterness. It tastes of the tomb.

That's never the wee frock I made you? she says. The satin rag is still in my lap and I shake it out so she can see that it is.

Oh, so lovely! I say. It's the loveliest material I ever saw.

It's far from lovely now.

I hand it across to her and she inspects her workmanship, running her fingers down the seams.

Hard to work, satin. Your two sides slip against each other so you've to put in a tight tacking stitch or your edges never stay together. Proper French seams but it's only plain work, this. It wants going in the bin. It's no use to anyone now.

She strokes it gently as it rests in her hands.

I pick up the newspaper cutting again. You're not in it, I say. You made all those costumes. You came up with all those ideas, you worked off tiny sketches, put in all those hours. And you're not in the picture. You didn't even go.

That's what I'm saying. A woman in my place couldn't go to a dance in those days, anyway you preferred not to. That's hard to believe now. I had my hair done to see you. They come on a Tuesday and a Friday.

What do you mean?

She looks at me with her receding, child's gaze.

As long as you wore a wedding ring folk were nice enough. They let you alone whether they believed you were a widow or not. You lived quiet but it suited you to, anyway. You hadn't the money.

What do you mean whether they believed you? Everybody knew Enid's dad was killed in the war. He was, wasn't he?

Aye, he was. But we were never married, and you'd never to come out with that, you'd be thought not nice. Enid would've had a terrible time. It's not a nice word, bastard. You don't want your wee one hearing that.

So Enid's dad, was he married already or something?

This is the wrong thing to say.

She drops her hands hard into her lap. What do you think I am? You think I had a dirty wee affair with someone else's husband? Who do you think you're speaking to?

She lifts the Liù dress in her hand. What do you think *this* is?

I'm sorry. I don't know.

It was to be a white wedding! All planned! Only we never got that length. I didn't know Enid was on the way till a fortnight after he was killed.

I'm sorry. I never meant that you—

She calms down, maybe because anger is so tiring, and drinks some of her coffee. She says, Here's where it went. See? My material.

My costume? You mean the material was for your wedding dress?

That's what I'm telling you. Don't know why I hung on to it. Maybe just to feel decent.

Decent?

Because I was meant to be getting married. There was only three months till the wedding. I didn't let him you-know-what till after we got engaged.

And you used your material for *my* costume?

Ach, I was daft to keep it. I suppose I was fond of you.

My face has started to tremble again and I have no handkerchief. I wipe my nose on my sleeve.

Enid's mum clicks her tongue and sniffs. You had your struggles. Mind you, you were a silly girl. All girls are silly.

People tried to pull the wool over my eyes.

Aye, well. Her eyes travel round the room and settle back on me. Never mind. After a while it doesn't matter, you have to just leave things be and never mind.

Not when they're that serious, not when something terrible happens.

Enid's mum snorts at this. It's forgotten now! I had my hair done to see you. They're very good, they come on a Tuesday and a Friday, they'll do you in your own room if you can't get to the place downstairs.

I haven't forgotten. I mean, I wish I could.

Listen, dear. Here's a thing. Nothing's tragic forever, if you just leave things be. Folk think you can't forget but you can.

But it was all my fault.

Well, just stop minding about it.

I can't.

She sighs. Then you're a silly woman. A silly girl turned into a silly woman, look at yourself. Lying there like that.

She is looking around the room again.

I had my hair done to see you, she says. They're very good, they come on a Tuesday and a Friday, they'll come up and do you in your room if you can't get to the place downstairs.

---------·-•-·---------

22

George was standing on a podium of upturned beer crates nailed together but the extra height was not lending him the authority he was owed. He felt exposed and under inspection, like goods on approval, no obligation to purchase. He laid his baton softly across the open score on the music stand.

'No, it would not be accurate to say that liberties are being taken,' he said to the crowd before him. Somebody in the back of the chorus had just said in a ringing voice that they were. 'Taking liberties is not the right way to put it at all.'

In the echoing shed his voice took on an impressive sonority; somehow the whiteness of the walls and the black of the stage backdrop added a tone of trustworthy depth to words uttered here. So it was puzzling that the company was restive. He had been rehearsing the principals, chorus and band separately for weeks now and they were quite used to the cuts and changes he was making to their parts, drastic though they were. They'd had several musical run-throughs of the whole show and nobody had objected then.

But this was the first big run-through on stage and perhaps he should have warned them that combining movement and music for the first time was bound to be difficult. The cuts might, temporarily, be making the action hard to follow; the show might even appear to be, this first time, a meaningless and cacophonous mess. He should have prepared them for the possibility that the whole thing would break down within fifteen minutes, with everybody blaming first one another and then uniting to blame him. Sandy Scott, President of the

Ayrshire Amateur Operatic Association, had lately taken to wearing his President's medal at every rehearsal and now there seemed to be a faction forming around him that was intent on picking holes in what George was trying to achieve. Now word was out that Puccini had left *Turandot* unfinished and there were ignorant rumblings about being short-changed.

'You never telt us it wisnae finished. And who's this Alfano character, anyway?' came another voice. 'Naebody's ever heard of him.'

'Alfano was . . . Look,' George said. 'Puccini wrote very nearly all of it. Alfano only finished the final love duet and the very last scene, after Puccini died. And of course he had to make certain judgements and decisions, based on Puccini's sketches and outlines. Was that taking liberties? Of course not. If he hadn't done it, we wouldn't have *Turandot* as it is today.'

He looked round for support, taking in Raymond and some of the stage crew stationed at the sides and the Mathiesons behind him, busy with paperwork at a trestle table. He spread his arms wide and raised his voice.

'So I, for one, am grateful that those judgements were made. And that is what I am doing, too. I am making certain necessary judgements, otherwise we would not have this production. Yes, I am making cuts. All companies do it.'

Puccini's *Turandot* was two hours long. For a number of reasons, some of which he was keeping to himself, George's version would run for half an hour less. With Gordon Black's help he had cut out swathes of music that the singers were simply not up to, he had trimmed away long, static exchanges that held up the story and exposed some of the cast's inability to act. He was speeding up most of the tempi, hoping that if he took the thing at a fair lick he could keep the audience's attention from wandering away from the stage to the buttock-numbing properties of the Burnhead Townswomen's Guild's borrowed chairs.

And because Puccini's cast called for seven male principals and George had only been able to find four, he had rolled the three parts of the courtiers Ping, Pang and Pong into one character called Pung. It was unfortunate that this new character was being sung by Sandy Scott, who was turning out to be a tedious purist. After all, the three courtiers didn't affect the plot, and it moved matters on considerably when only one character instead of three had to have his say. They – or more accurately now, he – merely commented on what was happening or issued dread advice and morbid warnings to Prince Calaf which of course he ignored, because if, when he heard

Pazzo! Va'via! Qui si strozza! Si trivella!

Madman, go away! Here they garrotte you! They impale you!

he were to pay any heed, there would be no opera.

George had also, by careful trimming of the scenes in which they appeared, made it possible for two other male parts – the Mandarin, and Turandot's father the Emperor Altoum – to be sung by the same person, an old man called Norman. George could not say so, but Norman's hand tremor fitted the role of the frail old Emperor perfectly, and for his appearances as the Mandarin (in a switch of cloaks and headgear and a different beard) George had found him a sword to clutch that kept him from shaking too much.

The changes might make events on stage a little more difficult to understand, but nobody would be following the story from what was being sung, anyway. For one thing it was all in Ayrshire Italian and besides, the synopsis would be in the programme. George hoped by means of these and other tricks to get away with it. It tired him out just thinking of the time and ingenuity he had expended on these people. They had all been so thrilled and charming at the start and now some were almost sour. He could walk out right now, how would they like that? Again, as he did several times a day, he asked himself why he had allowed it all to happen. Then he caught sight of Joe, standing next to Lila.

He stood up straighter and said again, 'All companies do these things. A production such as ours calls for certain concessions.'

'Disnae mean you've to hack it to bits,' came another voice from the chorus. 'Disnae call for a hatchet job.'

There were murmurs, even from the Bergsma sisters who sat at the front of the orchestra with their instruments on their laps. George thought that Willy's blind eye in its floppy socket looked wetter than usual. It shone brightly under the lights, shedding syrupy, reproachful tears that she dabbed with a tiny handkerchief.

'I haven't hacked it to bits,' he said. 'We have to make cuts so that we can manage with our reduced forces. And now,' he picked up his baton, 'I really think we should get on. We've hardly got started and it's already after three o'clock.'

Mrs Mathieson's voice behind him said, 'Are you still wanting to break for tea at half past? Because if you are I'll need to switch on the urn. It wants switching on at five past and it's already gone that. There's biscuits to put out as well.'

'Oh, what kind are we getting the day?' Jimmy Brock the coalman called out, peering round from his trombone. 'Is there any custard creams?'

'No, there's shortbread,' Mrs Mathieson told him, 'and Bourbons.'

A hand went up from somewhere. 'On the subject of biscuits, Mrs Mathieson, can I just put in,' said a woman whose name George kept forgetting, 'can I just say *re* biscuits any time it's ginger nuts please can an alternative also be provided as I'm sure my man's not the only one can't take ginger?'

'It's no the ginger, it's the hardness. They're too hard, ginger nuts,' said a man's voice.

'Away you go, Alistair, you know fine you get heartburn after ginger.'

'Thank you, Margaret,' Mrs Mathieson called. 'I've got that noted.'

George sighed. There was no point trying to get on with Act I while tea was in the offing. He spent the next half hour teaching them how to enter and exit without crowding or getting into jams, gliding noiselessly on stage and pouring off it quickly. They had to slip into the wings (which he explained were not in place yet, but would be suspended lengths of cloth held steady at the bottom by floor weights) and then the trick was to keep moving, flooding silently out through the open doors behind the backdrop and straight out on to the field. There were mutterings about the weather and the indignity. More promises were made; as soon as the scouts were back from summer camp they would be putting up two marquees just feet from the door for the chorus to use as dressing rooms.

After tea George conducted and shouted his way through Act II, now and then leaping on to the stage to pull people around bodily while still waving one arm in the direction of the orchestra and yelling at them not to stop. By twenty past four they had reached the middle of the act and Turandot's first aria.

Fleur missed her cue.

'Jesus, Fleur! Watch me for the beat. We're in two,' he said. 'It's a quaver rest and then you're in. "*In questa Reggia*"! Okay?'

'Oh, George! Oh, sorry, everyone!' Fleur said, running down the steps at the side of the stage and turning to face them. 'Sorry, sorry! Oh, George, it's not about counting beats, it's my *imposto*.'

She closed her eyes and made off down the length of the shed with her fingertips at her temples, swinging her neck from side to side and vocalising with her mouth closed to 'mee, mee, mee, meee'. She walked around, stopped, rolled her arms in the direction of the sound, closed her eyes, walked around some more. The chorus, murmuring, sank away to the sides.

When she returned she accepted a hand from Calaf and was

helped up the steps on to the stage. She smiled round again, too ready to be welcomed back, too much in need of compliments. She was emphatically made up; beads of sweat stood out on her powdered face like droplets of water on an apricot.

'I am so sorry, I crave your indulgence!' she cried. 'I must place the voice or I can't begin "*In questa Reggia*". I daren't take the voice there till it's ready. Don't look like that, George. Thanks, everyone!'

Lila, standing with Timur at the side of the stage, thought that she couldn't have grasped *l'impostamento della voce* properly. Uncle George and her mother had tried to explain it and she had pretended to understand, but all she really did before she sang was to imagine the sound she wanted to make and the space she wanted it to fill, and then somehow she didn't have to 'place her voice'. Rather it was her voice that took her there. When she was practising exercises and scales she did not think about the high notes except to look forward to them and when she was being Liù she pretty much forgot about nerves and the technical things; she no more thought about Liù's breathing and *l'impostamento della voce* than she worried about reminding Lila's heart to beat.

The afternoon wore on. George allowed a five-minute interval between Acts II and III because he was desperate for a cigarette but he refused a request for another tea break. It was after half past six before they made it as far as Calaf's and Turandot's last duet in Act III. At least a dozen members of the chorus had gone outside for another smoke and disappeared altogether.

'Calaf! Sing to Turandot!' George shouted. His hair was hanging in wet black tails and dripping sweat on to his shoulders; with every swing of his head the first desk of the first violins and the cellos ducked.

'Communicate! Turandot! You shouldn't be downstage, no, go up! Up! No, turn round only when he comes towards you! Oh, stop, *stop*!'

At the heart of Fleur's interpretation of her role was the idea that Turandot, as *Principessa*, should be free to stride or drift about the stage as she liked, her face wearing one of its two expressions, preoccupied or enraptured. Whatever she did she looked oblivious to her surroundings; Fleur's Turandot appeared to be listening to voices that nobody else could hear.

'Turandot! Get back! Stand where I put you!' George yelled, still conducting Calaf who was dragging the beat, and stirring his arms as if he were clearing his way through clouds of smoke. Joe's voice was hoarse. He had split every high note in '*Nessun dorma*' and now he was skipping anything above an E. But the final curtain could not go down until he had removed Turandot's veil, kissed her, taken her in his arms and melted her into submission.

George shouted, 'Turandot! Turandot! Go back to the steps!'

Joe's voice sank to a standstill and Fleur turned to face George with her hands on her hips. 'I'm entering the part!' she said. 'A princess contemplating her destiny would walk about if she wanted to.'

'Don't be ridiculous!'

'I know you told me to stay there till Calaf's aria's finished,' she said, 'but she's the *Principessa*! If it feels right for Turandot to move when he's singing "*Ah! Solleva quel velo*" to her, then why shouldn't she?'

'Because, my dear,' George said, his voice dangerously sweet, 'Calaf's aria is addressed directly to you, and he needs to know where you'll be. Plus the aria's all about *getting* you to move, which you are refusing to do. He's trying to get you to submit to him. To descend to earth – "*scendi giù sulla terra*". You see? And the point is – *the whole bloody point is* – that you don't. You don't move, you remain icy and aloof. And that means in one place. *On the bloody steps.*'

Joe said, keeping his voice light and pleasant, 'And don't forget, when the aria's finished I'm meant to rush forward and pull off your veil and I need to know where to rush to. It won't look right if I'm chasing you all over the stage.'

'But standing in one place all that time doesn't feel right. I just don't think Turandot would.'

George said tightly, 'Just do it. Let's go again. Calaf, from the top – "*Principessa di morte!*"'

Fleur said, 'But what am I supposed to do all the time I'm just standing there?'

'I don't care,' George said, leafing back through the score to the beginning of Calaf's aria, 'if you do a bloody strip-tease. Just don't wander off.'

For a while she tried, until her presence at the top of the steps became so oppressive that nobody said anything when she turned from Calaf and strolled away again.

Although it was Joe who was most affected by Fleur's wanderings it was impossible to tell if he were truly exasperated. For the last part of the final scene he was still using the score, and with his eyes glued to the music he couldn't pay much attention to her. When he glanced up from time to time he seemed more puzzled than anything else, and this was good acting, Lila thought; Joe was revealing the complexity of Calaf's feelings under all the princely bravado, for surely a person seized at first sight by a sudden passion for somebody else would, even in opera, be very taken aback. A person in that predicament might well find himself perplexed. She smiled encouragingly at him. But he was not looking at her; he was sending furious looks to George who was driving the tempo so relentlessly that he was having trouble keeping up. Angrily, he sang:

La mia vita è il tuo bacio! Non la temo! Hai vinto tu!

My life is your kiss! I don't fear it! You have conquered!

And then George fluffed the entry of the brass so that it was Jimmy Brock's trombone that led the orchestra in a blast of sound as the women's chorus, crowded offstage in the wings, sang of perfumed gardens in the light of morning, before the scene faded to silence.

George was now too tired to raise his arms but he tapped the top of his music stand with the baton again. 'Nearly there!' he called. 'Only the last scene to go! Cast, please. *La folla*, Calaf, Turandot, Altoum, positions, "*Diecimila anni*"!'

' 'Scuse me.' Sandy Scott stepped forward to the front of the stage. 'D'you mean we're going straight from Scene One into Scene Two?'

'More or less, yes,' George said.

'Because I think you'll find Scene One takes place in the Palace gardens, in front of a pavilion,' Sandy said, raising an eyebrow and looking round, 'and Scene Two takes place outside the Palace. That calls, unless I am mistaken, for a scene change.'

Several people murmured agreement. George coughed. 'I am aware of that. There are certain staging issues, and they are being dealt with.' He cast his eyes around. 'Stage manager? Raymond? Do we have a stage manager?'

Raymond emerged reluctantly from the wings, stroking his moustache.

'Ray, can you answer Sandy's query about the staging here?'

Raymond said, 'We've just the one set of steps. We move them from stage left after they're finished being the pavilion steps in Scene One to centre stage where they'll be the palace steps in Scene Two. Right?' He nodded at George and melted back out of sight.

Sandy stared after him. 'Well, in that case why aren't they being moved? Who's in charge here? Where's the stage hands?'

From the wings came Raymond's voice. 'Stage hands have buggered off. Move them yourself.'

George said quickly, 'That'll do, let's remember this is just a stage run-through, not a dress rehearsal. And moreover,' he said to Sandy, 'we shall further *suggest* the change of location by the use of lighting.'

Above the confused discussion he heard somebody say, 'Ach, it doesn't really matter.' George looked up and scanned the faces. 'I mean, if your man Puccini couldn't even be bothered to finish it . . .'

'I told you, Puccini died. He couldn't finish it because he *died*,' George said into the crowd. 'So Alfano completed it, so that we have a whole opera.'

'See your man Alfano, though. No guarantee he knew what way Puccini *meant* it to go.'

'Why can't we sing it in English?'

George let out a roar, threw his arms in the air and flung his baton across the room. 'For Christ's sake! Jesus Christ! Look, just shut up and do as you're told!' he screamed. 'Shut up, all of you!'

Nobody said anything. Slowly George crossed the floor and picked the baton up. Pulling his fingers through his hair, he remounted the creaking podium. He fixed hard eyes on them all and said quietly, 'Right. Thank you. Act Three, Scene Two. Cast on stage *now*.'

He was ready, baton raised, by the time the chorus and principals had flopped back into position. The orchestra cranked itself into the foursquare beat of '*Diecimili anni al nostro Imperatore!*' and the exhausted crowd sang in a peal of high, approximate notes and involuntary trills, at first subdued and tentative:

Amor! O sole! Vita! Eternita!

Love! O Sun! Life! Eternity!

But as George bent and swayed on top of his beer crates with wide swimming movements of his arms, the chorus's nervy squeaking swelled in excitement and volume as if a subterranean colony of disturbed bats, rising from darkness, had found the cave mouth and were flittering out and singing into the open sky:

Luce del mondo è amor!

Light of the world is love!

I'm reviewing a number of things since I saw Mrs Foley.

Did I really escape altogether feeling like *me*, jaded and alone?

No. There are days that summer – there are, of course there are – when I feel like my old self, when I wake up unable to summon Liù except as a passing ghost. The sensations of my own skin and clothes and surroundings – the damp and complex musk of old carpet, underarms, Woolworth's talcum powder, the smell of bacon in my hair – anchor me to Seaview Villas and the everyday pessimism that sours all my longings. Liù's ringing voice and her supple form in luminous silk stiffen into a mute doll as tawdry and dismayed as I am, lying in a patch of struggling daylight in a house of shrivelled hopes.

On such days, in gaps in rehearsals, I seek out Enid and other safe disappointments. I call in at Sew Right and if Enid's mum is these days a little less interested in me, I somehow think it appropriate, since I am not who I was. There may be something distracted and even forgetful about her, and she's always busy. Even when she's not reaching for pins or cutting difficult curves in material or serving customers, her mind seems fixed on some task connected to the costumes that is about to demand all her attention.

Och it's yourself, you'll be wanting Enid, is all she says nowadays.

Instead of delaying me with an offer of tea she'll say, She's away out with Senga and Deirdre, you'll be better trying the Locarno.

Senga and Deirdre dropped out of the chorus weeks ago but they still hang around on the fringes of the production, sneering or ogling, and Enid still hangs around them. If I do go to the Locarno and find her there, she comes and greets me at the counter as if I've returned from somewhere far away. She talks fast as if I may not be staying long, and usually I don't. She still says, glancing back at them, that Senga and Deirdre are fine when you get to know them and even if they call *Turandot* a load of shite, they don't really mean it. Anyway, she shouts over the jukebox, she's only in it herself because her mum says she's got to see it through and there's nothing else to do round here.

I don't care what they think. I don't even care if their company crushes me. I'm not sure it actually touches me, though my aloofness may be no more than the tacit gratitude of the benumbed. The only thing I'm certain of is that my real life won't begin until I'm hundreds of miles away from the thudding, steamy Locarno and the rest of Burnhead. After times like these when, back in the solitude of my room, I find that Liù has returned shining and real, I cry with relief at reaching her again.

Sometimes Enid turns up here and makes me walk up to the farm with her, to see what's going on, or so she says.

Fifteen's not too young to get engaged, she tells me. There's girls in the Bible were married at twelve. I was telling Billy.

This is the only time she mentions the Bible now and she hasn't been Gathered since early July. Billy's name crops up much more often now than the Lord's.

—◦—

23

J oe lay facing the wall with his back curled and his arms
tight around his chest. The wheeze of car tyres on the road
outside passed through the room like a cold whisper and
he shuddered; it was a satisfaction that he was soaked to the
skin and probably going to catch a chill. Then he wouldn't be
able to sing at all and it would be George's fault, because it was
George's fault he had walked out of the rehearsal into the rain.

He rolled over and groped under the bed for the bottle.
Instead of unwrapping it properly he had torn away only
enough of the brown paper to let him get at the cork, as if
the contents would be less vicious and disgraceful if he kept
them covered. He gulped hard, twice, set the bottle on the floor
and lay back. He shivered again and sniffed as the whisky
scorched its way down his throat, then he turned back to the
wall and curled himself up like a baby and sobbed.

He had strained again to sing 'Nessun dorma' all the way
through and failed; it was the third full run-through on stage
and still he couldn't get to the ends of phrases without taking
laborious breaths in the wrong places. Sometimes the high
notes were simply beyond reach and often his voice split and
wobbled in distress. His throat seemed full of chalk that he
could not clear no matter how much water he drank or how
hard he coughed, and even in some of the easier passages he
produced only a kind of quaint mewling.

And it wasn't just the singing. Even when he was managing
to do something quite well George yelled at him to budge or
show some feeling, and he couldn't; the music alone required
such concentration it was impossible to act. There were points

in the opera where he still didn't understand what he was saying and it was far too late to find out. His stance centre stage with feet apart, one fist clasped to his chest and his eyes on the roof felt as natural to him as any position ever would; what harm was there in being the one fixed point in a boiling sea of people? If his face betrayed little apart from the massive physical effort of the role, what could he do about it?

But this afternoon George hadn't let up, bawling about his boots being nailed to the floor and his face made of granite.

So what? I'm a singer, not an acrobat.

Nobody is asking you for acrobatics!

Oh, no? That's not my recollection, Maestro.

Just what the hell is that supposed to mean?

At the end of 'Nessun dorma' people had shuffled and looked away. George had scratched the back of his head with his baton and frowned at the score.

That was when Joe had stepped forward and said *George, I'm asking you again. We have to transpose 'Nessun dorma'. It's unsingable. A tone lower would make it much better for my voice. Changes the whole tessitura.*

Are you insane? Don't be absurd! You can't go transposing things willy-nilly. It'd make no harmonic sense with anything else.

But 'Nessun dorma' opens Act Three. It doesn't have to fit with anything else.

Of course it does! It's not the only bloody aria in the opera, you know!

Then George said the unforgivable. *Joe, you know it's a demanding role. If you put some proper work in, you might find the technique and stamina that's called for.*

Joe was pleased with the next bit. He sat up and took another drink and lay back down, playing it over as he squeezed a mouthful of whisky through his teeth.

Well, Maestro. If you won't grant a simple request to transpose 'Nessun dorma' down a tone then I'm afraid this production no longer has a Calaf.

It had been an exit worth getting wet for. A dignified walk to the edge of the stage in Calaf's big boots, a hop to the floor, swift strides down the shed towards the door, head high. The masterstroke, turning at the door to call out, *Please convey my sincere apologies to the entire company.*

And straight out into the rain, which was unfortunate, but he certainly could not have diminished the drama of it by going back to ask for an umbrella. Nobody had followed so nobody had seen him drag the neck of his pullover up over the back of his head, and as the rain came down harder, make off down the track still in Calaf's wide-topped thigh boots that forced him to run with his legs apart.

He stared at the arrows of rain spitting on the skylight and felt the minutes tick through his anger. He let it grow. An afternoon spent on it would not be wasted. This time he might even carry out the threat to leave. It would serve George right if he didn't go back. It was a mistake that he was here at all; his own mistake perhaps, but still George's fault.

You've got to come, I need you to. Of course it'll be better than staying in London, there's a beach on the doorstep, don't forget.

Standing in Crouch End with the telephone held to his ear and watching sunlight burn down on a bloom of mouse-coloured dust at the edges of the carpet, Joe had imagined himself laughing as glittering water washed over his bare toes, shrieking as blue waves broke on his shoulders.

George was always doing this to him, creating expectations that failed to materialise and then the failure was always, of course, Joe's. *It's not my fault the sea isn't blue. I only said there was a beach, you just assumed it'd be warm enough to swim in. You can hardly blame me for the weather*, he'd said.

Joe kept finding himself held unfairly accountable for his own disappointments.

He did hate the weather here, the malicious pattern of cloud, rain and wind broken by blasts of sun so scorching and short-lived that people stripped off and flung themselves at it like maniacs and spent the next week puce and crazed by sunburn. Come to think of it he hated the people too, the very sight of them trailing dumb and dazed through Burnhead, as if they'd been reared underground. They weren't designed for sunshine, not even short bursts of it; they had thin skin like uncooked sausages, just as liable to tighten and erupt under a touch of heat. He hated this creaking house too, with its cling of damp. He'd felt trapped from the moment he got here, tiptoeing about feeling secretive and restrained, because of course George hadn't warned him about his infuriating sister and mute Raymond and the girl who kept staring at him.

George rewrote things, that was the trouble. He glossed over the bits he didn't like and moulded facts to fit so that he could see life as he wanted it to be. Joe swigged from the bottle again and felt a sudden glow of whisky wisdom: George had re-written *him*. All the last Doge of Venice nonsense was George's. Joe had told him it wasn't an uncommon name and there were dozens of Foscaris in Italian telephone directories. But after a while he hadn't pointed that out so often. He'd studied his face in the mirror and seen there was another way of looking at it. Maybe he could detect in his features something ancient and noble, maybe he could be descended from the last Doge, who was to say? After that it had been easier to go along with George's version of the famous family restaurants until they could both imagine that people once converged on Glasgow from all points of the compass to eat at Foscari's; Joe let the photograph that he remembered from childhood, of his grandfather outside a fish and chip shop in the Gorbals, slip quietly from memory. It now occurred to him that the reason behind George's determination to elevate him was that Joe as he really was, one of a line of immigrant caterers, with a run-down café in a slum, was simply not good enough.

Nor was it good enough for George that he wasn't a great tenor. Joe had gone off the idea of singing within two terms and told George he might go back to technical drawing and just join a choir, but George had refused to let him treat what he called The Voice so casually. He insisted that his was a supernormal gift. His theory was that Joe was experiencing simple nerves over the commitment and responsibility of so huge a talent. Of course Joe was flattered, and stopped telling him that just because he was able to sing it didn't mean he wanted to and that actually, he found most of the music boring.

It *was* all George's fault. George had talked him into and out of so much that Joe didn't know if his opinions and tastes really were his or not. On every subject Joe could think of – opera, girlfriends, commitment, style, college, lineage, love, destiny – George had got him fired up with wrong ideas about what he wanted and was capable of and the person he could become, rolling his own ambitions up into one ball and tossing it to him in the shape of singing Calaf. Well, Joe was letting the ball drop at his feet. It wasn't his to begin with and he was no longer sure he had ever really wanted it. There it lay, George's fantastic bundle of expectations and Joe's confusion about his entire life, one and the same thing.

He drank deep from the bottle again and began to plan when he might be ready to hear George's appeasement speech, because soon he'd be begging at the door. The first time, naturally, he wouldn't listen. Joe felt a fresh surge of rage and his back tightened in disgust because he knew that he'd forgive George eventually, after a few more appeals, and that would be the point at which George would slide in a remark to suggest that really the fault was Joe's.

Of course I feel terrible about undermining you, he might say. *If that's what I was doing.*

But in order to get 'Nessun dorma' brought down a tone Joe would have to listen to a lot of that kind of thing. It was undignified and it clashed with his rebellious picture of himself; the thought of going through with it sickened him. But at least he had planned his walkout to leave enough time for the orchestra to get used to playing the aria in the lower key. You had to use tactics with someone like George or he would get the better of you, every time.

Joe eased himself up from the squealing bed, pulled off his boots and flung them so hard across the floor they hit the skirting board. Then he got under the covers. He wished that just by lying still and quiet he might be spared all that would follow George's knock on the door. He squeezed his eyes shut and wished he were invisible. Another car hissed by on the wet road, a dog barked. After a while, no other sounds came. Joe felt his mind begin to untangle and within a few more minutes he was asleep and snoring.

Day and night, I walk. I have re-learned the shades of this house. I am reacquainted with the sea-bleached brightness that glances off surfaces and I know the mere absence of light – the doomy, religious dark that sucks daylight out of corners – but I am drawn most to the kind of shining, greedy blackness that thrums through night air like a low whisper. As I walk, I consider that perhaps the strife I have raised here was not waiting for me after all but was brought. Perhaps it resides in me.

When the need for oblivion comes, I give in and sleep. I am less afraid of what awaits me when I close my eyes, because I find myself in the same dreams, the very same ones that came that *Turandot* summer, and in them I am again the girl I was. They are extravagant, restless dreams of flight and revelation in which I pass across landscapes I recognise but that turn out to be harbouring impossible surprises; I happen upon unlikely doors and unexplored paths that take me to places behind the ordinary surfaces of things. I am drifting through the garden of Pow Farm and I part the shrubs to find another garden beyond, lush with sunlight and fountains. When I look up through the sycamores the trunks become pillars meeting in splendid arches in the sky.

Sometimes I will discover a vast room coated in dust and with one finger trace a line down a wall to reveal a painted Arcadia of nymphs and trees and pools in silvery pinks and blues. I find objects of incredible fragility – confections of glass and beads, slippers and masks and fans of silk and feathers, frivolous, carnival trappings – whose only purpose is to adorn.

Even in the dreams I think my discoveries slightly absurd yet there is a ripeness in their beauty, as if the things I find have never before been thought quite as wonderful as I think them now. In another dream I meet obstacles, irrational wooden structures in the middle of fields or unnatural hills that rise up and push live, turfy smells in my face, smells like camomile or fresh blood that turn on me so suddenly that my stomach retches before my mind has had time to realise I am repelled to the point of nausea.

And still dreaming, I see some Lila or another in the act of gazing from my bedroom window across the moonlit ground. She watches as from the dead marsh between the house and the sea a city sprouts up, Gothic and toy-like, with winding alleys and steep roofs and soaring unreal towers. Her eyes are searching the spires and minarets for something and now the dream fills with longing, its atmosphere changes. I am not watching, but watched. My body and clothing are melding into the same supple gold substance, as if they are being drenched in the same warming paint, except that the trans-formation is deeper; not a gilding of surfaces but a meta-morphosis – skin and bone and fibre lose themselves and re-form as one melting body. It is nakedness of a kind, yet I am brave and happy to be watched and by whom or what I do not care – it may be the gaze of some vapoury, white-faced god – because all I want is more: more nakedness and shedding of self, more of this beautiful flaunting. When I wake from this dream I feel that I am being chased from it by a sadness that finally catches hold and clings to me like a chill.

Lila then and me now, there is little between us. I am still dreaming and waiting and wondering, as she does. The only difference is that now I know that disappointment, in my case, has not yet proved fatal.

24

During the day Lila lived in a hangover from her dreams. Another rainy spell descended. The continuing cold drip of the weather and the practicalities of five people living in the damp house, the sudden disagreements and ill-tempered stops and starts in rehearsals felt like slaps about the face after her slow, glowing dream world. Awake, she longed to be folded back into it and be kept warm and still. She craved swaddling for her mind but could not summon again the ability, that she remembered from childhood, to think of nothing at all.

She dwelled as much as she could in the opera, where the fusion of Calaf and Joe into a single being was as natural as the elision of herself with Liù. She luxuriated both in him and in a dream of him; the thought of him became as good as his touch, the promise of their life together as real as a glimpse of him, or as real as anything else that existed now. There was nothing to do but wait, because her life was now as predestined as an opera. All around her, time continued to pass in the usual way, but *Turandot* measured it in floating, supernatural lines of music; love, sacrifice and death unfolding in Puccini's oriental brushstrokes of melody, crackles of dissonance and murmured words of warning. Lila's future was another song, written but not yet sung. She had no idea of how very little she was managing to get by on.

She knew there was something demented in it. She wrote his name and hers in curling entwined patterns, doodled with their initials, worked out exactly how many days he had been on the planet before she was born. She read their horoscopes, made complicated connections of lucky numbers and the shared letters in their names. It was impossible to free herself. She chose dates for their engagement and for the wedding and planned how they would spend his birthdays. Christmas was organised in her mind, a mirage of snow and firelight and devotion, and in these fantasies she was neither just herself, the Lila who moved among the scenery and props of Seaview Villas, the farm and Burnhead, nor just Liù. She was simply the enchanted, most authentic version of herself, the one beloved by Joe.

Uncle George tried to look kindly on her sleepy vagueness. Though he was often irritated by her moonstruck face and her habit of not answering when she was spoken to, he softened every time she opened her mouth to sing, every time she moved gracefully across the stage. If the entire production turned out not to be a complete disaster, he thought, it would be thanks to her.

'Liù,' he told them all one day, 'as a character, is a paradox. She is both frail and strong. She yields wholly to love, and dies for it. She is the only truly tragic element in the whole opera, the only character who really moves us.'

'But you're making her sound like the heroine,' Fleur said. 'You're making her sound like the point of it all. She isn't. It's the turning of Turandot's hatred to love that's the point.'

Alec Gallagher, wearing old Timur's beaded shoes with curling ornamental toes said, 'Aye, but Liù's death is the most moving scene in the opera. After that there's nothing left for Timur. He even follows her body when she's carried off the stage. He's lost everything.'

'If you ask me the most moving bit's when Calaf finally kisses Turandot. When he starts to melt her ice and she gives way to love,' Fleur said. 'We should feel sorry for her because she submits to love against her will, remember. That's where the tragedy is.'

Joe said, 'Aha! But she falls in love! Nobody minds submitting to love then, do they? Isn't that right, George?'

'Yes, submitting to love is the most important thing in the world,' Lila said, earnestly.

'Exactly! And Turandot doesn't fall in love with just anybody. She falls in love with the handsome, heroic prince,' Joe said, 'and she marries him and lives happily ever after. What's tragic about that?'

'But I don't think they *would* live happily ever after,' Lila said. 'Not after Liù died like that. Calaf would never be able to forgive himself. Not really, not deep down.'

George said, 'You're running away with yourselves. The opera ends happily with the betrothal of Calaf and Turandot. There's going to be a wedding. Love triumphs.'

Lila said, 'But what about *after* the end of the opera? After the wedding. Even supposing they do get married.'

'I don't know what you're driving it. There isn't any after the end. The end is the end.'

Alec Gallagher said, 'Aye, the triumph of love. Nothing to greet about there. Veronica and myself are looking forward to our wedding.' Nobody heard him.

Fleur sighed. 'It's no good, none of you understand,' she said. 'Turandot just gives in. She doesn't have a choice. She's forced. That's tragic. George, isn't that tragic?'

'I was trying,' George said, with a soft look at Lila, 'to talk about Liù.'

'Yes, and we are,' Fleur said. 'That's my point. The difference between Turandot and Liù is that Turandot is forced to do what she does, but Liù does what she wants. You see? And everybody's sorry for her, and it makes Turandot look even more cruel. As if it's Turandot's fault that Liù's a servile little ninny.'

'Oh, Fleur, come on,' George said. 'That's ridiculous.'

'Oh, all right, then, maybe not servile. Maybe . . . maybe Liù just knew. She knew she was never going to get Calaf to love her, so then her life didn't matter. In any case, she wanted to sacrifice herself. And frankly, if people are able to go ahead and do what they want, why should we feel sorry for them?'

Lila looked dreamily away and said nothing.

'Spoken like Turandot,' George said. 'The point is this, all of you. All of you – Turandot, Liù, Calaf, Timur – everybody. Get inside your character. Think about them *day and night*. You have to know your character until what they do feels like the only possible way they could behave. Think about your character till you really know and understand them. All right?'

Lila nodded.

'You have to think about Liù,' George continued, 'until you know her as well as you know yourself. Will you do that?'

But Lila didn't think. Thinking in the way that Uncle George seemed to mean was unnecessary in the world that she had now entered. She continued to practise her exercises, to wash dishes and fold laundry and even to make strangely original meals, but she had already become Liù, slipping out of Lila's poor half-finished skin and into Liù's, while maintaining for appearances' sake the illusion that she was still merely Lila. In bed every night she would still calculate to the nearest minute when she would next see Joe; the creaking above her was still the last sound she heard before silence ruled the house. Then she would wait for the dreams, and in the very waiting there was something breathless and delicate, a hovering on the brink of something she could not name. Her heart ticked in her chest like a small bomb and in the welcome dark she half-felt the touch of his imagined hand until with her own, guiltily, she explored the dangerous wet tingle between her legs. Now and then in the middle of the night she would find herself wide awake, disturbed not by any noise but by a sudden sense of Joe's wakefulness above.

These days her thoughts careened off in every direction, her mind was too slippery to hold them down. Sometimes she felt there was no knowing where they might take her next.

Outwardly becalmed, I go every day to rehearsals. Apparently mellow and inattentive, I watch, listen and plan, being at the same time always elsewhere in a dream of Joe and Calaf and the future that is waiting beyond the day I am drifting through. I think little about technical matters. I do not need to be nagged about missed entries or dragging the tempo. Turandot and Calaf are much more difficult roles than Liù. They must be, because Joe and my mother are showing signs of strain.

In all our rehearsals now Uncle George makes us wear our characters' shoes, for the practical reason that we must learn to move in them naturally. My mother clicks about on red wooden sandals with platforms and Joe plants himself firmly on stage in leather thigh boots. But I do not wear Liù's silent, grey slippers to get used to them. I do not need to get used to becoming myself. The reunion of my feet with her shoes is a secret, the fit becoming perfect as my toes arrange themselves every day into the curves moulded by hers.

Oh, Liù and I are so alike! Liù is a dreamer, too. She also lives elsewhere, beyond the stage itself, beyond the observable world, somewhere in the wings or past the curtain in another life that is more real to her because in it is contained her love for Calaf. This is the world we inhabit, Liù and I, while we wait for our love to be returned. Maybe it is the world we inhabit after death. If Calaf does not love us in this one, then soon it will be the only one we will want.

Meanwhile we live out the relentless story. Turandot must

submit to the Unknown Prince unless she can discover his name before dawn. Liù claims to be the only person who can reveal it. Turandot orders the torture to begin; Calaf pleads for Liù's life and Turandot refuses. What does Calaf do? Does he see Turandot for what she is – the destroyer? Does he recognise the loving, brave Liù? Of course not. It is worse than that. He sees what Turandot is, and still he would rather have her.

So he sings to Liù, moved with tender gratitude:

Non piangere, Liù

Don't cry, Liù

But it is at most a pat on the head. He will see her tortured before he will give up Turandot.

And what can Liù and I do then, outrivalled and unloved? To push a dagger in the heart is nothing now, only a twist of steel through silk, the wrenching and the spill of viscera in ropes of bubbling red and a little time, a few seconds at most, for hatred. But with the spurting of blood comes a shock, because time stops. It simply stops. The moment will never pass. We will play it out like this forever, while unimaginable pain pours through us. When at last the thud of the clock comes once more it is a kindly, fading pulse, easing us into numbness. Now there is nothing but cool sky and silence in the sweet, ever-after place where Calaf loves us. Though we make the sacrifice willingly we do not die happy. We die to become so, to reach a place beyond the one where our hopes are already dead.

Is there also, I wonder, a baser satisfaction?

I'll kill myself and then you'll be sorry.

They will be sorry for the rest of their stained lives. Let them marry. No exchange of vows can clean up the blood that runs over the path they took to reach this point. When they meet at the altar they will not be able to look at each other without remembering that Liù lies in her grave; though it may lie far back in their story, they are rooted forever to that patch of ground where a tangle of wormwood twists up to choke them, the happy couple.

To me it makes perfect sense.

That's exactly how I feel, I whisper to Liù.

———◆———

25

L ila waited at Sew Right until the rain stopped because there was no telling with reds, Enid's mum said. It was only a shower but rain would go straight through brown paper and you couldn't trust reds in the wet.

It was the afternoon of the first night. Turandot's Act III headdress had been brought back to Sew Right for adjustments after Fleur had stopped yesterday's dress rehearsal more than once to complain that it wasn't dramatic enough. It needed to be more lavish if she were going to feel really princessy in it. Everyone was busy. It turned out there was nobody but Lila who could go to collect it in time for the evening. She sat on the bus, hot and shaking. For a few days now her throat had been hurting again and from time to time she was attacked by sudden shivering sweats that soaked her face and underarms, embarrassing her so much in front of Joe that she wondered if they were just an extreme, sick-making form of blushing. She walked from the bus depot in burning sunshine.

When she arrived and went through to the back shop she found Enid's mum partially hidden behind the winged head-dress on the table, still working on it. Exhausted by the walk, Lila sank into the other chair and breathed in the humid fug. Enid's mum felt the cold; even in August the back of the shop wasn't warm enough for her without the paraffin stove, but when it was lit it seemed to warm not the room but the water that lay invisibly in the air. Today the atmosphere was even heavier with glue and paint and floating fibre dust; the heat sent a tang so irresistibly chemical and narcotic around the room that Lila thought she might suffocate. She cleared the table in front of her of some scraps and pots and brushes, slumped forward and rested her head on her arms.

'I've just a bit more fringe to put on,' Enid's mum said. 'I wasn't going to bother, it's just a wee bit left over, then I thought, might as well be hung for a sheep as a lamb. Like it?'

Lila raised her head and nodded, and went on gazing. Working from a picture of Eva Turner as Turandot, Enid's mum had cut and twisted a wire lampshade frame, possibly two, into a sort of helmet shape with lethal-looking horns, like antlers, that branched out a foot at each side and ended in sharp points. The wire had been wrapped over and over with crimson silk and contrasting shiny red raffia and Christmas tinsel, all tied off with bows of red satin. Strings of red and gold beads hung in little swags down the wire bones of the antlers. Several ropes of red and gold braid and ribbon were attached at the pointed ends, from which they swung like loose trapezes across the top; from each of these strands were suspended paste jewels that shook as Enid's mum worked, sending tiny shivers of light to mix confusingly in the toxic, vibrant air.

'I can see your mum in it, right enough. She'll need to fix it on tight now it's a bit heavier. It ties under the chin. See?'

Fantastical as it was, Lila also could see her mother in it quite easily.

'It'll suit her, all right,' she sighed, laying her head on her arms again.

It was true that Fleur would wear it as a natural extension of her allure. On her, the suggestion of a Viking at a Christmas party would not cross anyone's mind for so much as a minute. The warm air of the room fell over Lila and wrapped itself around her like layers of gauze. She yawned. Outside, rain clouds welled suddenly in the sky and covered the sun. The yard beyond the barred window of the back shop grew dark, and Enid's mum worked on, and Lila's eyes closed.

'Aye, you'll be tired,' Enid's mum said, jolting her awake,

'and here you've your big night to come still. You're looking a wee bit peely-wally.'

'I'm all right.'

'Are you feeling a wee bit nervous?'

'Maybe a bit.' She was too limp and tired to feel anything.

'What did you get for your dinner the day?'

'There was toast and leftover raspberry mould.'

'Will you be getting your tea when you get home?'

Lila yawned again and said she wasn't sure. Enid's mum said she couldn't rise to a proper tea but she couldn't see her starve, and sent her out to the shops for rolls, ham and tomatoes and biscuits, telling her to hurry and get back before the rain came on. She was serving a customer when Lila returned, so Lila went out to the passage at the back and made ham rolls and a pot of tea. They ate with plates and cups set anyhow on the table among the scraps of material and ribbon and the pots of paint and glue. Lila could not find the energy to talk. After her tea she dozed on and off while Enid's mum worked away, pushing herself up from the table with a sigh when the shop bell sounded. While she was busy with customers Lila listened to the scrape and ring of the till and looked forward to her reappearance and more of her soft, drowsy atmosphere. Outside, heavy, pewtery drops of rain began to fall.

Enid's mum came back and took up the fringing again.

'Where's Enid?' Lila asked, for something to say.

Enid was off out, Enid's mum told her, looking past the needle she was threading and straight at Lila. Her and Billy, the two of them were off out in their peasant costumes, along with the Mandarin and Pung.

'In their costumes?'

'Aye, and the Mandarin and Pung, Norman and Sandy, they're in those *Mikado* ones we got the loan of, they're old but the silk's lovely. More colourful than yon pyjamas the peasants are in.'

'But what for? Off out where?'

'Down the esplanade. They're off handing out leaflets, for publicity. Senga and Deirdre, too.'

Lila was shocked. 'I can't see Billy doing that,' she said.

'Aye, sounds daft to me,' Enid's mum said blandly. 'Still, Enid got him to go.'

'They'll be getting wet,' Lila said. Now that she had Joe, how could the idea of Enid, Billy and the others larking about together leave her feeling so bleak and excluded? The shop bell sounded again. While Enid's mum served her customer, Lila swallowed the dregs in her teacup and tried to stop her throat hurting. She tried to lose herself in thoughts of Liù and Calaf, but they would not come.

When all the red fringing had been attached they made a bulky parcel of the headdress, wrapping it in several sheets of brown paper taped together and winding it in a complicated system of strings to use as handles. Enid's mum made more tea while they waited for the rain to stop.

The shower passed quickly. Water was drying in wafts of vapour off the pavements when Lila set off home, shaken awake by the fear that she was very late. In the steamy sunlight she felt nauseous and unhappy and her bones hurt; she had not meant to sit out the afternoon in the hypnotising air of the back shop, lulled by the to-ing and fro-ing of Enid's mum into forgetting how urgent life was outside. Now she felt unshelled and spilt, unprotected, back into a brutal day.

Hurrying along in short running steps, she tried to squeeze even five more minutes into the calculation of how much time there was. Her mother had wanted her back with the headdress by half past three and it was already after that. The performance was to start at half past seven and she ought to be at the farm at least by six or Uncle George would be furious. These days he was always furious about something. She was supposed to be using the front room of the farmhouse as a dressing room, sharing it with her mother who would take at least three hours over her costume and makeup, but Lila knew she could never manage the transformation from Lila to Liù in front of her. She had to leave Seaview Villas as Liù, so she had to get

back in time for a bath – and today a cold one might be
preferable – that would wash away Lila and her sweat and
soreness and the stain of a Burnhead afternoon, the running of
awkward errands with lumpy parcels. Even Enid's mum must
be rubbed from her memory of the day; Liù could not breathe
the homely air of Sew Right. Liù lived on a richer mix, wearing
her fate like a garment to which the slightest crumb of a back-
shop ham roll picnic must not adhere.

And on top of that, she was so tired. Would there be time for her
to rest for even half an hour? The strings of the parcel were cutting
damply into her palms and tiny, icy rivers trickled down her body.
Her face and throat burned. She began to fret that the brown
paper parcel would not hold. She worried that when she got home
the bathroom might not be empty. Her breath was coming in
jagged little gasps. She walked with her head down, praying she
would not run into Enid and the others. Part of her hurry was to do
with escape; Liù and Calaf waited somewhere up ahead.

Then, glancing round before she crossed the top of Station
Road where it joined Main Street, she saw Joe. She took a
breath to call out but he was too far away, walking away from
her, striding fast. He too was laden; one arm flapped from his
shoulder as he listed under the weight of the big holdall in his
other hand. He hurried into the wide turning yard in front of
the station and disappeared into the ticket office.

Lila watched the entrance doors swing behind him, then
slow, and stop. Already the station front was still and empty
again. How quickly he had been and gone, his entrance and
exit no more than an agitation of its surface; he could have been
made of paper, so lightly had he moved across it. Marooned on
the pavement, Lila felt that she was part of the emptiness he
had created simply by being no longer present. She was aghast
that he could assert his separateness from her so easily. How
frail it was, the connection between them, and how invisible; to
the ignorant eye she was no more than a girl in the street
watching an ordinary man with short legs disappearing into the

station. It appalled her to think that, beyond her sight, Joe might appear to be just anybody.

Now she could hear the thud of a train approaching from the left, the northbound Glasgow train. It lumbered under its cloud of smoke across the bridge that spanned Station Road with the ponderous chock, chock of slowing pistons and the wet sigh of steam. The smells of hot steel and burning coal punched the afternoon air.

Lila had no time to think beyond the obvious. He was leaving without her. She made off up the slope of the turning yard, running as fast as she could with the bumping parcel, tore through the empty ticket hall and up over the footbridge to the Glasgow platform where the train was still moving slowly, metal wheels screaming. The guard jumped out. Joe was a long way ahead, walking up the platform towards one of the front carriages.

'Joe! Joe! Joe, wait!'

He did not hear. With more squealing and grinding, the train stopped. Lila, half-blinded by smoke, nearly collided with the guard as she ran up the platform. He shouted after her, 'Hey, you! Slow down, you there! Stand clear there. You!'

As she turned at the sound of his voice, the parcel swung across in front of her legs and banged against the side of the train. She lost her balance and stumbled and with a scream went sprawling across the platform, squashing the headdress between her body and the ground.

'Joe! *Joe!*'

She couldn't get up because of a sick, swimming sensation in her head. Her mouth was full of dust; she gagged once and then gulped and had to swallow back the spoonful of bilious, hammy tea that flooded into her mouth. She coughed hard, then caught sight of the parcel and burst into tears. A moment later the guard was behind her, pulling her to her feet. Joe left his holdall on the platform and was marching towards them. She tried to stand upright as he approached, her legs trembling so hard that her skirt shook.

The guard said, 'You all right, hen?' He sounded shocked. 'You're a bit big to be falling over and skinning your knees, are you no?'

She turned her hands upwards. Her palms had taken the worst of it. They were scraped raw; welling beads of blood stood out from the ruts of torn skin and embedded grit.

'The lassie with you?' the guard demanded, as Joe came up.

Joe ignored him and stared at Lila. 'What are you doing here? What's going on? Are you all right?'

'Joe . . .'

He pushed at the headdress with one foot and a few paste beads rolled out. Where the paper was torn, red sparkling fronds of tinsel escaped and winked in the sunshine.

The guard looked at it and shook his head. 'You with him, hen? He's no giving you any bother?'

Lila couldn't answer. She felt sick and her nose was running. With a shaking arm she wiped a sleeve over her face, nodded her head, and then shook it.

Joe said, 'She's with me, okay?'

'Is that right, hen?'

'I told you.'

Lila nodded. 'I'm all right.'

The guard looked at his watch. 'Well, if yous are getting on the train, get on. If yous are no, get out the road.'

He dragged the parcel a few feet back from the train, hitched his trousers and returned to the guards van. As he blew the whistle a woman poked her head out of a carriage window and Lila and Joe watched her fluttering headscarf until the train disappeared round the shallow bend of the line.

'Well, then,' Joe said, over the top of Lila's head. He was staring after the train and would not meet her eye. 'So, you're all right, are you?'

She looked at him and said nothing. His voice had changed; it was now as rough as other people's.

He said, 'I'll have missed my connection to Euston now. I suppose I'll just have to get the next one.'

Still Lila did not know what to say. She watched him walk up the platform and pick up his holdall.

'Joe!'

He turned round. 'You should go home.'

'But, *Joe*! Why are you going? What about tonight?'

'Look,' he said, 'go home. That's what I'm doing. You're only young, there's things you know nothing about. Just go on home.'

'But what about tonight? You've got to sing. Oh, Joe, it's only nerves! You can't let us down!'

'I'm sorry if I'm letting anybody down, you'll have to excuse me . . .' His voice trailed off. 'Look, I'm not cut out for this,' he said. 'It's just not for me, all right? You'd better leave me alone.'

'I can't! I *can't*. What about tonight? And afterwards? You've got to sing. You can't leave now!'

'I'm not doing it, okay? Joey no can do.'

He turned and made towards a bench under a hanging sign saying BURNHEAD. Lila watched, trying not to weep. 'You can't leave. *Joe! Why?*'

Joe looked at her from the bench. 'Is it too much to expect you to mind your own business? Go home.' With a meaningless little smile, he looked away.

She picked up the disintegrating parcel with both hands, yelped with pain and dropped it. Joe ignored her. Watching him, she sucked on her stinging, torn palms, then blew on them until she felt light-headed. Carrying the parcel was out of the question. A film of sweat had dried on her face and her skin felt tight and hot. She was still shaking from the fall, she was in pain and she didn't know what to do. She didn't understand why everything she loved floated on ahead of her, forever out of reach yet not quite invisible enough, like a black veil fluttering in darkness. Sinking down next to the parcel, she collapsed in sobs that seemed to break from a desert inside her.

He's furious, Steve. He's at the door and Christine's behind him.

She says, Now, Steve, it's not the end of the world. It was my fault anyway, we were just walking past and Paris ran in, it's nobody's fault but mine.

Steve does not spare me the detail. As if it's not enough you wandering the neighbourhood all the hours. This afternoon, he says, Christine was bringing Paris back from playgroup—

Pow Little People's Paradise, you mean? I ask, smiling. I know, Paris's playgroup.

Steve glares. Aye. Paris pulled her hand away from Christine and ran into your front garden, and see that heap of rubbish? That big heap of rubbish you've got sitting there? That's why. That's the attraction. It's an eyesore and it's downright dangerous.

Dangerous, I say. You're telling me.

Steve, don't exaggerate, says Christine. Mind you, she says to me, it is getting bigger, isn't it? It's getting awfully big. What's all that that's on it now? I mean what's the point, what's it for, where's it all going to end?

Can my mother's wrecked piano, a heap of papers and notes and cuttings and sheet music, fusty rolls of cloth and ruined clothes and now some harmless stage props (papier mâché shields and helmets, painted banners and wooden swords) be thought dangerous? I mean, to anyone but me? As for where it's going to end, I'm the last person they should be asking. I really am the last person.

So Paris goes climbing right up over it before Christine can stop her, Steve says. And she hurt herself. She got a skelf in her finger. That heap's a danger and an eyesore and we're not folk to go complaining normally but it's been there days now. It wants shifting. At least you want to get the stuff in a skip. It's a bloody menace and I want to know what you're doing about it.

She was climbing in to get at the piano keys, Christine says, and lowers her voice to explain. There's a keyboard at playgroup. She's never away from it, I suppose she just made the connection, when she seen you know, your, er . . . piano.

What's left of a piano more like, Steve says sourly. Bloody mess.

She just wanted to hear what it sounded like. She was curious.

Steve won't let the matter go. He says, So, how long's it staying there? It's a danger to wee ones. I don't like seeing my wee girl in tears with a sore finger. I'll be back to see what you're doing about it, I'm warning you.

I clap my hands and say, Oh, sweet! She wanted to get to the keys, she wanted to hear what it sounded like! Well, that's a very good sign. Curiosity. She might be musical. Maybe it's not too early to think about piano lessons.

And Joe's furious. He drags me upright, takes the parcel and says, Oh for Christ's sake, stop crying! People will see you! Come on then.

All I can do is follow.

There isn't another train for an hour and a half so I suppose he thinks he can get me home to Seaview Villas and still make it back to the station in time; I don't know and I daren't ask. We're not quite over the footbridge before I'm thinking that if he's walking out of the production then there isn't going to be a performance at all, so why all the effort to get me and the headdress home?

I don't dare ask that either, in case it's because he hasn't worked it out yet. In no time I'm convincing myself it's simply because he cares about me, even if he doesn't quite realise it enough to say so. My mind calls up all the romantic moments in stories when hero sees heroine in distress for the first time and that's when he finally realises. I follow with a sense of anticipation.

I limp a little behind him, snivelling into my sleeve. There's no question of our holding hands because mine are too sore and anyway, he's now carrying the holdall as well as the parcel. He still has the holdall! He doesn't leave it at the station. This is the final proof. He will be staying after all; something is compelling him to stay, all he doesn't know yet is that it is because he loves me. He fishes for a handkerchief in his pocket and finds he hasn't got one, so he tears a strip of brown paper off the parcel and hands it to me without a word. I blow my nose on it and tear that bit away, then I spit on what's left and try to clean up my hands as we walk along.

We make our way up Boydfield Gardens. I keep my eyes half closed against the traffic of people and for once I walk in a straight line and make other people move for me; usually it's the other way round, me stepping round them. I don't care today if I annoy the women with lumpy beach bags and kids hanging on their sleeves.

At the bus stop Joe says, Okay, right, now I have to go. You'll be okay. He puts the parcel down. Somebody'll help you on with this, or the conductor'll do it. He swings his holdall up and holds it close against his chest.

I start to cry again. Go? You can't go! You're not going?

I'm trembling, ready to make another scene. Joe sighs and looks around to see if the people waiting over by the wall can hear. They can.

And anyway, *why*? Just tell me why. Oh, you can't go!

He stares across Main Street where the soot-stained sides of buildings that don't get cleaned and where the sun doesn't reach are still wet from the rain and look as hard as coal. He shivers with weariness at all the effort he makes to feel he belongs here but of course he doesn't, any more than I do. The bus rolls in from the far end of the street, tyres sighing through puddles in the gutter. He moves back from the curved wall of water sent up from the wheels, motions angrily to me to get on first and he follows, depositing the parcel in my lap and the holdall at his feet.

We ride along without speaking and when I try a small sideways smile in his direction he just glares. His eyes look filmy; the whites are lustrous and wet but also hard-looking, like the secret iridescent underside of a seashell picked off the shore and held up dripping to the light. When you don't know any better you bring them home, these shells, in a bucket of seawater. They rasp and gleam like treasure in the swing of your bucket as you walk, you gaze into it instead of where you're going. At home you set them on the garden wall and they dry off and turn dull and you see them for what they are, not so alluring after all. You were misled into thinking you'd found pearls.

Tears are still spilling out of my eyes, I can't help it. I must be the most watery person he knows. Maybe my face is wearing that lost rabbity look it gets when I cry. I try to weep attractively and look brave, so that he'll know this is unusual, that I'm not this person very often.

When we get off at the Pow Burn bridge Joe places the parcel on the ground and says, Okay, I've seen you home, all right? You go on home. You can manage from here.

But his voice is mellower. He gazes across the waste ground to the sea which today sparkles as a sea should.

But she'll kill me. I can't take it home like this, I whisper, touching the parcel. It's all bent and spoiled. You have to help me fix it, they'll kill me if I take it home like this.

He casts around for the words to refuse. I have no wish to cry now; I want only to keep him.

We can't fix it here, he says. You'd better go home.

Please, I say. Please help me. Come on. There's a place down the shore we can unwrap it and take a look. Come on.

I can hardly believe it, but he looks at me dumbly for a moment and then he does come, and my heart starts to thump because I am making things happen for once. Is it this simple? Can I just say come on, and he comes? Now I lead the way, walking across the scrub as fast as I can, too fast for him, laden as he is, to draw level and start objecting. The sun is hot again and shines through the silver marram grass in deadly splinters. I am full of dread in case the heat raises smells that can't be ignored, because Joe's continuing attendance is a fragile contract that will collapse if he is caused another moment's disgust, embarrassment or boredom. We cross the dunes and head up the shoreline towards the border of the tip. He had no idea I was going to bring him this far; I walk swiftly and do not turn round.

Since I was last here with Enid there has been a high tide and there are new deposits of seaweed that we have to cross. Joe starts to protest but I press on and he has to follow. The seaweed at least has dried and does not smell, but hidden in it here and there are dubious white fragments and remains that might have been fish or bird, bone, feather or egg. Whatever it is they are disgusting so I try to pick a path that doesn't veer too close. Then I take a step and I am in the middle of a black upward rush of raging flies, I scream and jump away, running, flapping my arms to get them out of my eyes and mouth and ears and hair. Not two feet away lies the split bag of a dead seagull. I was about to tread in a corpse. Joe laughs.

Up ahead, strings of smoke rise from the sprawling bonfires of the tip. The car seat is still lying in the place where Enid and I hauled it weeks ago, set against the bleached log and facing the sea. Another few yards closer to the tip and the stink of burning rubbish would drive us away; here, the smell puckers the air a little but does not encroach too badly. Joe flings down his load with some force, collapses into the seat and pulls a wrapped

PUCCINI'S GHOSTS

bottle from the holdall. My brain is working some seconds behind my senses, it seems. I hear the tear of the wrapping and the glump of the cork before I quite understand.

Why have you got that? Why are you drinking?

Go on, he says, I'll even let you have first go.

I shake my head.

You should. Helps you relax. He shrugs, takes a drink and gasps. That's the only time I ever take it, he says. When I need to relax.

The fume of whisky carries from his mouth and perfumes the air around me. I am concentrating on the sea and sky, whose blue is the only brightness in the landscape. A few hundred yards away beyond us the mottled scree of the tip rises like a loose wall, dripping bricks, broken fireplaces, furniture carcases and torn sheets of plasterboard from which rags of wallpaper in fleshy, private colours hang off like flayed skin. The shingle of the beach is the colour of wet concrete. Joe glances at me surreptitiously for a sign that I will give up on him and let him go. Without allowing myself to breathe any more freely, I bring the parcel over, sink down on the car seat and start to pull off the string. Again I break into a sweat, and some new weight in my head tips sideways and I find myself falling forward as if I'm being pushed. I try to right myself and find that I am groaning.

Here. *La bella* Liù. You need a drink, Joe says, almost tenderly.

Because he has used my special name I take the bottle. Then I catch in his eye a look that I feel stupidly unprepared for, as if from the day I met him I have been ignoring the direction he has been bringing me in all this time. Somewhere along the way to here, he and I uncoupled ourselves from normality and joined each to the other, so I shouldn't be surprised that we have ended up here. I take an experimental drink from the bottle and then a longer swig and I hold my breath to stop the coughing. Then I swallow and my head is full of a taste so dense it seems

349

to stick to my face. Although the stinging in my hands has abated I hurt in several new places: I did scrape my knees, and I banged my hip, and an old ache in my chest is now reaching round into my spine. Not just my throat but my whole neck is sore. Again heat breaks out all over me and I picture the squalid little rolls of paste that must be lying in the folds of my skin where talcum powder mixes with sweat. I try to stretch, and can't. Joe takes the bottle from me and drinks hard. Even though I am hot I am shivering, and when I hug myself to try to stop, in my armpits I find tender swellings, like rubbery little beans. My mouth curls with distaste at myself.

Joe is still drinking.

Looks like that's fucked, he says amiably, nodding at the headdress at my feet.

No! No, we have to fix it. It'll be okay, I say, reaching forward and picking it up. Look, you just have to straighten it up and bend the horn things back the right way. You're stronger than me. My hands are too sore anyway.

The effort of this speech makes me belch and my eyes water with the sharp backbite of whisky. Pardon me, I say.

Joe actually smiles. He takes the headdress and does as I ask, with surprising care and gentleness, pulling the red wire back into two equal points. He dusts off the silk, picks stray threads away. Some of the beads and paste jewels have come off but there were so many to begin with that a few less won't matter. When he's finished he sets it down on the brown paper and we both have another drink. I hate the taste but the whisky is helping me to feel less. I'm trembling all over and my heart is beating hard, sending painful vibrations through every rib and up into my head.

Thank you, I say, handing the bottle back. I close my eyes to sense how alone we are. There is no noise but the slurring of the sea and the guttering, wandering voices of the gulls that sound like lonely children. I try to blink away the dust that has gathered under my eyelids.

Joe says something or maybe I dream that he does, but I can't open my eyes even if he is talking to me, not yet. His voice and the birds and the tide grow fainter; sounds sway above me, they come and go slyly. When I open my eyes again the world is heartlessly bright and again my eyes are not working properly or maybe all movement is slowing down to a pace I can cope with. I watch a murmur escape from the side of Joe's mouth and his head slips back as the hand with the bottle drifts up to his lips. I close my eyes again and float, then I feel the bottle on my mouth and Joe's breath flowing round me as I drink, wet and whisky-warm. He pushes against me, getting to his feet. He stands up and staggers a way off. His moving makes me giddy. The car seat smells bad and dirty and maybe I'm mistaken that it's a car seat, maybe I'm in the stinking hold of a ship lost in the swell of an ocean. Behind me I hear Joe cursing and unzipping and the rattle as he pees into the sand, followed by his deep sigh. My mind has wandered too far for anything like shock, so I close my eyes again and let my body stretch out, even though it's painful and the seat is rough and scratches my thighs. It feels as though little wire spiders are breeding just below its surface. But I marvel that all squeamishness has left me. I must cling on no matter how the boat rocks, my little rocking boat is all I have. Joe returns in a flurry of kicked sand and slumps down, his hands flopping against my legs. We'll be safe even in this ruin as long as we cling on together. I'll be all right as long as Joe stays, lying here with his head next to mine like an offering, his body's bulk against me. I fall asleep.

———————

26

Lila's mouth flopped open and slapped shut. She gave a rasping cough and struggled to get up. 'Is there some water anywhere?' she said. 'I'm not well. I need a drink of water, there must be some somewhere.'

Her voice sounded coated, as if she had a mouthful of wet paper. She dragged herself to her feet and turned towards him. It was true she didn't look well, but how was he supposed to come up with fresh water here, on a beach? She tried to smooth down her clothes; she was in some pink and yellow things that Joe hadn't taken in before. He didn't understand her clothes at all. She wasn't made for this kind of place, or for hard drink either. That wasn't his fault.

'Look at the state of you,' he said, uncorking the bottle again. It was half finished already and that *was* her fault. He drank greedily, in his mind merely keeping pace, getting even.

'Please,' she said, peering hard at him, pushing her hands down her thighs. 'Isn't there any water?'

'There's only this,' he said, lifting the bottle and patting the seat. She sat down again, took the bottle and raised it slowly, closing her eyes. Joe watched her mouth open and search and close around the opening. She drank, her lips puckering and licking round for an escaping trickle, and then she gave a sigh and let her head loll back, her eyes still shut and the line of her throat stretched white and bare. Warmth spread through him. He took the bottle from her and set it carefully in the sand. Her closed eyes looked like small fruits, lemon-shaped, the eyelids just thin peel guarding the juicy pulp underneath. He studied her slightly open mouth and let it suggest to him other round, open waiting places in her body. Or in bodies, generally; lips, specifically. All bodies had those. He felt himself starting to get hard. What a surprise she was. It could even be her body he was thinking of, but it didn't matter. Poor kid, *la bella*, out of it now, she couldn't hold on to her stupid little poses any more, not with a skinful in her and Christ, no more could he. Something unaffected in her was coming to the surface, through her sleep, and it appealed to him. Poor kid. *La bella*.

He let his hand glide over and touch her hands that were folded together across her lap, pointing down between her legs. She murmured, her eyelids wavered. Joe held his breath, his mind considering in more detail the wet and hidden possibilities under her clothes, ready. She wanted it all right. The thump of heart and whisky and blood was beating in his head and little trembles broke out all over his body, a curiosity of nerves. So did he, all right. No reason why not; George was no reason why not. George might be a reason why he should. His hand skated over hers again, traced a line up her arm and moved across, slipping up under her blouse. Maybe not all the way. He was very hard now. Under the stiff cones of the bra her breasts had subsided into their own velvety swell. He was not familiar with breasts but hers were so soft – too soft and welcoming to be quite foreign. He withdrew his hand and undid the blouse buttons and as he slipped a finger back inside and found the nipple, he moved his other hand down to unzip himself. She was awake. With a tug of her clothes he pulled her breast free and fixed his mouth over it.

'Joe, oh Joe . . . *oh.*'

He sucked, letting the edge of his teeth graze the nipple, then he bit, and without letting go he lifted himself up and lay down alongside her, pushing her into the seat with his knees. He wondered what the moans coming from her meant, what it was she wanted. She moaned as he nibbled some more and freed the other breast and squeezed it hard, and he moaned too; it seemed a courtesy to supply an echo. Now she was rolling around neither resisting nor helping. Perhaps she wanted to make it easier for him, it was hard to tell; she was taking to this in the same way she had to the whisky, as if she needed it so much the question of liking it or not did not come into it. He pushed a knee between her legs and then, in case she should be about to speak, he moved up and planted his mouth on hers. It didn't matter whether she wanted to stop or encourage him; he simply could not bear to hear her voice. Trying to move his hand slowly, he felt under her skirt. She seemed to freeze for a moment. Then she shoved her tongue into his mouth and his hand pushed inside her knickers and landed on her belly and immediately she spread herself, drawing up one leg and hooking it over the back of the seat. He was so surprised he lifted his head and tried to look at her but she closed her eyes and buried her face in his neck.

'It's all right! Do it. Go on, do it,' she whispered. 'Do it, do it if you want.'

He had no idea what he wanted. His hand was resting on what felt like a nest of warm straw. Her skin tasted a little sour but with a memory of sweetness, not exactly meat or fruit but something that had come from an animal or had been lately growing, like buttermilk, or overblown flowers. Was that what he wanted? She lifted herself and pushed hard against his hand and then he felt it under his fingers, the bold nub as slippery as syrup, a little peeled strawberry. She was holding her breath, raising herself; he thrust a finger inside and heaved himself on top of her, fumbling, and as the second finger went in hard she cried *Oh!* He had not got rid of enough clothes yet. He squeezed himself with his free hand and tried to hold back but just as he was about to push in, the warm spilling began, smearing her thighs and wiry hair and stomach and his fingers, slipping into the creases of their clothes and raising its usual raw, sad, wasted smell. He collapsed away from her and lay with his head turned to the side, allowing dismay to settle, feeling emptied of any further point in being here.

She didn't seem to realise. After they had lain for a while she sighed in a way he found annoying, as if she'd been enlightened, shown the sacred mysteries or something. He reached over for the whisky bottle and drank. He didn't offer her any and she didn't notice that, either.

'I don't mind it happened,' she said. 'I'm glad. I thought we wouldn't before . . . I mean it's supposed to be better to wait, sometimes. But with us it's different.'

'How come, diff'rent? B'fore what?' Joe said. Half out of malice, he wanted to know just how cock-eyed it was, her idea of what was going on.

'Oh, Joe! You know,' she said. '*You* know, you . . . You know, before . . .' She obviously thought she had bestowed upon him something priceless. 'Before the opera. Before it's all official, when I get to sixteen.'

'Look, I told you,' he said, 'I'm not doing the opera. I can't. Far as I'm concerned it's not happening.' He turned on to his back, perching uncomfortably on the edge of the seat. He pushed himself, cool and sticky, back into his clothes and zipped up. 'There is not going to be no fucking opera. I told you.'

Lila struggled to sit up. 'You can't say that *now*,' she cried. 'You can't!' She grabbed his shoulder. 'Not now we're . . .'

'Not now we're *what*.'

'Well, not after . . . not now we're everything to each other!'

'Aw, Jesus.'

'We are! We're in it *together*. How can I go back now? What am I supposed to tell them?'

'You don't need to tell them anything. You *mustn't* tell them anything.' Joe tried to smile at her. He tidied a strand of hair from her face. 'It's our secret, okay?'

'And I'm not well, either,' she stated wearily, settling back, aware of stinging between her legs. Feeling bad was all she was really sure of. 'I think I'm getting tonsillitis again. You'll probably get it too, now,' she added miserably, and began to cry. 'Still, that won't matter if you're not going to sing, will it,' she sobbed. 'I'll never get to London. I'm all packed and ready and everything and I'll never get to go.'

'*Oh*, Jesus,' Joe said, and let his voice trail away. He patted her leg. 'Come on. London's not all it's cracked up to be.'

He got to his feet and handed her the whisky bottle. 'Here,' he said jovially. 'Thirsty work, eh?'

Lila took the bottle, drank and coughed. She said, 'Is it because you think I'm too young? Sixteen's too young to get engaged? I wouldn't mind waiting. Are you thinking we should wait a bit longer?'

Joe stared at her. 'That's not what I'm thinking at all,' he said. Was that what she was on about, was she really that naïve? Had it really not occurred to her that she was under age? Not that it had actually happened – not properly – but she seemed to think it had. She could say anything.

Lila swallowed. 'I don't think my voice works any more.' She sat up and sang a scratchy scale and then she sang another, stronger and clearer. 'Well, Liù,' she said. 'She's still here, anyway.'

She wrapped her arms round herself and tucked her hands under her arms. 'You've got to sing,' she said fiercely and suddenly. 'You've got to. Otherwise I might as well kill myself. Otherwise . . .'

'Aw, Jesus.' Joe's head throbbed. He was too drunk to weigh up his chances accurately; perhaps he could get away right now and that would be an end of it, but what if she talked? George peeved and jealous anyway, plus George's underage niece interfered with would mean real trouble.

'You've *got* to. I mean it. If you don't I'll kill myself, and then you'll be sorry.'

'Aw, stop that, will you?' Joe got up and stood facing the sea, steadying himself. He turned to her. She was sitting bolt up-right, her eyes glittering. 'Look, I'll think about it. I need to think. I need to see how I feel.'

'There isn't time. We have to go back and get ready. You've got to come *now*.'

Joe sighed heavily. 'Jesus! Look. Suppose I go back. I'll go back, but no promises, okay? I'll . . . I'll go back to the house and see how I feel, okay?'

'We can go back together.'

'No! Don't you see, if anyone sees us together they might start wondering where we've been. They might ask what we've been up to. See? I'll go first.'

'And we keep this a secret?'

'Exactly.'

'Until?'

'Until . . . until later. Till afterwards, till we don't have to any more.'

'And you promise you'll go straight back. You really promise.'

'Okay, I promise.'

'And you will sing.'

'I promise I'll go back to the house.'

'You've got to sing! You've got to!'

'Okay, okay! Jesus. Okay, for fuck's sake, I'll sing. You stay here a bit longer and then you follow, okay?'

'Okay, Joe. I trust you. You *do* promise?'

'See you, then.'

'See you on stage,' Lila said. 'See you, Calaf.'

She lay back and closed her eyes and when she opened them again Joe and the holdall had gone. Sunlight cut a sparkling path through the water, sliced low across the beach and into her face. A translucent snip of moon hung high in the sky, miles above the salty whisper of the tide. She stood up on rigid legs, arranged a fold of her skirt like a bandage over her hand, picked up the parcel and set off back towards the dunes, too absorbed by the task of walking straight and protecting her hands to think very hard about anything.

Steve's got a point, Christine says, banging cushions together and setting them back diamond-fashion into the chairs. I've given her permission to do what she calls a quick once-round before the funeral but it doesn't seem to me either quick or once. We're arguing about clearing away papers and so on, and I don't think we're getting anywhere.

She keeps saying, about this and that and the next thing, that it's only decent to do it right. You only get one go vis-à-vis a funeral, she adds.

(That's why, since midday, the coffin has been sitting on trestles in the music room. By rights he shouldn't go from the undertakers', he ought to leave from his own home, Christine says. It's more fitting. So I let her arrange it that way. I wanted to remark on her being surprisingly old-fashioned for one so young but I'm wrong about that. It's only the young into whom death strikes such awe.)

I mean Steve has got an important point, she says again. All that mess out there. Still there, cluttering up all the front, right up against the window near enough, I don't know what folk'll say. He'd have got it shifted for you before today, he'd have been only too pleased to get the garden nice. You'd only to say. For a nice send-off. Fitting.

And it washes over me that after eighty-five years of life and most of them spent in 5 Seaview Villas my father finally leaves this house for the last time and the garden's a mess when his coffin goes past, and it's not good enough. Again I fail him. Very little grows here in the sandy ground and salt wind but can't one flower open, might not a single bloom rise from the place where he sat his life out, cultivating his philosophy of not expecting too much, making a virtue out of being overlooked? Och, Lizzie, I'm happy enough, he used to say. Yet again the right thing to do evades me or doesn't come until too late.

But if we are to mark his passing in sausage rolls, I'm on top of it. Sheena of Party Fayre arrives. She's come early to get on so that she'll be ready for when we come back from the service. She pokes her head out of the kitchen at us.

You'll no mind, she tells me, you'll no mind only I've got my mum coming later to give me a hand?

She disappears to get her microwave in from the van.

Anyway, Christine says, turning her attention to me, look at you, where in God's name have you been now? Have you been down the shore? It's time you were getting ready. Goodness sake.

I lie in a bath that she runs for me and I feel that there is a smudge in me that I shall fail to wash away before this afternoon's performance of the funeral; the purpose of this bath is not to cleanse but to obliterate myself, smudge and all. I dress carefully. The clothes Christine has kindly cleaned and pressed are costume. I have not worn makeup for days and it does me good to paint some pride back on my face, to dab over my consternation with a subtle, daytime, all-over base tone for the maturer complexion. Since I have not managed since I came here either to wash or to sleep away my stained self, it helps me to hide. I must hide in broad daylight, in the guise of his blameless daughter. I want to step out of this room at least looking like a worthy mourner of the last of my gentle, immaculate ghosts.

But this last funeral, my father's, goes off with more than a touch of grace. Odd how the most fugitive quality in a person may be the one that asserts itself just as he is leaving, when it's too late for speeches because you might choke on all you should have said long ago. At the Evangelical Lutherans' hall there is a sombre courtesy present among us that withstands the falling and swooping of Luke's voice and the furrowing and lifting of his brow. We let him tell us there is no emotion inapplicable and no response inappropriate 'at this time' and that we may share 'all that is in our hearts'. There may be a moment when I almost believe it. Whatever we feel, Luke will flush it from us and wring it out, he will hang it up to dry and bless it. We are to look back with gratitude, smile beaming smiles for my father's remembered quirks and nod with nostalgic respect for the dutiful, stoic times he represents. And take our tears to Jesus. Nobody seems to notice that there is no music. The part with the prayers and the box is over soon and before I know it we're back here at Seaview Villas, right about where I started. Luke seems satisfied. We accept, we trivialise and we wipe our eyes.

Today must be the first day since the *Turandot* meeting that the house has been full. I stand in the hall and listen to the decorous sway of conversation in the music room where for so long the air has been still. Luke and Christine and Mrs Foley and Dr Chowdry are here, plus two couples from Seaview Villas, perfect strangers whom Christine tells me I have met. They came to pay respects some days ago only I was not just at my best, one of them says. There are others, a few pew-fillers, Luke's church mainstays, but also quiet old gents who say they always held my father in high regard. One says they very seldom spoke but they used to nod to each other at the surgery.

A party of fifteen or twenty or so will have its lapses into silence; there are pauses in conversation while people get tea and a dram down them, not to mention the finger sandwiches. The place is ripe with the smell of elderly bodies in winter clothes and the whiff of toasted cheese from Sheena's pizza bites. She comes and goes from the kitchen with plates and cups, and through the open door I see her mother stationed at the sink with her back to the gathering. Sheena's five-year-old

is here too, for reasons that were apologetically explained and I
have forgotten. Her name is Jordan. She and Paris have been
stuffing themselves and are now sugar-fuelled, snickering and
hyperactive, running around groups of people and poking out
tongues stained bright pink from the muck they've been eating.
Jordan crashes into my legs, looks up and gasps; her breath
smells like hot plastic and raspberries. I turn her round and
steer her back up the hall.

I observe a general absence of solemnity. It is not the presence
of the children that dispels it. Funerals used to be what they were
meant to be, drab and frugal. People would take a dram like a
tonic to bring them round after an unpleasantness, but they
don't any more; they propose quiet toasts, eyes already tracking
the whereabouts of the bottle, working out how long till the next
snootful. They raise and clink glasses in a display of enjoyment
that once the dead had the power to constrain. Not even for the
afternoon of their disposal may the dear departed be anything
but celebrated. Mourning may no longer show. It has joined
grief in grief's true place, weeping and pacing an empty room in
the small hours, face hidden in the hands. We may not even say
dear departed any more, it's all first names now. But I don't feel
like celebrating. The obligation is being foisted on me, as if I'm a
child given a flag on a stick and commanded to wave it while
something she doesn't recognise goes by. Here I am, doubtful,
with the stick cutting into my hand, standing on the edge of the
parade.

I wander away to the kitchen. Sheena's mum, a woman in
trainers and aquamarine trousers and sweatshirt, is still at the
sink. Her hair is cut so short the back of her neck looks like a
man's. She turns around looking for more cups to wash and I
see that it's Senga McMillan. Her hair is strangely dyed and the
face and body are heavier but it's her. We both break into
smiles. She peels off her rubber gloves and plumps her hair.

You're Sheena's mother?

Aye, Sheena's my second. I've just the three. Grown up now.

How wonderful.

Aye, see when Sheena says it's a funeral tea for Duncan at Seaview Villas, here's me thinking it must be the same Duncan.

She talks quickly, as if she's nervous. And here it *is* you. Sorry about your father. So how're you doing? You're a stranger here these days, are you not?

Yes, well, it's been such a long time! Life's pretty hectic still. Actually, I *never* get back! I . . . I live in Antwerp. And how are *you*?

We chat for a time, two women in their late fifties talking safely of the usual subjects and each assessing what damage the years have done. I can hardly believe this is Senga who ripped the flowering currant bushes to shreds on the last day of school, who was the first to go all the way, who smoked and shoplifted and swore and is now Senga the grandmother, who breaks off mid-sentence at the sound of Jordan's sudden wail from the next room and hurries to see what's wrong.

One of the Seaview Villas neighbours has her hands clasped over both of Jordan's and is trying to persuade her to give up what she's holding.

No, dear, we don't want that broken, do we, dear? Better let me have that.

Jordan protests and snivels and clutches her prize tighter. At the sight of her granny she wails even more, the neighbour lets go and Jordan dives wet nose first straight into Senga's legs. She wants rid of what's in her hands now and she allows her fingers to be eased away from the heavy glass paperweight she's holding. It's smeared with snot but it's in one piece. Senga takes it carefully, breathes on it and rubs it on her sweatshirt. Jordan's already over at the sideboard selecting another one from the two dozen or so set out in a row. Senga smiles apologetically and goes to reason with her.

No, Jordan, leave those, Nana says leave those alone. Those are the lady's, they're not yours. Want a marshmallow? Go and get a marshmallow, on you go and get one for Paris as well.

Jordan scowls and exits and for a long time Senga lets her gaze rest on the row of paperweights. When she looks at me her eyes are wet.

Oh my, she sighs. Oh my, there they all are. They take me back! I cleaned those for years.

Cleaned them? What do you mean?

Aye, I'd forgotten. Nice to see them again.

Forgotten what? What do you mean?

Oh, I'm talking about when they were still Audrey's. Years ago, before she died. Not remember? Audrey Mathieson's paperweights.

Audrey Mathieson's? They were my father's, I tell her. He kept them in the sideboard.

Oh aye, but they were Audrey's before. I remember him getting them, I brought him them down myself in the car. Audrey Mathieson's paperweights, not remember? You must have heard he got her paperweights.

I think I may have forgotten, I say. I assumed he bought them, over the years.

There may be a shade of the old Senga in the look she gives me, just the merest sly pleasure in being ahead with a piece of information that she knows and I don't – like what really happens to a boy's thing when he wants to do it to a girl – but it doesn't last. She tells me that for eighteen years or so she has been a cleaner and general assistant at North Beach Court.

The sheltered flats. Where Mrs Foley stays now, she says. Nice wee flats. Anyway, Audrey Mathieson was there. She was there from when she was widowed till she died. Liked it well enough, and she'd no family to take her.

I didn't know she'd died.

Oh, aye, a while ago now. Maybe eight years? Though it's always longer than you think, isn't it, could even be ten, eleven. Aye, more like ten. Anyway she left these to your dad.

They worked together for years, till he left the firm. They were work colleagues.

Aye, I know. But they were still friends after, weren't they? They went about together from when she was widowed. Before I even went to work there, I'm talking years and years ago. You'd know that.

Oh, of course, certainly I did, I lie.

He was coming in every day to see her, right to the last. I mind he brought the paper and read to her. Oh, we saw an awful lot of Mr Duncan. They were close. He was awful good to her. You could say devoted.

Jordan reappears, wraps herself round Senga's leg and stares up at me.

Jordan, I say, come with me. Would you like one of these to keep? One to take home and keep?

I lead her by the hand to the sideboard.

Christine is suddenly at my side, telling me that Mr and Mrs Lennox from number two are about to go. I thrust a paper-weight into their hands and say I hope they will accept this as a . . . as what?

As a memento of my father, I say.

Oh I couldn't, dear, says Mrs Lennox. It was your father's. There's no call.

Oh yes you could! You must, I cry. Here! Take another.

Jordan pulls at my skirt. Can I have this one? she asks, pointing.

I stoop down and hand it to her and say, Yes, this one is yours.

Senga says, What do you say, Jordan?

Mrs Lennox says, Seems a shame to break up the collection.

No, you're wrong about that. It's right to break up the collection, I tell her. Everyone's to take one. Spread it out, spread the prettiness around. They're all pretty, just pick one, any one you like.

This seems to prompt the putting aside of teacups and a general exodus but I won't let anyone go until they're weighted down with one or two of these dubious lumps of the glassma-ker's art. A loose line-up forms; I shake hands and insist each person chooses a paperweight from the diminishing number on the table. An embarrassed quiet settles on us as the queue shuffles along but I am inwardly ecstatic, feeling I have found, quite by accident, a gesture to equal the day. Among all the objects in this house only the paperweights, crude as *objets d'art* perhaps, have a lustre that I think they owe to Raymond and Audrey, to the pair of them.

Two dozen Vasart paperweights: not much as a gift to the world goes, but I want to send them out beyond this dead house. I want to put them in careful hands of any age (this has nothing to do with posterity), hands in whose care they may shine. I want them gone from here and placed in lives not yet wearied as mine has become.

27

Lila stepped through the back door. The kitchen looked sulky and abandoned as only an empty room painted red, sage and lemon could, its gaiety inadequate; bright, but abandoned anyway. She ran the cold tap and swallowed mouthful after mouthful of water. She let the water pour over her cut hands and dabbed some on her burning face.

She was aware of a five o'clock stillness; it was nearly half past. In the mirror inside the pantry door she saw that she didn't look as ill as she felt. Her skin was rosy – dewy, even – as if the heat and pain pulsing through her had filled her cheeks out. Her eyes looked back brightly from the mirror and she paused, holding her breath. There was not a sound. Joe must have got back at least twenty minutes ago, found the house empty and gone up to the farm straightaway to get into his costume. Everyone would be there by now. Joe would tell Uncle George that she was coming later. He might even say he had seen her returning with the headdress. But should she go to the farm at once just to make sure he had come back?

No need. Joe had promised. And she was too altered and feverish and exhausted, too deep in this new strangeness about herself; if she slept for an hour or so, perhaps she would wake up more used to it all. A sleep would also help her hold off the tonsillitis long enough to sing, and if she stayed here to rest she wouldn't have to see anyone before she was ready to go on stage; she could bath and change and go straight there and arrive just in time for the curtain. After the performance Uncle George wouldn't dare be angry that she had cut it so fine, because after the performance everything would be different.

She sang a few notes and swallowed, and sang again, louder. The stinging and aching between her legs was worse, just at the moment, than her throat. But she would get over that. And now that it had happened, now that she and Joe were a couple, it was going to be even easier than she thought. Though she would put aside the costume when she left for London she would never quite put aside Liù. Liù would be somewhere inside her from now on, a strain of underground music that would ripple through her life, singing of love that did not fail.

Just then she heard the music room door and her father's scraping footsteps along the hall. Why couldn't he lift his feet? He stood in the doorway looking at her.

'Well, Lizzie?'

Did it show? Lila had a sudden memory of Joe and the feel of it, the thick, weighty tube rubbing along her leg and pushing against and nearly, very nearly, right into her. It was an intolerable idea that her father had one, too. How could he have one and be standing there, looking at her so smoothly? But if he hadn't, her mother wouldn't live here like a bird trapped in his hands. Now she knew why her mother shuddered when she looked at her father's hands. He had large fingers that moved too fast, and her mother must look at them and remember where she had let them go and how eager they had been, that one drunken night. And because she had allowed it, she was having to spend the rest of her life with someone she probably couldn't even tolerate gloved. Lila blushed furiously.

'Och, Lizzie. You all right?'

'I'm just tired, I'm going for a sleep. Where is everybody?'

'I couldn't say. I'm er, just five minutes back from Burnhead.' He glanced behind him. 'I'm just away to put the kettle on. Your mother was having her hair done, I believe. Moira Mather was giving her a lift straight from the hairdressers'.'

Another pair of feet trotted down the hall and Mrs Mathieson appeared.

She said, 'Hello, dear. We're just looking over the production account. Getting a few costings for props jotted down. Then we're away to the farm.'

'Where's Joe? Is he up there already?'

Her father said, 'Joe? I couldn't say. I suppose so. Is that there the headdress?'

'Oh. Yes. Some bits came off.'

'Oh, it'll do,' Mrs Mathieson said, coming forward and picking up the tattered parcel. 'It'll pass. I'll take it up when we go. So your mum isn't worrying about it.'

'Sure you're all right?' Raymond asked.

'I don't feel very well. I need a sleep.'

'Well, on you go up, lassie.'

Taking care to avoid his eyes, Lila moved past him to the stairs. He turned and watched her, stroking his moustache.

'I'll pour you a wee cup of tea and bring it up before I go.'

'It's all right, I just want to sleep.'

'I won't disturb you. I'll leave it outside the door. Hot drink's good for a throat.'

'Oh, okay. Thank you. Maybe I should take some aspirin too.'

'I'll bring you some. Lizzie,' he said, in a different voice. He was embarrassed.

'What?' Her heart was thumping. Did it show? How could he tell? Could he smell the whisky?

Mrs Mathieson smiled at him.

'Lizzie,' he went on, 'I'm proud of you, lassie. You sing your best now, and I'll see you later.'

Upstairs she dropped into sleep and was thrown out of it at intervals, hearing the sounds of trains and the waves of the sea and distressed cries. Shapes rose out of bright light and sank into darkness. She turned on to her back and tested her underarms again for the lumps – still there, more tender now – and she stroked her lips with one finger and found them warm and dry. Her mouth felt gluey. She assessed the ache between her legs and found it came back when she pressed herself, as if there were bones down there that were now bruised that she hadn't known she had. The stinging had stopped but the heat in her face now seemed related to it; somehow that had more to do with it than the smear of blood on her knickers did, because nothing technical about what had happened was as important as what Joe had really done, which was to declare himself. She had been left in no doubt. Though he had got carried away (the way they will) he had not got carried quite all the way, and it was the greatest compliment that she aroused in him passion and respect equally. She lay in bed and imagined – or rather designed – the next time, which would take place magically without the obstruction of clothes and, she thought daringly, with more words from Joe, among which 'passion' and 'respect' would predominate.

She got up and went to the door and opened it. On the floor was a cup of tea, stone cold, a skin wrinkling its surface. There were aspirins in the saucer. Next to it was the blue and white Spode vase with another bunch of dark red and orange pansies in it. She picked them up and took them back to bed, placing the vase exactly where it had stood before. The cold tea was disgusting but she was parched again and drank it. *Thirsty work, eh?* Joe said. Her mind fought it. Her father had left the tea but he couldn't have left the pansies, too. Or was it a coincidence that he had picked the very same flowers and put them in exactly the same vase as Joe had done the first time she had tonsillitis? It was Joe who, being of few words, left her flowers, smoothed her bed, brought her chocolates in a heart-shaped box. He did those things to tell her without words that he loved her.

She dozed for a while longer and woke to the sound of voices downstairs. Her head was clear. She smiled up at the ceiling, hearing Joe's voice. Then it grew utterly quiet again. A mistake then, to think she had heard him.

But she got up and opened her door silently and stepped on

to the landing. A disturbance of dust scurried and climbed and fell in the slant of light that bled down from the skylight in the attic stairwell. Joe was in the house. Lila could feel him somewhere near and if she wanted to she could sing out, shout his name and claim him. The forbidden things were permitted now.

More sounds came: of feet on the staircase below her and urgent laughter and someone falling against the wall. A lull, a murmur, and then the footsteps pounded upwards, nearer. One of the two voices was Joe's. Lila darted back into her room and stood against the wall behind the door. She heard two people reach the top, breathless, drunk, excited; they must be holding one another up. As they lurched around on the landing Lila caught a sound that was animal, involuntary and male, and it was familiar but uttered out of place because it belonged – it could only belong – to what was theirs: to the afternoon, a car seat, their little survival raft on the wet shingle below the tip, their private wreckage, hers and Joe's. The sound came again and this time it was more pressing. She heard two people stagger along the landing. A door opened but did not close.

That spare room door won't close. It swings open.

You just need to push it till it clicks. I'll tell him he just needs to push it hard.

Lila moved closer to the threshold of her own room and stood listening to the murmurs and smothered grunts of soft, mutual attack.

Shsh . . . doesn't matter, come on . . .

You're drunk . . . hey, all right . . .

She heard one voice arguing gently and then the other came, floating underneath it. Joe's voice.

Yes, there's time . . . I want you to, you want to . . . oh, yes. Joey likes that. You like that.

She crept forward a step or two and stood like a rock in the stillness. Joe's voice reached out beyond the room.

Unnhh . . . oh. Oh, God.

As his voice grew louder she made herself look across the landing and through the angle of the open door of the room opposite.

She thought it was a wonder she did not scream. But later it seemed a greater wonder that as she shrank back into her room they did not start up and follow, alerted to her presence somehow, for how could they inflict such lethal agony and be unaware? The annihilation she felt going on inside her should make a noise of some kind. How could love bleed away so silently?

Later I leave the house dressed in Liù's creamy silk clothes and over them her disguise, a rough grey cloak. I am wearing the slippers and the sharp cinders of the track help me remember her exile and feel my own.

I do not go to the farmhouse, or to the marquees behind the shed where the chorus are getting ready in a twitter of noise and excitement. I come here, to a spot just behind one of the black drapes at the side of the stage. I will wait here in the wings until it is time for me to go on. I will not speak to anyone, and all they will think is that I am too nervous. Let them. I'm wearing Liù's white pure face and looking through her black-rimmed eyes and my mouth is her perfect red; nobody can tell that what I am is a solitary girl cornered in a dream from which she does not expect to wake.

Behind me the wings are crowding with the chorus of guards, Chinese peasants, executioners' servants; chorus members and stage crew drift and form knots, whisper, giggle, tense up, preen. The noise from out front swells and swells. I peep out now and then to see how the shed is filling up. The place is nearly full. The chairs were set out neatly but the rows are growing ragged as people shift round to talk and turn seats sideways for a better view and sprawl for extra legroom. Under the lights, with the chatter and the passing of programmes, the place has the air of a huge and crowded waiting room.

The orchestra is in place tuning to the oboe although the oboe sounds not all it might be. Both the Bergsma sisters are sitting like upright seals in tight black evening dresses. Joanna has taken out her plaits and her hair is wound into an obedient French roll underneath a black evening toque with a curling feather and a diamante pin. From my hiding place in the wings I watch Willy as she cranes round to get a proper look at the audience with her good eye, presenting her décolletage from all angles and revealing a cluster of moles that hang on her neck like a family of Rice Krispies.

Uncle George has cut Act I by several minutes to get us straight into the story. In his version, instead of milling about in the crowd first while the chorus sings at length about the imminent execution of Turandot's latest unlucky suitor, Timur and Liù appear on stage after a few minutes and we're straight into the rising of the moon and my first aria, '*Signore, ascolta!*' It'll have more impact that way, Uncle George says. You'll have them in the palm of your hand right from the off.

I notice that Timur – Alec Gallagher – is lurking behind me in the wings, ready for our entrance about twelve minutes into the first act. My eyes are sore but I can see across the stage to the wings opposite, from where Enid sends me a large, circling wave. Billy is next to her and I also make out Senga who seems to have opted back into the chorus and stands with her arms folded, wearing a homemade wig of black wool. I long to rub my eyes but dare not upset the makeup. My father waves across too and gives me a double thumbs-up. Then he signals to the man operating the stage lights, who nods to the lad at the shed door, who checks with Uncle George, and then switches off, one by one, all the overhead lights. The stage is in darkness. In the twilight of the shed the audience settles, murmurs, coughs, falls silent. From the very front, down the length of the shed strides Uncle George in bowtie and tails, baton in hand, nodding around in a way that prompts rapturous applause. He mounts the podium and stands swaying foolishly and bows so low he nearly loses his balance. His mouth must be very dry; when he grins his lips do not return to their proper place, they stick to his teeth.

He raises the baton. This is the cue for a slow, emerging, dawn light to bathe the walls of the great Imperial City of China. But the light comes on stickily; it stops, flickers, recedes and then floods the stage in a burst of vibrant yellow. There is a click of annoyance and a sigh from the lighting desk, from the audience come a few sniggers. George turns and scowls at the lighting man, swipes at the air with the baton and brings in the brass with the first five strident fortissimo chords. People run past me onto the stage. I am nearly knocked over. For the next ten minutes I stand dazed by the moving colours and swirl of sound. My mind is writhing with thoughts; I have a head full of snakes. Behind me Timur speaks and I hear nothing.

Stooping in our cloaks, he and I slip onstage and press our way through the crowd and straight into the white beam of the lights. Beyond the silhouette of Uncle George there is a restive darkness in which I sense people breathing and living, different from us. Up here in the glare we are not alive, we are moving figures – only puppets – in a tale of love and death, a fairy tale of something glimpsed, half understood and nearly forgotten.

I glide forward. I draw myself up very straight and tall and shed my cloak. There is a shiver from the audience as it drops to the ground because in one split second they know they both love me and must be afraid for me. Calaf in his gilded coat with his boots and cutlass is sweating hard. Even from this distance I smell the whisky off him. His pale eyes, set in the artificial ochre of his made-up face, burn colder than I have ever seen them. Now he is singing:

A me il trionfo! A me l'amore!

For me, the triumph! For me, love!

Because he is still drunk he is shouting rather than singing. From his mouth arc delicate flecks of spit whose parabolas of descent on to the stage are caught prettily in the beam of the lights. Then there is a slow fizzing noise and half the lamps over the music stands in the orchestra suddenly go out. There are whistles from the audience and cackles of laughter. Uncle George waves his arms and refuses to stop, though the strings and woodwind are already collapsing into disarray. I turn upstage, bowing my shoulders and wringing my hands with fear for Calaf. The sombre chorus parts to make way for me and I catch one or two people looking sympathetically, but whether at Liù or Lila I cannot say. With my back to the audience I vocalise almost soundlessly as Uncle George has taught me to do:

Just so there's no frog there when you hit your first note, pick one of Timur's fortissimo moments and sing a scale up your sleeve, less than half-voice.

As Timur finishes:

Non c'è voce umana
Che muova il tuo cuore feroce?

Is there no human voice that can move your fierce heart?

I turn and pace my way perfectly, as rehearsed, down to the very front centre stage, where I am supposed to kneel to sing the plaintive, pleading aria to Calaf who stands a way off at the side. I am ready. Uncle George, ignoring the panic in the orchestra and grinning stupidly, nods me in and stands poised with the baton to follow my first, unaccompanied *'Signore, ascolta!'*.

I sink to my knees, open my mouth and raise my hands in entreaty to Calaf. No sound comes. Uncle George swings towards me from the podium and waves me in again. I do not sing. Not because I cannot, because I am considering whether or not I care to. Uncle George yanks the baton through the air once more and waits, darting wild looks at me. Slowly I get up from where I'm kneeling, and stare at him.

'Signore, ascolta!' he mouths at me.

When I take no notice, he hisses it. I turn my attention from him and gaze at Calaf and then I walk slowly towards him and place my hand on the cutlass hanging from his belt. At the best of times Joe moves on stage as if he has artificial limbs and now, rather drunk and terrified because I am not following the correct moves, he is paralysed. I seize the cutlass from the scabbard and walk back to centre stage.

I'll kill myself and then you'll be sorry.

Liù understands this perfectly.

'*Signore ascolta!*', for God's sake! Come on. *Nil desperandum*! Uncle George says, loud enough for the first six rows of the audience to hear.

I turn back and look at Calaf. I let myself enjoy the silence. The long, long silence. There won't be much silence for a while to come, after this.

Pointing at Joe with the cutlass, I say loudly, I saw you. I saw you. I saw you . . . I turn to George and raise my voice even louder. I saw *you*. Both of you, you and him together.

Joe steps forward and now I really shout.

He sucked your thing! You let him suck your thing! You pushed it in his mouth and he was sucking it, your thing was in his mouth!

My voice rings right to the back of the shed; the words soak in like poison. Joe strides towards me but I raise the cutlass and scream and he stops.

I'm not singing to you! I'm not singing anything to you. You were smiling! I hate you! I hate both of you!

I feel a pounding in my throat and the cutlass is shaking in my hand. Uncle George is gesturing madly to the lighting desk and suddenly the stage goes dark. Behind me, some of the chorus stand staring while others begin to surge to the wings. The orchestra are putting down their instruments, members of the audience are getting to their feet. A few people are already rounding on George. Somebody on stage strikes a match and there is a scream, people stamp out a flame that could take hold of the drapes. The overhead lights of the shed are suddenly switched on, blinding me. I look down at my tawdry, stained dress, pull a hand down my sweating face and look at my palm; it is greasy with black and red and white, the colours of the grit and blood of the afternoon. I am gasping. My fever has taken on liquid form and courses behind my eyes, flooding my head and melting my grip on what is really happening. I doubt if I can walk but I make my way to the edge of the stage and concentrate on the chaos. All around me ancient Peking falls apart, lengths of cloth are dragged down in the confusion. Everywhere is mayhem and distress although the costumes and coloured silks of the falling banners under the lights make this a very pretty kind of riot, I observe, almost coolly. Now the white clad apparition of my mother as Turandot comes into view at the far end of the shed, appearing from the farmhouse just in time to witness the collapse. She will never get on stage now. With the last extant corner of my mind I take in what I have done and am aghast at the power I wield. But all is as it should be; the only unanswered puzzle is that I should be singled out to know such power. Liù made the ultimate sacrifice for love, but I? I sacrifice love itself. I will destroy love, and myself along with it. I am watching the messy, bewildering result, the bloodbath I wade in, because I love the wrong people in wrong ways for wrong reasons. I throw the cutlass as far as I can across the stage, at which there is a new outbreak of screaming.

But for a moment the only sound I hear is a roar in my own head as though I am plunging into deep water and wish to drown. Everything slows and darkens and I become clear and separate from the world in a way that I know will last all my life. I put out arms to steady myself but there is nothing to catch hold of before I faint and fall.

———•◦•———

I'm back at the window. I'm dressed for the journey back to Antwerp. My black leather trousers have a tiny split on the inside of one leg but I suppose I shouldn't be surprised. They are old now.

Is it Antwerp you stay, someone asked me at the funeral, and the answer is yes. Antwerp is where I stay. I stay and that's all, because there's no reason not to, but no reason to either: I'm too old to sing in any more choruses, I give lessons to no more than three or four occasional amateurs, there are lots of people I'm friendly with which is not the same as having friends. Nothing much else. Antwerp was just the last place I had a job, and when I was made to leave, I stayed. If my life had come about in a different order it would be Stuttgart, Bologna or Lille where I stay.

I liked the illusion of progress that moving from chorus to chorus every few years created in my own mind, if not in anyone else's. I could be quite fierce about my career, aggressive in that little yapping dog way that people of some, but moderate talent often are.

Just a few more papers and things to sort out.

Burnhead & District Advertiser Thursday 1st September 1960:

OPERA FIASCO:
OPENING NIGHT IN RUINS

Curtain Comes Down
As Indecency Alleged

Amid allegations of gross indecency BAST's first performance of *Turandot* on Friday descended into chaos within
minutes. Claims that musical director and conductor George
Pettifer committed sexual offences of a serious nature involving a minor were made publicly from the stage by another
minor. A shaken Mr Pettifer tried to continue the performance but was forced to leave the building after threats were
made.

Shock

Members of the cast and audience were treated for shock as
the performance was abandoned in front of an audience of
several hundred who witnessed the startling revelations.
Claims are circulating that the production was already in
difficulties. Chorus member Moira Mather commented, 'It was
a shambles anyway.' Another said, 'A lot of people put their
heart and soul into this. We've been badly let down.'

Breach of Trust

Mrs Mather commenting on the allegations of indecency said,
'What kind of man does this? He had close proximity with our
youngsters, it sickens me to think what was going on, he has
abused our trust for his own ends.'

Death Trap

A report has been sent to the Procurator Fiscal. It is expected
that Scottish police will travel to London where Mr Pettifer
was believed to have travelled overnight. Police also say the
performance may have been illegal. A spokesman said, 'The
premises were unlicensed for entertainment and do not ap-

pear to be covered by a fire certificate. These are serious matters that will be investigated thoroughly particularly as young people may be involved.'

By Staff Reporter Alec Gallagher

I spend two nights in hospital and then they say I can go. There's no treatment for glandular fever; it just has to run its course. Enid's mum brings me back to the flat over the shop and by then George and my mother are off to London and Joe has disappeared, nobody is certain where to. I don't see any of them again.

My father calls to see me at the flat a few times and sits there, helpless. We find ourselves unable to speak. We've never done small talk and this certainly isn't the time to start big talk. He embarrasses me and I pretend to be tireder than I am. Before long Mrs Mathieson comes instead but she isn't very forthcoming, either. In my lucid patches it's Enid, usually while her mother is busy in the shop and I am too exhausted to stop her, who keeps me maliciously supplied with the latest stories making their way round Burnhead.

Apart from Alec Gallagher being on the warpath, Mr McArthur feels taken in and out of pocket and curses the day it all began. The Townswomen's Guild were promised their chairs back and have to pick them up themselves because Jimmy Brock isn't having any more to do with it. The scouts and guides are interviewed by the police, one by one. The police come to talk to me too and though still feverish and upset I have to tell them exactly what I saw and heard. I am instructed to use the word 'penis', and I ponder the possibility of actually dying of embarrassment. But soon it is decided that Uncle George will be prosecuted in England. I don't think they can find Joe and the police in London discover, by talking to some of Uncle George's students, that there's enough to go on there, anyway.

Moira Mather puts it around about my father's prison term

just after the war. This is the kind of family we are. Her husband is furious with her because it reflects badly on the firm although paradoxically – perhaps he feels guilty for telling her about it in the first place – he refuses to sack my father. So he stays on for a while, his contact with clients cut to the minimum, and Mrs Mathieson says to Enid's mum – Enid overhears and brings it straight to me – that they're all keeping their heads down and you could cut the atmosphere with a knife. It's no good, though. Not long after, my father resigns and gets a job in Kilmarnock selling insurance.

Mrs Mathieson and Enid's mum are quite good friends by now and I grow skilled in looking wan and preoccupied so that they talk in front of me as if I cannot hear. Mrs Mathieson likes to speculate on who's keeping my mother in the manner to which she's accustomed now that Uncle George has been suspended without pay. Enid's mum has to lower her voice when she utters the names George or Joe. She's sorry to say it but she can't give the time of day to that kind.

By the time I'm well again, returning to school is impossible. It's too late after all that's happened for returns to anything; it's time for me to start learning the moves I need to master on the way to appearing to be someone else.

But it turns out that all I can do is sing. The elderly owners of Sew Right and the three other Sew Rights down the coast between Burnhead and Glasgow live in a big house in Paisley next door to a widow who takes lodgers and will do an evening meal, so off I go to live in one room and to take proper singing lessons and, to be on the safe side, a course in shorthand and typing.

In the months that follow, I picture George wondering how the police will come. He'll spend his time waiting. He'll chain smoke and drink too much, and when he's drunk he'll swell with bravado. He'll start inventing how things will be, which is what he is still best at. He'll say 'nil desperandum' and make jokes about nancy boys and tease my mother that at least in prison he'll be popular. She will try to stay calm but all she'll do is fret away the hours between one nervous headache and the next. They'll sleep in the afternoons and wake when another day is drawing to a bitter, unsatisfactory close.

Will the police barge in almost comically, or will they crash through the door at dawn or do they creep up with a stealth that he's not alert enough to notice, so gentle and slow an invasion that he's leaving the flat handcuffed before he knows what's happening? When it comes, surely it's a relief. For months he'll have been studying the papers, following all the trial reports from the mundane to the most lurid. He'll plead guilty but will that mean six months, a year, two? He will have acquired a smattering of the law but won't be able to divine the formulae that govern mitigating, aggravating, and 'other' circumstances; he'll reel off the sentences handed down but won't understand how they're arrived at. A lot seems to depend on the judge. What he will understand, from careful study of grainy newsprint photographs of the convicted, is what the expression on their faces means. Forgive me if you think forgiveness is what I need, and if you care to, their faces say, but I'm tired, so if you don't care to, go away and let me sleep. He gets a year.

He's the first of them to go. The cutting's here.

Burnhead & District Advertiser Thursday 19th October 1961:

JAILED OPERA CONMAN DEAD AFTER TURANDOT FIASCO

Died in Prison

Fraudster George Pettifer (31) imprisoned in April under the Homosexuality Act has died in Wormwood Scrubs Prison following a sudden collapse. Welcomed in Burnhead last year in a bid to bring 'opera for all' to the town, Pettifer's offences were exposed from the stage on opening night amid dramatic scenes that police later described as 'a threat to public order'.

Debts Unpaid

Pettifer's death spells the end of hope for several local traders as well as Glasgow and London firms who remain unpaid amid financial chaos following Pettifer's disappearance from Burnhead. Several contracts including the hire of stage lighting and musical scores remain outstanding.

Family Turmoil

Florence Duncan, sister of Pettifer, who also played a major role in the opera fiasco now resides in London estranged from husband Raymond Duncan who resigned from local firm Kerr, Mather & McNeill following further revelations concerning fraudulent trading.

By Staff Reporter Alec Gallagher

It's Alec Gallagher's indignation and sense of betrayal in print, I suppose, though admirably toned down to be merely judgemental and inaccurate. The editor's interest in an old scandal is waning and this is, it turns out, the last vicious little flurry of attention from the paper. It could be worse. It could go further on the abuse of effort and goodwill of the good folk of Burnhead, it doesn't recount the details of Ricordi's threat to sue for BAST's breach of copyright, unauthorised abridging of the score and libretto and withheld royalties. It doesn't hint that our youngsters were lucky to escape George's perverted clutches and that there was no telling how far he might have gone.

I don't think Alec bothered to find out that George's death was due to acute respiratory failure as a result of a collapsed lung. Who'd be interested in hearing that his tuberculosis went undiagnosed or rather ignored by the prison doctor, because the nancy boys were notorious for malingering, always trying to get themselves admitted to the hospital wing for a few days' escape from what was done to them by other inmates?

It's not much of a funeral. In these circumstances the prison only lets you have four people. My mother is nominally in charge of arrangements.

He wanted to forget you were ever born, she puts in her only letter to me, in which she also spells out how he died. Don't come. I don't know how you can live with yourself. You killed him.

As if my presence at his funeral would alter that, but I don't go. My father doesn't go and if Joe does, I never hear about it. Actually, I don't know how I live with me either, but I know how I try: I pretend not to notice dates. Around the time of his birthday, and the trial, and when he died and was buried, I take special care not to think. I strive to make those days pass with nothing more than a tightening around my heart, which at least doesn't show on the outside.

She's next, in 1964, and I don't go to her funeral either. She'd want me to carry on, I lie to myself (crediting her with a capacity for forgiveness that she never possessed in relation to me), feeding my burgeoning self importance because I'm a proper music student now and I've got a job for the summer – bed and board and little else but experience in the chorus in a Gilbert & Sullivan season at Abersoch. She dies in London and if I ask for time off for my mother's funeral they'll ask me what she died of and I don't care to go into it. She doesn't leave a note. She leaves her record collection scratched and cracked, some tattered sheets of manuscript, a collection of clothes that the moth is already into and some split and faded gloves, now laughably old-fashioned.

Hers has to be a quiet one, too. My father manages to get her a service and a minister rather than the usual suicide's dispatch – quick and ashamed by authority of the coroner – and even gets it done without a mention in the *Burnhead & District Advertiser*. He doesn't even put in a death notice because surely there's been enough fuss already. He reports back in a short letter to me what he finds out: how on the day Dickens & Jones decide they will turn half their ladies' fashions floor into a boutique staffed by seventeen-year-old girls in white boots and lipstick, and relegate my mother to a lower paid job in the stock room, she returns to her bedsit, tapes over the window and door, feeds the meter with coins, turns on her two gas rings, closes the curtains and goes to bed. It's a sunny day about a week before her fortieth birthday. When I hear about it I imagine the buses passing on the road outside her window and people on the top deck noticing how motionless the curtains hang, for can't it be seen somehow: all that sorrow in one person sealed in the world of a tiny room, taking her leave as the buses trundle by?

I think nothing moved her as much as the pathos she detected in her own life, a life that should have grown towards some blossoming, accumulating beauty and value, but didn't. I think she withered from the inside, using herself up on grievances about her hungers and wishes and desires, and in the end it was too much, the vague though massive deficiencies of her life whining in her head like the echoes of huge whimpering animals who had died in a cellar.

My father doesn't comment on either death except to say that they're at rest. We both need the thought that they're tidy in their graves now; we use it to avoid further discussion. We don't care to wonder out loud how long George gasped for breath on the concrete floor of his cell, or to plot her descent, after he died, from single room to worse room and job to more demeaning job. Coincidentally her death certificate reads 'acute respiratory failure' too. Not a word on either one about hearts and pride and promises fatally collapsed and broken.

No idea about Joe. I imagine him still at the seaside, though I'm not sure why. I see him as older than his sixty-three or -four, I suppose because twenty is so very much older than fifteen. He'll be a fastidious, nautically-dressed old bachelor and the life and soul of a senior citizens' club, outnumbered about eight to one by the ladies, who adore him and whom he still likes to keep guessing. It still won't be his fault that he is a natural taker of attention, though perhaps by now he will have learned how to exploit it more graciously. I imagine he still looks past people so that they can feast their eyes on him as he talks, and I'm sure that still nobody ever quite knows how long they'll have him for. In any gathering, in any room with other people he'll somehow always be the one nearest the door. But if he is now a happy man he will also be genuinely kind-hearted. He'll be stout and his lips will be very thin and he will choose ties and cravats to match his eyes, which he will consider his best feature. And they are, although these days they will tend to get pink and wet very early into a tumblerful of relaxing whisky; they may well contain the dim, frantic light of the intractable drunk living always somewhere between sobriety and oblivion and scrambling for shore without knowing which way it lies. Or perhaps his drunkenness these days is casual and innocuous. Or perhaps he's dead.

I've packed what I arrived with and put my luggage in the car. There's nothing else I want to take, except maybe this. Fancy him keeping it. It was right at the bottom.

The World As I See It Today
Today as I sit in this classroom on Thursday the 23rd of June, 1960, the world looks a hard blue colour. That is because it is a Thursday. Monday is pale green and unripe. Tuesday is beige, Wednesday is white, Thursday see above, Friday is grey like a man's suit, Saturday is a different blue from Thursday and Sunday is that dark green that old people paint their houses. I would rather not do this but I can't help it. I think if I lived somewhere else that was better and a more definite, proper place, I might have other things to think about and not get the colour coming straight into my mind the minute I think what day it is. This is the first time I have mentioned this.

Other people would laugh and as I get teased quite enough anyway! By certain people who shall remain nameless though everybody in this school knows who they are. I would even get teased for my name, the one my mother uses on me, which is Eliza. That is her sort of name. I don't feel like an Eliza. I stick to Lizzie at school, that's what my dad calls me, an ordinary name. He is ordinary himself so it suits him to use it but I don't feel like a Lizzie either. I used to get called Lila but that was a long time ago.

Best friends don't tease one another or at least they shouldn't, but I still wouldn't tell even Enid Foley (about the colours), though she is my friend she takes things the wrong way and she's only interested in God at the moment, since Easter she is OBSESSED. She thinks everything is a sin and only Jesus can get you out of it. Most people are obsessed by something, Elvis Presley is one, Cliff Richard ect, who I really like but being obsessed is going a bit far and makes you look stupid. My mother hates them, she only likes classical music and opera, the rest is just noise according to her. My father likes Lonnie Donegan but he doesn't play the records in our house.

Anyway, the world as I see it today, it's a stupid idea because I don't see the world today in any way at all. Nobody can see the world. We only see the bit we're in ie this bit of Scotland called Burnhead. And if you only had Burnhead to go on you would say the world is a dump. Burnhead is neither one thing or another and I am the same. Anyway who cares? How I see the world isn't important as I am only me and it doesn't matter what I think, so I will just go on seeing the world my way, you can't change. Why I have to live here I don't know, there must be thousands of places more interesting where people really enjoy living there. But wherever you go you have to take your own head with you. What I mean is wherever you go it's the same you inside. You can't get away from yourself, it all comes down to what goes on inside your own head unfortunatly, changing that is your only hope of changing the way you see the world.

The lines of dried ink sparkle like graphite – the faded, dry river of one afternoon's lazy thoughts fixed in its meandering across paper. Written on my second last day at school, as it turns out. I remember Miss whatever-her-name-was the English teacher saying a lot can change in a summer and that is true, but a lot doesn't.

Wherever you go you have to take your own head with you. What I mean is wherever you go it's the same you inside. You can't get away from yourself, it all comes down to what goes on inside your own head unfortunately.

The truth is I am exactly the kind of singer my mother would have become. I can't sing without feeling it's a perilous undertaking. I can sing loud and I can sing soft, but I never go to the limits. I want a quiet, a liveable kind of life, not one that might have in it anything that is bigger than I feel myself to be. Turning away from the huge and frightening open sky towards the dark, contained air of opera houses is not so high a price to pay for remaining free and lonely; I've been safe all this time from having anything more taken away from me. I do not want, ever again, to make too much noise.

So I fear that most of my performances have been obstinate or smug. It's not that I can't act; it's that it never looks like anything else. I never seem to mean it, and it always shows when a singer doesn't mean it. I try to use my imagination, but my imagination though vivid is not agile, and is not drawn to originality; it still follows the rules as it did that summer, as children's imaginations do, but unlike a child I no longer believe in angels and devils or that there is any logic in goodness and love.

It's done now, the last chest sits atop the high pile in the front garden. At this time of year as soon as darkness comes the wind gets up. But at least it's dry. I have made a tight cluster of the newspaper so the *Burnhead & District Advertiser* will be the first thing to go up in smoke, which seems only right. I push the wad deep into the pile, arrange the last of the papers and boxes and debris around it to keep it out of the wind, and light a match. It takes three or four attempts, and then the flame catches. I return to the house to watch at the dining room window but it's not satisfactory; I cannot hear or smell the burning or feel the heat so I try to raise the window and of course it will not budge. It has not budged in years. I'm suddenly angry that there has been no fresh air in this room all this time, and just then the glass shatters from the heat of the fire and there is a warm inrush of smoke.

The wind is always blowing somewhere in Burnhead. It conspires in corners, it whips rubbish into unruly eddies and drops it in roiling heaps or it ambushes you on a high corner and catches in your hair like twisting fingers. You could scream at it. But now the wind is sucking through the fire and there is a bed of pink and orange flame at the core of it and a roar pulling up cloudy plumes of smoke into the air. The night splits with sounds and smells of bursting wood and white-hot piano wires and cracking varnish. Burning veils of muslin are lifted by the wind, they sparkle, disintegrate and fall over the garden and waft through the window in smoking wisps. Glowing flakes of ash drift around me and the wind throws a speck in my face that hits my eyes and I cannot move. Tears pour down my cheeks and dry tightly on my skin. I'm back at the window, stranded and weeping. There's no place in the world like Burnhead for chucking grit in your eye.

———•◦•———

ACKNOWLEDGEMENTS

I would like to express my gratitude to the staffs of the Mitchell Library, Glasgow and the Carnegie Library, Ayr; the Department of Printed Books, Imperial War Museum; Helen Smailes, Senior Curator of British Art, National Gallery of Scotland; Veral Marshall of the Stone Gallery; Bruce Ritchie, Director of Professional Practice, The Law Society of Scotland; Miranda Jackson and Nick Cutts, BMG (Ricordi). I was greatly helped by varied enlightening writings on *Turandot* by John Black, Mosco Carner, Jürgen Maehder, Mary Jane Phillips-Matz, Jeremy Tambling, Eva Turner and William Weaver.

Very many thanks also to Judith Murray at Greene & Keaton Limited and to my editor Carolyn Mays at Hodder & Stoughton.